The Other Side of JACKEL ISLAND

by Amy L. Benevento

AQUABROOK PUBLISHING HOUSE
WALTHAM, MASSACHUSETTS

AQUABROOK PUBLISHING HOUSE,
87 Washington Ave., Waltham, MA 02453

ISBN-10: 0-985-62070-6
ISBN-13: 978-0-985-62070-7

Book Cover by Richard Green
Map by Debby Owen

For deleted scenes, character symbolism, and further details, visit:
jackelisland.com

Published by Aquabrook Publishing House
Waltham, Massachusetts

Printed in the U.S.A.

Dedicated to Max, my friend and editor
who shared the world inside Jackel Island with me.
Also dedicated to the man from New York.

Characters in
JACKEL ISLAND

JAMIE

Horse Trainer.
Assistant in the
Equestrian Dept.
Age 22

TOM

Head of
Administration.
Island "leader"
Age 34

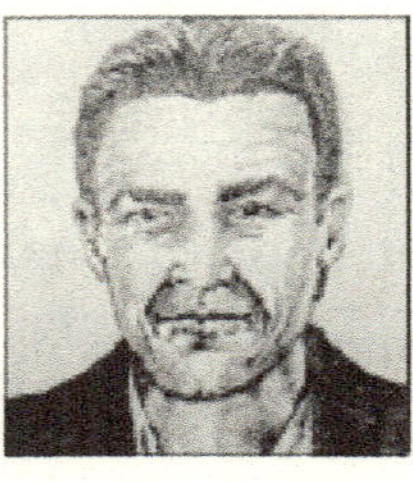

ADRIAN

Chief of Security
Late 40's

EVAN BRONTE

Head of Research.
World Renowned
in the science world.
Age 38

JIM

Doctor
Age 56

GRADY

Security Team
Age 36

EARL

Head of
Equestrian Dept.
Jamie's boss.
Age 52

KANE

Head of
Maintenance

DARCY

Works in
Administration
under Tom
Age 32

BRIAN

Assistant Cook
Age 25

JEREMY

Assistant in the
Maintenance Dept.
Age 20

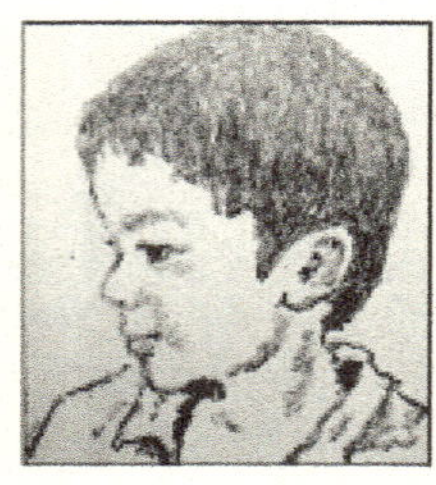

DEREK

Joel's son
Age 9

Illustrations by Amy L. Benevento

Characters in
JACKEL ISLAND

JOEL
Head of the Computer Dept. Tom's twin. Age 34

TARIQ
Head Cook
Age 64

STEVE
Security Team
Age 39

SHEILA
Administrative Assistant

ALICE
Nurse

BRITTANY
Nurse

HENRY
Jamie's dog

MR. HYDE & MR. EDWARDS
Bronte's Bodyguards

PHILIP
Research Dept. Bronte's right hand man. Age 56

MARVIN
Research Dept. Science wiz. Age 33

PAULINE
Research Dept. Physician Asst. Age 44

SANDRA
Research Asst. Age 28

Illustrations by Amy L. Benevento

JACKEL
Stables
Main Campus
Lagoon

ISLAND
N
W
E
S
Research Center

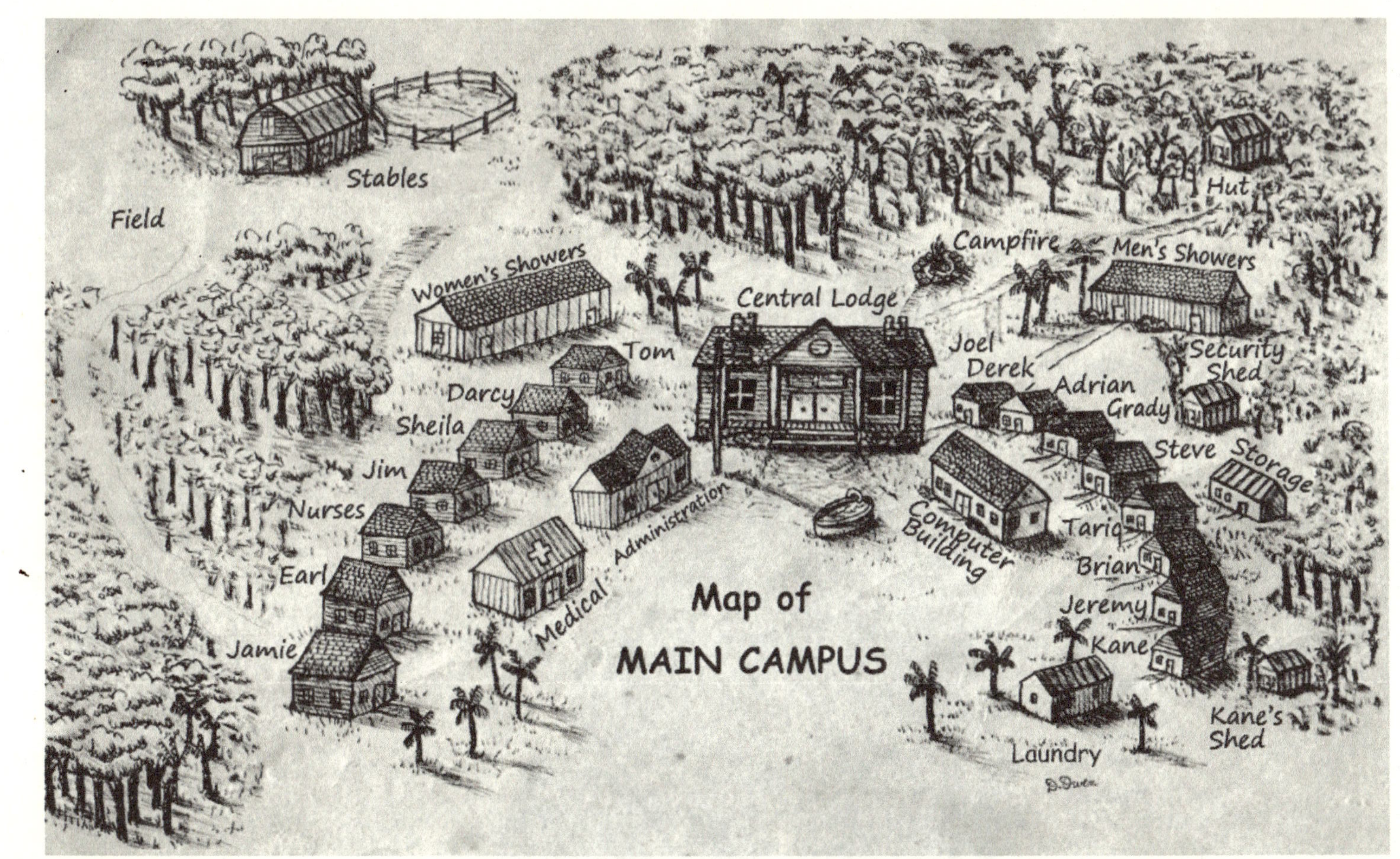
Map of
MAIN CAMPUS
Stables
Field
Hut
Campfire
Men's Showers
Women's Showers
Central Lodge
Tom
Darcy
Sheila
Jim
Nurses
Earl
Jamie
Administration
Medical
Joel
Derek
Adrian
Grady
Security
Shed
Steve
Storage
Computer
Building
Tariq
Brian
Jeremy
Kane
Kane's
Shed
Laundry

ACKNOWLEDGMENTS

A heartfelt THANK YOU goes to my editor and friend, Max Chalmers. She was with me every step of the way, editing this novel chapter by chapter, encouraging me, and living their world with me. To not even *begin* to express my gratitude, I give her free Tai Chi lessons for life!

I'd also like to thank Donna Brown for inviting me into her home to educate me about horses. Donna owns a farm in Raleigh, North Carolina, and has been training people how to ride horses for several decades. She is a wonderful lady! I wanted to compensate her for her time, generosity and kindness, but she wouldn't take my money. So I gave her corn muffins.

My gratitude goes to John Catalano, a chemical scientist at GlaxoSmithKline, and to Jim Kennamer, who is Vice President at Talecris Biopharmaceutical. Jim has studied biochemistry and molecular cell biology. Both these gentlemen shared their knowledge when I needed science questions answered in order to write this book. I bought Jim a margarita for his time and attention. John – I owe you one!

A special thanks goes to young Eric Mullen, my fourteen-year-old martial art student who is more knowledgeable about cultures and religion than any professor or historian I've known. Talk about walking encyclopedias! I so much enjoyed our talks on religion and spirituality. Eric helped me with my character Kane, who was central for this story. In an attempt to express my gratitude, I treated Eric with sushi!

Further thanks goes to the Honorable Judge James Brown who told me what sentences some of my characters would receive for their federal crimes, and Mohammad Soetomo for his knowledge on lifestyles in Indonesia. Last but not least, a huge thank you to Rick Green for putting up with my many changes with the book cover. Rick was patient and understanding when I needed to get this book cover exactly right. You rock, Rick!

JAMIE'S SONG

I don't care if I ever get home.
I don't care if we just keep on living
our lives on this distant sand,
in this foreign place, in this unknown land.

I don't care for the ways of the past.
I don't miss the times when I asked
for this and for that, for right and for wrong,
for him and for her, for weak and for strong.

We caused a disturbance when we came ashore,
we cut up the ways of this land.
To survive in a world full of darkness and greed
is to live a life that's too savage for me.

By land, by sea, by heart, by soul.
And now, will this place make us whole?

I have a feeling deep down inside…
I have a feeling part of me died.
I'll make a vow to never again be blind,
now that I see with crystallized eyes.

I tried to make sense for years and for years,
I tried to see what's for real.
It's time I see what this place can reveal,
if I just let go, release steering wheels.

Lyrics by Jamie E. Robinson

A bird doesn't sing because it has an answer.
It sings because it has a song.

by Maya Angelou

West vs. East

The West Side

The East Side

The East Beach

The Lagoon

Campfire

The 3-mile trail that connects the west side with the east

The stables

Wild Przewalski Horses

CHAPTERS

PART ONE

PART TWO

CHAPTERS

PROLOGUE

Elongated shadows fell on the path that cut through the woods. I quietly kept in the path's shadows so as not to be seen. I was approaching the campsite from the woods when Kane materialized from the black air, emerging from the darkness like a bat. He grabbed me, his arm holding me against him, and I gasped.

"It's not safe!" he whispered. He had his forearm around me just below my neck and my back was pressed against his chest and stomach. It was as if I was slammed against a metal vending machine. "They're in the woods."

"Who?" He released his hold on me. "Who's in the woods?"

"Go now. Go to your cabin. Lock the door."

"You're scaring me. What's going…"

"Go now! That way." He pointed towards the water basin by the stone lodge, beyond which were our cabins. He nudged me forward. I took a couple of steps, then looked back at him.

"Kane?"

"Go. Go now!"

All he did was point, his long finger showing the way to my cabin, like a Charles Dickens ghost with the spectral finger pointing to the grave.

"I don't want to go that way, Kane." He shook his outstretched finger towards the water basin, and with his other hand, he gave me a gentle push.

As I approached the water basin, the men, in unison, lifted their rifles in a clamored flurry, and I heard the clicks of metal and stock. All rifles were aimed at me! I felt the sour gush of adrenaline. I held my breath and stared at them.

Chapter 1
ARRIVAL
Several Months Earlier

As I awkwardly stepped off the boat and onto the dock, I had no idea what was going to happen in the following months. The humidity and sweet smell of jasmine hit me hard, one weighing me down, the other lifting me. Solid steady land lay below my feet at last, though I still sensed an artificial sea sway. Seagulls screamed. A heavy salt breeze swept by me, and I saw large blue–gray hills and swaying teak trees beyond a half dozen people who were standing on the dock waiting to greet me. I let the breeze, the jasmine, and the humidity wash over me before I focused on the people whom I would be living with for the next six months.

I wasn't sure where in the world I was, literally. They only told me that I would be stationed on an island east of India. I suspected that some of the information they gave wasn't entirely accurate, like, for example, the name of the island. Jackel Island. That wasn't its real name. I tried getting information on *Jackel Island*, and there was none to be found, though there was a Jackal Island, as in the wolf–like animal, and there was a place called Jekyll, as in Jekyll and Hyde. They were purposely vague for security reasons. Therefore, I was unable to tell anyone where exactly I'd be living for half a year. For the past three months, Jao Institute had put me through a grueling interview process, and then hired me for this 180-day project. Bio–CMAT was the name of the two–year project, and I had no idea what the acronym stood for.

A hundred and eighty days. What could happen in that time? It was now early June, and I'd be home by Christmas. I was the last to arrive on the island, and was assigned to work the remaining six months of this project. Roughly twenty employees who had arrived at the beginning of the project were already living and working on Jackel Island.

Jao Institute, a multi–billion–dollar pharmaceutical research firm, had staffed the island with a five–man research team, a three-man administration department, a computer consultant, medical and security personnel, two cooks, and a cleaning crew of two. I was hired to domesticate the wild horses that ran native on Jackel Island, taming the horses so that we would be able to ride them. This would provide transportation between Main Campus on the west side of the island, and the Research Center on the east. Three miles of jungle lay between Main Campus and the Research Center, with a single path that connected the two work areas. There was not adequate funding to build roads on the island's rough and rocky terrain, and jeeps were costly to ship in.

I tame horses. That's what I do. I grew up on my Uncle's farm. I have a feel for horses. As a child, I started training dogs for neighbors and school friends, and was surprisingly adept at it. I was the girl who could not only get their dogs to do tricks, but to behave and listen. Training dogs led to training horses. As a teen, articles were written about my abilities in the local paper. I eventually made the national news, though it was just a couple of articles. I even had a television appearance once. I believe that's how Jao found me.

I am wounded inside and thus can sense when other animals are, and I soothe them.

A tall, thin but sturdy man with jet-black hair and a serious look stepped towards me on the dock, extending his hand.

"Welcome to Jackel Island, Jamie. I'm Tom." He smiled a toothy grin, his mouth and skin boyish, but his eyes looked a little hard. Before his introduction, I knew that this man was either Tom or his twin brother Joel who was also stationed on the island. I knew this from his bio in the Jao corporate folder I was given, which I read multiple times during my voyage. Besides a photo along with a description of staff, the folder gave company policies, guidelines, rules, compensation, insurance information, and safety tips for the island.

Tom was head of Administration, our leader of sorts on the island. He was 34, twelve years my senior. I took his hand, which was refreshingly cold and dry, and looked him in the eye as I smiled and thanked him. He firmly took my bag from my other hand, which surprised me considering his high rank, and motioned me away from the boat.

I was out of my element, never having traveled out of the United States, unless you count Canada or Mexico. So this was quite the journey for me, and I strangely felt a need for his leadership at the moment. He was starting to ask about my voyage, but was cut short when my foot caught an uneven board on the dock, causing me to lose my balance and lurch forward very awkwardly. He caught me under the elbow to steady me, then laughed a bit, and I felt ridiculous. This was my introduction.

"You all right?" he asked and let go.

"Yes, I'm fine, thank you. I'm just a bit weary from the trip." I'd traveled by ship for weeks, but had transferred from the ship to a local boat hours ago. The waters were too shallow for a ship to dock so close to shore, so a smaller boat was needed.

"Well come on, then. Let me introduce you to the others." Tom grinned, and I followed him towards the small group that was gathered behind him, looking at me with half smiles.

Adrian stood in front of the others, with his arms folded across his chest, leaning back slightly, smirking at me as if he knew something about me that I didn't know. I knew his name from his bio in the corporate folder. Looking at him now, I could see that Adrian was comfortable in his body. Being Chief of Security, he was hardy and solid. He looked like he pressed iron regularly, had a military haircut, and was one of those people whose age was hard to tell, though he was no longer young. He had an animal awareness.

"Hello young lady!" I smiled weakly at him, nodded, and then looked to the ground. I am confident with animals, but not with people.

Grady was by Adrian's side but back a step, tucking his chin out some with one hand on his hip. He didn't command the intense presence that Adrian did, but it seemed he tried. I recognized Grady from the photo in the folder – the wispy light brown hair, the dimples, the mischievous look. Grady was also in security working under Adrian.

"Well hello!" he chimed at me. "I certainly hope we get better acquainted later on." This man was too familiar, and I cautioned myself to keep my distance from him. I responded formally.

"Hey, I'm the doc. I'm Jim. Welcome!" An older and gentle–looking man with a soft grin stepped forward, and I immediately warmed to him. I'd say he was mid–fifties. I went to shake his hand, but he said "ahh…" and hugged me instead. It was warm, not creepy. I heard Grady mumble "I'll be damned" under his breath, which made me laugh, expelling some of the awkwardness. I could see that this man offered more than medical attention to our Jao staff.

"You must be hungry."

"Umm…" But before I could answer, Tom's twin caught my attention. The double effect caught me off guard. This man held himself differently, focusing more inwardly than Tom did. Wearing khakis, he had his fists jammed in his pockets, and he grinned awkwardly, looking from the ground to me, then back to the ground again. It was as if he were figuring out a math equation.

"Hello" he said quickly in a low voice. "I'm Joel."

"Hello," I said. It was then I saw a small boy appear from behind Joel's leg. Joel took one hand out of his pocket and put it behind the boy's head. Looking down at the boy, Joel said, "This is my son, Derek." Derek looked to be about seven years old, and seemed slightly Asian, his Oriental features softened. I gathered Joel's wife was Asian and wondered if she was here on the island.

"Hey there!" I said to the boy.

"Hello Ma'am." I believe that was the first time anyone called me ma'am and felt I was still too young for that title. I smiled down at him, then looked at the others.

"Is Earl here?" I asked, and looked among the people whom I would work along side for the next two seasons. I had a special interest in Earl because he was assigned to be my immediate supervisor.

"He's at the stables, I believe," the doctor answered, and Tom confirmed with a nod.

"There's definitely too much testosterone here, don't 'cha think?" A dark haired woman with red lips and cheeks stepped forward. This grinning girl, who was maybe ten years older than I was, stood eyeing me, amused.

"Oh, definitely," I said, and I heard Grady moan as the doctor laughed and Tom playfully flicked his fingers at the woman's shoulder. Looking about, I saw only men besides she and me, and I wondered where the other women were.

"I'm Darcy in Admin," she said. "Here's a kit for you, compliments of Jao." Darcy gave a mock bow as she held out a large thick plastic bag with a colorful tropical tree on it. 'Jao Institute' was written in block letters across the top. "It has your towels, soaps, island shoes, a few bits of clothing that should fit, providing you gave your correct size."

"Island shoes?" I asked as I slowly took the bag from her.

"Don't ask" Grady said. "It's top secret."

"They think we women pack high heals and delicate sandals," she said. "Something Sheila and company wear."

"Excuse me?" I asked, my eyes raised.

"Sheila and company – the other women here at Main Campus." I heard a few snickers from the others. I looked at her confused. She sighed, then extended her hand. "Welcome to Jackel Island," she said, and I took her hand in mine. Her skin was hot and she griped like a man. "I run administration under Tom."

"Wait, who's under *who* again?" Tom asked, tilting his head.

"Ha-ha, funny" Darcy said blandly.

"I can take that two ways," Grady said, and Darcy slugged him hard in the gut and told him to shut up. My jaw dropped, but no one reacted as if anything was unusual.

Ignoring Grady's "Oww!" Darcy said to me, "See me if you need anything, anything at all."

"Thanks!" I said to her.

"Come on, let's get you situated," Tom said as he joined his palms, and they all turned away from the sea. I followed them off the dock and into the heart of the island.

Chapter 2
ENTERING THE ISLAND

As Tom led us away from the ocean, we passed a giant black man in baggy tan pants and a stained sleeveless T-shirt chopping wood. Working in perfect rhythm, he never looked up at us as we passed him. He looked surreal, this giant of a man.

As I followed these strange people, these who would become my group, my pack, I fought to remember their names and faces. I silently reviewed them in my head. I only met about half of them, not counting the five people who worked at the Research Center on the other side of the island.

Tom, our Leader with jet-black hair and a firm handshake, walked in front of us. He had put forth effort to see that I felt welcomed on this new team, and he was easy with the woman who worked under him, not asserting his seniority, almost flirting. He seemed strong and practical, and I got a sense that he was a good man. Time would tell.

Adrian, who walked next to Tom, had a smooth gait. Adrian was striking and left an impact on me. Towering over me, he had an air of confidence and natural sensuality. Weathered somewhat with age, I watched him walk with Tom as he cut through the sea air with grace and poise, his movements rooted and instinctual. Some people aren't good looking, but they are very attractive, as was the case here. Adrian was Chief of Security. I wondered if he took orders from Tom, but something told me he truly took orders from no one.

Grady had an "I'm so cool" walk, and he turned around and caught me looking at him. I was angry at the timing. He winked at me. My mouth opened a bit, and I quickly looked down at the sand. He gave a two-syllable laugh. This man loved his dimples too much.

I maneuvered to walk by Jim, the doctor. From him, I sensed calm. I thought of a horse back home who gave off such serenity. Jim's sandy hair was longer than Tom's and Joel's cropped hair, definitely looser than Adrian's crew cut, and it blew in soft wisps in the ocean breeze. He looked down at me over his shoulder and smiled.

"Is Main Campus a long way from the dock?" I asked the doctor, and he assured me it was just a little bit longer.

Joel kept his eyes to the sand as he walked, with little Derek at his side. I was surprised that children were allowed on the island. Derek was not mentioned in the company literature. I struggled to remember Joel's position with Jao, and then it came to me – he oversaw the computers and was known in the geek world as some sort of techno wiz.

I have this ability to know when I meet someone whether or not we will become friends. Darcy and I would. She had dark thick shoulder–length hair as opposed to my longer straight light brown hair. Darcy and I both wore no make up, but she was naturally very pretty and sassy looking, where I was still girlish looking.

As we walked, I wondered if the showers would be clean, what my room would be like, and the personalities of the animals I'd be training. With the hours upon hours of answering their questions during the extensive interviews, of reading up on Jao Institute, of all the psychological and medical testing I undertook, I never learned about how my day–to–day living conditions would be on this island. I would certainly find out.

I had left it all behind. I thought of my dogs and my horses, the Maine coast, Friday night lobster, Melinda and Jack from the stables... I had left it all behind.

As we walked, they asked me the standard questions about taming animals, and I gave the standard answers, which now came by rote. Everyone asks the same questions – how do I train a wild, disturbed, or undisciplined horse? How old was I when I knew I had this ability to tame the wild? Did I ever get injured? Was there ever an animal I could not train? What did I think of Cesar Millan, the Dog Whisperer?

It took me a moment to realize that Tom stopped, and the others slowly did too. I brought my eyes up from the sandy path.

We had arrived.

In front of me stood our settlement, my new home, referred to as "Main Campus" in Jao's literature. A modern Jamestown. The two developed areas on the island were Main Campus in the west, and the Research Center in the east, with three miles of thick woods in-between the two areas. The scene before me now looked like an upgraded summer camp for boy scouts, or some church retreat area. I saw a clearing before me with packed dark dirt on level ground. Square in front of me was a large stone building with two chimneys on either side, probably the gathering place and dining hall. A hand written banner hung above the thick wooden door, and it read "WELCOME JAMIE!" This made me smile.

To the left and right of the main building were a few office buildings with small wooden cabins behind them. These buildings and dwellings formed an open semicircle around the clearing, with seven or eight cabins on each side of the large main stone structure, not counting the three larger office buildings. A flagpole with the American flag stood in front of the main stone building, a bit to the left. It comforted me to see our flag after being on foreign waters for over three weeks. In front of the main building to the right was a graystone water basin, and I saw three women milling about it. They turned to look at us, and two of them rested their eyes on me. I gave a small wave to them. Before they could respond, a loud sound came from the right, like a rock clanking against a pan, and it made me jump.

"That's Tariq, our cook. He's making something nice for tonight in honor of your arrival" Jim said to me. I shot him a quick smile, then took in the site of my new little community. It was rather quaint and warmly inviting to me, after having spent twenty-three days on the ship.

"Home sweet home," Tom said loudly, looking straight ahead.

"Which cabin will I be staying in?" I asked.

"That one on the end," Tom said, pointing to our left, the cabin furthest from the main building. "Cabins are grouped by department. Admin and Medical are on the left side, and the other four departments are on the right side, over there."

"Which other four departments?"

"Security, Computer, Maintenance, and the cooks," Tom said. "Admin and Computer are right next to Central Lodge, on either side. Medical and Security are sandwiched in the middle, with Maintenance and the cooks on the end over there." Tom pointed.

"What are those three larger buildings in front of the cabins?" I asked.

"The one on the left next to Central Lodge is the Admin building," Tom explained. "The building next to it is the medical building, the one with the huge red cross." I gave Tom a sarcastic look. "The larger building on the right is the computer building."

"What are the smaller structures?" I asked. "Not the cabins, not the admin, medical, or the computer buildings, those over there on the right."

"Well, that's the laundry room, over there by Maintenance," Tom said. "Then there are a few storage sheds."

"Showers are behind Admin and Security, near Central Lodge," Darcy said. "Women's is behind Admin, and Men's is behind Security. If you see Grady in our shower, kick him out."

"Hey! I highly resemble that!" Grady said, and I wondered if I heard him correctly.

Jim smiled, then said, "We sit around a campfire every evening after dinner. Our campfire pit is behind Central Lodge."

"The stables, where you'll be working with the horses, are about a quarter mile back behind your cabin," Tom said. "There's a path, then you pass an open field to get to the barn."

My mind was swimming, trying to take it all in. I shook my fingers around my head to illustrate my exasperation. Tom and Adrian laughed.

"It's a lot to take in all at once, huh," Adrian said.

"I'd be happy to give you a private tour," Grady said, and he winked at me.

"I'm sure you would!" Darcy said sarcastically. "Creep!"

"You'll get the hang of this place in no time," Tom said. "Darcy, please show Jamie to her cabin," then he handed me back my bag and said to me, "Go ahead and get settled in. Take a nap if you'd like. We'll see you at dinner."

"Make sure you're hungry. From what I hear, Tariq's prepared a welcome feast," Jim said.

The others murmured their welcomes and "see you laters" before going their separate ways. The three women by the water basin kept looking at me, but never came forward.

"This way," Darcy said, and I followed her to the left towards my new home.

Chapter 3
NEW HOME

I stood just inside the wooden door of my cabin, finally alone. I was looking at a simple one–room open space. It would be enough. Anything larger would lose the intimate feel this cabin had.

In the back left corner was a small single bed with a dark green and maroon plaid comforter on top. I preferred sleeping against a wall, I felt more secure. Two windows with knotty wood frames were above the bed, one looking out back, and the other looking off to the side on the adjacent wall. I would be watching the trees and sky as I fell asleep. A small nightstand stood by the bed, and on it was a child's lamp with a giraffe imprint. Odd. A card table with a chair stood against the back wall in the middle. I supposed this was for visitors, and wondered if I'd ever invite someone inside. I pictured Darcy and I becoming close, with her telling me secrets of the island as she sat at this table, and me on the bed. On the table was a single clay vase that held three gerbera daisies – one red, one orange, and one yellow. That was a nice touch; it had to be Darcy's doing. In the far right corner was a small closet with a dorm–style sliding wooden door. A dresser was placed against the right side wall near the front of the cabin.

I looked up. Thick wood beams stretched across the ceiling, and directly below lay a large oval tabriz rug, giving the room a warm and snug feel. I walked across the room and laid my two bags on the bed, noticing a single moon orchid laid across my pillow. Darcy?

Turning around, I saw that there was no bathroom, and wondered how I would deal with this during the monsoons that would come near the end of my stay here. According to the literature that Jao supplied, temperatures averaged in the 70's to lower 80's year round, so there was no need for a chimney or an air conditioning unit. Indonesia's warm waters ensured that temperatures on land remained fairly constant. In case of harsh weather, Jao instructed employees to go to Central Lodge. Jao's handbook indicated that we would need a couple of weeks to get used to the high humidity, which was already starting to bother me. I pulled off my light blue button-down blouse, white pants, and plain white sneakers. Unzipping my bag, I laid out fresh clothes. I had packed two raincoats, as monsoons typically blow in around the holidays and last until early spring, so we would perhaps be catching the beginning storms. But compared to the harsh blizzards I was used to in Maine, a monsoon would be a breeze. Jao had instructed us to pack extremely lightly, saying that most new arrivals often brought clothes and footwear that were not suitable for the climate.

I found a place for my clothes and belongings. After putting most of my folded clothes in the dresser, I hung my button down shirts and pants in the closet. I didn't know what to do with my shampoo, toothbrush, and other toiletries, so I arranged these items along with my deodorant, lotion, powdered Jean Naté, suntan lotion and nail polish neatly on top of the dresser. Could I replace Jean Naté and other specifics once I'd used it all up? I placed my backpack, insect repellent, extra lotion, and some horse texts and books on plant life in Indonesia in the closet on the shelf above my clothes. I read a lot, and placed the novels I'd brought on the table. Was there a library of sorts here?

I put Mr. Dody, a stuffed brown dachshund dog with a zipper along the top of his back where you could slip in 3 egg-sized pups (a white, black, and brown pup) on the bed by the pillow. Now this was my home.

Suddenly, there was a rapid knock on the door. I jerked, ran my fingers through my hair, smoothed out the fresh clothes I'd just put on, and then answered the door. Standing there were two wide–eyed blond boy–men who were roughly my age – one younger, one maybe older.

The younger one was skinny; the older one was heavy.

Before I could say hello, the younger one said "Hey! You must be Jamie!" Before I could confirm, he asked, "Can we come in?" and he proceeded to walk inside. His heavy friend rolled his eyes.

"Come on in," I said to the older guy, smiling. He entered reluctantly. As I shut the door, I turned to find the thin boy looking around eagerly while the heavier guy gave me an apologetic look.

"I'm Jeremy. I'm twenty and single." I would have guessed Jeremy to have been younger than twenty. Jeremy was full of nervous energy, with blond hair and green eyes. His lower lip extended a bit further than his upper lip, and both lips and nose aimed for one point. Jack-o-lantern Jeremy. He was quick to smile, a mouth full of scrambled teeth that gave him a puerile look. "You married?"

"No."

"Boyfriend?"

"No."

"That's totally cool."

"I'm Brian." I turned around and felt his gentle eyes soften on me. Jeremy embarrassed Brian, but I gathered the two were like brothers and that Jeremy was harmless. Brian was overweight with blond curly hair. I would guess him to be older than I was by a few years.

"What do you do here on the island, Brian?"

"I'm just the assistant cook."

"Well that sounds fun, not stressful."

"Yeah, I guess."

"When did you get in?" Jeremy piped up. I spun around. Jeremy started walking about the cabin, looking.

"Around 3:00." Jeremy opened my closet and looked at the contents up on my closet shelf.

"Why do you have lotion? Isn't it humid enough here for you?"

I walked up to Jeremy and shut my closet door. "Dinner should be soon, right? Is there a set time?"

"In about an hour and a half," Brian answered. I spun around to look at him. "Dinner's at 6:30 each night. Tariq yells at you if you're late." Brian looked at Jeremy who continued snooping, now with his hands behind his back, whistling. "You'll really like it here, Jamie. There's something about this island, the air or something. It energizes you better than coffee. Everyone here says."

"Hey look!" Jeremy shouted, and we zipped around. Jeremy had snatched Mr. Dody. "She's got a stuffy!"

"Hey!" I yelled, and then Jeremy threw Mr. Dody to Brian, who caught it on reflex and gave me an apprehensive look, like he was just caught holding stolen goods. Brian handed it back to me and I hugged Mr. Dody close to my chest.

"No worries, Jamie, it's cool" Jeremy said. "Even if you're over six years old now, it's cool."

"Ahh, you're a pretty funny guy," I said blandly. "Don't you two dare tell *any*one about Mr. Dody." As soon as the words left my lips, I realized my mistake.

"Mr. *Dody*?" Jeremy leaned forward. "You actually *named* that thing? Ha!"

"Don't worry, we won't say anything to anyone," Brian said.

"Mr. Dody, ha!"

"Jeremy, why don't you just..." Brian said, but Jeremy had already forgotten about it when something else caught his interest.

"Look! It's the giraffe lamp! Oh wow!" Jeremy said, backing up, as if it were a bomb.

"Oh no, sorry!" Brian said.

"What? What's with the giraffe lamp?" I asked.

"You gotta sit down for this" Brian said. I looked at the two of them. Jeremy had finally stopped buzzing and was actually standing still in the center of the room, looking rather somber. He raised his eyes and nodded at me, and so I sat on the edge of the bed, still holding Mr. Dody. Brian took a chair at the table, and Jeremy leaned on the dresser at the front of the room.

"Well, the giraffe lamp gets passed around," Brian said.

"Excuse me?"

"The giraffe lamp gets passed around to the new guy. Or girl, in your case."

"I still don't understand."

Brian explained. "The giraffe lamp started out in Tom's cabin when we all first arrived."

"Yeah," Jeremy continued. "Well, Tom moves the lamp to Adrian's cabin, and Adrian storms out yelling 'who the *hell* put this damn *thing* in my cabin!' And Tom said 'I did. I didn't want it in my damn cabin.' And Adrian yells 'well I certainly don't want it in *my* cabin either.' So Adrian shoves the lamp back at Tom, who then puts it in the doctor's cabin."

"Well, the doctor moves the giraffe to Darcy's cabin as a gift. He said he thought it was more a girl's lamp," Brian said.

"He denies the fact that he just didn't want the damn thing in his place," Jeremy added.

"Let me guess… Darcy didn't want it either," I said.

"Hell no. So she moves it back to Uncle Tom's cabin, as those two are having a fling," Jeremy said.

"Those two are having a fling?"

"Yeah, you don't know?

"I just arrived two hours ago."

"Fair enough. Well, they move it back and forth, Tom wins, and so Darcy is stuck with the lamp. Darcy moves it in Grady's cabin. Bad move. Grady thinks she's hitting on him."

"But she's with Tom, right?"

"Doesn't matter. Grady's Grady. Anyway, Grady moves it to Tariq's cabin, another bad move."

"Tariq?"

"Head cook."

"Oh yeah, that's right, that's right. Why is that a bad move?"

"Because Tariq has a temper and yells. You don't want to get on Tariq's bad side. Never piss off the guy in charge of food. So Grady has to take it back."

"What if he refuses? I mean, isn't Grady 'Mr. Muscles' in security?"

"Doesn't matter. Tariq makes the food. And no one can tolerate Tariq's screaming. I tell ya', don't piss off this guy."

"I'll certainly keep that in mind," I said. "So what happens to the lamp? I mean, before I get it?"

"It gets passed around to just about everyone, except for Kane."

"Kane?"

"Head Maintenance guy. Only black guy on the island. Huge guy. I'm talking giant. I'm guessing he's six–foot–six or so. You probably saw him chopping wood. He does that when he's not working. He says it's meditative"

"Kane is Jeremy's boss," Brian clarified. "Kane and Jeremy make up the cleaning crew."

"Maintenance crew," Jeremy corrected.

"Why doesn't anyone give the giraffe lamp to Kane?

"'Because he'll put a curse on you or something," Jeremy said. I looked questionably at Brian, and he slowly nodded.

"What about the little boy? The lamp's perfect for him."

"Tried it. The lamp scares him."

"Oh."

"Anyway, Tom made it official that the new arrival gets the lamp. So you're stuck with it, dear," Jeremy said. "And you can't give the lamp away. That would be considered a crime."

"And there's like zero crime here," Brian said.

"But if you *do* commit any sort of crime, Adrian will tie you to a tree overnight and put snakes at your feet."

"Really?" I asked.

"No. Not really, don't worry," Brian assured. "Though little Derek actually believes this to be true."

"Derek? The little boy? How old is he?"

"He's nine."

"Nine? Really? He looks a couple years younger."

"He's Filipino. You know, from the Philippians?"

"You mean the Philippines?" I asked, but my sarcasm was missed.

"They're tiny people, not much bigger than Hobbits," Jeremy said. "But Derek's like Jack of all trades. He's actually becoming quite the computer wiz, along with helping the doctor out. He's learning to cook, too!"

"He's Joel's son, right?" I asked. "But why is he here on the island? I mean, why isn't he with his mother?"

"Joel got custody when his wife had a problem with over doing pain meds while driving," Jeremy explained.

"Joel is just about the best there is with computers," Brian said. "One of the conditions Joel made when he agreed to work on this project was that he got to bring his son."

"Derek's the man!" Jeremy said. "Derek should be in charge, not Tom's daddy."

"Tom's *daddy*?"

"Girl, you don't know anything," Jeremy said. "Tom's father *owns* Jao Institute."

"He does?"

"Richard Gordon's two sons are Tom and Joel. That fact is not spelled out in the corporate literature, probably at Tom's request. Gordon is a common name, so people don't connect." Jeremy explained. "Tom is kinda' touchy about people thinking it may be a case of *silver spoon*."

"Though the folks over at Research have better housing, better equipment, more staff," Brian said. "Tom's father gave them the better deal than his own two sons. I think it's because Dr. Evan Bronte, who heads the research department, is this huge big shot. You've heard of him, right?"

"Oh, don't get me started on *Bronte*..." Jeremy said.

"Why?" I asked. "And what's with his name – *Bronte*? What's up with that? Sounds like something from English Lit 105."

"I feel like drinking brandy out of a pewter glass and saying 'jolly ol' chap' whenever I hear his name," Jeremy said.

"Anyway, his bio is quite impressive," I said. "I don't read science journals, but from what I understand he's world-renowned in the science world, right? He's got like two Ph.D.'s in biochemistry, and I forget what else, something I can't pronounce. He's written all these books on... what is it... brain stems and quantum physics, stuff like that. I'm surprised that he has only four people under him here on this project."

"Four that we *know* of. Everything's a secret over there. They're holier than thou. We're immaterial to them." Brian said.

"Don't get me started," Jeremy warned, then pushed himself off the dresser. "Hey, gotta' go." Brian stood, puzzled. "See ya at dinner."

"Remember, don't tell anyone about Mr. Dody!" I said only half jokingly as the cabin door slammed.

Chapter 4
FIRST NIGHT

Tariq came crashing into the room from the back kitchen, pounding the door with his back as he held a large pewter platter with steam snaking out into the air. He was a short sturdy man with wild masses of black hair, thick lips and eyebrows, and a blotchy complexion.

"Get ta living hell outa my *way*!" he yelled as he almost ran Jeremy over. Jeremy jumped. "What da matter wit you?"

Brian meekly followed Tariq carrying a tray of assortments for our dinner. Young Derek came next, carrying as much as he could hold in his arms. They made several trips through the door in the back of the lodge, a door that apparently led to the chef's kitchen.

"You gonna' HELP or jahss look stupid!" Tariq barked at Tom as he passed him. I was quite surprised that Tariq spoke to our leader in that manner. Amused, Tom smirked as he ran his long fingers through his short black hair, then went to the kitchen in back. "All ah you… help breeng food out!"

Dr. Jim, who sat at one of the back tables with his legs crossed as he spoke with Joel, stood, smoothed out his pants, and went off to the kitchen in back to also help. Joel, the computer wiz, stood and followed him. I saw Darcy march off to help as well.

I wanted to help, but I stood frozen by the lodge's entrance door, having had arrived not even a minute prior. I hesitated venturing deep into the large room, not eager to merge with a world of strangers. I watched about a dozen people fill the room with the hollow buzz of conversation, as if at a cocktail party. No one seemed too concerned with Tariq's fussing. While most of the faces were now somewhat familiar, I didn't really know these people. I recognized Leader–Tom who was now bringing in food from the kitchen, Dr. Jim and

Computer–Joel, who disappeared into the kitchen, Lively–Darcy, Little–Derek, who carried a platter that seemed to weigh more than he did, and of course Jeremy and Brian, the two blond boy–men whom I had met in my cabin an hour ago. All of them, except for Jeremy, were helping Chef–Tariq bring in food from the kitchen. I wondered if all this food and all this help was the norm.

I noticed the two beefy but trim security men I'd met at the dock, Adrian and Grady. Oblivious to anyone else, they stood in the middle of the room talking with each other along with a third man. My eyes fell on this third person. He was a serious looking red–haired man with a square face and narrow eyes. I assumed this was Steve from the Jao bio, the security guy I hadn't met yet.

Darcy hurried to help Derek with his heavy platter, as he had almost dropped it. Setting the platter down on the table, she then noticed me from across the room, smiled, and headed my way. Her gait and animated demeanor were welcoming.

As Darcy walked across the room towards me, I noticed the three women who I'd seen by the water basin earlier this afternoon. They clung together at the side of the lodge, looking around the room, their eyes darting like birds. When they saw me standing alone by the door, they whispered and giggled among themselves.

"Don't mind those flakes," Darcy said to me when she reached me. I looked at her and she rolled her eyes. We smirked at each other.

"Where's Earl?" I asked Darcy. I was dying to meet him. I would be working directly under Earl for the next six months.

"He's probably still at the stables. He often takes his dinner there. He prefers the company of animals to people."

"I can relate." Darcy shot me a look. "And where's Jeremy's boss, the head cleaning guy?"

"Head *maintenance* guy," Jeremy piped in. I hadn't noticed that he had joined us. "That would be Kane. Kane rarely joins us for dinner. Tariq brings him his food privately. Most of the time, he doesn't even join us for Campfire. He prefers to be alone."

Darcy started arguing with Jeremy as to whether or not Kane was a vegetarian, with Jeremy insisting he was, and Darcy swearing she saw him eat meat. I drifted off and looked around the room. Central Lodge was huge. Couches and chairs were grouped in the front of the lodge, with two ceiling–high stone fireplaces at each side wall, giving the lodge a snug feel. The crystal–clean fireplaces didn't look like they were ever used, and I wondered why they built a fireplace in a tropical lodge. I noticed a male and female bathroom on each of the side walls in the front of the lodge.

So it seemed that this Central Lodge was the dining hall, gathering room, conference hall, library, and living room – a place to read during monsoons, a place to gather when our cabins got too small, a place to escape the sun, or a place of security should an emergency occur. I read in the Jao handbook that a non–denominational Sunday morning service met here, for those who were interested.

In the back of the lodge, where several people were scurrying to get the last platters of food on the table, was a long head table. It spread parallel to the back wall and was fancier than the table at Jesus's Last Supper, but not as elaborate as a wedding's head table. Two smaller side tables jetted out from the longer head table on either side, forming an upside–down U.

Tom, his brother Joel, Dr. Jim, Adrian, and his two security assistants, Grady and Steve, started to get seated at the head table. Apparently, this table was for the Department Heads and the Security Team. There were two empty seats at the head table, and I wondered if they were for Earl and Kane, or perhaps Tariq. One of these men was left out. The three girls sat at one of the side tables, and Darcy directed me to the other side table with Jeremy, Brian, and Derek.

Tariq had prepared a feast. It amazed me that Derek knew the name of each dish, which he promptly informed me. We had babi guling, Balinese–style roast pork, along with cakalang fufu – grilled smoked tuna skipjack fish stuck on bamboo. Darcy confided to me that all this was unusual, especially having two meat dishes, and added that I should feel honored. I did indeed. Instead of potatoes like we'd have back home, Tariq had prepared nasi kuning, a rice dish cooked with coconut milk. In a large turquoise dish was gado-gado, a mixture of vegetables, crackers and rice with peanut flavored sauce. Jeremy called it salad. I did not try the sambal goreng teri because Darcy told me it was spicy salted anchovy with peanuts. She didn't eat it either, as anchovies are rather nasty things. I loaded my plate with fruits – water apple, mango, banana and jackfruit. We washed it down with teh botol (bottled tea). Dessert was pretty – jello-like squares of red, green and yellow clusters called *cendil*, a flour-based sweet rice dish cake, molded and colored, served with fresh grated coconut.

Halfway through the meal, Tom stood and said words of welcome to me. The others clunked their tea bottles, and I smiled and nodded, hiding my self–consciousness. When I feel uncertain, I can hide emotions from people, but not from horses. Horses can always tell.

Campfire came after dinner every night when it wasn't raining. I walked with Darcy, Brian, and Jeremy down the lodge's steps and around back behind the lodge, following the security team down a narrow path that led to a small clearing. Though cooler, the air was still heavy, but the others didn't seem to notice. I was the only one who was wiping my forehead and the back of my neck. Dr. Jim and little Derek trailed behind us as we entered the cleared area. There were camp chairs on packed dirt, a stacked wood pile, torches sticking out of the ground like miniature telephone poles, and a little man–made shed. I watched Adrian as he unlocked the shed and took out an iron rod and matches.

Tom and Joel had retired early. Tom had said he had a report to fill out, and Joel had some computer work. As we sat down in the chairs near the fire pit, Darcy told me that Kane and Tariq rarely joined in at our campfires, nor did Sheila or the nurses. She added that Tariq always cleaned up after dinner, then would promptly go to bed, and Kane would go off to do his thing, whatever that was. However, Kane was with us tonight. Leaning against a tree a short distance from us, I watched Kane sharpen a wind instrument he was making, using his kīlaya knife for fine–tuning. This giant of a man worked his knife gently. Adrian started the fire, along with his two security assistants, Grady and Steve. The doctor stood next to them by the fire, and he lightly kicked Brian's foot and suggested he help Tariq with the dishes.

"I tried to, but he shooed me off, told me to get out of his way."

"That's his way of wanting you to relax after dinner" Jim said.

"I don't know about that." Brian squinted his eyes.

"Mm, I think so," Jim smiled, then leaned towards me and said, so only I could hear, "You might want to thank Tariq sometime for making such a feast tonight. He really fussed over your arrival." I looked up at Jim as if he were crazy. Tariq scared me. Jim straightened up and said, "Aww, his growl is ferocious, but there's a big heart in there. He'll be damned if you see it though."

I looked away and watched Derek swinging his legs as he sat on a log behind the camp chairs across from me.

"You know what, you don't *seem* like a horse trainer," Grady said to me as he brought a log from the stack to the fire. Derek looked up at Grady, then at me.

"What do you mean?" I asked.

"Aren't female horse trainers rugged and hard, overly assertive... you know, kind of... manish? I mean, you don't seem like that. Or are you? I mean, of course you're not. You're... well... soft, and girlish." Adrian shook his head. I think I caught Kane smiling, or maybe it was a grimace from working his knife into the flute.

"Do you always have to be such a creep?" Darcy asked Grady.

"Me? What do you mean?" Grady was wide–eyed.

"You just keep out–doing yourself, Grady," she said.

"So the food at dinner isn't always like it was tonight?" I diverted.

"Uh–huh, yeah right," said Jeremy.

"We had twice as much food tonight!" Derek said from the log.

"It was special tonight, but we generally eat well here," Jim said. "You just have to be punctual, which is nice because it forces us to all be together. Breakfast's at seven, and lunch is at noon."

"So what else about the island should I know?" I asked. "Does it rain a lot? Is there ever a break in this humidity?"

"It doesn't rain so much during the summer months, but we can get a quick downpour in the afternoon. Seconds later, the sun is shining." Jim said. "And I suspect that you'll get somewhat used to the humidity."

"When does mail come?" I asked.

"Every day by rowboat," Grady said. Darcy kicked him.

"Mail comes in on the supply ship, which comes about twice a month," Jim told me.

"Is the water warm for our showers in the morning?" I could now ask questions that I didn't feel comfortable asking during the interviewing ordeal last spring.

"Get to the showers before Sheila and company get there, because they use up all the warm water," Darcy said, then added, "I always flush the toilet over and over again when they're showering."

"The showers are to the left and right of the lodge, behind Admin, and also behind Security over there," Jim pointed. "What are there… five or six showers in each stall?" he asked the others.

"Five," said Brian.

"Six!" corrected Jeremy.

"Five," said Darcy.

"Who cares," said Grady. "I just know that I'll share my shower with any lady any time."

"Okay, you're being creepy again," Darcy said.

"How do we wash our clothes?" I asked.

"There's a laundry room behind Maintenance, but good luck finding a machine that isn't being used," Brian said.

"I wash my father's clothes and mine, by myself," Derek said.

"You wanna' wash mine too, kid?" Grady asked. Darcy kicked him again. "Oww! Chirst, woman!"

"Is it hard getting personal computer time?" I asked.

"Every employee gets twenty minutes a day computer time, which includes email," Adrian said as he stirred the fire with his iron rod. I noticed that when Adrian spoke, the others got quiet. "Our computer signal can be quite temperamental here on the island."

"Do we get Netflix?"

"No Netflix, but we get a variety of movies from *Happy Friday* delivery. No streaming, obviously, just DVD's from Jao's video library. And we can make movie requests," Adrian said. "We're not hermits from the outside world."

"I watched Jurassic Park!" Derek said, swinging his legs.

"Happy Friday?" I asked.

"A supply ship arrives every other Friday. We call that day Happy Friday."

"Kinda' like McDonald's Happy Meal." Jeremy equated.

Ignoring him, Darcy said. "They bring items that we requested – a specific shampoo brand, our favorite toothpaste, a requested DVD, socks when ours are worn, books, etc. You can fill out the form for requests. I have them on my desk in the Admin building. *Maybe* the items will arrive on Happy Friday, if you're lucky."

"The supply ship honors only about half our requests." Brian said.

"Someone started calling this Happy Friday. Was it you, Jeremy?" the doctor asked.

"Wasn't me," Jeremy said.

"Yes it was," Darcy said.

"No it wasn't."

"Yes it was!"

They bantered on back and forth as the rest of us sat and listened to the fire snap. The whole while we talked, no one really looked at anyone. All eyes were in the fire, except for Kane, who continued to work his knife into the wood. He and Steve had said nothing all evening. Steve always maintained a sense of seriousness, even when some of us were silly. We continued to stare in the fire. What was it about fire that was so mesmerizing?

Jeremy broke the silence. "Be prepared to have a little stomach upset from the strange diet here," Jeremy said to me, then to Jim, "remember when I first came, Doc?" Jim just smiled.

"I don't think you want to share that experience," the doctor said, chuckling.

"He gave me a blow by blow update, including all the colors," Brian added.

Derek stopped swinging his legs. "I think I just heard someone coming from the woods," Derek said. "I think it's the research people."

"Derek's afraid of the research team, though he's never met them," Darcy whispered to me."

"I think I hear them coming. I think they're going to hurt us," Derek said, and he hopped off the log.

"Come here, baby," Darcy said, holding out her arms to him. He shyly walked over to her, and she held him. Derek seemed vaguely embarrassed, but was more concerned with what may be out there in the woods.

"That crew is a bunch of bad–asses." Grady said.

"Enough of that." Adrian cautioned. "Grady, the boy." Adrian motioned his head over to Derek.

"Oh yeah, sorry," Grady apologized with mocked sheepishness.

"I've heard the word *ass* before," Derek said.

"Enough!" Adrian pointed a finger at Derek, and Derek slumped.

"Why is the research team three miles apart from us?" I asked. "And why don't they *eat* with us?"

"Who knows," Darcy said. "Ask Jao Institute. Lord knows why they do half the stuff they do."

"They're too good for us." Jeremy said.

"Come on, Jer, they're part of our *team*." Jim said.

"No, *you* come on, Jim!" Darcy snapped. We all stopped and looked at her. "Why do you defend them, especially Bronte, after what he put Tom through? A *lot* of us through." There was a silence and I waited for an explanation.

"Okay Derek, time for bed," Adrian commanded. Derek fussed a bit, but Adrian was firm, and Derek marched off. What a safe world it was here where a child could walk off by himself through the night woods unescorted by an adult.

"You folks really need to be a little more careful with your talk around the boy," the doctor said. "No wonder he's afraid."

"I'll drink to that," Grady said, then reached behind a rock and retrieved a bottle of bourbon. Adrian grinned, and Jim shook his head. Grady took a large swig, went "ahh!", then passed it to Adrian, who threw his head back. Adrian passed it to Steve, who took a healthy swallow before passing it to the doctor, and I was surprised to see the doctor take a drink. Adrian laughed at the face I made when I took a sip. The bottle got passed around to everyone, that is, except for Jeremy, who kept reaching for it, but no one passed it to him. Darcy winked at me as she purposely by–passed poor Jeremy, who said "Come on now, hey!" I watched Brian pretend to drink, and understood. The stuff tasted nasty. Darcy drank like a man.

"I just don't know why you defend him," Darcy continued as she passed the bottle to Jim, who studied the label. "You know what he *did*!"

"Darcy, we need to all get along here, east *and* west side," Jim said. "We shouldn't be divided like this. We need to…"

"There you go again, defending him! I can't believe it!"

"He can bully, but he's actually quite harmless. I see no real threat." Adrian said, and playfully snatched the bottle from Jim. "You gonna' drink or you just gonna' read?"

"Actually, his work is quite impressive," the doctor said. "He has two Ph.D.'s, one in neurophysiology, and one in biochemistry, not to mention an M.D. in psychiatry. The man is world–renowned in the science world with his study on human brain cells, not to mention the books he's published on the subject, selling over a million copies in several languages."

"We don't even know what his work *is*! Everything's such a damn *secret*!" Darcy said, and she walked over to Adrian and reached for the bottle.

"You need to calm down some." Adrian said, and he held the bottle out of her reach, then stared at her as he took a swig. She stared him down, her eyebrows digging into her eyes. They argued back and forth, with Darcy and Jeremy venomously attacking Dr. Bronte's character for some bullying he apparently did to them in the past, Jim crediting the man's reputation, and Adrian admiring his military achievements with his biomedical research for the Department of Defense. Grady enjoyed the excitement of it all and added fuel to the fire for his amusement.

For some unknown reason, the research area was divided from us. My job was ironically to link our two worlds, providing transportation via the horses who would act as a three–mile umbilical cord between Main Campus and the Research Center.

Kane continued to lean on the tree, working his knife, just listening. I walked over to him and offered him the bottle, and as I did, the others got quiet. I felt the weight of their eyes me. As I held the bottle to him, Kane just smirked and vaguely shook his head.

"I mean, don't they *eat*?" I asked, walking back to the group. Adrian, Jim, Darcy and Brian looked at me as if I'd just done a double back flip. "They're human, right?"

"Yeah, well I'll give them *that*," Jeremy said. "They're human, I *think*. Hey, hand over the bottle, dammit!" I handed Jeremy the bottle and he held it with two hands as he drank, reminding me of an infant.

"That's enough!" Darcy grabbed the bottle from Jeremy.

"Hey!" Jeremy yelled.

"They have kitchens in each of their living quarters," Adrian explained.

"We don't!" Jeremy said.

"They also have bathrooms in each of their homes," Darcy sneered.

"We don't!" Jeremy said.

"*They* have chalets. *We* have cabins," Darcy commented.

"If communication between Main Campus and the Research Center is so infrequent, I'm wondering why I'm training animals for transport."

"Well, we hope to bridge that gap between the east and the west side," the doctor said.

"I wonder if they have to give blood for drug testing as much as we do," Jeremy said.

"I'm sure they do," the doctor said.

"I bet they don't," Darcy said. "I bet they somehow get around it."

"Everyone on the island is tested once a month," Jim said. "No exceptions."

"I hate blood tests!" Brian said.

"Oh, it's not so bad, Brian," Jim said.

Again, a silence fell as we all stared into the fire. The flames seemed to feed on our emotions, growing in waves when we got upset about the people across the divide, angrily giving off sparks, and then quieting to a tickle when our talk became friendly or comical.

Jim leaned back, holding the back of his head in his palms. "So Jamie, what do you miss about home so far? You've only been on the island several hours, but you've been away from home for roughly three weeks."

"I don't know… my dogs. My horses."

"What about you, Brian?"

"Chicago pizza," Brian said without thinking.

"California women!" Jeremy said.

"Here here," Grady said, holding the near–empty bottle in the air.

"I miss my bed," Darcy said.

"Tom's isn't soft enough?" Grady asked, and she threw dirt at him.

"What about you, Adrian?" Jim asked, as Adrian studied the fire.

"Oh, I don't know," Adrian said. "Sure, I miss Alaska, but I rather like it here. The mountains, the ocean, the jungle... no taxes. I can think better here."

"I miss my wife," Jim said. "And the farm back home. That, and holidays with the family."

"You grew up on a farm?" I asked Jim. He nodded and proceeded to tell us a bit about his childhood in Illinois. His farm was pleasing and affable where he worked in rhythm among people he loved. My work on the farm as a child was filled with toil and anguish, working among people I feared. I said nothing.

We continued to blurt out what we missed about home – sport teams, snow, local bands, luxurious bathrooms, drug stores, our favorite restaurants, Christmas...

We also revealed what we did *not* miss – rigid work schedules, concrete, writing monthly checks for bills, traffic, grocery lines, frozen dinners, cold weather...

Perhaps it was the alcohol talking, or perhaps it was the dead of night which caused us to reveal demons from our past, with all our faces in shadow as the fire flickered dim orange shadows on our bodies. Surprisingly, we all seemed to have some sort of trauma from our past! Adrian was lost in the Alaskan woods for three days when he was twelve years old, having ventured off from a camping trip with his father. He said the tragedy changed his life. Jim's little sister died of leukemia when he was in high school. Grady said he was beaten by his father on a regular basis when he was a boy, and said Earl shared the same misfortune, a tragedy that Earl shared with Grady one night over a bottle of whiskey. Darcy told us that Tom's father disowned him for about a week when he was thirteen because the cops brought him home after he'd gotten involved in a bitter fist–fight at a McDonald's parking lot. Darcy also told us that the same father threw Tom's brother Joel off a rowboat to teach him to swim, and Joel nearly drowned, swallowing so much lake water that he was sick for days. Darcy added that little Derek was in the car when his mother fell asleep at the wheel from an overdose of painkillers, but thank God no one was seriously hurt. Darcy did not, however, reveal any personal tragedy that happened to her, nor did Brain or Jeremy. I didn't tell them that my parents were killed when I was nine years old.

As the night grew on, one-by-one we went off to our cabins. I walked with Jeremy and Brian down the short path towards the front of the lodge, and thanked them for not telling anyone about Mr. Dody.

"Who's Mr. Dody?" Jeremy asked.

"Never mind." It was good that he forgot.

"Oh yeah, your stuffy!" Damn!

As they veered off to their cabins, I saw Tariq washing something in the water basin by Central Lodge. I was surprised he was still up. I slowly approached him. He did not turn around when I reached him.

"I..." my voice cracked. "... I want to thank you for tonight, for the meal you served." There, I'd said it. Still, he did not turn around. I stood awkwardly behind him for too long. "It's me, Jamie." Nothing. "Okay then, umm... I just... Thanks again!" I slowly backed up as if he were a bomb, spun on my heels, and went towards my cabin. Just before I hurried away, I thought I heard him say something to me, but I don't think it was in English.

I opened the door to the cabin. My room. My space. Tiny area, but it was mine, all I had now. Sounds hollowed from being inside, gone was the outsize buzz of insects. I went to the nightstand and turned on the lamp. The giraffe illuminated to a yellow–orange. I was alone. Exhausted, I felt my life back home was no longer real.

I slipped into sleeping clothes, carefully putting away my pants, blouse and shoes. I slid into the small bed. Looking at the thick sturdy ceiling beams, I watched shadows from the flickering lamp dance on the wood. I reached to turn off the lamp and settled back in bed. Sounds quieted and intensified. I looked through the window above my bed and watched and heard the tree branches blow against my cabin, seeing the shadows they cast in the room when my eyes had settled to the dark. I took a breath. I then thought I heard ruffling just outside the window... an animal behind my cabin? I was afraid. I missed my dogs fiercely. I hugged Mr. Dody to my chest and one of the pups popped out of the zipper. If any of the others found out I slept with a stuffed animal, I would be mortified.

Chapter 5
FIRST DAY ON THE JOB

I woke to the twittering and chirping of a thousand birds giving off a thousand decibels, each of whom sounded utterly delighted. Their sounds made the air and my soul full and rich.

When I returned to my cabin from the showers, I noticed that Mr. Dody was gone. I looked under the bed and around the room. Nothing. I stood dazed.

When I entered the lodge for breakfast, most everyone was there already. Grady had his arm poised to throw something, but stopped mid–air when he saw me. He called out "Morning Sunshine!" He then proceeded to throw something at Tom, who caught it, looked at me, and grinned. In fact, Darcy, Jim, and even Adrian were looking at me funny, as if I was unzipped or unbuttoned.

"What?" I asked as I walked in the room. No one said anything. Tom told Derek to be alert as he was about to throw something to him. Derek stood to catch it, missed, and Mr. Dody landed on the ground.

Earl wasn't at breakfast. After breakfast when Tom, Darcy, and I were walking down the lodge steps, Tom told me that Earl often took his breakfast at 5am so he could hit the stables early, cowboy that he was.

"You'll meet Earl later this morning, after your tour of Main Campus," Tom said. "I assigned Darcy here to show you around the different departments before you start your work with the horses."

"Come on!" Darcy locked her arm in mine and led me away from Central Lodge.

Darcy pointed to the right. "That's the Administration Building. Behind it is Tom's cabin, the closest cabin to the lodge. My cabin is next to his." Darcy led me into her cabin briefly to get keys to the department buildings, and I got a quick glance at her red–themed room.

"How'd you get the red curtains and red throw rug?" I asked.

"I ordered them. Cost a bundle. C'mon, let's go to the Admin building."

Inside the brick Administration building, the off-white walls in the open room had a retro feel, as if I'd find a lady with a 1940 hairstyle at a typewriter, and a man in suspenders operating a morse code decoder. Sitting at her desk, Sheila seemed surprised upon seeing us, then quickly shot her face down at the papers on her desk, appearing quite busy and preoccupied. Two lounge chairs were angled towards each other in the front corner, with a standing lamp between them. Darcy told me that she, Tom, and Sheila worked here during the day, where Tom made all the decisions, with her pointing out his mistakes. "Sheila just does the grunt work," Darcy whispered so only I could hear, then walked to the file cabinet and looked at it as if it had horse manure smeared on it. "We have modern computers, but we still use filing cabinets, can you believe it?" She then led me to the back of the room. "Tom has his own office over there. My cubical is here."

I noticed that Sheila eyed Darcy, looking up from the papers on her desk when Darcy wasn't looking her way.

"See us for supply requests, if you need to leave the island in an emergency, if you ever have a problem with your health insurance records, if you see that money isn't adequately deposited in your account back in the States, anything like that… see us in Admin and we'll take care of it."

"Sure. Thanks."

We left the office and I followed Darcy towards my cabin.

"Hey, what's up with Sheila?"

"Sheila? Oh, she and her groupies, the two nurses, just annoy me to no end. They don't pull their weight around here; they flirt with Grady, which is like stealing candy from a baby. They actually gathered around me one night in the showers to warn me to stay away from Grady. Now *there's* a disgusting thought. Grady, eww!"

"They con*front*ed you?"

"Yeah, can you believe it? Three of them against me. They gathered around me like a herd of she–thugs. There was some shoving, some bruising, but I won. They now know better than to mess with *me*!"

"I'll keep that in mind."

"And her cabin is next to mine, of all people," Darcy said.

"There's the medical building," Darcy said, pointing with her chin. It was pretty obvious that the brick building we stood before was the medical building because it had a large red cross painted dead center above the door. "The doctor's cabin is just behind the medical building. The two nurses live next to Sheila, over there. They share a cabin."

"Do they have names?"

"Alice and Brittany."

"I'll never remember that."

"Just think "A" and "B." Those two and Sheila make up Sheila and Company."

"Does the doctor share the annoyance you have with these girls?"

"No, because he's male. Guys don't see stuff like that. But Jim's a sweetheart, pure gold. Brian sees it, but he's gay."

"Brian is *gay*?"

"Yeah, everyone knows this but Brian," Darcy said. "Let's go inside the medical building. Come on!" I followed her inside.

Pale greens dominated the large cool room with smooth hard floors. A couple of metal tables and a cushioned exam table that reclined were set against the side wall. Microscopes, AED's, a stand-on scale, a centrifuge, and other medical equipment were in the room.

Surgical lights hung from the ceiling above the exam tables. Dr. Jim, who was seated in a light brown vinyl chair, looked up as we entered.

"Well hello there! What calls for this nice surprise?" Jim asked. "Are you here for your monthly blood test?" Darcy explained she was giving me the standard tour, and had to decline his coffee offer. One of the "A-B" girls sat at a table in back writing something on a form. She looked up, weakly smiled at us, then got back to her writing.

"So this is the place I don't want to need to be in," I said.

"Unless you're coming in for a social visit," the doctor said, "Which actually I urge you to do anytime." Jim raised his mug, then sipped his coffee.

"Thanks, Jim, but we gotta' go. I need to show this girl the rest of the compound."

We left Dr. Jim's office and went behind the medical building and behind the doctor's cabin. We stood at the edge of a long thin wooden structure that reached from Medical to Admin, the showers.

"This bathhouse is girls only. The bathhouse on the other side is for the guys. Tom and Jim have to trek across the way to use the bathhouse. Grady sometimes treks across to use *our* bathhouse, pervert that he is. I think Earl cleans himself in a stream, he's such a damn cowboy."

Darcy showed me the buildings on the other side of the clearing. The computer building was next to the lodge. Joel, who was in charge of the computers, had his cabin behind the computer building and close to the side of the lodge, and he shared his cabin with his son.

Inside, the computer room strangely smelled like oil and disinfectant, with five computers atop college-type desks. A broken computer with its guts spilled out lay in back of the room, while Joel sat on the floor and worked at the computer with a small tool. He nodded as we entered.

"Just giving Jamie the introductory tour. Ignore us!" she called to him, then she quietly said to me, "It kills me how he's Tom's double. They're night and day! Joel is so damn quiet and serious. Tom certainly isn't."

As Darcy played with a computer wire, she explained that as Jao employees, any of us could use the computers when we wished to email back home, keep personal files in our own password–protected folders, or search the internet, but were asked to limit our time to twenty minutes a day.

"This time limit is only enforced when someone obviously abuses it, like Sheila and Company." Darcy ran her finger through the dust on top of one of the computers. "Also at night, it's a little harder to get computer time."

Outside, Darcy quickly explained the rest of the structures. The three men who made up the security team had their cabins near Joel's. A shed belonging to the security team sat next to Steve's cabin. This shed was always locked. "Only the security guys and Tom have a key to this shed." I gave her a quizzical look and she shrugged.

The men's bathhouse stretched behind the computer building and Security. This marked male territory. "It must be nasty in there," Darcy said under her breath.

Our chefs, Tariq and Brian, stayed in one cabin down from Security, and Tariq kept meats, pots and pans, and cooking supplies in the storage shed behind their cabins. Darcy confided that she once found a box of chocolate bars in the shed and stole it. "Since then, Tariq locks the shed."

At the end farthest from Central Lodge was Maintenance, where Kane and Jeremy worked. "There's the laundry room. Good luck getting laundry time," Darcy said. "Kane and Jeremy's cabins are behind the laundry room. Don't go inside Jeremy's cabin or you'll need a tetanus shot." A bird from a high tree above us gave a piercing shriek, as if emphasizing Darcy's point. "Kane's storage shed is behind their cabins. I can show you inside if you'd want, but it's just shovels and brooms and cleaning supplies, and sometimes a dead animal that Kane is skinning. Oh, not to mention Kane's knives. There could be a voo–doo head in there, too… I don't know."

"I'll pass."

"Okay then." She slapped her palms on her hips. "That about ends your tour of our humble compound."

"Well done! Thank you, Miss Darcy!" She took a bow and we both laughed. "The stables are about a quarter mile or so behind your cabin. Just follow the path."

I was about to meet the horses. And Earl.

I changed into my heavy jeans, yellow cotton shirt with the v–neck, and sturdy shoes, then went behind my cabin and followed the short path through the woods. My life was once again changing, but this time, for the better. I hoped. I thought of my introduction to the horse world when I was nine years old. It was just after my parents were killed in a boating accident off the coast, when I was brought to my Uncle's house to live on the farm. I remember finding solace and strength in the horses after being ripped from my life and thrown in with Uncle Calvin, who shook me awake at dawn until my teeth chattered in my head, who smacked me in the back of my head when I mixed the horse grain incorrectly. The horses stood unremitting as they braced the same rough handling and desecration I withstood, and from them I learned.

The woods gave way to a meadow, and as I passed the field of flowers, I stopped to look at the stables ahead of me. Low against the mountains' feet sat a dark red A–framed barn that settled on a mixture of compact dirt and sand. Tan worn wood showed through in spots under the Indian–red, giving the structure the appearance of being beaten by weather, surrendering to the mountains that towered behind.

I quietly walked forward and stopped a short distance from the fence. To the right of the stables stretched a white horse–fence that encircled a containment area for the animals. Immediately inside the area, a tall thin long–limbed man close to fifty bent scrubbing a water trough. Beyond him three horses, or, on closer inspection, ponies, were feeding in the paddock – one white, one black, and one brown. A breeze swept by from the meadow, and the white pony looked up.

I watched the bony man work the scrubber with the vitality of a man half his age. He wore weathered filthy jeans, scuffed boots, and an open green–striped collared shirt over a black T-shirt.

"You going to just stand there, or are you going to help out?" He called over to me, without ever looking up. How he knew I was there bewildered me. I slowly approached.

"Hello. I'm…"

"You can start by grabbing the broom that's in the barn and knocking down the cobwebs in the corners." Still, he never looked up. I stood there for a moment, watching him clean the trough without missing a beat.

"All right," I said slowly, and backed up.

Inside the stables, sunrays pierced through the cracks of the wood in sharp angry lines. I smelled hay and wood and horses. I found the broom in the corner and began working on clearing the cobwebs, ripping them away. I thought of the ponies I had seen at a glance, and wondered if the white one was a Sandalwood pony, a fine animal noted for its speed and endurance. I couldn't wait to lay my hand on the pony's barrel, and when I did, I could tell how tense or relaxed the animal was. This would give me an indication of how difficult my job would be in the upcoming months.

I was done clearing cobwebs soon enough. I put the broom back and left the stables, walking outside to the animals. The white pony looked up at me as the black and brown ones continued to feed.

"Done already?" Earl called out, still working the troughs. "Now you can wash out the water buckets. Scrub 'em real good, you hear me? Then fill 'em back up with clean water." I stood there for a moment.

"What are you doing, catching flies?"

"Where are the water buckets?" I asked blandly.

"Over there. And the hose is over there." He didn't look up from the trough. He just pointed.

When I finished cleaning and filling the water buckets, he had me muck out the stalls, clean the saddles, then clean them *again* because they weren't polished well enough, and then I had to put out bales of hay for the animals.

A bell sounded. Noon. Never thought I'd be this happy for the lunch hour. I looked at Earl who was working out a knot on a saddle. "Go on, get!"

"You're not coming?"

"Too much damn work to do here."

"So should I stay and help you? I pull my weight."

"I said *get*!"

I was late entering Central Lodge for lunch. I worked further out than the others, and I'd left the stables filthy so I had to wash up and change clothes.

It was wonderful seeing Darcy, Brian, Jeremy, Jim, Tom, Adrian, and even Joel and Grady. Little Derek, of course, too. They were already seated and eating, but called out warm hellos when they saw me. It was like I'd known them longer than a day. I hadn't even been on this island for 24 hours yet.

Tariq had prepared ayam kalasan, a Javanese fried chicken of sorts, with some kind of yellow rice, and cut pineapple. I slid into a seat next to Darcy.

"So how's the first day on the job going?" Tom asked from the other table.

"Nice!" I lied.

"You getting the horses in line?" Jim asked. I didn't correct him by telling him that they were actually ponies. I also didn't tell him I had no feel for them yet, as I hadn't gotten within ten feet of any animal this morning.

"They're fine animals."

"Working here on the island has its own tempo," Aidan said, not necessarily to me. "You find it, you hear it, and it grabs ahold of you and kind of guides you along."

"Sounds like we should put those words to a song," Darcy said.

"I know what you mean, Adrian," Jeremy said. "I used to get tired at times back home in California. It seems I never get tired here."

"You're too young to get tired anyway," Jim said.

"No Doctor, Jeremy's right. Even at my age, I don't seem to feel the afternoon slump I used to feel back home," Adrian said.

"I don't even tire from the drudgery of the budget reports," Tom said. "Who needs coffee on this island?"

As I approached the stables for the second time, I watched Earl work the ponies. He had command of the black and brown animals, but as he circled the white pony, the animal eyed him with ears plastered back. The animal kept his distance. I drew closer. The white pony was terrified, some past trauma. This I could see. This animal held no trust and certainly no appreciation for humans. So it was an abomination when Earl struck the pony with a leather strap.

I remember the feel of the table edge banging my hip when Uncle Calvin shoved me aside for not answering him. While he never out and out struck me hard, nor did he ever leave a visible mark on me, his treatment of me was bitter and my memory of his company was afflictive. Aunt Priscilla was forever silent and never protected me from his malice.

I now felt hot liquid behind my eyes, which I held in. I had an urge to rip the leather from Earl's gloved hands. I hated myself for standing still, as my Aunt had done for so many years.

"About time you returned." Earl said as I opened the gate.

"Someone needs to spread manure, and I'm busy breaking this here pony."

It was several hours after lunch when Earl announced he was taking a short break, but not before giving me enough work to keep busy in the stables. From the barn window, I watched him walk through the meadow until he was out of sight. Grabbing a carrot, I then left the barn and walked into the paddock with the ponies. It was the white one I was interested in, though the black and brown ponies were interested in the carrot I held. Ignoring them, I very slowly inched towards the white pony, avoiding sudden movement, avoiding eye contact. I spoke softly, letting him sense me and get used to me. Could this animal know that I was different than Earl, or did he distrust all humans? That depended on his experience with humans when he was a foal, and I had no way of knowing his past. When I got within ten feet of him, he tensed and was about to bolt, or perhaps attack. I stopped and turned away. I made sure he knew I was no threat. Forever keeping his eye on me, he eased a bit. I continued to talk softly to him so he would later find my voice familiar. Ever so slowly, I bent down and gently tossed the carrot to the side of his hoof. He did not accept this treat. I sat on the ground for fifteen minutes, at which time I decided to return to the barn in case Earl returned. I slowly rose and headed back to my labor. When I turned around, the white pony took the carrot.

It was five o'clock when I left the stables for the day, my first day of work here on this island in some corner of the world. I walked through the meadow and down the path that led behind my cabin, but I didn't enter our camp. I veered right and headed towards the ocean. As I approached the water, I heard music, a flute of sorts. I went closer to the music and saw Jeremy, sitting barefoot on a rock facing the waves, playing a soft melodic song. It was what I needed. I climbed on the rock next to him. He only moved his eyes to acknowledge me, but kept playing, not missing a note. I just listened as the sound calmed me. His fingers worked the simple instrument, and when he was finished, he said, "You smell bad."

"Thanks. Stable work. What's that you're playing?"

"A tin whistle." We just sat and watched the waves for a moment. His presence eased me, like the song had. I resisted an urge to lean against him for comfort.

Leaning against people was a strange habit I got into as a child shortly after my parents were killed. Back then, I hadn't even realized I was doing this. I once attended a birthday party where Charlie was the only kid I knew, and when one of the kids badly cut his hand on the cake knife, I hadn't realized I was leaning on Charlie until he shoved me away. I had no idea how odd my behavior was until the other kids told me so in no uncertain terms. When I got to be a teenager, I had mostly stopped this affliction, unless situations were extremely stressful. In eighth grade, our math teacher threw an eraser at one of the kids, and the kid started screaming bloody murder at the teacher. Before I knew it, I was leaning into a boy who had given me a mood ring, and when we both realized what I was doing, I shot off him as if he had lice, leaving him most confused. Even as an adult, I sometimes literally clung to people while my mind was on something else in a type of oblivious haze. When I *did* find myself leaning against another human being, it was often mistaken for a sexual advance, an occurrence which left me mortified.

I hate this about myself, this leaning I do.

"You okay?" Jeremy asked.

"I think so. Yeah, now I am."

I stared out at the ocean and let the day drift off me. I listened to seagulls, and didn't know if they were calling from contentment or if they were complaining.

Chapter 6
SECOND NIGHT

I looked forward to our campfires. I looked forward to sitting in the semi–darkness with these new people who were becoming familiar to me, perhaps more familiar than people from my real life back home. I should have been tired from all the stable work, but like Adrian and Jeremy and the others, I simply wasn't. It was the island; it breathed new life into us.

Tonight, Tom was with us. He stood by the fire with Adrian and Grady. They were talking in hushes, with Grady kicking a fire log as he snickered over something. I sat with Darcy, Jeremy, and Brian, and the three of us were arguing over how to work our hands in "Here's the church. Here's the steeple. Open the door and see all the people!" Brian was having difficulty with this. Jim was showing Derek how to tie a fishing knot, but Derek ended up correcting Jim, causing the doctor to lift his chin and laugh up at the stars. I wondered if Earl was still at the stables. Joel preferred his time away from people, which was so unlike his twin brother Tom. Kane and Tariq also preferred their solitude tonight. Sheila and the two nurses were together, no doubt, or perhaps with red–haired Steve, the quiet guy from security. He was getting awfully familiar with them at dinner earlier.

"So why Jackel Island?" I asked no one in particular.

"What do you mean?" Tom asked.

"I mean it sounds so much like Jackal, the devil wolf," I said.

"It's spelled differently," Adrian clarified.

"I know some jackals here on the island," Darcy said.

"Oh yeah? Who?" Grady asked.

"Well, you're the king jackal," Darcy said. And they bickered back and forth as to whether or not Grady was a jackal, while all agreed he was certainly a devil. Meanwhile, I finally got Brian to "see all the people" with his hands.

"Okay Jamie, help me pick out who the hottest guy is here on the island." Darcy said loudly. I dropped Brian's hands.

"What, is it '*put the new girl on the spot*' night?" I diverted. I noticed that Grady stopped kicking the log, and Adrian, Jeremy, and Brian were looking at me. Tom took a seat by the fire. "Oh great."

"No really, help me decide," Darcy said. "We got Tom over there, who's got my vote."

"I'd *better* get your vote," Tom said.

"For you, Jamie, we have Adrian over there with the body. Then there's Grady and his dimples." Grady took a bow. "If you like cowboys, vote for Earl." That made me smile. "If you like sweet, vote for Jim or Brian." Jim smiled down at the fishing knot in his hands.

"Oh gee," Brian said, looking away.

"Joel looks exactly like Tom, but watch out for those quiet ones," Darcy continued. "If you're into cute, vote for Jeremy or Derek."

"I vote for Derek," I said.

"Oh man!" Derek squeaked.

"She plays it safe, I can't believe it," Jeremy said.

"I'm not finished!" Darcy said. "There's Kane and Tariq too, if you like the foreign mysterious type."

"I'm sticking with Derek."

Grady started giving reasons why he should win, listing specific details, with just about everyone else giving counterpoints. The men started shedding light on each other's defects.

"Not to undermine this enlightening conversation, but where on earth *are* we exactly?" I asked. The bickering stopped and there was quiet.

"On an island, sweetheart," Grady said.

"Thank you Captain Obvious!" Darcy said.

"No really… I mean where *are* we? Why can't they tell us? Are we in the Indian Ocean, or the Pacific Ocean? Are we near Java? Malaysia?"

"We're probably a little off the coast of New Jersey," Grady said. "The ship that brought us all here probably just took a really big loop."

"We're not supposed to know," Brian said.

"Does *any*one know?" I asked, not sure if I was out of line. I looked at Adrian, who was poker-faced. I looked at Tom and he raised his eyebrows.

"Oh, I already tried him," Darcy said. "He *says* he doesn't know."

"I've studied the vegetation and the trees a bit," the doctor said, "and it falls in line with Indonesia, but perhaps more the western part."

"Why don't they tell us?" I asked.

"Seeing that we communicate to our family and friends in the States through the internet and phones, they'd risk word getting out and unwanted visitors coming to the island. There can be no contamination with the bio–testing going on here," Adrian explained. "When the project is over, they'll let you know."

"Do *you* know where we are?"

"Now why would you ask that?" Adrian peered at me, cocking his head. I eyed him back, looking for clues, an aversion on his part. All I saw in his eyes was amusement. He stirred something in me, the indistinct brush of whiskers starting to poke through his boxlike jaw, the downward slant of his eyebrows, the firm way he held himself... Adrian lifted his chin a little but kept a steady gaze on me. It suddenly got still, and I felt eyes on us. I hadn't realized I was staring, so I broke his gaze. Jeremy looked at Adrian, at me, then back at Adrian again. Grady whistled into the fire. Darcy elbowed me.

"Well," I slapped my palms on my legs, then stood. "I better get going. I have to get to the stables early tomorrow."

Darcy walked with me as we left the campfire. The voices of our friends back at the fire slowly dissipated as the trill of the cicadas and bush-crickets in the woods intensified.

"So what's with you and Adrian?"

"Nothing!"

"Don't give me that, something's happening between you two."

"No, really, nothing! He's more than twice my age!" I kicked the sand as I walked, aware of the smell of smoke, the moist foliage around me, and the humidity on my skin. "Everything I feel, lately, has been…"

"Intensified?"

"Yes! Yes! You feel it too?" I asked.

"Oh yeah. All of us do. We don't know why."

We reached the clearing in front of the lodge and hung by the water basin. I kicked at the bottom of the stone basin with my foot.

"Listen, I've been wondering something…"

"What?" Darcy asked.

"Two things, actually."

"Shoot."

I continued to kick the basin. "Why doesn't Tom mention his father? Why doesn't he like it known that his father owns Jao Institute?"

Darcy sat down on the dirt and sand, leaning her back against the water basin. I slid down next to her. We were shoulder–to–shoulder.

"Tom had problems with his father when he was growing up," Darcy explained. "You gotta' understand that they grew up filthy rich. Jao Institute is no minor firm. Tom told me it was all suits and ties at dinner. As a boy, he saw more of their maids than he did his own parents."

"Ouch."

"As a teen, Tom got into petty trouble… not stealing or breaking things, just mostly fights and mouthing off and breaking rules like curfew or loitering. A couple of times, a local cop would bring Tom home because he had gotten in a fight, which embarrassed his father to no end. He was more concerned about his reputation than his own son. In high school, Tom wore ripped jeans and wanted to be an auto mechanic of all things. His father was dead against this, and things between them got hostile."

"What about Joel?" I asked. "Was their father like this to both of his sons?"

"Tom says that Joel and his father were fine. He kept his mouth shut. Growing up, Joel was the 'wiz kid' while Tom was the troublemaker. Joel helped out with the high school computers, while Tom was helping to stir things up. Joel was fixing everything mechanical, while Tom was fixing to fight."

"So Tom was the black sheep."

"Up until about ten years ago when their father didn't like Joel mixing with an Asian lady. He told Joel if he married her, he wouldn't consider him his son anymore. Joel married her anyway. And now, their father desperately wants Derek in his life, his only grandson."

"So how is it that Tom is now working for Jao Institute?"

"At some point, Tom and his father reconciled." Darcy looked up at the stars. "When his father's appendix burst, it jarred something in Tom. They communicate now, and his father put him in charge on this project. But Tom's awfully touchy about it."

"Why?"

"I don't know. Past baggage, I suppose. I think Tom still has some anger with his father, and doesn't want to be linked with a man he finds to be somewhat unethical. He doesn't want us to think he's been handed something for free." Darcy sighed. "Sometimes he confides in me that he's not sure if he's a *leader*."

"Really!? Because when I first arrived, and I saw him standing there from the dock, *that's* what he looked like to me, a leader."

"You need to tell him that."

We looked square at each other for a few seconds. I nodded, then looked ahead at our cabins with the lit lanterns by the doors. The glow they made and the shadows they cast gave an eerie yet cozy feeling.

"What's all this about the head research guy, Dr. Bronte? What did he *do* to you guys?"

"Oh Jamie!" Darcy dug her heel into the sand, then drew a full sigh. "When we first arrived, we were all so very excited. I can't describe it. It was like we'd entered a new world, you know?"

"I *do* know. I feel it now."

"Anyway, we all got close right away, except for Sheila and the nurses who cling to themselves. I mean, there are the loners – you know, Earl, Tariq, Kane and even Steve, who only talks with Adrian and Grady. Steve's okay I guess; I never had a problem with him. And I really like Kane, though he scares me sometimes, the way a witch doctor would. Just stay out of Tariq's way and you'll be fine with..."

"Darcy, you need to stay on track here." I laughed. "What about Dr. *Bronte*? I'm dying to know what he did."

"Oh yeah. Sorry. I do that, I wander off track." She lightly punched my shoulder. "Well, when we first arrived, we all got really close, right away. All of us except for those in the research department. I just thought it was because they were three miles away, and that they were over–worked. I think we all thought that. We just didn't see them much, with them being over on the east side of the island."

"Okay."

"Well, Tom decides to invite them to dinner, and they accepted. Tariq prepared a feast similar to your welcome dinner last night."

"In Central Lodge?"

"Yeah. Central Lodge. And things were going well. Actually, I found Evan Bronte to be quite charming, very well mannered. We thought he'd be super stiff and arrogant, being such a big wig and all, but he wasn't, at first. He even had a sense of humor."

"At first?"

"Yeah," she said in a low gutter voice. "After dessert came the cordials. The men started drinking. Well, I did too. I had a glass of red wine, *two* actually…"

"Darcy, stay with me."

"There I go again." She hit my shoulder again. "Tom said something about it being easy to be the leader here, because everyone did their job so well. Bronte raises an eyebrow, and asked him if he truly thought he was the leader here. Tom looked at him and grinned and said yes he was. From there it fell apart."

"What happened?"

"They argued over who was actually the leader."

"Tom is!"

"Bronte questioned that. Bronte said that Tom's father was little more than Bronte's puppet."

"Wow! He said that?"

"Yeah," Darcy said. "It got a little ugly. Let me just say that when they left, it wasn't all handshakes and hugs." I took a deep breath and looked up at the trees swaying in the night wind.

"So that's it?"

"No, it got worse. Much worse. The next day, we had no electricity. Tariq wakes us up before the sun comes out, screaming that his kitchen isn't working. Earl actually leaves his stables rushing to us saying he has no power in the barn. This is how we all woke up. None of the lights worked, and all of Joel's computers were down. The jerk was making a point."

"How did he turn off the electricity?"

"None of us knows how."

"Man! Tom should've contacted his father."

"He couldn't. No power."

"So what happened?"

"Adrian, Grady, and Steve head over there by foot. The horses weren't trained yet."

"Ponies," I corrected.

"Whatever." Darcy hit my shoulder for the third time. "Tom went with them. They had to *walk* through the woods and the meadow. When they arrived at the research center, Tom said that Bronte was expecting them, sitting in a chair just outside their main building. The two men who assist him stood by him more like bodyguards than fellow researchers. Adrian believes that's their role."

"Little bookworm can't back his own threat."

"Oh no! Oh no! Just listen. Tom and Grady start yelling, while Adrian and Bronte remain calm, but Bronte doesn't budge. He's not going to turn the power back on until Tom admits who the real leader is, and that his father is a mere puppet… all this in front of the other men."

"Oh wow."

"Bronte is calmly telling Tom that it's simply a minor request of manners. Tom doesn't do it. He told me that he never felt such rage, that he was so close to pounding Bronte with his fists regardless of Bronte's two thugs who stood by his side the whole time. Tom told me that he looked to Adrian for support, but Adrian just stood there holding his forehead with his fingertips. Then Adrian told Tom to just say what Bronte wanted, that it was just words and false pride. Adrian said Bronte was just toying."

"Oh my God, I don't think I'd give in to Bronte, would you?"

"Hell no! Tom was furious at Adrian, and Grady couldn't believe Adrian either. I don't know what Steve, the other security guy, was doing, because Tom didn't really mention him, just that he was there. All Tom said was that before he knew it, he had rushed at Bronte, and Grady was there by his side in a flash, and Tom threw his fist at Bronte."

"You're kidding!"

"No, I'm not. Tom said it all happened so fast. He saw red. Adrian *did* step in to protect them, but before anything got started, Tom was on the ground with Bronte's knee on his chest and his knuckles on his throat, and Grady was held by one of Bronte's thugs."

"I can't *believe* all this."

"No one got hurt, but Tom couldn't believe the fighting skills of these guys, especially Bronte, who we all thought was just some super science geek. They're super trained. Adrian, Grady, and Steve are highly trained fighters too, but I guess Bronte's people are even *more* skilled. What amazed Tom was that Bronte was able to take him down in half a second. Tom admits that he's not a trained fighter like the security guys, but said he's been in his share of street fights, and Bronte's *not* a big guy."

"Though Dr. Bronte has military background, if I remember correctly," I said, remembering Evan Bronte's profile from Jao's package.

"You know what the tragic thing about all this is, Jamie? When Tom was later telling me what happened, he started crying a little, the humiliation of it all. He tried so hard not to. That was the first time I kissed him. I kissed his eyes when he started to cry. That's how we got together. Wow, I can't believe I'm telling you this."

"That's okay," I said softly.

"Tom said he hadn't cried since he was a pre–teen." We were quiet for a while. I listened to the insects buzz, creating a tiny symphony. "Tom is sincerely a good guy, through and through."

"I can clearly see that," I said. "What about Adrian? What was *he* doing all this time?"

"He'd stepped in to protect Tom when he rushed at Bronte, and was at a standstill with the second thug. There were words. Adrian later said that his prime purpose was to restore power to Main Campus, and to keep the peace, and that Tom had over–reacted, adding fire to a bad situation. He and Tom argued for days about how all this was handled. Adrian thought Tom was hotheaded, and Tom needed Adrian to back him. Tom's right, Bronte needed to be firmly stopped. Adrian thinks Bronte was just bullying."

"Seems a little bit beyond bullying," I said. "Borderline

dangerous."

"Ya' think?'

"So what would it take to make Adrian actually take action?"

"I don't know… probably a hydrogen bomb."

Tired as I was, I did not go to bed right away. Grabbing a flashlight from my cabin, I headed out into the night and through the woods behind my cabin, past the meadow, and back to the stables. I didn't know if Earl was sleeping inside; hopefully, he was in his cabin. When I reached the barn door, I pressed my ear against the wood. Hearing nothing, I slowly opened the door. If Earl caught me, I was prepared to tell him I'd lost something, but he was not inside. The ponies were, and I headed towards the white one. This time, I got a few feet closer to him, but still, he did not like for me to be too near him. I sat and hummed to him for almost an hour. Before I left, I threw him another carrot.

Chapter 7

WORKING THE STABLES

It was early morning when I was walking down the path to the stables, passing thick brush and blue ferns that were still wet with dew. Already it was humid. The neem and durian trees swayed and danced with the sea wind. I was not far from the stables, at the spot where the path cleared to a grassy meadow dotted with purple and yellow blooms, when I saw Adrian with Derek a distance off at the meadow's edge. At first I thought Derek was angry with Adrian, as they were swatting each other's hands, but it looked too choreographed, as they together moved their hands up-down-left-right. It seemed to be some type of intensified Indonesian paddy-cake game. As I watched further, I noticed they moved in unison and rhythm, as if they were one person. They then moved so that they stood side by side with their feet apart in the grass as if riding a horse, while their fists hung at their sides. Together, their palms rose to their chest like they were lifting an invisible object, then with their palms facing outward, they moved their hands forward in front of their chest, pushing, all the while in perfect cadence with each other. In unison, both their hands glided above their heads, as if praying. After a brief pause, their prayerful hands soared down, fingers pointing to the heavens. White-tailed seabirds from the sky circled around the man and boy as if curious. Both bird and man moved with a flow that was beautiful.

From the path's edge, I could hear the waves in the distance, how they swooshed out, then paused as the water drew in, only to swoosh out again. I took tai chi in college, but only for a short time. I did not continue with it because there was too much memorization with specific moves. There was one thing I loved about tai chi, and that was connecting hands with one other person, pushing and receiving their push, leading and yielding, reaching and drawing in, like the waves going out and in. The instructor was amazed how I, a beginner, took to this pushing of hands when I had so much trouble with learning the specific moves of the form. When I joined hands with the instructor, I could perfectly and entirely connect to him, all the while listening and sensing, the way I've done with animals since I was a small child. When he tried to push me off balance, I swayed off each of his advances the way water rolls over a rock. This was precisely how I worked with the horses. I thought of one of my horses back home, and how she'd become spooked and would dart forward at me, though I knew that she'd advance a split second before she did, and I darted back, matching her timing exactly. By the time I was 16, I was gaining popularity for the knack I had with horses, and my Aunt sought out a professional trainer for me in hopes I could bring in some income for the farm, or for college should I not receive the scholarships I had hoped for. I was coached by a professional horse trainer who commanded the horses by force and not by yield, by control and strength and not by gentleness and softness, which he mistook for weakness. He was all push, all take, and no give. I could not connect to the horses this way.

This gentle way was the connection I wanted to have with the horses and ponies here on Jackel Island. *This* connection was the reason I came.

"You can start by sweeping out the tack room". There was no good morning. "Make sure you wipe off the counters real good. After that, put the hay out for the ponies to feed." I stood still staring at him for a moment.

"Good morning to you, too," I mumbled before I turned to go.

"What was that?" Earl said.

"Nothing!" I kept walking.

"Girl, I asked you a question!" But I had left Earl to sweep out the tack room, wipe the counters, and spread hay in the feed buckets. I heard him say "Christ!" as he slammed something hard on the stable floor.

In the late afternoon, my clothes were once again stained with the filth of doing stable chores. I had had two chances to be alone with the white pony earlier today when Earl was away, as I continued to allow this animal to get a sense of me. But now Earl was back, and he was out in the paddock where I wanted to be, where I should have been. It was five o'clock and I needed to head out to clean up for dinner, and perhaps rest a bit. I leaned against the stable supporting post, wiping the back of my neck with a light blue hand towel as I welcomed a gentle breeze. I watched Earl walk a circle around the white pony, who held his ears back, eyeing Earl's whip. This pony was never halter broken, so of course he was never rugged, and I doubted if his feet were trimmed or if he was wormed. It seemed that to Earl, he was an untouched and unpredictable wild beast. This animal was never imprinted by human touch when he was a foal. Earl was attempting to put a halter on this animal when he should have just been trying to lay a gentle hand on him first. He was trying to saddle and bit the pony before building trust with him. I knew that a feral horse was easier to train than a domesticated animal that had distrust for humans, and this animal was both. Earl was giving body language to the pony that the pony had no way of understanding. The man was fighting the animal, threatening him with a whip in anticipation of the pony finally giving up. No actual communication or bond was taking place. It was a sin. It was an abhorrent sin. I had to look away, and a tear dropped by my shoe making an oval imprint in the dust.

Chapter 8
GIRL FIGHT

I decided to skip dinner. After witnessing the offense with the white pony, I had no stomach for food. I had no stomach for any of this, or for anyone. I left the stables, crossing the meadow with its honeyed smell that clashed with my despair. As I left the meadow and entered the path in the woods that led to my cabin, I welcomed the damp darkness with the late sunrays slanting through.

As I approached Main Campus from behind my cabin, I saw Grady leave the Medical building and enter the camp's clearing. Seeing me turn away from him, he called out to me, "Bad day at the races, Sunshine?" I continued to walk away from him. "Was it something I said?"

I decided to go to the beach.

I left Main Campus and walked towards the sea, wanting to lose myself in the tide's rush. At the edge of the clearing, I breathed the clean base scent of new forest. I then saw Kane chopping wood with a broad maul ax. I caught his smooth movements and was reminded of the fluid scene I'd witnessed early this morning between Adrian and Derek. As I passed Kane, we didn't look at each other, but I felt his surge as vividly as I felt a wind, and strangely I welcomed it, a breeze of strength passing through me.

"Southeast of India," I heard him say in a low guttural voice, emphasizing every syllable. What was that accent? I stopped in my tracks.

"Did you say something?"

"Last night you asked," he said, and then he simply continued with his ax. This large man had never lost his rhythm nor did he turn his head to look at me. This man went by feel. I saw a small brown mouse run over the toe of his boot. I stood and watched him for a moment, wondering how he knew where we were in the world, and I also wondered how he knew that I had asked this specifically last night. I didn't know if I should speak to him. The muscles in his upper arms glistened with sweat and labor as he worked the ax.

"Thank you Kane," was all I said, and he gave a slight single nod at the wood before the ax fell on it. I left him and proceeded towards the beach.

I stood staring at the sea, allowing each wave to wash a layer of gloom off me, purging, trying to clear myself of disheartenment and anguish. I felt a love towards the white pony that pulled at me and ripped in me at the same time. I should not be feeling this so intensely. I did not understand why everything I felt and sensed was magnified here on this foreign island. Also unclear was how I became attached and endeared to Kane in a matter of a moment, and this brought me to question the validity and correctness of my senses. Why were Jeremy and Brian like brothers to me, and Darcy suddenly a best friend, when it was a mere three days of my knowing them? And then there was Tom, our protector, once a rebellious youth who was now mostly tamed but still with spirit. And what were these stirrings in me that I felt towards Adrian, a man more than twice my age; this brought me shame, confusion, and ill repute. And excitement.

"Hey!" I jumped. Sheila from Administration was directly behind me, accompanied by her two nurse friends. I was surprised that I hadn't heard them approach. One of the nurses had a stick, which she dug in the sand.

"Hey," I said back. I looked back at the ocean. I wanted to be alone.

"So what's with you and Grady?" Sheila asked, and she got too close to me. Her forced casual tone unnerved me.

"Huh? Nothing. What are you talking about?"

"You and Grady!" the nurse with the stick said. Her name started with an A or a B...

"Me and Grady?" I asked, showing a little disgust in my voice. "Keep dreaming." I searched my brain, wondering if their names were Arlene and Beatrice. Or was it Amy and Bonnie? Alison and Brandy?

"Yeah, you and Grady!" one of them said and I turned to look at her. Alice and Brittany! That was it! But then I saw her face, serious and bitter, and I remembered Darcy telling me how these girls confronted her in the shower. I was in trouble.

"Listen, you got it wrong..."

"No, *you* got it wrong!" Sheila jabbed a finger too close to my face. "Stay away from him. We know what you're doing." Alice and Brittany started circling me, taunting, as Sheila glared a death-stare at me. I looked at her in disbelief, then turned my body to the other two, who lifted their arms and wiggled their fingers at me to provoke me, a mocking torment aimed to ridicule me. Alice or Brittany jabbed her stick towards me and I jumped. They laughed.

I had never been in a physical fight before.

"Are you for *real*?" I shouted. "Stop, go away! Jeez! What's the *matter* with you?" I remembered Darcy telling me that there was some bruising when she had encountered these three women a few months ago, and I was afraid.

"Woooh!" they sneered as they wiggled their fingers, imitating a ghost, and they approached me, half snickering. I backed up. "Woooh!" One of them thrust her stick at me and I jerked back. My heel caught a rock and I landed flat in the sand, half of me falling into a brush of nettle that angrily scratched my face near my eye, stinging. They laughed.

"Just stay away, okay? That's all." Sheila said. "Come on, let's go." And they left me lying on my back propped up on my elbows in the sand.

Some speak of "breaking a horse." I never use those words. I *train* horses. But now I lay broken in the sand looking up at the clouds. I was beaten by Earl and by Sheila and the nurses, and my heart ached for the white pony, and I hated it here. I drew my knees up to my chest and rested my forehead on my knees. I cried.

I heard a soft rustle and fear stabbed me. They were back. I looked up from my knees. But it was only Derek.

Derek appeared over the sandy hill carrying a conch to his ear. He stopped suddenly when he saw me, letting his arm that held the conch fall from his ear to his side. Then he ran and dropped to his knees right before me.

"Are you okay?" he asked. His voice was sweet.

"Yeah, yeah, I'm fine."

"You've been crying."

"No. I fell. The twig here scratched my eye. It stings. It made my eyes water."

"Both eyes?"

"Yeah." I scrambled to stand, then brushed sand off me. Derek stood too and looked up at me, squinting.

"Do you want my shell? Here." And he held it out to me. I was about to say no when I remembered something my father told me when I was small. He said to always accept a gift if it came from the heart, and that to refuse such a gift was an insult to the giver. It was one of my few memories of him. I took the conch with two hands and held it to my chest.

"Thank you, Derek," I whispered. Derek turned and kicked the brush that had scratched me moments ago. His actions confused me at first, and then I understood. Following his actions, I then kicked the thorny brush too, and doing this made me let go a bottled up laugh. Derek smiled and gave it a hard kick. I laughed harder. "Oh Derek!"

"Come on. I know who can help you." He put his hand in mine and pulled. "Come on!" And he pulled me towards Main Campus.

Derek led me back towards our settlement, holding my hand and pulling as we hurried across the grounds. I smelled Tariq's dinner that I would miss, a sweet spicy smell mixed with herbs. Once again, I passed Kane at the same place he was twenty minutes ago, only this time, he stopped chopping wood as we approached. He squinted as he looked at my cut face, and said nothing. He readjusted his grip on the ax and slowly shook his head as we passed him by.

I felt a little embarrassed being led by Derek through Main Campus. When we reached the medical building's doors, I hesitated.

"Come on!" He pulled me in, having to use a majority of his weight.

The doctor was sitting in his tan vinyl chair. He stood when he saw us, setting his coffee down. "Ooh!" he said to me after he saw my cheek. Derek had told me that four tiny drops of blood came from my one cut line, but not enough blood to drip off my face.

"Come in, Jamie. Sit down here." The doctor put his hand behind my shoulder and led me to a cushioned exam table. I climbed up on the exam table, sitting with my legs over the edge and my hands on the table as the doctor turned on the surgical light above my head. "Let's have a look here." His thumb lifted my chin as his fingertips lightly touched my face around the scratch. "Aww, it doesn't look serious at all, but it must sting, huh. Just missed your eye. What happened?"

"I fell into a bush."

"Uh huh," the doctor said blandly, and he stepped away to get a small glass bottle from the shelf.

"You mean you just *fell*?" Derek asked.

The doctor pressed cotton at the opening of the tiny glass jar and tipped the bottle upside down. He came to me and lightly pressed the cotton on my wound. The pain was sharp.

"So what happened?"

"I fell."

"How'd you fall?"

"Hmm?"

"How'd you fall?"

I opened my mouth to answer, but no words came. I couldn't think that fast. He stopped dabbing cotton on my cut and looked at me. He saw it in my eyes, a wavering hesitation. His eyes softened on me. It was too late for me to say anything now.

"Derek, why don't you run along now and go get ready for dinner," Jim said.

"Okay. See you Jamie!" I told him thanks and good-bye, and he hopped from the chair and was gone.

Jim went to get something from a drawer and came to put a small bandage over my wound.

"Are you all right, Jamie?" he asked softly.

"Yes."

"You sure?" He drew out his words in a slight sing–song manner as he smoothed the bandage over my skin. I thought of Sheila and the nurses, of Earl and the white pony he struck, of my uncle shaking me awake by my shoulder. I thought of the boat accident.

"I've got to go," I said abruptly and hopped off the table.

"Jamie!"

"No, I just have to go. Thank you for..."

He looked at me puzzled. I wished he was my father, and I feared if I stayed, I would tell him so, or worse, I would lean on him, the way I do. The way I hate. He opened his mouth to say something, but I was as confused as he was. I turned on my heels and quickly left the medical building.

Ten minutes later, I was lying on my bed when I heard three soft knocks on my cabin door. I didn't answer. The knock came again, this time five rapid but quiet raps. I held my breath.

"Jamie? Can we talk?" It was the doctor's voice. I made no sound. "Are you in there?"

Eventually, he left.

I missed dinner, which left me with a feeling of solitude and weighted melancholy. I sat on the bed in my cabin, looking at the ceiling beams. More than an hour later brought another knock, louder and more urgent this time.

"I'm not feeling too well… I'm trying to sleep," I called out. I felt a little bad that I had avoided the doctor when he had shown me nothing but kindness. But it wasn't the doctor.

"Okay, sorry. Jeremy here. Brian's with me. Just seeing if you're all right. Missed you at dinner."

"I'm fine. Will see you in the morning."

I heard mumbling, then their feet leaving.

Fifteen minutes later came the third knock. I tried to ignore it but the knock persistently came again, then again.

"I'm not feeling too well," I called out towards the door.

"It's Darcy!" She gave a loud whisper. This time I got up from the bed and let her in. She slowly came in the room carrying a small bag, which she handed to me. I was glad to see her. She eyed the small bandage below my eye.

"Dammit, Jamie! Why'd you let Sheila and her hussies do this?"

"How'd you know?" Darcy sat at the chair at the table in the back of the room, and I sat on the bed. "Jim…"

"He was just concerned, really," Darcy said. "He remembered when the girls confronted me a while back."

"Who else knows?"

"Well, just about everyone." I felt miserable and let my face show it. "Small island Jamie, sorry." I looked down into my lap at the bag I still held. "I brought you a sandwich," she said. "Listen, I don't think Joel, Grady, or Steve knows. Neither does Tariq. We kept it from Derek too. And Kane and Earl are never at dinner, so they don't know."

"Kane knows," I whispered. "How did everyone treat Sheila and company?"

"The men all pretty much left the girls alone, you know how oblivious men are, though I kept glaring at Sheila and her death queens. Really, I wanted to throw pineapple at them!" She studied me. "Jamie, you really shouldn't take their shit."

After Darcy left, I spent some time staring at the cabin's ceiling beam. After a spell, I ventured out into the night to be with the white pony. I still could not touch him, but he let me get closer than I had before.

Chapter 9
LEARNING TO BREATHE

It was still dark when I woke the next morning, my fourth day on the island, my mind still troubled. I wanted to arrive at the stables before Earl to have more alone time with the white pony. I couldn't take another day of stable work without animal contact.

I quietly left my cabin, taking the dark path through the woods that soon reached the meadow's clearing. I stood in the still silence as the sun materialized where sky touched land, turning the meadow to gold. Day was breaking. I was at the wood's edge under a dicksonia blumei tree, wondering the mystery of this island. A thick of dark green lush spread behind me, and ahead of me, an open land sprinkled with floral color with an early morning wind that sighed over the land.

I was not alone. Perhaps eighty feet to my left was Adrian, who worked his body with kicks and punches under the emerald sun that touched his face and shoulders. Did he exercise this way every morning? I watched him as he slid through the air with an exuberance and fervor I admired. I slowly walked over to him.

When I was just within earshot, Adrian stopped moving and stood still, breathing hard. I stood behind him, watching his back move up and down while he caught his breath.

"Hello Jamie." He hadn't looked at me so I wondered how he knew it was I. Now he turned and looked over at me, smiling, self-assured, with the new sun's rays tickling his eyes.

"Good morning Adrian." I walked up to him. "What was that you were doing just now? Some kind of kickboxing?" Adrian picked up a towel from the ground and dabbed the sweat off the back of his neck.

"Oh, just a bit of silat. Hey, I heard you had quite a time of it yesterday afternoon." He continued patting the towel on his skin.

"Oh that." I looked down and kicked at the grass. Earlier, I had removed the small bandage from my face. The cut was clean, though very visible – a thin red line followed by another faint red scratch, the larger cut with slight bruising underneath. "You heard?"

"Yeah, I heard something about it." He put the towel in his back pocket. "It's nothing to be ashamed of, Jamie."

"No, I know." I looked up from the ground. "Can you teach me?"

"Hmm?"

"Can you teach me? The stuff you do here, can you teach me? I saw you teaching Derek yesterday morning."

He sighed and looked up at the sky, putting one hand on his hip. "Why?" He looked down at me. "So you can knock down the other girls here on the island?" My jaw dropped. Insulted, I was about to say something, but he spoke before I could. "This would be a pretty big undertaking, Jamie, more than you know. To do it right, it'd take me until Christmas to teach you just to breath properly, and then it'd take until next summer to teach you to stand upright, not even considering learning how to move and to think correctly…"

"Look, never mind." I wanted to tell him that I was already breathing and standing and moving on my own, thank you very much. I turned to leave.

"Jamie, hold on a minute, please," he said calmly. I stopped. "Please." I turned around and faced him but didn't step his way. I put one hand on my hip and tilted my head. Adrian seemed to focus on my scratch, and then he walked over to me.

"Breath in, like this," and he breathed deeply. I hesitated, feeling awkward. "Come on," he urged, "like this." I looked at him a few moments, then meekly imitated him. "Deeper, in through your nose. Have your stomach rise, not your chest." I did, not sure where this was going. Were we going to do this until Christmas? "And move your hands like this." Following him, I had my palms by my hips face up to the sky, and I brought them up to my chest, all the while keeping them an inch from my body, all the while breathing in. "Now bring your hands like this and breathe out through your mouth." I turned my palms out and pushed. I gave him a questioning look. "You're doing fine." We spent several minutes on breathing, and my apprehension slowly lessoned. After a minute, I felt a little bit more relaxed.

"Now stand as if you're on a surf board riding a wave. Have you ever been on a surf board, Jamie?" I shook my head no. "All right then, just pretend." I stood as he stood, firmly locked to the ground, only I was unsure, and I felt a little silly. When he gave each of my shoulders a firm shove, he unbalanced me a bit. "No, like this. Imagine roots under your feet that latch in the ground." Feeling more foolhardy, I braced myself for his nudge to my shoulder. When it came, his force made me side step, losing my composure, just like I'd lost my composure to Sheila when I fell into the bush. "Sit into your stance, lower your weight." I didn't know what he meant, just like I didn't know what Earl meant by using his whip on the white pony, just like I didn't know what Sheila meant when she and the nurses bullied me. When his jab again came to my shoulder, I tumbled. I quickly regained my balance, and when I came up in an instant, I swung at him, without thinking. And again. And again. I was aiming for his face but I couldn't land. "Woh!" he said holding my wrists. I could no longer move my arms, just my hips. I was crying. I wasn't sure when the tears had started. I tried with all the effort in me but couldn't stop crying. So he wouldn't see my face, I rested my forehead on his chest.

"It's all right Jamie." He put his palm on the back of my head. "It's all right." My breathing slowed but I didn't want to release my head from his chest, probably because I didn't want him to see my face.

"I don't normally cry like this," I said into his chest. "The last time I cried was yesterday, and the time before that, it's been years, I think."

"You've gone through quite a change in the last few days. You've been totally uprooted." We were positioned in this manner for several seconds, and I felt the warmth of his hand on the back of my head. I drew back from him and dried my face with my finger, forgetting about the scratch until my finger rubbed against it.

"What's going on, Jamie? Is all this because of the girls who tangled with you yesterday?"

"No, not really."

He drew a breath. "I didn't think so. Seems like you've been bottling up a lot of stuff."

"Adrian – it's… I don't know. I feel so weird here, everything's so… *intense.* I haven't gotten to even *touch* any of the ponies yet. So what am I doing here? Now I'm wondering if I should have even come. Should I quit? Should I leave? I don't even know what it is I've left behind. I mean, I miss my dogs more than any person back in Maine. So…" Adrian studied me. He cocked his head slightly to one side. "I'm not making any sense, I know. And I'm awfully sorry I hit you. It's not you I'm mad at, not at all."

"I realize that."

"I hope I didn't hurt you."

"No, but you sure as hell startled me," and we both laughed a little. "I've had worse attacks, Jamie."

"I'm sure you have." I stepped back from him. "Listen, I have to go. I gotta' clean muck from the stables." I rolled my eyes.

As I approached the stables in the early morning before work started, I was hoping Earl wasn't there. Come to think about it, I never saw him around his cabin, which was located right next to mine. Did he sleep in the stables or in his cabin?

The sun cast a gold smear on the side wall of the barn. When I looked from the barn to the fence and beyond, my heart sank a bit when I saw Earl. He was turning the ponies outside.

"Tack's gotta be cleaned," Earl said when he saw me. "I like my tack cleaned after every ride. I use good old basic saddle soap and a knuckle brush. You'll find both of those in the barn on the shelf in the back." Earl began throwing hay to the outside ponies. "Clean out the leather pores real good. As long as the soap suds keep turning gray, you need to keep cleaning. And make sure you work the leather real good. It's going to take some elbow grease."

So I spent my morning cleaning the tack, getting more and more enraged as I worked the leather with hard thrusts. What little healing the breathing and crying and talking to Jim, Darcy, and Adrian had done was now being scoured away as I scrubbed. I dug the knuckle brush into the pours with violent abrade as I questioned the heavens why I was being kept from these animals.

Earl poked his head in. "When you're done there, you can put fly spray on the ponies." I said nothing. I didn't look up. I bit my lip. "I gotta' step out a bit. You have enough here to keep you busy." When he left, I looked up.

I stopped working. I held my breath, listening. When enough time had passed, I stood, brushed myself off, and ventured out of the stables into the open air.

There before me were the three fine ponies. I took in my surroundings, the stables, the horse–fence, the ponies inside the paddock under a bare sky, the wide meadow behind me, the abundant trees encircling us all. Mountains poked behind and above the trees between the forest and the sea.

I was alone with the animals.

Slowly, I crept forward to be near them. The white pony, always observant, considered me. I looked away and loosened my walk, not directly walking towards him so as not to threaten him. I then drew my attention away from the white pony and studied the other two animals.

The brown pony was closest to me, a female. This animal was slender and looked to be of fine breeding, perhaps of Arabian blood, and she proudly held her tail high. She nodded her head up and down at me, and she let me rub her forehead. The black pony lifted his head. This animal was the largest of the three and looked resistant and unyielding, but what caught me was that this animal had the most expressive eyes. I rubbed the black animal's muzzle and cheek as I glanced at the white pony who was furthest back, who continued to check me out.

The brown and black ponies were saddled.

I gently put a bridal on the brown pony and led her out the gate. My heart pounded, but without further thought, I mounted the brown pony. As I rose on the saddle, my heart lifted and fluttered. I tested this animal by riding her in a tight circle, and she obeyed with ease. Minimum pressure on the bit was required to cue this pony. I surveyed the surroundings once more, looking for the best escape route. I then quickly gave the forward command, and the brown pony and I raced off along the white fence and beyond, traveling away.

We raced along a path in the woods that led to the heart of the island. I had no idea where I was heading; I just knew I was heading east. I bolted away from Earl, from Sheila and the nurses, from Grady's looks and advancements, from this place not being all I had intended it to be, and from my past. I plunged ahead through the fertile trail flanked by shoulder–high bushes, through this arboretum of wild jungle in this eminently foreign land. I felt so very alive.

Chapter 10
LOST IN THE WOODS

The brown pony and I crossed through bengal bamboo, wild eucalyptus, and silk–cotton trees under a canopy of foliage. The sun streaked through from the sky, riding on rays of mist. I had slowed the pony down a while back after I considered myself to be a safe distance away, and now, we proceeded at a gentle pace alongside the jungle's thick garden with the thrush brushing my legs and saddle. I rode eastward at least a couple of miles until we had come to a clearing that stretched out towards a low silver–blue mountain, where I dismounted and let my pony drink from a creek.

What I saw next I will never forget.

As I stretched my legs to remove the saddle ache, there before me at the far end of the field stood a herd of wild horses! But these horses were like none I had seen before. Somewhat furrier with manes that stood up like mohawks, these horses were stocky with shorter legs and white muzzles. They were astonishing. I looked for the dominant stallion, but this herd, from what I could tell, consisted only of young males. I knew that sometimes young males group to form bachelor bands before they acquire females for their harem. This alluring group of animals stood dazzling under the sun, bewitching me with their striking beauty. They were so very free. They had sensed me, but I was far enough not to be a threat to them, so they continued to graze.

I tied the rein of the brown pony to a tree and slowly stepped out into the field, putting as little initial weight down as possible so they wouldn't detect me. I wished I had washed the saddle soap off me so I wouldn't be so pungent to them. Nature turned quiet as I crept toward the wild horses in a vacuum of silence. I was entirely and perfectly focused on the animals. Sounds ceased. Suddenly, as one, they all jerked their head towards me, wiggled their muzzles, then they turned and scampered off, leaving me standing alone in the center of the clearing.

"I believe they are przewalski horses." I zipped around. "They're the last surviving wild horses." Standing before me was a royal man, as if he'd be a prince or a king if it were another time. He stood squinting his eyes from the sun as he tilted his head at me. The suddenness and firm nature of his presence caused my heart to race. How had I not heard him? I just stood there with my mouth open, waiting for my heart to calm down. He held an off–white pony by lead.

"I'm afraid they're very rare and very endangered," he said, playing with the lead in his hand. "Not too long ago, they were considered extinct."

I finally closed my mouth and leaned my head back a bit, studying this man. He wasn't particularly tall, or short… he wasn't heavy or thin. His lips were firm, a lawyer's lip; his nose was straight and average–small, and he had green eyes that gave a square look and danced with life. He looked to me to be in his late thirties. He had brown hair, the kind you could tell was lighter when he was a boy. A few loose strands fell softly on his forehead, tossed out of place from riding in the wind. He was dressed smartly in white khaki's and a sky–blue button–down shirt, clashing with the relaxed land. He held himself sharply and distinctly.

"Excuse me, who are you?" I asked.

He smiled with his lips pressed together, a condescending smile. He looked to the ground, but only for a second.

"These animals are native to central Asia, specifically China and Mongolia. How they ended up here on this island I have no clue. And I would like to ask the same of you. Who are *you*? You're not supposed to be here."

This man had to be from the research department, as I must have been close to their compound. He remained still with his head slightly cocked, waiting for me to answer, but I didn't want to tell him who I was before he told me who he was. I had asked first. So I stared at him, this man who stood firmly.

"Are we playing a staring game?" he asked me.

"I don't know, are we?" I couldn't keep all the sarcasm from my voice, as this man unnerved me. He slowly smiled and his face gave way to a full grin showing nice teeth, which brightened his face, turning this man into a striking and alluring individual. Hollywood good looks. But then his lips relaxed and his face returned to one of bland firmness.

"You shouldn't be here," he whispered.

"Why not?" I whispered back, mocking. I'd leaned forward a bit when I spoke.

He looked down the clearing. His hair moved in the wind. "The security boundary line is clearly marked. You people from Main Campus aren't to cross the line." He looked back at me. "Did you not see the markings?"

"You're from research?"

"Did you not see the markings?"

"Are you from research?"

He smiled big again, and while I found him to be most provoking and somewhat annoying, his smile was remarkable. But he only smiled for a moment, and it was gone, his radiance vanished.

"What, do you play chess?" he asked. I was confused. Actually, I did play; I beat a teacher once when I was in Middle School. "Yes, I work in the research department."

"You're not the *main* guy, are you?" I asked.

"Main guy?" He smiled, his lips pressed. "No."

I was relieved. From what I had heard from Darcy, Jeremy, and the others, Bronte was a monster. This guy who now stood before me was simply odd. "So what's with the main guy, Bronte?" I asked.

"Dr. Bronte?"

"Yes, Dr. Bronte, the guy you work for, right?" I said. "What's up with him?"

"What is it you want to know about him?"

"Is he... is he as..." The man tilted his head to further read me. "Just what's up with him?"

"I'm not sure I follow you."

"Is he like... a badass?"

"A *bad*ass?" The research man was amused. "How so?" He laughed under his breath.

"Well, I don't know for sure. I just heard. I never met the guy. I'm... new here."

"If you never met him, how would you know?" I looked out into the field. Out of the corner of my eye, I saw the man play with the lead in his hand. "You really don't want to cross Dr. Bronte. If he catches you crossing the boundary line, well, it wouldn't go too well for you."

"What do you mean?" I quickly asked without moving my lips.

"He's been known to lock people in his lab and do biochemical testing on them."

"No way! That's illegal! He wouldn't... No way. Would he?"

The man nodded, raising his eyebrows.

"You're kidding me. You've got to be kidding me. I know you're kidding me."

The man shook his head, his eyebrows still raised. I looked at him, expecting him to laugh, but he didn't. He looked dead serious. Oh my God, what the others said about Bronte was true, that he was dangerous, possibly evil. I didn't know the extent of his maliciousness.

"I don't believe you," I said, trying to hide my doubt. But he just gave me a steady grave look. I swallowed. "He locks people in his *lab*?" The man gave several quick faint nods. "Biochemical testing?" The quick nods came again along with his deadpan stare. "I think I need to go now," I said softly.

"Okay," he whispered back.

As I rode back towards Main Campus, I thought of the strange man I'd met and how he had stirred something in me the same way Adrian had, only this eluding man was curiously more exciting, though definitely more dark–spirited than Adrian. I never even got his name. It didn't matter because I wasn't planning on seeing him again.

I pondered over what he told me about his boss and decided that Dr. Evan Bronte was also a person to avoid, lest I end up in his lab brain dead. Were all the people who worked in research creepy?

I cleared my mind of these two men and thought about the wild horses. He had mentioned that they were przewalski horses, and I seemed to remember reading about them, that only about a thousand or two now exist. I had seen these astonishing creatures, and I planned to see them again.

As I trotted through the brushwood and shrubbery, sea green juniper and curry leaf brushed my leg, and the smell of night blooming jasmine was piquant. I realized it was early afternoon and I hadn't eaten anything yet today. Thus, I hurried home. As I neared Main Campus, I saw Adrian at the brink of the woods, cutting calcutta cane with a bamboo splitter. His black pony was near him. When he saw me, he stood and held up a palm. I slowed my pony down.

"Girl, everyone's looking for you." Adrian looked up at me as I sat on the pony. "I believe you are in serious trouble with Earl." I looked off at the tops of the pines. I saw an unfettered bird land on the exact apex of the tallest tree. I had no intention of seeing Earl today. That adversity I would deal with tomorrow.

"Adrian, I just had to get away." I took my eyes from the bird and looked down at him. The sun cast a dot of white in his iris.

"I figured that was the case." Adrian played with the splitter in his hand. "I would advise laying low for the time being." Adrian patted his black animal.

"Exactly my plan," I said, and started to give my pony a kick to get moving. Then I stopped myself. "Oh, Adrian, I saw wild horses!"

"You did?"

"Yes. They were quite awesome."

"I bet they were." Adrian spun his spinner in the air and caught it. "Jao knew there were wild horses on this island before the project began. That's where you and Earl fit in. Instead of delegating funds to build roads through woods and import vehicles, Jao hired Earl to domesticate these wild horses for transport between Main Campus and the research center. But breaking these wild animals has proved to be impossible. They have never been successfully domesticated by anyone. That's why Tom had four semi–domesticated ponies transported here from the Indonesian islands. When Jao became aware that Earl was having difficulty breaking these wild horses, they added you on, knowing your reputation with animals." Adrian gave another spin of the blade and again successfully caught it. "Where did you see the wild horses?"

"Over in the fields by the research center."

Adrian's face dropped. "Over in the fields by the research center?" he repeated. My face sobered to match his. "Jamie, you're not to go over there." I continued to look down at him. I didn't want to displease Adrian. My pony, sensing my tension, hoofed the path. "I mean it. I'm telling you to stay away from the research center. Do you hear me?"

"I hear you. I'm sorry."

He bounced his index finger at me twice, then turned to the calcutta cane.

"Adrian –"

"Hmm?" He didn't look up.

"I met a research assistant."

"Hmm?" Adrian stopped with the cane and turned to me. "Who? Which one?"

"I didn't get his name."

"Big older guy?" he asked.

"Not particularly."

"Was he a goofy looking guy?"

"No, not at all." Adrian creased his eyebrows. "He warned me about Dr. Bronte. He said that if Dr. Bronte caught me in their area, he'd lock me in his lab and do scientific experiments on me."

Adrian looked at me dumbfounded for a second, then let go a laugh. "That's ridiculous. He's pulling your leg."

"I don't know. He seemed pretty serious."

"Oh Jamie," he laughed. "I'm afraid this research assistant has a twisted sense of humor and has pulled a fast one on you." Adrian's smile faded. "But listen carefully to me now, you are not to go over there again, okay?"

"Okay, okay. I won't."

"Jamie, I mean it."

But I was already trotting off.

Chapter 11
ALL QUIET ON THE EASTERN FRONT

It was awkward but also comforting to once again join everyone for dinner. I sat with Darcy, Jeremy, and Brian as we ate Bakwan malang (soup with meatballs and wonton), ketoprak (vegetables), and for dessert, gemblong, a sticky rice drenched in Javanese sugar. Tariq hurried about the room complaining that the food was getting cold because people wouldn't god damn stop talking, and the familiarity of his carrying on soothed me. Jim gave me two pats on the shoulder just before I sat down, and that broke the uneasy feeling I had after having left him so terribly abruptly the day before in the medical building. Tom put me at ease by acting as if nothing at all had happened.

I was relieved that Earl was not at dinner. I would have to receive his wrath tomorrow morning, but I could put that out of my mind for now. Sheila and the nurses sat on their side of the room and I never looked over at them, but Darcy sure did, and I kept elbowing her to stop. All the while, I was watching Adrian as he moved about the room with an ease that was all his own, with a commanding air of a high–ranking officer. Derek ran up to me to show me a shell he'd found with a unique purple color on it. So I was once again joined with these people in an interlaced bond that connected me with them and the island, a connection I hadn't felt since I was nine years old.

At the campfire after dinner, Jeremy continued to call our research project "Bio–Cement" and Brian continued to correct him. "It's Bio-CMAT!" Grady continued making crude comments, and Darcy continued to snap at him. I had not seen Kane. When I asked about him, Jeremy shrugged and said, "Don't ask me. Kane never says two words to me and I *work* for the guy!"

I watched Adrian stir the fire with relaxed concentration, and when I looked away, I noticed that Tom was looking at me. Tom then leaned back, put his arm around Darcy, and said, "Do you all remember the security team's hunting trip when we first arrived on the island?"

"Wait a minute now..." Grady said, objecting. "You're not going to tell *that* story again, are you?"

"I think we are." Adrian smiled and jerked his chin up at Steve, who actually smirked. Everyone else chuckled under their breath.

"We all heard this painful story before," Grady said. "No need to tell it again."

"Well, Jamie hasn't heard the story yet," Tom said, and he pushed back his black hair with his palm. "Days after we arrived on the island, Adrian, Grady and Steve planned a hunting trip early one morning, an hour before dawn."

"Didn't you all share a bottle of whiskey the night before?" Jim asked, and he winked at Darcy. She laughed.

"Oh, here we go," said Grady.

"Everyone *shared* the bottle, but it was only Grady who was drinking," Steve said quietly. Derek looked up at him. I don't think I'd ever heard Steve say something to the group, only to Adrian or Grady directly.

"Why?" I asked.

"Adrian and I were only pretending to drink," Steve said, and he held an imaginary bottle up to his lips, but his mouth was closed. "The two of us were merely making drinking motions."

"Grady, you didn't last much past ten o'clock," Adrian said. "Steve and I had to put your sorry ass to bed."

"Yeah, but it was *your* sorry ass who set the clock ahead five hours," Grady said. "I still need to get you guys back for that. I'm still scheming."

"You keep on scheming, then," Adrian laughed.

"Adrian and Steve woke Grady up at midnight," Tom said, "only he thought it was five o'clock in the morning."

"Man, I felt like absolute dog shit!" Grady said.

"Grady!" Adrian warned, and motioned his head to Derek, who was fixing the rocks around the fire and seemed not to be listening.

"Oh, sorry. Forgot."

"Be careful, man!" Tom said. "That's my nephew."

"Sorry. Don't be so touchy!"

"Anyway," Tom continued, "the three of them took solo posts in the woods. Grady kept waiting for the sun to rise, and couldn't figure out why it took six hours!" Everyone laughed, with Grady snarling that it wasn't so damn funny.

That evening, as I lay in bed listening to the night crickets, I thought of the strange research assistant I had met in the field earlier today. "You people from Main Campus aren't to cross the line," he had said. "You shouldn't be here," he had whispered. He had warned me about Bronte, as had Darcy and Jeremy and some of the others. I was hoping that I would be able to go the entire six months of my stay here on the island without having to meet this Dr. Bronte. It seemed that the research team stayed in their own little world at the east end of the island, and that was fine with me.

I got out of bed and got the Jao folder from the dresser, and leafed through until I found Bronte's bio. I got back in bed and read it again, holding the paper against my bent knees.

EVAN BRONTE PROFILE

Evan Bronte, Ph.D. in neurophysiology with distinction, Ph.D. in biochemistry, and M.D. in psychiatry, is an internationally renowned researcher who has gained worldwide acclaim with his numerous publications and with his study of human brain cells and human consciousness. Bronte's works show extensive study in protein cytoskeletal structures and microtubules that organize interiors of the brain's neurons and other cells. His texts have sold over one million copies internationally in 12 languages. Bronte's publications include: *Findings of a Science of Consciousness*, *Bio-molecular Altering Consciousness*, and *A Look Inside Neurophysiology*. His most recent book, *The Quantum Brain*, explores the interface of cell biology, neuroscience, and quantum mechanics.

In 1996, Bronte served in the United States Air Force with the Walter Reed Army Institute of Research (WRAIR), the largest and most diverse biomedical research laboratory in the Department of Defense. Specializing in the Department of Biologics Research, Bronte worked with other researchers to develop vaccines for mission-related disease threats. Bronte's work in the Pilot Bio-production Facility (PBF) provided research, development, production, and testing of vaccines for human use. Vaccines that were produced at PBF protected soldiers against diseases they could have encountered in areas of deployment. In his last four years of military service, Bronte served as an Air Force psychiatrist, becoming top advisor at the U.S. Mental Health Advisory Team. Bronte's research, which was performed in collaboration with the Departments of Neurology and Psychiatry, has focused not only on specific disorders, but also on various activation studies designed to explore how brain function is associated with various mental states.

Bronte is presently conducting research for Bio-CMAT, a two-year research project for Jao Institute, a multi-billion dollar pharmaceutical research firm based out of Berkeley Heights, New Jersey. Bio-CMAT, under the direction of Richard Gordon, pursues new techniques in the prediction of chaotic biochemical changes, with applications to cell biology and micro-organisms.

It was quite an impressive profile. How unfortunate for such a brilliant man to possibly be so jaded.

Chapter 12
THE ODIWANCHI WAY

I woke up very early again, two hours before breakfast. It wasn't like me to wake up so early, especially three mornings in a row, and I wondered if it was because of the peculiar energy this island seemed to give, or because of my worry and dread over facing Earl. Rather than remain in bed and brood over it, I rose and got out of bed. Alone in the shower building, I washed in the dark.

As the air turned from black to silver to gold, I headed towards the ocean, feeling the dew from the jambu bush and red wax ginger as I brushed my fingers along their leaves. I trudged on along the path to the sea. How would I explain my stealing a pony to Earl? How could he possibly begin to understand when even *I* could not? Like suffering through a root canal, facing Earl was something I simply had to endure.

I trekked on, only to stop short when I almost stepped on a little brown mouse. It was then when I noticed the rich earthy smell of fresh cut wood, then immediately heard the ax. Kane! I bent to look at the mouse, who surprisingly didn't scamper away. I laid the back of my hands to the ground, and the mouse came into my palm.

"I'll be damned, a tame mouse!" I said, scooping up the mouse, and I followed the sound of the ax until I stood before Kane. He wore dark green lightweight pants with a tan open shirt. His bronze skin was damp from either the humidity or his labor. He continued to work his ax, though I am sure he was aware of me.

"I believe I have something of yours," I said. "Or some*one*, I should say." This time, Kane stopped working and looked over at me as I cupped my hands carefully to my chest. I approached Kane to hand the creature over to him, and then kissed the top of my hand that held the squiggling mouse. A memory came to me, a time when I was very small and my mother was telling me not to kiss a cat or dog, due to the germs they carried. While I loved and still love my mother, I never heeded this advice, and have yet to become sick from kissing an animal.

He looked down at me curiously as I held the mouse to him, and when his hands met mine, I felt a breeze of strength move from Kane into myself, and I welcomed but feared this bizarre sensation. Kane took the mouse from my hands. At contact, Kane's charged touch pulsed a voltaic nerve in me. It felt strong enough to jolt a small creature, but the mouse was fine as it nestled in Kane's palm.

Kane sat on a log. I sat next to him. He turned to me and gave me a puzzling look. Did the electric touch confuse him as well?

"What is it?" I asked.

"You kissed the mouse." He seemed bemused.

"Is that bad?"

"No. It is very *good*." Kane turned from me and stared straight ahead. Again, I noticed that he had an accent that I could not place. Was it a British accent? French?

"Kane, where are you from?"

"Mauritius."

"Where's that?" Kane sat straight and still as he looked out at the foliage beyond the small clearing where we sat. He was an unusually large man, with mild African features, and he had a hint of slanted eyes that held a fixed piercing gaze. He looked almost Egyptian. Kane was strong and soft at the same time, intense and mild, keen and fluid.

"Mauritius is an island nation off the south coast of Africa."

"Is that where we are now?" I whispered.

Kane merely smiled and shook his head. He bent and let the mouse run free from his hands to the ground. "This land is very *very* different."

We sat in silence for a few moments, as I watched the mouse clean himself in quick jerky movements. "Kane, why do you always chop wood? We're not exactly in Antarctica."

"It calms me." He took a deep breath. "It is my religion."

"Religion? Chopping wood? What religion is that?" Kane only looked ahead contently. I watched the mouse explore the woodpile. "Is it a Mauritius religion?"

"A little more than half of the people from my island are Hindus."

"So you're Hindu?"

"No, but from Hinduism we learn that good begets good."

"Okay," I said slowly. The mouse quickly dug its front feet against the wood. "Are you Christian?"

"No, but from Christianity we learn love and forgiveness."

I didn't know how to respond to that.

"Are you a... Buddhist?"

"No, but from Buddhism we learn to free our minds from clutter, something that chopping wood helps me to do."

"So you're a little bit Buddhist?"

"I am a little bit of everything."

"Kane," I laughed. "A person can't be *every*thing. That's like saying you're a Jewish Muslim who's a Taoist... Confucianist" I stumbled for words.

"From Judaism, we learn to wait for a divine message. From Islam, we learn to submit to God."

"Why are you giving me this religious lesson here?"

"From Taoism, we learn balance and harmonizing. From Confucianism, we learn a code of honor with which to live among each other."

"You're not going to start calling me 'Grasshopper' now, are you?"

"From Baha'i, we learn spiritual unity of all humankind. From Shinto, we learn to respect nature."

"Okay..." I said very slowly.

"From Sikhism, we learn a sense of community and serving."

"Kane…"

"From Jainism, we learn of the eternal and rebirth…"

"All right! Enough! How do you *know* all this?" Kane finally stopped. "I mean, why don't you teach religion at Harvard instead of being head cleaning guy here?" Right after the words left my mouth, I was hoping I hadn't insulted him. But he only smiled.

"This is exactly where I want to be."

"So what religion *are* you?"

"I am not any of the religions I mentioned."

"So what exactly *are* you?"

He laughed. I hadn't heard him laugh and it startled me a bit. "You are persistent."

"I hope I'm not being rude."

"You are being *inquisitive*. That is good." Kane drew a deep breath. "I follow the Odiwanchi way."

"What's Odiwanchi?"

"It is a religion of non-religions. It is where a person learns to hear their heart, to see with their inward eye. Though there are countless claims, no *one* person knows all things. Every religion is a thought or an interpretation that comes from a *person*, a human being. Sometimes, this thought is shared and believed by millions of people." He looked down at me. "Every person is on a different path. One person cannot tell another person the truth, though he *can* tell him his *own* truth. Truth must come from within each person. It is not something that is told or taught, but self-discovered."

I held his gaze for a moment, then looked at my hands in my lap. "That's interesting. I like that. But you may upset a lot of people if you spread that around."

"I am telling you this now because you are troubled."

My head shot up to him. "How do you know I'm troubled? I mean, why do you think this?"

Kane rose from the log, picked up the ax, and chopped wood.

"Kane, why do you think I'm troubled?"

But Kane simply continued to use his ax, leaving me sitting alone on the log.

Chapter 13
A NEW RESPECT

"What in tarnation is the *matter* with you?" Earl yelled when he saw me. After I'd left Kane, I went to the stables and found Earl bent over, working with barbed wire. I had slowly approached him from behind, and when he stood, he'd seen me for the first time since I had taken the pony yesterday afternoon. "I said, what in tarnation is the matter with you, for Christ's sake!" All I could do was stand there. From his gloved hand, he angrily threw down the coil of barbed wire, and when it hit the ground, I jumped. "You stole one of my ponies, Girl!" A vein protruded in his neck as he hollered.

"I brought him back," I said.

"It's still stealin' in my book!" Earl shouted. "I have a good mind to request that you go back to wherever it was you came from! Maybe you should consider getting on the next ship that leaves the island." I stared at the ground, burning. "You hear me?" I was starting to feel fire in my chest and throat. "I asked you a question, Girl!"

"You'd like that!" I yelled. I balled my hands into fists that hung at my sides. "You've been keeping me from the ponies since I *got* here!" We stood staring at each other, with me breathing hard.

"This is no place for a girl," he said. He took his gloves off and tossed them on the barbed wire. "Especially a girl like you," he said under his breath and started walking towards the stables.

"What's that supposed to mean?" I followed him.

He stopped and turned to me. "You're soft. Too soft. I noticed this the moment I laid eyes on you. You don't have the farm–way about you. There's not a callous on your hand. Your hair is soft, your eyes are soft, your *look* is soft, you speak softly, except for now, I may add. You're not cut out for this line of work." Earl looked up at the sky. "I tried. I tried to toughen you up with good honest hard work, but then you go and take one of my ponies on a *joy* ride."

I opened my mouth to speak, then closed it, then blurted, "I'm here to train horses!" I held my palms up, reaching out to him a bit.

"Oh, are you now?"

"Yes I am! I'm not here to be your… your *slave*."

"Is that a fact?"

"Yes! Yes, that's a fact." I was breathing hard again, and as I looked at him, and he kept my gaze.

"You *do* got some spirit in you, that I gotta' say." He pushed back his hair and looked out at the animals. "Well, the way I see things is that I got some girly–girl who doesn't know squat, and I gotta' find things for her to do. It's not personal, and I suppose it's not your fault being here, seeing they hired you and all. It's just that no one asked *me*. I've been doin' just fine here. I don't need a helper."

"Well it seems to me you *do*."

"Oh, do I now?" He looked back at me.

"Yes, at least with the white pony. You're having trouble training this animal," I said. "And by the way, I'm not a girly–girl. I don't *like* girly–girls. And why do you assume I don't know squat?"

"'Cause you're not more than a kid."

"I'm twenty–two."

"Like I said, you're not more than a kid, and you don't weigh more than a newborn foal."

"A person's size doesn't matter when they train a horse, you of all people should know that!"

"Talk to me when a thousand pound beast comes charging at you. If it weren't so dangerous for you, I'd give you a shot at the white pony. It'd teach you a lesson or two." He started walking away from me again towards the stables, and again, I followed him.

"Earl, *give* me that shot," I said, now excited.

"What are you talking about?" he said, still walking away from me.

I hurried to keep up.

"Let me work with the white pony."

"Ain't gonna' happen. You'll get hurt."

"No I won't. I *know* I won't. Let me at the pony, *please*."

He stopped at the barn door and looked at me, either in disbelief or in consideration. Then his face straightened. "I'd be crazy to let you at that wild beast."

"He's not wild. He's just scared. *Please* Earl." He looked at me, unsure, then pushed the barn door open. He went to a barn shelf and grabbed barbed wire shears. I leaned on the door watching him.

"Tell ya' what," he said, looking down at the shears in his hand. "Go feed the brown and black ponies. Lord knows, there ain't enough good grass here on the island for them to graze properly, so give 'em a good mix of gain and hay. Do you think you can do that?" He shook the barbed wire shears at me. "And listen, don't get close to the white pony, but leave some feed out for him as well, then keep your distance, ya' hear?" He put the shears in his pocket and walked towards me to get to the barn door. I had to step out of his way. "If you don't get trampled to death and I see that you half way know what in tarnation you're doing, I might let you get within ten feet of that white pony, as long as I'm right near to keep you from getting killed." He headed out into the paddock.

"I already got within four feet," I mumbled, but Earl was out of earshot and hadn't heard me.

As I was setting out hay in the red wheelbarrow by the fence, Jeremy came half running towards the stables with his blond hair bouncing on his forehead and ears, and his wind instrument jetting out of his pocket. He had on tan cotton pants, no shirt, only suspenders, exposing a rib-poked chest and a tiny flat stomach. I think I weighed more than Jeremy. I'd never seen anyone but Earl at the stables, and welcomed the sight of my young friend who always seemed to be smirking. "Jeremy!" I stood.

"Hey Jamie! Kane and I just finished sweeping and dusting Central Lodge, the Admin Building, and Medical, so I thought I'd take a break and see what you're up to."

"She's workin', Boy!" Earl called out.

"Sorry, Sir! Won't be long!" Jeremy called over to him, unbothered. Then he said quietly to me, "That Kane never says two words to me. He just points." I continued to lay out the feed for the ponies as Jeremy propped himself on the gate.

"Get off that gate!" Earl yelled. "It ain't a rockin' chair!"

"Sorry Sir!" Jeremy said without emotion and hopped off. "How ya' like working here?"

"It's all right," I said. "Do you like working for Kane, even though he doesn't say much?"

"Sure, he's cool." I was hoping he'd tell me more about Kane, but Jeremy simply took the tin whistle from his pocket and hopped back up on the gate, ignoring my warning that he was about to hear from Earl. I skeptically looked over at Earl who was now busy with the coil of barbed wire. Jeremy began to play a Celtic song. Both Earl and the white pony looked over at us at the exact same time, in comic unison.

"Boy, what the hell is that noise? And get your sorry ass off that gate!" Jeremy hopped down without missing a beat. He continued playing as he leaned a shoulder against the gate. Earl rolled his eyes and went back to his barbed wire. He didn't yell for Jeremy to stop playing.

I rolled the wheelbarrow over to the ponies, listening to Jeremy play his whistle in the background. I passed Earl, who was still working with the barbed wire. I noticed that Earl was keeping an eye on me as I spread hay out to the black and brown ponies, who ate immediately. The white pony was in the back corner of the paddock, keeping as much distance from Earl as he could.

I had been alone with the white pony several times. The first time was my first day on the job when Earl took a break in the afternoon, and I could only get ten feet from the animal. That night, I had approached him again and got a few feet closer. The next day, I was able to be alone with the white pony two times when Earl took breaks, and each time he allowed me to get just a little bit closer to him, as I let him hear and smell and sense me. Two nights ago I had ventured off to the stables late at night to be with the white pony for the fifth time, and I had felt less anxiety from him, though he still kept a guarded eye on me the whole time. I was finally breaking through.

Slowly, I walked towards the white pony, holding a little bit of hay in one hand. Earl stood.

"Girl. That's about enough. Don't you get too close."

Hearing Earl's voice unnerved the white pony a bit, so I stopped and looked away. When the animal calmed a bit, I took one easy step after another.

"Girl!"

Ignoring Earl, I eased forward, stopping only when the white pony tensed, continuing when he relaxed. I prayed that Earl wouldn't speak or advance, as that would break any trust I was now building. As fragile as cards held up by toothpicks, this shaky bond between us could collapse and crumble. Miraculously, Earl remained still.

I got within three feet and stopped, staying at the pony's side so he could see me. He hoofed the ground and breathed out loudly. I felt his warm breath. Then he dropped his head and relaxed his ears. I inched forward, avoiding direct eye contact, keeping my hands low. Two feet. The white pony eyed the hay. I summoned thoughts of happy times with my dogs, and filled my mind with visions of the beautiful Maine coast. I knew my mindset would transfer to the pony. I willed the consoling thoughts to envelop and consume me, immersing myself in complacency. The pony reached for the hay. As he chewed, I patted him on his firm shoulder, the area where horses nuzzle each other. First contact with this animal filled me with awe, reverence, and wonder.

"I'll be damned," I heard Earl say.

I don't remember when Jeremy stopped playing.

"Never met a horse I couldn't break, until that there white pony," Earl said to me. "Damn, Girl... amazing how you marched right up to him like he was a kitten." We walked across the paddock towards the stables to get a halter. "I was hired a year and a half ago to train the wild horses that run free on this island. Nobody knew that those horses simply can't be touched, not by anyone." We entered the stables, and our eyes adjusted to the darker air. "When I told Tom that the island horses here can't be domesticated, he then had four local ponies from Indonesia sent in."

"Four?" I asked, stopping by the barn door. "I thought there were only three."

Earl turned to face me from the center of the room. "You never saw the other white pony. Off-white, I should say. That one was broken pretty damn easily. Dr. Bronte in the research department has that animal." Earl turned his back on me to go pick out a halter. "Some of the folks here are a tad bit sore about that, seeing that Dr. Bronte gets two ponies, and the fifteen of us share the remaining two."

"What other pony is he going to get?" I asked.

"The white one."

"Dr. *Bronte* is going to get our *white* pony?"

"Yep."

I stood with my mouth open.

"Girl... Jamie is it? Gotta say, I was damn shocked when you marched up to that animal and touched his neck, sure as day!"

I smiled. "I didn't exactly march."

"Pretty damn shocked." Earl untangled the straps on the bridle, then reached for a halter. "Seems Indonesia yields *ponies*, not horses. Ahh, these ponies here ain't much smaller than horses – the white pony is thirteen hands high. Most of my horses back in Colorado are fourteen hands. Anyway, all the ponies we got here on the island came half broke except for the white one. That one sure has a wild streak. I broke all the other ones just fine, though it took a little bit of doing." Earl left the stables and I followed him.

"Who gets the other ponies?" I asked.

"The black one is Adrian's pony. He's a Java pony, a real tough guy, robust. He's quite willing and has a good temperament, that one. He's mostly Arabian. He's our largest pony, strongest too, I'd say. Hell of a lot of endurance. That one can work all day."

"He's got almost human eyes," I said. "What about the brown one? Whose pony is that?"

"The one you stole?" Earl held up his hand and looked at the ground. Then he scratched his head and looked at me. "That one belongs to Adrian's assistant... Grady is it? He has the brown one, though he rarely rides. That there's a Batak pony. She's a fast one, I tell you. She's mostly quiet and docile, but woof, she can get a mean temper, then watch out. It's probably due to her being female. But she was easy to break, and though she's slender, she's strong and sturdy."

"What kind of pony is the white one?"

"A Sandalwood. Finest pony in the country, cream of the crop. They're mostly used for racing and can go several miles, if I can ever saddle the damn thing. They say that Sandalwoods are friendly and easy to manage. Ain't that a laugh."

"This one's just been spooked, is all," I said.

"We've been waiting to get another pony in for months now, and that one will go to Tom. Guess that one will come in by about the time our project is finishing. Figures. Damn corporations... never could figure out their line of thinking. Anyway, Tom just figured that transportation should go to Security first, and those ponies are our only transportation here on the island!"

We were interrupted by the sound of the gate opening when Jeremy came hurrying from the field towards us, with an entourage of five. Tom and Darcy, Adrian, Dr. Jim, Brian, and little Derek were with him. Earl and I gave a puzzling look to each other as they approached.

"What the…" Earl said.

Jeremy reached us first, out of breath. He rested his hands on his knees, bending down slightly as he breathed hard.

"I told everyone how you touched the white horse!"

"Pony."

"Whatever. I heard that horse couldn't be broke."

"Pony." I corrected again.

"Whatever. How'd you do it?"

"What are you rambling about, Boy?" Earl asked, wrinkling up his face.

"I'm talking about Jamie! How she touched the white horse!"

"Pony!"

"Whatever!"

By now the others had reached us. Adrian and the doctor seemed amused, and the others were curious.

"What's all this commotion?" said Earl. "We got work to do here. Don't you all?"

"Well, Jeremy came rushing to us, all excited…" Tom said.

"Something about Jamie touching the untouchable," Adrian smirked. "What'd you do exactly, Jamie?"

"I want to see!" Derek said.

I looked at Darcy and she was smiling at me. "Well? Let's see your magic," she said.

"Whatever you did, you impressed Jeremy," the doctor said.

"Oh for cryin' out loud, what are ya' all ramblin' about? Don't you all have work to do?" Earl asked.

"We're on island time, Sir!" Jeremy said. "No nine–to–five here!"

"I don't work." Derek said.

"Well shouldn't you be in school somewhere?" Earl asked.

"My dad trains me, from the workbooks."

"Well I just think there's too much *gabbing* and not enough *working*," Earl said. Then Darcy did something that surprised me. She went up and hugged Earl.

"Aww, don't you just love us anyway," she said. Earl mumbled something about foolishness, but no one took him too seriously, not even Derek. Darcy had an ease about her with people that I did not have. My bidding was with animals, not people. I took the halter out of Earl's hand, and he opened his mouth to protest. Before he could, I turned to the gate, leaving them to their quibbling. I entered the paddock, halter and lead rope in hand, and headed towards the white pony.

As before, I inched towards him with my eyes lowered, seemingly distracted. I conjured calm and peaceful thoughts. I stopped on cue whenever I sensed tension of any sort from the pony. He looked for a carrot or hay, but I carried the halter, which was foreign to this animal, causing him to throw his head in the air. I hummed a bit to calm him, and stood still. When he calmed some, I took a step closer, but the bull snap made a metal clinking sound, and the white pony jerked back. I quickly closed my hand over the clip. Sensing my alert nervousness, he backed up again and gave a quick walk around the back end of the paddock. When he tired of this, he stopped in the other corner, further away from me. I slowly approached the white pony again, looking back at the gate, and I was surprised to see that the others were still watching, Earl among them. This could take some time. I crept forward as if on thin ice, positioning the halter a little behind me. When I got close enough for the lead rope to reach his neck, I stopped. I talked softly to him, but looked away. When the time was right, I gently put the lead line over his neck. He jerked back, and again circled the back end of the paddock. He stopped in his original corner, and once again, I slowly paced towards him. I made two more attempts with the lead rope before it stayed over his neck. When he became aware that the rope wasn't hurting him, I took the final step forward, standing by his head on the left side, and slowly reached for the other end of the rope. I had him! I heard a couple of the others gasp.

It took more than several tries to slide the halter over his nose. He tried to bite it, and even me, but I took gentle command with the lead rope until I had slid the halter over his nose and behind his ears, all the while holding firmly to the lead. After it was on, I let him get used to it while I rubbed and patted his shoulder, making cooing sounds to him.

When he stopped bobbing his head up and down and quieted a bit, I turned to the others at the gate, leading the white pony towards them. They all clapped.

"I'll be damned!" I heard Earl say.

Chapter 14
FALLING INTO RHYTHM

As the nights fell into days, and the days fell into weeks, I fell into a gentle rhythm here on Jackel Island. I could feel the beat of the island and I flowed with it. Waking to the symphony of birds each morning, I felt a heightened sense of everything – the feel of shower water on my skin, the smell of the sea air with all its rich foliage, the awe of blue and white and yellow and violet fields, orange and pink sunrises, the weight of humidity that lingers in the air and fills it, the taste of food where each sensation, sweet–sour–bitter–salty, was amplified, the mournful call of seagulls by day and merbau crickets at night, the tropical sun tingling and dancing in my pores, the feel of the ponies with their arista yet soft coat that was taut over their muscle, and the way the animals' muscles moved under my legs when I rode them... Brian often said that Jackel Island's air was honey with nutrients. Darcy said the island was infested with romance, but hoped she wouldn't become like Grady. I could think more clearly and quicker in the last several weeks, and I needed less sleep. Concerned over the mere four or five hours of sleep I was getting each night, when before I was accustomed to eight, I went to the doctor. I was due for a blood test anyway.

"Are you tired during the day?"

"No."

"Then don't worry about it."

Jim went on to add that Tom and Brian had also visited him about a month after they had arrived, concerned when their need for sleep had drastically lessened. He said he had experienced the same thing and welcomed the more conscious hours to his life.

I also experienced a deepened affection for these people on the island with me. Darcy, Brian, and Jeremy had become my closest friends ever, each in their own and unique way. Darcy understood me like no other, and I confided everything to her, and she to me. Brian, who was only three years older than I, had the biggest heart of anyone I've ever known, with perhaps the exception of Dr. Jim. When I needed compassion, I often went to Brian. In a silly way, he reminded me of the Tin Man. His quiet disposition gave way to a tenderness of soul, a friend who was serene enough to truly listen and not judge.

"Brian, does Tariq scare you?" I asked him one day when it was just he and I sitting in Central Lodge. It was an hour before dinner, and it was raining hard. "I mean, Tariq being your boss and all. When you're preparing meals with him in the kitchen, does his constant carrying on scare you?"

"Well, he used to scare me a lot at first, and he still does kind of." Brian adjusted his shirt over his large stomach and pushed back his curly blond hair. "But mostly, Tariq is just full of hot air, kind of like Earl." We were both half–laying half–sitting on the same couch at opposite ends with our knees bent, our sneakers touching in the middle of the couch. "Why? Does Earl scare you?"

"He used to, at first," I said. "But I'm getting used to him." I lightly kicked Brian. He kicked me back. Then we kicked each other about twenty times.

"Brian, can I ask you something else?" I asked.

"Hmm?"

"Please don't take offense, I'm just curious, no biggie..."

"What?" Brian sat up from the couch and looked at me.

I stared at the high ceiling beams that stretched across the lodge.

"Are you really gay? Not that I care one way or the other, I really don't. I'm just wondering."

"No! I'm not! Why does everyone think that?" Brian flopped back down on the couch. "Even in High School, everyone said that. Why does everyone think that? Gee!"

"Okay, okay. I just wanted to hear it from you if it was true. No major deal."

"Gee!"

Jeremy was like a little brother to me. He was totally oblivious half the time, always mispronouncing words and facts, not getting it when people became annoyed with him, childish, immature, not aware of boundaries or personal space, but totally lovable and he would do anything for anyone he considered a friend. Often after work I would go to the beach and find Jeremy sitting on a rock playing his tin whistle. I would sit next to him and listen, letting the mellifluous sounds wash the stable grime off me. Once, he stopped playing his song and matched his whistle to a seagull's cry in perfect pitch, making me giggle uncontrollably. That day, I had extracted a worn photo of my father from my pocket to show Jeremy, only a huge wind gust snatched the photo from my hand and soared it bouncing along the sand towards the sea. Jeremy flew off the rock and ran to get it back for me, but the wind carried my photo further out and away until it finally landed in the water. I screamed. Without thinking, Jeremy ran after it as the waves crashed into his teen–thin body, and he thrashed about, grabbing at the square glossy paper that bobbed in the waves and glittered in the sun. After several minutes, he came back to me holding the dripping and ruined photograph of my father.

"Here. Sorry!"

I really took to nine–year–old Derek, not just because he was always giving me his treasures from the island, but because he always seemed to be bouncing up to me when I least expected it to show me a conch, a butterfly, a unique twisted limb from the woods, an interesting bug, a colorful flower, discarded snake skin that lay like torn tissue paper in his hand, a tortoise shell, bamboo… and he would give these items to me as gifts. I didn't have the heart to throw them away, but I didn't know what exactly to *do* with them. I didn't have space in my small cabin, and I figured it wouldn't be good for a tortoise shell or snakeskin from a dead reptile, bugs, or tiny insects inside tree limbs to lay where I slept. So I kept a little "Derek Garden" outside just behind my cabin with all the treasures he gave me. As I lay Derek's recently dead butterfly against a teak tree, I thought of all the gems inside the tree knot that Boo Radley had given to Gem and Scout in *To Kill a Mockingbird*.

One night at our campfire, Derek presented a live banyan tree frog to me in his cupped hands. When he passed me the frog and I tried to take it, the frog slipped out between our hands and jetted in the woods in one huge desperate leap. Derek looked terribly upset. I was touched and pulled him to sit on my lap, which he respectfully declined, telling me he stopped sitting on laps ages ago. "Well Jamie, *I'm* not too old for laps," Grady said from the fire pit, to which Darcy said, "You're such a creep of huge magnitudes!"

I visited the doctor as often as I could, usually during mid–morning or afternoon breaks from the stables, before dinner, or on my days off. He always welcomed me affectionately, his face unfolding to a gracious beam when he saw me. "Jamieee!" he'd say when I'd pass through the Medical doors, the last syllable of my name ending on a lower note. Then he'd pour coffee into the dark green mug for me.

I felt comfortable in the Medical building, despite the nurses who didn't appear to be too close with Jim, or with anyone else on the island, for that matter. They did their own thing with Sheila, and rarely, if ever, joined us at our campfires.

My visits were either a medical need like the monthly blood test I had to take, or more frequently, a social visit. Derek also came to visit the doctor frequently, as did Tom, Darcy, and Brian. Derek and the doctor had a special grandfather–grandson bond, with Jim giving him sweets he'd ordered just for Derek, and Derek swinging his legs as he sat on the exam table telling the doctor all about his fishing adventures, wonders he found on the island, or how Adrian was teaching him silat. Tom's visits were short, but he came often enough, frequently asking an administration question or two, or to check on the medical status of one of us. Personally, I think Tom just sought Jim's company. Darcy confided in me, but she sought advise and comfort from the doctor, too, when something bothered her. If she came in while I was visiting, I would often leave so the two of them could be alone, if I felt that Darcy needed this. Brian would come in just to "hang out", as he put it. Brian didn't say much, but seemed to enjoy his time with the doctor. Jim sometimes slipped one of Derek's treats to Brian as well. Of course, we all visited the doctor when we needed medical attention – a stubborn splinter, a headache, stomach problems, a nasty cut, sunburn…

As we sipped our coffee, we told each other about how our day was going, earlier times on the farm and how we grew up, and what we missed from home. Jim confided in me that he missed his wife terribly, so much it had become a physical ache. When he described her to me, his face softened and saddened, where his lips smiled but his eyes didn't. He wrote to her every day from the computer room. He said after he returned home, he had promised that he would never leave her again.

I told him the kindness I remembered from my mother and father, and then the harsh contrast when I was forced to live with my Aunt and Uncle.

"Did your Uncle ever draw blood when he hit you?"

"No, I can't say that he ever did. And it wasn't like I was bruised really either. It was just a lot of shoving and pushing and yelling and ignoring." I picked at my thumbnail. "I don't know…" After some silence, Jim reached over to pull my one hand away from the other.

"Do you stay in touch with them?" he asked.

"No, not really," I said. "I sent them Christmas cards for a while, and my Aunt responded, just signing both their names. There was never a note, just their names."

"Do they know you're here?"

"No."

"They must have been proud of your accolades with your work with the horses in the States, weren't they?"

"I don't know. I suppose, I guess... maybe a little. What I remember most is their trying to get me to capitalize on it as best I could. College money."

"Well, Jamie," Jim said, setting his clay coffee mug down, "I am proud of all you've done. I truly am. And until my time is up," he said, touching his finger on the table with the words *until*, *time* and *up*, "I'll send you a Christmas card every year. With a note."

I was no longer afraid of Tariq, at least not totally. There were times when an after–work pony ride in the late afternoon on the sand by the ocean would fall into early evening, and I'd miss dinner. The first time this happened, I had tip–toed into the kitchen during campfire to ask for a grilled cheese sandwich, thinking that would be easy for him to make. Tariq was finishing cleaning up the dinner plates. When he saw me, he sounded off about how I was late for a dinner he labored over. "What da matter with you? Why you miss dinner? This is not good!" I had stood there waiting for him to pause so I could ask for the sandwich, but he never stopped complaining to me. He just continued yelling, and while carrying on, he went to get a plate of leftovers that he had prepared for me. "Missing dinner is no good! It's just no good!" he hollered as he handed me my covered plate. He had kept it warm. Later, in my cabin, when I had uncovered the dish Tariq had prepared for me, I discovered that he had placed a pink lotus flower diagonally across the plate and over the food.

Another time, on my day off, I had planned to go on a morning pony ride into the woods to see the wild horses on the east side of the island, with intentions of spending most of the day out by myself. I told

Jim. Jim told Tariq. Brian came to my cabin door early that morning with a picnic lunch that Tariq had prepared for me. Brian relayed a message from Tariq, stating if I didn't eat it all and brought back any food uneaten, there'd be hell to pay.

While Jim was like a father to me, Tom was like a big brother and was most protective of Darcy, Derek, and even me. Jeremy too, or anyone he considered weaker. One time, Grady was being hard on Jeremy, calling him a girl, telling him he needed to bronco up, until Tom finally told Grady to knock it off. While Tom was tall and thin and somewhat solid, Grady, like all the men in Security, had a marine body and was well trained in hand–to–hand combat. When Tom stood up to him, Grady looked at Tom in disbelief with his mouth open, but he said and did nothing to Tom, and stopped teasing Jeremy.

When administration matters arose, which occasionally called for a meeting at Central Lodge, Tom was most professional and did well in taking charge, not in an over–bearing way, though not weak–mannered either. His leadership was a comfort to me, but sometimes I felt that Adrian was equally in charge, a strong force in the background. At our campfires, everyone let their armor down a bit, Tom most of all, and he told us animated stories of his rebellious teen years, stories that surprised as well as entertained us. With a boyish eagerness that was quite charming and captivating, Tom told us of a time when he told his father that he had "found Jesus," just to spite him. As a teen, Tom loved fixing cars, and believed at the time that he wanted to restore classics for a living. His millionaire father strongly opposed, believing that life as an auto mechanic was not befitting for any son of his. The two of them frequently argued, mostly at the top of their lungs, with Tom's twin brother Joel running off for solitude. So when Tom pretended to find Jesus, quietly telling his father that being an auto mechanic was his calling, and keeping all his verbal arguments at low volume, his father simply didn't know how to handle his sixteen–year–

old son, now soft-spoken and filled with the Lord. Joel would silently observe all this from the dinner table, or from his bedroom, and would roll his eyes and shake his head at his brother when the two of them were later alone and Tom was howling with laughter.

Tom got in his share of high school fights. Coming home a bit bloodied with ripped shirts would enrage his father. Joel once asked his brother "why all the fights?" and Tom had responded "I just can't stand it when people are wrong." Joel remembered a time when they were in second grade, and fourth graders were verbally picking on them. Joel and his brother were tall and thin for their age, and one of Joel's attackers was a stocky ten–year–old. Joel only reached the other boy's chin, and the third boy had a reputation as a contentious bully. Being called names and shoved a bit didn't bother Joel much; he just tuned them out. But it incensed Tom to no end, and at seven years old, Tom swung fists and pulled at the three fourth graders, attempting to land each of them in the mud under the swings, to which he surprisingly succeeded.

One evening in Darcy's cabin, she and I got our hands on several bottles of red wine and proceeded to get drunk, a rarity for me but not so much for Darcy. She confided in me about a personal tragedy that happened to her when she was in High School. Darcy told me that she went to a rough school, and one day as she was at her locker, three girls dumped a bucket of red paint over her head, then ran. It stained her skin for days, but the tragedy was that she had to cut off most her hair. "I couldn't even get the red out of my eyelashes." Darcy told me it affected the rest of her days in High School. So this was her personal tragedy. Everyone on the island seemed to have a dramatic story from their past.

Tom came into Darcy's cabin, and to his surprise, found us drinking. He quickly caught up with us, his two gulps to every one of our sips. When the bottles were empty, Tom revealed that as a teen, he had hated his father and believed him to be an evil man, claiming that his father slept with a couple of neighbors' wives, took business bribes, and unethically adjusted financial figures. Darcy stroked his short black hair as Tom looked off in the distance with a hardened face.

Darcy and I would sometimes irritate Tom by murmuring non–sensible garble to each other, then laughing to the point where we lost control. "What? What?" Tom would ask, but we were laughing so hard we couldn't speak. Also, it wouldn't be funny had we explained. Darcy's mind often trailed off topic, and she also often mixed words up, so when she tried to say the word "people" but "feaple" came out, and Tom thought she said "fecal", we couldn't stop laughing. It wasn't even funny, but seeing her drool because she was laughing so hard was, and hearing Tom asking so intently what all this was about made me drop to my knees in laughter. At some of our campfires, Adrian, Grady, and Jim would look over at us with a puzzled look during our first dozen giggling fits, but soon learned to simply dismiss these spells of ours. Jeremy tried to join in but kept missing the point. Darcy told me that later on, when she and Tom were alone, Tom would ask what it was we were laughing about. "I never tell him, just to drive him crazy."

Joel was an enigma to me. Like Kane and Tariq, Tom's twin kept mostly to himself. Only a good eye would be able to tell Tom and Joel apart in a photograph. Seeing either of them move or change facial muscles was a dead give–away, as they held and carried themselves radically differently. Tom was animated and gregarious; Joel was subdued and an introvert. I used to think that Joel was a bit cold and aloof and I worried for his only son, Derek, but I later learned that it was just shyness. I could now see a sweet side to Joel which was passed to Derek, only Derek didn't know enough to hide this quality in himself yet. Being sweet was not manly, or at least Joel apparently didn't think so.

Joel was an absolute genius with computers and anything mechanical. He took apart and fixed my Nook. When he handed the tablet back to me, Joel asked me something I'll never forget.

"Listen, ahh... if anything were to ever happen to me and my brother, heaven forbid, could you... could you look after my son? He takes to you, and you're so good with him."

I was proudly astounded, though I wondered why his offer wasn't passed to Joel's wife, or his father.

"Why Joel, of course I will. I don't take this lightly. I... I'm touched that you asked me this." Then I added, "What about Derek's mother?"

"She..." Joel stared at his hand. "She's out of the picture. She's trying to handle her own demons."

The whole time we spoke, Joel stared at the tablet that each of us held between us.

Never again did Kane and I exchange so many words as we had that day when we sat on the log together and he told me of his spiritual way of looking at things. But since then, we had a non–verbal bond which I strongly felt every time I passed him in the woods, in our camp's clearing, or in Central Lodge. I often thought of all he had to tell me that day, of seeing with your own human heart instead being guided by learned words. Twice, I felt a need to simply sit on a log near him as he worked his maul ax, his way of meditating. As he worked the ax, I'd sometimes see his little mouse peer out of his pocket. Giant man with little mouse. Another time I picked up a spare broom and helped him sweep the laundry room behind his cabin, just to be near him. We all often helped each other with our work. As Kane and I worked in the laundry room, I saw a hint of a vague smile while he swept up dust, an upturn of the lips so very faint that I wasn't sure if was actually smiling at all.

Adrian, Grady, and Steve made up the three–man security team and were often together, though while Adrian and Grady intermixed with everyone, red–haired Steve kept more to himself. Jeremy called them the Three Musketeers.

Marine–bodied Steve, whose shirt was always too tight, kept company only with Adrian and Grady. He reminded me of one of those colorless soldiers in a bad movie that didn't develop their characters. He'd pass me by the water basin or by the breakfast table with a nod, carrying absolutely no emotion on his face. He spent a lot of time in the computer room when he wasn't working out.

Grady occupied himself with Sheila and the nurses after hours in their cabins, but he also enjoyed our company and socializing at the campfires. Grady was one huge hormone with his constant innuendos, but like Earl and Tariq, he was pretty harmless, so I no longer went out of my way to avoid him. Darcy kept him in line with her verbal attacks every time he cared to utter a colorful suggestion. Tom once told me that there was no need for him to punch Grady's lights out when he was out of line, because Darcy took care of him.

Grady smiled easily, was quick–witted, and was eager to hop into bed with anything that wore a skirt. And he was fearlessly loyal to his boss Adrian.

Adrian. Back in my former life in Maine, if anyone had ever told me that I would be interested in a man more than twice my age, I would have adamantly disagreed and told them they were crazy. A month ago, I would have said that I would not have *ever* even con*sid*ered dating *any*one over thirty. But Adrian was the first person I thought of when I woke up, and the last person I thought of before I fell asleep. I thought of the way he walked, leading with his hips. I thought of the way he always remained calm when anyone else was excited or spirited. I thought of the way he'd look at me when I spoke, with his half smirk and scintillating eyes. I thought of his tight hips and solid chest and his smooth even voice. I wasn't one for crushes or foolishness with men, and I fought these feelings, though Adrian planted seeds in the fruitless soil of my heart. I wondered if these stirrings were the effects of the island. I both savored and frowned upon this churning in me.

On my way to work at the stables in the morning, I would often pause to see Adrian and Derek in the west fields in front of a newly rising sun, with Adrian showing martial art moves to the boy. I would stand at the woods' edge, half–hidden, watching the two of them glide through the early morning air. If I wasn't running late, and if Adrian was alone, I would go to him in the western fields before my work at the stables, where he would show me a method of breathing and meditating, and a way to stand firmly. As soon as he explained "it's like sitting in a saddle," I immediately understood, and I could now withstand Adrian's firm pushes. No longer did I lose my balance so easily with him.

With his touch, I felt a surge. When he straightened my wrist, or tapped my abdomen to show where the breath came from, or straightened my head to properly align me, I ached for more. I felt a tingling or flickering, a burn of a candle skimming my skin. Alone with Adrian in the early morning fields, or sometimes late at night just before I fell asleep, I thought of pressing my stomach into his, pressing my face into his neck, and then I'd quickly push the thoughts away. I did not want to feel this towards Adrian. He was too old! I avoided his eyes lest he read my feelings. I kept comments formal and impersonal. It unnerved me when he got physically or emotionally close.

People think that it is always warm in the tropics, but nights at Jackel Island sometimes got chilly, especially if one sat still for a period of time away from the campfire. Since I was a small child, I had a tendency to become easily chilled. One evening when we were all sitting around the campfire, my teeth began to chatter from my bare arms being exposed to the evening air. I was unable to get close to the fire, as Adrian and Grady stood on one side of the fire pit, and Jeremy and Brian sat close to the fire's rocks on the other side. There were several conversations going on – Tom was talking with Darcy a little ways away from the fire, their foreheads pressed together; Jeremy was hitting Brian in the arm and Brian kept yelling "Ow!" which made Jeremy hit him harder still; Jim was playing cards with Derek and reminding him not to cheat; and Adrian was talking with Grady. Adrian stirred the fire with a metal rod while Grady kicked at the outer logs with his shoe. All the sounds washed into one as my teeth chattered while I was trying to catch any warmth from the fire between Grady and Jeremy. I was vaguely aware that Adrian's voice got closer to me as he went to get something, all the while speaking to Grady. I was not focusing on anything in particular, and if I wasn't so cold, I may have nodded off. I was vaguely aware that Adrian was behind me. I then felt the weight and tickle of his long sleeved shirt, which he placed over my shoulders. I snapped my head up at him behind me, noticing that he now wore only an undershirt and his cotton pants. He gave me a close–mouthed grin, then turned away and finished his sentence to Grady as he walked back over to the fire. I clutched at his shirt, still warm from his skin, and it felt wonderful and almost wrong at the same time, like a sensual act.

These people were becoming my family and I grew to love them dearly.

Earl continued to give me jobs at the stables that made me sweat and dirtied my clothes, but he also allowed me to work directly with the ponies. And he talked to me. We sometimes worked side by side as he'd ramble on about whatever was on his mind – the laziness of youth today, how no one in America eats a good healthy meal anymore, how parents don't wallop their kids when the kid certainly needed a wallop, how movies are no longer as good as they were back in the day, etc. I would stick up for my generation and remind him of benefits *we* had which *his* generation never did, like video games, iPods, internet, and cell phones. "Exactly my point!" was his response. We'd banter back and forth, and I was hoping that Earl saw the humor in our debates the way I did.

I'd sometimes bring a picnic lunch for Earl and me to eat, prepared by Tariq who threatened me with a verbal thrashing if I didn't bring the basket back. The way the food was aesthetically presented in the basket made Tariq an artist of sorts, and Earl never once complained about Tariq's Indonesian cooking.

If I got my stable chores done to Earl's satisfaction, he'd let me take afternoon rides to "get the run out of 'em", as he put it. "You need some getting' the run out of *you*, too," he'd say. I treasured the afternoons when I'd race the ponies with the wind sweeping the humidity and sun's heat from my skin, riding off and away through the long stretch of the island. I often rode to observe the wild horses in the east field.

The white pony only allowed *me* to ride him. The first time I rode him was bareback with a halter, and after several rides, he trusted me enough to put a saddle on him. Soft and responsive, the slightest shift of weight was more then enough to get a response. His mouth was like butter as he responded to the reins I held. He spun circles for me. A slight squeeze and he would halt and back up for me. A twitch with my little finger would yield a perfect turn. He responded to my voice commands; a click of my tongue would send him forward. When I led him, all I had to do was point in a direction of choice, and he'd march on. Beneath that frightened defensive exterior there had always been an intelligent and willing animal.

As the bond between the white pony and me grew, we would ride the three–mile stretch to the forbidden east side of the island, into research territory. I was now watchful for any person who might come into view, leery of seeing the research assistant again, or worse, Dr. Evan Bronte. I did not seek human contact when I ventured out there. In fact, I hid from it. It was the wild horses I sought, and was always awe–struck when I'd see them grazing off in the distance among the gold wisps of the field. I would sit in the tall grass and watch them for hours. I began to recognize individual horses in the herd, the horse who nuzzled the neck of the animal with the bounce to his walk, the horse who lifted his muzzle to neigh, the horse who rolled on his back in the grass. Walking like a crab, I'd inch forward to get as close as I possibly could, stopping to rest if any one of them looked over towards me. They remained distant from me, and the lightest inkling would cause them to bolt.

Quite by accident, I discovered a small jade lagoon with a waterfall roughly a mile and a half from Main Campus, deep in the heart of the island. I surmised that this lagoon was just about dead center of the island. When I was returning from observing the wild horses, I followed a different path in the woods than I had taken before, just to see where it would lead. It led to the emerald lagoon with the waterfall that sprayed rainbow colors. I was pretty grimy from the stables and from the ride, and so I removed my socks and shoes to feel the cool water. Did anyone know of this lagoon? Looking around, I saw no one, and heard nothing but birds and insects and a rustle of bush when my pony grazed. Do I dare? I stood still, debating. Then I walked over to a tagar shrub and hovered against it as I quickly undressed, then hurried in the pine-colored glass water.

The days I spent observing the wild horses, and my swims at my own private lagoon were a real treat. I had covertly named this aquamarine pond *Emerald Lagoon* and claimed it as my own. As much as I treasured my private swims and observing the native horses, I spent most of my time at Main Campus with the others simply due to circumstance. Jeremy was right; we were on "island time" where there was no time clock, no "nine–to–five" mentality. We started our work early, worked hard, and quit when we finished and not before, taking breaks to recharge our internal batteries and to visit. We helped each other out, and the divisions between each department blurred. Earl got used to Jeremy or Brian visiting the stables, Derek too, as long as they had a rag or a tool in their hand and worked, and as long as they "stayed the hell away" from the ponies. Brian, Derek and I often helped Jeremy and Kane sweep out a building or a porch, dust, or scrub what needed scrubbing. Derek preferred *any*thing to his studies – cooking, cleaning, working alongside his father with the computers, visiting the doctor, training with Adrian, even mucking out the stable. Joel had a hard time getting Derek to do his schoolwork. So I often came over to the computer building and sat with Derek, going over his school workbooks. He was frightfully bright, but bored with school.

Darcy, Jeremy, and I helped Brian in the kitchen quite a bit. Even the doctor and Derek would sometimes come to help chop vegetables, stir, or clean dishes in Central Lodge's back kitchen. Dr. Jim liked to cook and was quite talented there, but knew enough to stay out of Tariq's way and to keep any suggestions or cooking insights to himself. Jim told us that back home, it was *he* and not so much his wife who did the cooking, though they often cooked together. Jim would wink at us as he added an herb behind Tariq's back, or add more spice than Tariq wanted.

Derek trained me on the computer, and I helped with mundane data entry at the computer in the Administration building. Derek, Darcy and I entered figures, leaving Joel to tinker with the computer's innards.

The Three Musketeers, as Jeremy called the security team, and Tom would be at the dock to meet the delivery boat that arrived every other Friday. Happy Friday. Our waters were too shallow for a sizeable ship to dock, so the supply ship would anchor in the distant waters as items were transferred to a boat, which would then come to our dock. We all anxiously and enthusiastically waited for our requested supplies – batteries (we were *always* in need of new batteries), food cravings we never anticipated, food that Tariq didn't have such as Twinkies or red licorice, a new swim suit to replace a worn one... There were items we hadn't foreseen that we'd need – a compass or a whistle or tweezers.

We were fervent with anticipation, often cheering when we first sighted the ship in the distance. When the boat brought an extra heavy load, Kane, Joel, and Earl would help Tom and the security guys unload supplies from the ship to Main Campus, and the rest of us would eagerly rip open the boxes to claim our loot. It was like Christmas.

The men from the supply ship sometimes stayed overnight, and would bring their spirits to share at dinners and especially at our campfires. Bourbon or Jack Daniels would stimulate an evening full of stories and extra laughs. We all were thirsty for any news from back home.

After I'd first arrived, I used to take my computer time in the evening to email people back home, especially Melinda and Jack from the stables. As the days added on, my evenings were instead filled with visits to the doctor, Darcy, Jeremy, Brian, or Derek immediately after work. Then I'd see everyone at dinner, followed by Campfire, until I dragged myself off to bed. I squeezed in computer time during breaks or my day off, but more and more, emails became a chore and not so desirable. Life back in Maine became unreal and no longer important. Jackel Island was now my home, my life, my world. The thought that all this would end in a few months, and I would be returning to the hollow emptiness of the States, was almost unbearable.

PART TWO

Chapter 15
TO TOUCH THE WILD

I itched! Yesterday, I had rubbed against a strange plant while I was walking in the woods with Brian. He was telling me he thought he might be in love with Darcy as I scratched, and I was trying to explain to him that she was with Tom, as I scratched some more.

In the shower, I fiercely scrubbed my leg with soap trying to rid myself from this itch, trying to rub the irritated *skin* off me. I meshed the soap to my skin, scrubbing so hard I shook the shower stand.

"What's all that noise?" Darcy called from one shower over.

"It's me scratching," I said. "I have poison ivy or something."

"Go see Jim!"

"Brian's in love with you, by the way."

"I know. Go see Jim!"

I *did* go to see the doctor, and he gave me some ointment that he said would work like a charm. "Isn't this your day off?" Jim asked me.

"Yes it is!"

"Then why are you up and about so early?"

"I'm going for a ride today. I want to get an early start."

I wasn't two feet from the medical building when Brian rushed over to me, hurrying across the camp's clearing, carrying a bundle that bounced against his leg as he jogged. He was out of breath when he reached me, and handed me a stuffed red–checkered cloth with a big knot on top. "This is from Tariq," Brian said, huffing. "It's your lunch for today. He said if you lose the scarf he's going to clock you."

"How did he know I was missing lunch today?" I asked Brian.

"Hell if I know."

"Nothing's sacred around here."

"You got that right," Brian said. "Hey, you didn't tell Darcy anything about me liking her, did you?"

"Gotta' go!"

When I climbed in the saddle and jiggled the reins, the white pony blew out a jet of steam from his nostrils before blasting off. Like a dog who was excited to go on a walk, this pony loved to run. My job for the next couple of weeks was to have him trust others so that Dr. Bronte could eventually take ownership of him. But for now, it was just the white pony and me. Earl yelled something to me as I cantered off, but I didn't hear him, and he quickly faded in the distance. The tin–blue morning air was electric with the promise of seeing the wild horses.

The world buzzed by in a green blur with pine and brier and thicket as I weaved through the woods on the white pony. The trail lay covered with dirt and scattered leaves and twigs as I flew past the trees. I was deep in the heart of Jackel Island, dead center, mid-point between our Main Campus at the west end of the island, fast approaching the east side where the wild horses grazed, beyond which the five–man research team lived and worked.

I started to notice that my responses weren't as quick as usual. I felt slightly jittery. I wondered if it was from the plant that had caused the itch, or if I was having a bad reaction to the doctor's ointment. Perhaps it was nothing, just slight fatigue from lack of sleep that might have been finally catching up to me. I trudged on.

I stopped where the dense blackish woods opened up to the sunlit clearing. The white pony stomped and blew out air as I looked out into the golden field, and there, two baseball fields ahead, grazed the wild animals. I felt tingly, either from the strange affliction that recently fell upon me, or from the sight of the wild horses, a sight that always grabbed at me as if a million electrified ants wiggled in me. The wild horses!

I got down from the saddle and felt a thump in my head as my feet hit the ground. I was slightly dizzy. I figured I should eat something, so I went to the bundle that Tariq had prepared for me which was tied to the side of the saddle, untied the red–checkered cloth and unwrapped a sandwich. I loosely tied the pony's lead around a tree, then stepped out into the field's edge. I chewed my sandwich as I leaned against a tree and watched the animals glisten under the sun.

I heard the horses buzz and stir, and it seemed to me that the herd was gathered together like a majestic ensemble, so far unconquered by human hand. Only sun, flies, earth, and each other ever touched their bodies, and they claimed Jackel Island as their own. I pushed myself from the tree and slowly advanced toward the herd.

Recently, they had allowed me to venture closer to them than I was able to get before, but still, I could not get too close or they would bolt. As I drew nearer to them, I noticed that their behavior was off. Something was wrong with them, a disturbance. The horses nervously pranced as they grazed, and they became easily agitated, some jerking their heads up and down, their movements too quick. I wondered if there was a snake near them, coiled up among the herd. I crept closer. Normally, their attention would be keenly on me, but now it was also on something else.

It was then when I saw movement on the ground, a fallen horse on his side, his leg unnaturally caught between two fallen logs. The poor creature wiggled desperately to free himself. I feared his frantic movements would break his leg. It was the horse who nuzzled the neck of another horse, the young male with eyes that settled in his face like two black marbles, only now his eyes were wide open and wild with fear. I stood still before the gold void in the middle of nowhere. A Banggai crow called out, mocking, and the sound broke my transfixion.

Suddenly, the world was a blood–red panic, and I ran forward to free the fallen horse, running as if in a dream with thick legs that weren't working quite right. I was vaguely aware that my advancing could trigger an attack, especially from male horses protecting their females, or females protecting their young. However, upon hearing me, the herd instantly galloped to the far edge of the field and beyond, leaving the lone horse on his side and vulnerable.

I stopped when I saw him, this horse with tiny erect ears and a stand–up bristly mane, this wild horse who violently jerked and twisted to free himself from the log and from me. With demonic and turbulent thrusts, the horse lurched uncontrollably and hysterically for escape. The poor thing gave a single shrill like a human scream.

I dropped to my knees and leaned to see exactly how the logs had trapped his leg. The poor animal was filled with murderous terror, jerking his leg up repeatedly in the wrong angle. A thrashing hoof to my head while he was in this frenzied state would surely kill me, so I allowed distance.

He stopped thrashing, but only for a moment. His savage jerking motions came in spurts, then quieted, then would start again. As I examined the log, I was relieved to see that all I need do was to simply move the log to the side and he would be free! Stockier than the average horse, his leg did not appear to be broken.

I placed my hands on the log to move it, but suddenly, an urge to touch this wild przewalski horse, this untouched species, was strong in me. Crawling around to the back of the creature and out of kicking range, I sat in the caramel grass, reached, and traced my fingertips along the curvature of the animal's back, ever so softly. I touched this wild animal! I made contact with this feral creature, and had formed a joining where none existed before between human and przewalski. Surprisingly, he didn't thrash about with my touch.

Suddenly, my sight went black on the edges, and I shook to regain awareness. I would no longer allow him to be trapped. I crawled back to the log, moved it aside with my feet, and he immediately scrambled to stand, struggling for a moment to find his footing, then bolted off, bouncing in rapid gait through the honeyed flat field and beyond the auric horizon. I sat in the grass and watched him disappear.

All was quiet and still, but only for a moment.

I then heard a metronome of pounding earth behind me. I turned to look, but vision came in and out. Was it a man on a horse? Was it gold hair that blew in the wind, or field straw that swayed with the breeze? I grew very confused. I stood, felt nauseous, and faltered.

A man on a horse drew close to me and said something, and I cocked my head to understand his words while I struggled to stay on my feet. He hurried off his horse and rushed towards me, frightening me with his urgency, but I was more concerned with my physical state. When I couldn't find words, I held out my palm towards him to hold him away. I saw black at all four corners of my vision until the blackness merged in the middle and consumed my sight, and I fell into the field.

Chapter 16
THE MYSTERIOUS MAN

Bits and pieces came to me... my head being lifted slightly from the ground... a mineral taste as thin metal was placed to my lips and water dribbling down my chin and neck, tickling... a scrambling as I was lifted too quickly, and then nothing. More fragments came... jouncing that hurt my upper legs and lower spine as my back leaned against something that was both soft and firm, and one arm firmly holding me around my middle, wanting to lay down but unable to, all the while catching glimpses of a vast landscape swimming in colors, and then nothing. Later... confused hushed voices... houses or scanty buildings like a dwarf town back in the States, and I wondered if I was dreaming... a confined hum and still air where I sensed I was no longer outside. And then nothing.

I woke looking at a surgical light near the ceiling that emitted pulsating white illumination. I squinted. Was I in our doctor's office? I looked for Jim and for his chair, then realized that the room was all wrong, with unfamiliar tables in incorrect locations, strange equipment, and gray walls instead of pale green. I wanted to smell Jim's coffee, but I smelled ammonia. Where was I? My heart jolted, and I shot up from a cot as a light green blanket slipped off me in my haste. I felt suddenly queasy. I saw the back of a man as he stood by a counter, and he was preoccupied. He was writing something in a large black notebook. I feared it was Dr. Bronte formulating chemicals, chemicals that were meant for me.

"Welcome to the world of the conscious," he said calmly, his back still facing me.

"What's… what's going on? Where…"

"You're safe." He turned around. I was relieved to see that it was the strange research assistant who appeared in the fields the first time I'd seen the wild horses, the man who had warned me about Dr. Bronte. I recognized the dancing green eyes, the firm lips, and wispy light brown hair. "You gave me quite a scare." He came to me with a little cup of water.

"What happened?"

"You fainted. You don't remember?"

"Kind of. Why did I faint?" I sipped the water.

He laughed. "Well, I don't know. I didn't see any bruises on you. Did you fall or hit your head?"

"No."

"Were you dehydrated?" He bent to pick up the blanket that was on the floor

"No, I don't think so. I had plenty of water."

Folding the blanket, he asked, "Are you diabetic?"

"No."

"Do you have any medical conditions that aren't indicated on your employee profile?" He placed the blanket on the end of the cot.

"No, not that I'm aware of. I'm pretty normal." I said. I finished the water and he took the cup from my hand.

"Hmm." He went back to the counter and leaned against it, studying me as he absently held the empty cup by his hip.

"How long have I been out?" I asked, rubbing my head. "Where's my pony? Where am I?" He started patting the air with his palm to abate me as I fired questions at him. "Am I in the research center?"

"You've been in and out of consciousness for a little less than an hour. And yes, you're in our research area." He sighed. "Of course, I couldn't leave you lying in the field. I had to bring you here as it seemed you needed medical attention."

"Maybe I should have been taken to *my* doctor."

"There was no time for that. It made more sense to bring you *here* instead of traveling with you in my saddle the two and a half miles to your side of the island."

"My pony… I left him tied to a tree."

"I'm sure he's fine," he answered quickly. "And by the way… *Whose* pony?" He tilted his head and smirked. "Isn't that white pony technically mine?"

"Yours? No. I'm training him for Dr. Bronte, not the whole research department." I said. "Where is Dr. Bronte, anyway? I don't want him to find me here."

"Oh…"

"Listen, I'd better get going." I stood from the cot, feeling woozy. He quickly put the empty cup down and hurried towards me.

"Ooh, not so fast," he said, and put his hand on my shoulder to steady me. "You need to take it easy." He gently pushed my shoulder down until I sat on the cot. "I want to make sure you're okay before I release you."

"Release me?" I leaned my forehead into my fingertips, then looked up at him. "I can go when I want, right?"

He sighed and looked at the floor, then at me again. "Jamie, I had *told* you that you weren't supposed to be in this area." He scratched his head, then sat next to me on the cot. "I was hoping that just a warning would be enough. Do I need to take further action? Hmm?"

"How do you know my name?" We sat looking at each other. His face was stone and I couldn't read him. "Look, I really need to get back." I stood, then immediately he stood, like two jack–in–the–boxes popping up. He pushed my shoulders down again to get me to sit. I closed my fingers around his wrist to resist, but again felt lightheaded and flushed. I sat, and then he sat, the two jack–in–the–boxes receding back into their boxes. I held my forehead.

"There you go, that's better," he said. "You okay?"

I held my head for a moment before I spoke. "I think I had a bad reaction from the ointment our doctor gave me this morning."

"Ointment?"

"I got poison ivy or something. So the doctor gave me ointment."

"There *is* no poison ivy on this island. Can I have a look at your rash?" I leaned forward to lift my pants at the ankle so he could see some of the irritated skin. He got off the cot and squatted to have a look.

"Hmm," he said, "looks like some kind of tree nettle... I'm thinking nilgiri nettle, or perhaps rengas." He looked further, pulling at my pant leg. "But that wouldn't cause you to faint." He stood. "Do you have the ointment? Can I see?"

"It's in my bag that's tied to my pony." I shrugged.

"Well, come to think about it, that's no matter. Ointment wouldn't cause you to lose consciousness." His voice trailed off as he stared into the center of the room, thinking.

"It itched like crazy this morning. I tried scrubbing it clean in the shower, but I'm sure it was already in my pores by then."

He zipped his head at me. "With soap?"

"Yes, of course. Why? Why do you ask? Does soap have a bad reaction to... to nettle–whatever, or ren-grass... what was it?" He looked at me as if he hadn't heard me.

"Do you mind if we take some blood, just to run a test or two?"

"Blood? Why? I just had a blood test."

He smiled kindly, then sat down on the cot next to me. "Pauline here is a medical researcher with a PA, far more equipped than your nurses. I'd like for her to run a few simple tests on you, if you don't mind."

"Ahh, that's okay. I'll be fine. I don't want any tests."

"Oh, I insist!" He put his fingertip towards my knee but didn't touch me. "There has to be a reason why you fainted and we just want to determine what that is. I'm going to call Pauline in."

"Umm, please... I'd rather you wouldn't." I was starting to feel uneasy. "I just want to get back."

"I'm sure you do. I'm sure you do." He slapped his knees and stood. "If you don't mind, I have a few questions before I get Pauline in here." He went to a desk, got a pad of paper and a pen, and sat back down next to me. "Can I ask what it was you were feeling before you lost consciousness?"

"What was I feeling? I don't know... weak."

"Weak, okay." He wrote it down. "I would gather you were lightheaded too. Were you?"

"Yes."

"What else?" he asked. I studied my knees. "Were you nauseated?

"Yes, a little, in waves." He wrote. "I also felt tingly."

"Tingly?" He said with volume, slightly high–pitched on the first syllable. He seemed surprised. "How so?

"I don't know, just tingly. Like... live wires in me."

"Hmm." He wrote. "What else?"

"Why do you want to know?"

"Please..." He looked at his pen that was lifted from his paper.

"Umm, dizzy, I felt dizzy." He scribbled. "Ah, let me see... my reactions were slow." He looked at me. "Yeah, like sometimes there was a fraction of a second delay before I could move."

"Interesting," he murmured to himself and went back to his pad. "Anything else?"

"Why do you want to know all this?"

"Anything else?"

I thought. "The air got black before I fell." I said. I leaned and saw him write "affects vision" on his pad. He slowly moved the pad out of my line of sight.

He tapped the pen on the paper twice before he stood.

"We're going to make you feel better, okay?" he said, smiling with closed lips but his eyes were still, his mind, elsewhere. He crossed the room and took something from the counter. He went to the far side of the room, poked his finger at the object in his hand, which I now recognized was a wireless phone, and put it to his ear. He started talking in low tones. I could not hear what he was saying. When he finished with the phone, he came over to me.

"Jamie, Pauline will be coming in here in just a moment. She's going to take a small sample from your arm, and then give you something that will alleviate your lightheadedness and nausea, all right?"

"A sample of my blood?"

"Mm hmm."

"I told you, I don't want this." I crossed my arms and held my upper arms tightly.

"Don't worry, it will only take a moment, and then we'll let you go."

"You'll *let* me go?" I stood.

"Sit down, Jamie."

"I really need to get going!" I remained standing.

He said loudly and firmly, "Sit *down*, Jamie!" His voice vibrated in my chest and held an authority that chilled and rattled me, and I looked at him open–mouthed. I sat down.

"That's better," he said softly, and he turned calm and poised. The switch in him confused and alarmed me. A polar disposition in animals is usually a red flag.

Just then, there was a knock, and he turned to the door.

"Oh, that's her now," he smiled kindly at me, and his fire–to–ice manner daunted me further. He went to the door and let a dark–haired middle–aged woman in. She carried a small metal tray with medical objects on it, and walked over to me.

"Jamie, this is Pauline." His voice was sweet but all I could think about was his yelling "Sit down, Jamie!" at me.

"Hello Jamie," she said. I looked from her to him, then back to her again. "Dr. Bronte tells me that you had quite a spell today."

"Dr. Bronte? How does *he* know?" I asked.

"Excuse me?" she asked me, then looked at the research assistant, who widened his eyes and shrugged.

"We should proceed," he said.

"If you can give me your arm, please," Pauline asked me.

"I'd... I'd rather not. I'd really rather not." Pauline looked genuinely confused.

"Jamie! What's the matter?" he said, bewildered, then he turned to Pauline. "I'll take it from here. She's upset, understandably." His tone was soft and kind. "I'll be by with the sample in a moment."

I wanted to protest, but I said nothing. Actually, I wanted to yell. I just sat there while wanting to run out the door, afraid to speak, afraid to stand, afraid to see this man turn from human to something else in a half a second, then back to being most charming. Pauline said something quietly to the research assistant, then left.

He took a hypodermic needle from the tray, tapped it, then, as he held the syringe in the air slightly above his eyes, he examined it for a moment. When he seemed satisfied, he turned his head and looked at me. An animal sense filled me, a fear, a strong warning. I pushed back on the cot so my back hit the wall behind me and my shoes faced him. He bit his lower lip before walking over to me.

"Heavens, Jamie, you're not a child. You really shouldn't be afraid of needles."

"It's not that."

"Then what is it?" I looked up at him from the cot, trying to find words. I couldn't say what it was I felt, this gut feeling that told me to take caution. He raised his eyebrows and slightly tilted his head when I wouldn't answer. "Ahh!" he said quietly in exasperation, then went to get a little white cotton ball from a jar. I picked at my fingernail

"Please give me your arm."

"No."

"This is childish, Jamie. It'll be over with in a moment. I am your employer and I'm telling you to..."

"You're not my employer! You're just a research assistant."

"Oh for crying out loud." He absently and a little angrily tossed the cotton away towards a waste paper basket and missed. He then put his foot on the cot and rested his arms on one knee, bending towards me.

"Jamie, listen. An hour ago, I found you half–conscious in the field. I took you in. You're still not well, and you want me to simply let you go when you can keel over in a heartbeat. Now, I have the means here to easily treat you, but you, for some illogical reason, refuse. What would you have me do? Release you so you can fall flat on your face?"

Now I was confused. Maybe this man was trying to help me after all. Maybe in my confused state, I had twisted things.

"I just don't like to be forced." I said quietly, barely moving my mouth.

"You don't like to be *forced*."

"Now you're mocking me."

"Oh for heaven's sake!" He removed his foot from the cot and stood, rubbing his hair in exasperation. I was starting to feel a little guilty.

"Why do you have to take blood?" I asked.

"To make sure the treatment will do what it's supposed to do," he said emphatically and slightly sarcastically to the center of the room, nodding with the words '*treatment*' and '*supposed*', then he added, "which I feel pretty confident it will. We just like to be one hundred percent sure on these matters."

"Okay," I said faintly.

"Hmm?" He looked over at me.

"I said all right."

He nodded and got another moist cotton ball from the jar. I didn't give him my arm but he slowly and gently took it, then dabbed my inner arm. I looked away. His hold on my arm became very firm, firmer than when Jim held my arm to take blood, and I felt the needle go in and linger. My eyes watered and I squinted. I wanted to cry, not from pain, but from defeat. I wanted to sit among Adrian, Tom, Jim, and the others around the fire. I wanted to rest on a log and watch Kane with his ax, where the breeze blew sweat off our skin, where the sound of the sea was near. I wanted to lean my head against Kane's bicep and feel his strength. Most of all, I wanted to know what was happening here. My thoughts and feelings were so very clouded. I did not sense ill–intent from this research man, and I believed that he actually wished me well in his own twisted way, but he was hiding something. He was not who he portrayed himself to be, and beneath his calm was a fire. And secrets. This is what I sensed from him. But then again, my senses were off and I was not myself.

"All done." He said. He took my hand and led it to a fresh cotton ball that he had pressed on my arm. "Here, hold this tightly." Our eyes locked and his face softened when he saw my moist eyes, but then he turned from me and held the syringe filled with my blood above his head. He briefly looked at me and said, "I'll be back shortly," and left for the door.

I let out a huge breath when he was gone. I hadn't realized how tightly I was holding my stomach muscles until I released them. I was alone in the room and I breathed easier now. I stood, and the vertigo came, but to a lesser extent. It passed. I thought of leaving this room and somehow heading back to Main Campus, but I didn't know how to get to my pony. And would I bump into this man outside?

I felt like a prisoner.

I began to explore the room. This room had a colder feel than our doctor's room. While Jim's medical room had a homey feel, this sterile room was more like a lab with trays of labeled test tubes, microscopes, calculators, a two-foot high plastic human anatomy model, unfamiliar equipment and machinery, a globe, and graph paper scattered on a table with scribbles. I went to the counter and rested my hand on the formica, still feeling somewhat unsteady.

On the counter next to my hand I saw a black notebook titled "JAO

PROJECT." I opened it, and on the first page, it said "Bio–CMAT". I thought of Jeremy saying "Bio–Cement". At one of our past campfires, Jeremy, Brian, Darcy and I were guessing what "CMAT" stood for, making silly guesses like "celibate men are thugs" or "chocolate milk at Tariq's" or "crazy madness at Tom's" (the last given by Darcy). As I looked further at the page, I saw the words "Bio–Chemical Mind Altering Test" written in smaller type under the bold "Bio–CMAT." So this is what it stood for! I found this interesting, perhaps even a little spooky. I was anxious to tell Darcy, Jeremy, Brian and the others.

I turned through more pages and saw chemical equations with notation, graphs, diagrams with words and arrows, illegible scribbles, line graphs, strange illustrations, bar charts, and summary paragraphs, some typed, but most of it hand–written.

Flipping further through the notebook, I stopped at a page that had military letterhead, and it had a heading in bold written at the top: "SPLIT BRAIN". I glanced at text underneath, reading portions of sentences – "...bridging the gap between brain hemispheres..."; "...severe childhood traumatic event..."; "...dissociate disorder..."; "...increased production of opiates, dopamine and serotonin...", and "...causing the death of neurons."

I had no idea what all that was about.

I leafed through further pages, but stopped suddenly when I saw our names written in bold type – Adrian North, Grady Galinger, Steven Taylor, Tom Gordon, Joel Gordon, Kane Jabari – with writing next to each listed name. I was about to read further when I heard footsteps. My heart surged and I quickly shut the notebook, then hurried back to my cot, fighting the dizzy spell caused by my haste. The research assistant came in, smiling.

"This," he said as he held up a thinner needle than before, slightly bouncing it in the air "will make you feel better in a heartbeat."

"Another needle?" I said, turning up a corner of my mouth. I was hoping that he hadn't notice that I was breathing a little hard.

"Yes, another dreaded needle," he said with exaggerated emotion, teasing. "Come on, you survived the last one, didn't you?"

As he held my arm and gave me the injection, I thought of the notebook, and wished I had time to read what was written about Adrian and the security team, Tom, Joel, and surprisingly, Kane. I jokingly thought of asking him, "Hey, I got a question for you... How do you bridge the gap between brain hemispheres? And by the way... what's with all our names in your black book?" I wondered what his reaction would be. But he most likely would not find it amusing, and he may even become mad.

After the injection, I *did* feel instantly better, and being true to his word, the research assistant said I was free to go. He did say that there was one condition – that he escort me to my pony a half a mile away.

Being outside where the air was lighter ameliorated the somewhat restrained and captive feeling I experienced in the lab.

"Hey, what was in that shot, anyway?" I asked, but his only answer was a smile.

I looked around as best I could to get a feel for the research grounds, but he hurried away from the lab building, and I had to double–step to keep up with him.

"Come on, now," he said, but I wanted to look around, and when I did, I was quite astonished and impressed. While our Main Campus looked more like a polished campsite for elite Boy Scouts, this research area was like a miniature European vacation center. I saw neatly laid red brick paths cutting through grass, coral–colored small houses in polished stucco with dark green doors and shutters, a greystone main building with Doric columns rooted into the porch that jetted into the ceiling, and a black iron fence to hold the community snugly in. I even saw a picnic table and a grill under a large waringin tree. This was Jao's exclusive commonwealth district. Our area was for the common people.

Here in the east, it was open and sunny, and you could see the bouldered sea from where we stood, whereas most of our main campus sat eclipsed under trees. The sea here was abundantly rocky, with undersized mountains breaking free from the water and into the air. Turquoise waves smashed against stone, forging ocean foam to swirl on the banks. I whistled, then felt a hand on my upper arm, which brought me back to reality.

"Come along, Jamie." I hadn't realized that I'd stopped to gaze.

"No wonder," I whispered. He continued walking, and I followed.

"No wonder what?"

"Well, I take it that my friends at Main Campus aren't exactly enamored with you guys in research." I had to practically skip to keep up with this man.

"That would be a fair estimate."

"I guess it's a case of the haves and the have-nots," I said. He looked back at me briefly, but did not slow down.

"In every society, there's always a divide between the rich and the poor," he said. "I didn't know you were somewhat into sociology."

We passed through a gate, leaving the research compound and we were now entering a wide path in the woods.

"Hey, what's with the marathon? Now that you cured me of the jitters, I'm going to die of a heart attack trying to keep up with you." I sprung over to him, gripping his arm just below the elbow in an attempt to hold him still for just a moment. He stopped and turned around to me. He looked at my restraining hand, then up to my face with his mouth slightly open and chin tucked, staring. It was as if I had attempted to high-five the Pope. I immediately let go. He shut his mouth, gave me a slight supercilious look, then turned on his heel and continued walking down the path. I followed.

"The fact that you guys live in the Taj Mahal and we live in the ghetto isn't really the problem between our two groups, I don't think," I said.

He laughed. "Jamie, you're quite dramatic. You're reaching to extremes, don't you think?" He stopped abruptly, and I nearly bumped into him. He turned and faced me. "Please tell me… what do *you* think the underlying problem is between your group and mine?"

"Well…" I watched a sparrowhawk soar above us on the right, soaring towards the ocean. "I think it's a power play."

"You do?" He seemed amused. "How so?"

"Well…"

"Well?"

I opened my mouth to answer, then squinted at him. "You're mocking me again."

"No, I'm not."

"You are," I insisted.

He looked at the tree tops, then down at me. "I humbly apologize if you think I am 'mocking' you." He continued walking, this time more slowly. I walked by his side instead of behind him. "So what about this power play?" he asked.

"Well, you heard about how Bronte turned off our electricity, right?" I asked.

He paused. "Tell me what happened."

"It seems he… why are you smiling?"

"Am I?" he said. "Go on."

"This all happened a year and a half ago, well before I arrived. So I don't know the details, but our group invited your group to dinner. Weren't you there?"

"Mm."

"Well, everything was going fine until Bronte questioned Tom's authority."

"Why would he do that?"

"I don't know. Male ego."

"Excuse me?"

"I don't know why guys do the things they do. He just did."

"Oh, Jamie," he laughed.

"I'm so glad I'm amusing you," I said. "Anyway, Bronte turned into a real jerk, Tom got mad, and…"

"A jerk?"

"Yeah. Bronte started saying he was king of the island, or leader, whatever. He wanted everyone to admit that."

"You make him sound rather arrogant."

"Isn't he? I heard he was." I said. "You work for the guy. Is he a real jerk?"

"Are you asking me if he's arrogant, or if he's a jerk?"

"You're mocking me again." We walked on, and I saw him smile and shake his head. "So is he, or isn't he?" I asked.

He sighed. "He may perhaps have an arrogant streak. I wouldn't say he's a jerk."

"Really? Because when Tom wouldn't admit that Bronte was King, Bronte turned off our electricity."

"Now how did he accomplish that?" he asked.

"No one has any idea."

"What a prankster."

"No, what a *jerk*." We approached the east field. He stopped and put his hands behind his back and looked out at the meadow. I noticed that the wheat-colored grassland was the same hue as his hair, when sunlight hit both.

"I assume he eventually turned it back on."

"It took some doing," I said. "Tom and the three guys from security had to hike three miles to get Bronte to turn the generators back on. You didn't hear about this? Didn't you hear about the fight?"

"I believe I *did* hear something to that effect. If I remember correctly, Tom Gordon was quite the hothead and charged at Dr. Bronte."

"Yeah, and when he did, Bronte put Tom down on the ground in half a second."

"Imagine that."

"Our security guys could have flattened Bronte if they wanted to."

"You think so?"

"Yeah. Besides, scientists aren't usually fighters."

"They aren't?"

"Adrian's buffed, Bronte's not, not at all."

"Ouch."

"Bronte probably just learned some tricky move in the army," I said. The research assistant put his hands on his temples and laughed. I didn't understand what tickled him so much and I looked up at him, squinching my eyes together. He stopped laughing, looked at me, then started up again, slowly shaking his head.

"Oh Jamie, I haven't laughed like this in... years," he said. "And I believe Dr. Bronte was in the Air Force, not the army."

"Whatever."

"Oh my," he said, then started walking into the field. "So tell me about this, ah, *buffed* man, Mr. Adrian North."

"How'd you know his last name?"

"You don't miss a beat, do you?" he said. "Jao profiles."

"Oh," I said, absently looking for the wild horses. There was no sign of them. "What do you want to know about Adrian that's not in the files?"

"What would cause a level–headed trained fighter like Adrian North to get agitated? What do you think?"

"I'm thinking this is a strange question." He looked down at me, contemplating, as if he was working out a math equation in his head. Breaking his gaze, I ventured a few steps further into the field and snapped off a thick blade of grass, then held the grass taut between my thumbs and blew hard. No sound came. I turned and found him looking out into the field lost in thought. I tightened the blade of grass between my thumbs and blew again, and again no sound came.

"Adrian doesn't get upset easily," I said. "He even stayed calm when I started punching him." The words left my mouth too soon, and it was too late to take them back. The research assistant quickly moved his head towards me with a curious look. I tried to whistle through the grass again to distract, but no sound came.

"You *struck* your Chief of Security?" He looked curious, and amused. "Heavens, why would you do that?"

I put the blade of grass to my lips and gave one more blast of air, and this time it took, shrieking through the air. The research assistant jumped. This amused me.

"Look, I… I have to go. My poor pony has been tied up for way too long," I said as I backed up. "Thank you for…" I couldn't find the words. Still looking at me with curiosity, he gave a vague nod. I nodded back, then turned and hurried across the field to the white pony, half expecting this man to follow. When I reached the pony, I removed the lead from the tree and climbed in the saddle. As I looked back through the field, I saw that the man was still standing there, watching me. Again, I never got his name.

As I rode away, I wondered why this man wanted information about our Chief of Security.

Chapter 17

THE SCENE AT THE LAGOON

I eased into the beryl water and felt protected by the columns of thick tree trunks that surrounded me, trunks with variegated bark that twisted and turned like dinosaur muscle. I was alone. Branches, limbs, and leaves towered over me, and while some of the branches sunk down towards the limewater like an umbrella, most of them clawed into the sky. Vines coiled around still more vines like boa constrictors. All living vegetation battled for sunlight, starving each other out. Tree trunk gave way to branches, branches gave way to limbs, and limbs gave way to tender green flower. Sunrays and speckles of blue leaked through any space that wild life didn't occupy. The air was filled with life, almost choking on it.

I had touched a living wild horse.

Here in the lagoon, all was still. Forest, plant, and wilderness could not stretch to the water or the air immediately above the lagoon. The cool vert water permeated my skin, washing away humidity, dust, and tension from the three–mile ride through the woods.

I had left the strange research man less than an hour ago. I had felt somewhat controlled, intrigued, and charmed by him. Also, strangely, I felt tenderness mixed with curiosity and even fear towards this man. I did not fully comprehend him or what it was I felt. One thing I *was* sure of was the fascination I'd felt when I had touched the wild horse. I remembered the feel of my fingertips tracing the horse's backline, the coarse hair with fire–life underneath, savage bristle over untouched skin and muscle which enveloped untamed and primitive life. I had touched the wild przewalski horse.

From the thicket I heard something, a rustling of leaves. I froze and became fixed on hearing. No one knew about Emerald Lagoon, so I wondered if it was an animal, and if so, was it a harmful one. Were there bears here? Boar? Tigers? I heard the rustle again, coming closer. My heart pounded. I was not dressed, not at all. I was completely under water except for my neck and head. Could an animal smell me while I was immersed in the lagoon? I did not move, I did not breathe.

A shrub was pushed to the side and Adrian appeared. It was Adrian! Only Adrian. I felt like screaming at him, or hugging him, but I simply let out a lungful of air.

It was then I realized the gravity of the situation; I had no clothes on.

He had not seen me. He dropped his tan burlap bag on a rock and kicked off his shoes, as if it was a routine for him. He ran his fingers through his hair, what cropped hair he had, and I saw his chest rise and fall as he sighed deeply. It was then he noticed me. He was startled, but only for a second, and he quickly regained his composure.

"Hello there," he called over to me.

"Hey," I called back, then added, "You surprised me!"

"You surprised me too. I see you found this treasured place."

"I did! I didn't think anyone else knew about it."

"Nor did I," Adrian said. "Mind if I join you?"

The air chilled. I did mind, given my awkward situation, but there was no polite way to prevent him from coming in the water. My only option was to wait him out, have him swim until he had his fill, and hopefully he would leave before I got out of the water without him ever noticing my dilemma. I was hoping he wouldn't notice my clothes by the tagar bush. I held out my palm, which faced up towards the sky, and tucked my chin down with raised eyebrows, motioning for him to come on in.

Adrian removed his shirt. I was surprised at how conditioned he was, especially for a man of his years – tight skin over polished muscle. I looked away and watched two butterflies flicker over a bush. When I looked back over at him, Adrian was ankle–deep in the lagoon and coming my way. He had only his pants on. When the water reached his stomach, he dove in. For a moment, all was still, and I became fearful he would get too close to me or see me under water. I backed up. Where was he? He quickly surfaced a few feet away from where I was, shaking water from his head. I kept backing up, then stopped when I was a safe distance from him.

"There you are!" he said, smiling. "The water is wonderful, hmm?" He ran his palm over his face.

"It is."

"What's wrong?"

"Nothing!"

I swam away from him and stood under the waterfall as its splash pounded on me, protecting me like a thin shower curtain. The spray gave off a prism of blue–green–yellow–red, and I hid in its transparent film. I kept my eye on Adrian who stood in the center of the lagoon, water dripping from his jaw and chin. He gave me a puzzling look, then he dove under the water again, startling me. I held my breath until he broke through the surface three feet from me.

"Amazing waterfall, huh," he said.

"It is."

"You all right?"

"Yeah."

Adrian grew closer to the rock wall near me and stood directly under the waterfall's blast, shutting his eyes as he let the water pummel his head and shoulders. I noticed freckles on his shoulder and wanted to run my fingers over them. Instead, I quickly and quietly swam away, back to the center of the small lagoon. When I looked over at him, he had just opened his eyes. At that moment, he looked for me, expecting me to be right next to him, where I was just before he shut his eyes. He seemed to be caught off guard when I wasn't there and scanned for me, and looked surprised to see me back in the center of the lagoon.

"There you are!" he said. "My word, you keep running away from me!"

"The waterfall's spray got to be too much."

I watched a film of color act as a halo around him. Here was this man who I thought of in overly familiar ways, who I had imagined holding me as I slept and feeling his hot breath on my neck, pushing back my hair, and feeling his jaw hard against my face. Here was this man who I had wanted to touch and be touched by, and now I was avoiding as if he were an enticing snake that could bite and release poison throughout my blood. I did not want him like this.

Or did I?

Was I later going to regret avoiding him when I was safe in my bed, alone? But no, this situation was too real. And he was much too old for me. I now had to wait for Adrian to leave the lagoon, however long it took. I had to work harder on acting as if everything was normal, because he was starting to see that I had a dilemma. And this dilemma had to be kept hidden.

With a blast, Adrian dove from the waterfall and emerged before me. I was surprised at how hard I was breathing as I stared at him, watching water drip from his face and shoulders. A breathy wind blew against us.

"Jamie, can you just stay put for a second so I don't have to keep chasing you around this lagoon?"

"What do you mean?" I quickly asked, then I slowly swam to the side of him. He turned to face me. I continued to swim around him, trying to get behind him, and he kept turning to face me.

"What are you…" he started, looking confused and curious. I continued to swim a close circle around him without really understanding why. When I reached my starting point, I started swimming a second circle around Adrian. I didn't want to swim away from him again, and I didn't want to stand still before him, so I circled him, and was unsure when I would stop or what my next move was. What I wanted was to get behind him and wrap my arms and legs around him, while at the same time I wanted to swim away from him. I wanted him to leave. I wanted him to stay.

With a lunge, he reached out and grabbed me just above my elbow.

"Good Lord, stop it! You're making me dizzy!"

When he let go, I did the unthinkable. I burst at him with one quick leap, pressing my head against his shoulder with the freckles, holding his ribs. I simply held on, shutting my eyes, closing out the forest–green lagoon, the wild vines above, the burly tree bark and twisted trees that surrounded us, the buzz of insects and the flickering butterflies… I shut out the world as I held on to Adrian.

"Jamie – " I didn't dare speak. I had no idea what would happen next. My actions surprised me. This was not me.

A heavy wind pushed at us, followed by a speckle of raindrops. I then felt his hands on my shoulders. Was he going to push me off him? That would be a harsh slam. But he simply kept his hands still.

"Jamie," he whispered. I didn't answer right away.

"Hmm?"

"You *do* realize I'm more than twice your age."

"Mm hmm."

Adrian then ran his palms up and down my arm, not exactly in a sensual manner. I couldn't read him. I kept expecting him to pull me off him, and I simply held on, afraid to run my hands along his skin, afraid to move at all. His hands went from my upper arms to my back, and his fingertips moved up and down, now in a romantic way. It was then I circled my palm on his skin below his breast along the side of his stomach. Under his skin his stomach muscles were as hard as the tree bark. I brought my arms around his back and squeezed, pressing my face into his shoulder, taking him in. I felt his fingers under my chin, pushing my face up. Following his lead, I let go, and he led me up to his face, his mouth finding mine. Our teeth accidentally clunked together as he kissed me. He tasted earthy, like the forest. His hand went behind my head and under my hair and he pressed me to him. His other hand traveled up and down my spine as I held his lower back. I felt my body flush, the heat giving way in the water.

He then took his hand from my spine and reached below his stomach, and he shuffled a bit. I felt his knuckles at my lower stomach as he guided and pushed part of himself towards my inner thigh, almost dead on.

"Woh!" I quickly pushed off him. "Woh!" I said again. I was not expecting this.

"I'm sorry, I'm... I thought..."

"It's just..."

"I'm sorry."

"It's just you're a little fast. I'm not that fast."

"It's okay. I'm sorry." We both spoke in rapid succession.

Was this the norm? Were most men and women this quick? Was I leading him on? Was I being too easy? A prude? We had no protection. Should I remind him of that? Did men think women have that taken care of? When it came to romance, I was simply ignorant. So we stood before each other, still with the taste of each other in our mouths, awkwardly apologizing to each other.

"Well now," he said. "Where do we go from here, Jamie? It's your call." He leaned back in the water and treaded. I then did the same.

"Why is it my call?"

"Well, I'm finding it a little hard to read you, if you want to know the truth."

Just then, the sky cracked and it poured with vengeance, and water pounded down from the suddenly gray sky. I yelled "Whoa!" and ducked down into the water, and the last thing I heard was Adrian laughing at either the heavens or at me.

I popped back up for air.

"What is it that you want, Jamie?" He had to yell to be heard above the rain. I bit my lip. "The last thing I want to do is to pressure you," he said above the rain. The fact that Adrian had to shout clashed with this tender moment. I wanted to answer him, and I was trying to find the words, but this was most difficult because I was very confused over how I actually felt. "We can pretend this never happened, or…"

"No." I sighed. "I don't know, Adrian. I just don't know."

"What?" he yelled.

"I said I don't know!" I hollered, but the rain abruptly stopped, leaving my voice to echo in the sudden quietness. "I just don't know," I said more quietly. "I really wish I did. I'm sorry. I…"

"Maybe you just got caught up in the moment. I can understand that. If you don't like me romantically, that's fine, Jamie. I'm just confused…"

"No, it's not that." I cut him off. "I *do* like you."

"Romantically?" he asked.

"Yes, but I just don't know…"

"You do?"

"Yes! But I just don't know if we should act on it."

Adrian stopped treading water and stood. He ran his hand through his hair. "Why the hell not?"

"I don't know."

"Our age gap?"

"There's that." I circled my finger in the water and I heard him exhale. Just then, the sun poured out from the sky. "Well, what do *you* feel for me? Do *you* like me?" I asked without looking up.

I heard the water stir and then Adrian was right before me, his hands on my shoulders. He brought his head down and kissed me, and I pressed into him.

Chapter 18
ADRIAN'S GIFT

"No dog!" Tariq yelled at me. "No dog near my kitchen!"

"Aww, he's just a puppy," I argued.

"No dog inside! Dog *out*side!" Tariq insisted.

"You don't think he's cute?" I asked, holding the pup out to Tariq, his paws dangling in the air.

"Outside!" Tariq yelled, and he stormed off, heading for the kitchen.

"You better bring him outside," said Jim, who was kneeling next to me just inside the lodge entrance door. He put a finger under the dog's chin and lightly bounced the dog's head.

"Dog outside!" Jeremy mimicked Tariq. He was on the floor with me, along with Jim, Brian, Darcy, and Derek, all of us cooing over the seven or eight–week–old kintamani as we waited for breakfast to be ready. Derek lost his fingers in the animal's thick white coat, and complained that Adrian gave *me* a dog, not *him*. Jeremy told Derek that Adrian probably liked me better than him, in which Derek did not see the humor.

Tom burst in the door and practically tripped over the six of us sitting on the floor.

"Hey, what do we have here?" Tom asked, looking down at all of us.

"Adrian gave me a puppy!" I said, beaming, as I rose and held Henry out to Tom. Tom took Henry from my hands and raised him way above his head, laughing. Henry looked dazed and sleepy.

Yesterday afternoon, Adrian and I were together in the lagoon until the sun got low. We never discussed if we were going to let the others know about us. So I had felt unsure and awkward at dinner, until

Adrian arrived late, came right over to me and shook my shoulder, giving me a sweet grin before going to his usual seat. While Adrian and I sat apart at dinner in the seats we always sat in, we exchanged frequent glances. No one caught this but Darcy, and her eyes beamed into me like lasers forming a huge question mark. That girl never missed a beat. Throughout dinner, I kept warding off Darcy's questions, telling her "later!" and "shh!" and "not *now*!"

Adrian and I sat next to each other at last night's campfire. We didn't hold hands or anything like that, but Brian later asked, "Is there anything up with you two?" I denied everything to Brian. He didn't believe me. Jeremy and the others were oblivious, except for maybe Jim who kept looking at me funny. Meanwhile, the usual jokes and stories flew around the fire.

After Campfire last night, I had gone in Darcy's cabin and filled her in, telling her just about everything. When you're a girl, the "don't kiss and tell" rule does not apply to your best girl friend.

Later on, after I had left Darcy's cabin and had settled in my own place, I had heard a quiet knock. It was Adrian, as I had suspected, and I felt mixed emotions. I wanted him to come in, and wanted him to go away. He told me he came only to bid me good–night. I was hoping that none of the others watched as we held each other just outside my cabin door.

Early this morning, as I woke to the orchestra of screaming birds in surround sound, Adrian stopped by to give me a special gift, Henry. I named the white little fluff on the spot. Henry's mother was native to the island. She had dug a hole just outside a small rock cave near the center of Jackel Island to nest her young.

I was in love. With Henry. Maybe with Adrian in time, but definitely with Henry. Adrian would now have to compete for my affections.

Derek followed me out of the lodge, his hand on Henry as I held the dog to my chest.

"Why didn't Adrian give *me* a puppy?" Derek asked. "I thought he really liked me."

"He does, very much!" I said, and sat on the ground by the water basin in front of Central Lodge. Derek sat next to me on the packed dirt. "Can you help me raise him?" I asked. "I'm Henry's mother, and you can be his big brother."

"Sure!"

"So Henry's family is just you and me, no one else."

"Wow." Derek didn't take his eyes or hands off the puppy. "Hey, that kind of makes you my mother, sort of."

"Yeah."

"So my father's now your husband, sort of."

"Don't push it."

Kane then emerged, carrying a shovel. I put the puppy on the ground for Kane to see, and Henry hobbled over the packed dirt towards him. Kane stopped, and rested his hands and chin on top of the shovel's handle, watching the animal play with his shoelace. I half expected Kane's mouse to appear, and wondered how the mouse and puppy would interact.

"Kane, are you going to breakfast in the lodge?" I asked. Kane raised his melted almond eyes at me and slowly shook his head. "Then can you watch the dog for about a half hour?" Kane nodded. "Come on, Derek," I said as I got up off the ground, dusting off my palms and pants. Derek and I entered Central Lodge for breakfast.

I didn't realize it then that Kane would always watch over Henry when I could not.

"Go sit next to him!" Darcy said to me, sitting next to me at the table. Darcy pointed her chin to Adrian, who was sitting next to Tom and Grady at the head table.

"Who?" Jeremy asked. He sat on the other side of me.

"Shut up," I said.

"Me?" Jeremy asked.

"No, not you. Darcy," I said.

"Just go over there!" Darcy insisted.

"Shut *up*!" I said.

"Me?"

"Not *you*. God, Jeremy!"

We ate Nasi Goreng for breakfast. Tariq came out of the kitchen briefly, angrily burrowing his brows into his eyes at me, making sure my new little fury friend wasn't with me. I just smiled at him, and Tariq shot his eyes up to the ceiling as he mumbled something in his language, then he scurried back off into the kitchen.

Darcy jabbed her elbow in my ribs hard, and I turned to her to yell "Ow!" in her ear as loudly as I could, but she was looking straight up. Adrian stood before us in front of our table.

"Hello Romeo," she grinned at him, and I elbowed her hard in the ribs.

"Hello ladies, Jeremy, Brian." Adrian said. His face fell a bit, and his eyebrows creased. "Listen, are any of you having problems with your email?"

Brian, Darcy, and I started talking at once. We all had problems receiving our email yesterday. Adrian looked at Jeremy who was simply chewing. Jeremy looked up at Adrian, then stated he doesn't really deal with email, talking with his mouth full.

"I didn't think much of it," Darcy said.

"Me either," Brian said.

"I only had about five minutes to check my email yesterday before dinner," I said, "and it wouldn't load."

"The internet is down as well. Well, I'm sure Joel's aware of the problem and is working on it. Where *is* he this morning?" Adrian said. "Anyway, our computers should be back up sometime today, I imagine. Tom was just wondering how widespread the problem was. We'll talk with Joel to see what's going on."

"Doesn't concern me in the least," Jeremy said, still chewing.

"Speak of the devil," Darcy said, and we followed her gaze to the front door. Joel hurried in. He eyed Adrian, and pointed his head to the head table. Adrian followed Joel to the back table, and the men talked as if in a football huddle.

"Wonder what that's all about?" Darcy asked.

"Don't care," Jeremy said, still chewing.

I watched Joel talk rapidly with concern to Tom, Adrian, Grady, and Steve. Jim was on the side listening in, his eyebrows knotted with distress. Tom and the security men fired back questions at Joel, who raised his eyebrows and shook his head. Adrian, who was leaning on the table, pushed off it and stood upright, then gave a weighted sigh. He looked troubled. Tom looked over at us, then huddled further with the men, and they spoke in frenzied hushes, several of them looking over at us. After a while, the men broke away from each other. Adrian nodded at Tom.

"Listen up, everyone," Tom said at the end of breakfast, standing. The hum of conversation quieted. "Seems we have some sort of computer glitch and so we don't have email or internet access. Our phones are down, too. But Joel is working on it. So sit tight."

"Do you know when our phones and computers will be working again?" Sheila asked. Tom looked at his brother. Joel simply raised his eyebrows.

"We're working on it and will let you know," Tom told us.

Chapter 19
TROUBLE IN PARADISE

Two days later, it was the Fourth of July, and we still didn't have email, internet, or phones. Even Jeremy was feeling a bit uneasy. Darcy, Brian, Jeremy and I sat with Jim in the Medical building before dinner, as Derek played with Henry in the corner. Henry hadn't barked yet, but was learning to snarl at Derek's playful attacking hand.

"It's like we're cut off from the outside world," Brian said.

"It's creepy," Jeremy added, rolling a string around and around his finger, then untangling it, only to wind it back around.

"Do you know anything, Jim?" I asked.

"Nada," he said. "I know only what you know."

"Would you tell us if you *did* know something?" Darcy asked. Jim gave her a look out of the corner of his eye, with his chin tucked low.

"Did Tom say what the problem is?" I asked Darcy. "Anything at *all*?"

"Nothing!" said Darcy. "All he keeps saying is that they're working on it. The men just keep whispering among themselves. Something serious is up."

"Did someone contact anyone in the research department?" I asked. "Are their computers down too?"

"Yeah, they are, at least that's what Tom told me." Darcy said. "Adrian rode out there to ask them if they had connection to the outside world, and they said no. No one knows why the computers aren't working, not even the research team."

"I'm sure Joel will have our computers and phones up and running this week," Jim reassured us.

"How do you know?" Darcy asked. "Joel told Tom that he's never been stumped like this before."

"Well, Joel's the best there is with computers," Jim said, and then added, more to himself, "I haven't corresponded with my wife since Monday." He looked sad.

I never saw Joel so nervous. For the last two days, I, along with several of the others, went in the computer room a couple of times a day to see if there was any news. Joel worked non–stop at the machines, stopping only to eat one or two meals a day, and to sleep for a few hours. He looked rough, with dark smears under his eyes, his hair scraggly, his skin unshaven, and he was rather pale. He wore a desperate look. He reminded me of the wild horse who had lain trapped on his side in the field. Derek clung to me, saying his father was acting scary.

"Joel, maybe you should take a break," I said to him.

"Wish I could," he said, never taking his eyes from his work.

"I kind of worry about Derek," I said, wondering if I'd misspoken. Joel stopped and was still, but never looked up at me.

"Sorry," he said quietly.

Adrian was preoccupied since our computers and phones went down. I hadn't trained in martial arts with him in days, as he was nowhere to been seen in the fields in the early mornings, not even with Derek. He didn't bid me goodnight last night, or the night before. We each put in a full day of work the last several days, seeing each other briefly at meals, where all his focus seemed to be with Tom, Joel, and his security team. The men had not joined us for our campfire the last two evenings.

Things were very strange on Jackel Island.

Even Sheila and the two nurses were asking Darcy and me if we heard anything. Jim and Earl missed talking to their wives terribly. While Earl wasn't one for computers, and therefore, he didn't use email,

Earl told me he always called his wife every evening, and not being able to speak to her before he went to bed the last two nights was unsettling for him. Earl busied himself with his work, and I tried to do the same. I wasn't particularly missing anyone back home in the States, but was concerned over what seemed to be happening to us here on the island.

Kane was most watchful, but said nothing. He didn't use computers or the phone, but he seemed to be studying us. Tariq was the only one of us who seemed unaffected. He seemed oblivious.

At dinner last night, Tom again announced that they were continuing to work on the problem, and they were doing all they could. His smile was forced. He skirted over our questions, giving vague answers. Adrian stood by Tom with his hands on his hips, looking serious.

I'd walked back from dinner last night arm–in–arm with Jim, my head against his shoulder. I knew this was not my childhood affliction. No, this was intentional, on both our parts. For those few moments when we walked from Central Lodge towards our cabins, I allowed myself to imagine that he was my father.

It took effort for me to get Adrian alone after dinner last night, and he was cold and distant to me when I asked him what in God's name was going on. As I tried getting his attention, Adrian kept looking over my head and telling me not to worry, that things would be worked out.

This morning, I had spotted Adrian by the water basin, and hurried up to him. I proceeded to tell him about Henry's paws wiggling as he slept, though I could tell he wasn't listening. When Adrian saw Joel leave the computer building, he said "Excuse me," in the middle of my sentence, and left me for Joel. It was then and there I decided to quit excusing Adrian's preoccupied manner. I would be polite if I happened to bump into him, but nothing more.

That night at dinner, tensions were high. Our dinner hour in the lodge was usually loud and carefree, but the quiet was now darkly haunting. Everyone eyed each other. Even Kane was present at dinner, sitting by himself, eating pieces of fruit off his knife. Tom finally stood and cleared his throat, and we all silently waited, looking at him.

"By the way, I bid you all a happy Fourth of July. There'll be no fireworks tonight, as planned. Sorry folks." No one was surprised. Tom continued. "I know you're tired of hearing me say this, but we really are working on the problem as best we can. I wish I could tell you when we'll be up and running. But rest assured, our shipment comes in two days, and we'll have communication then."

I turned to Darcy and quietly asked her, "Darcy, doesn't Tom tell you *any*thing about what's going on?"

"Absolutely nothing. He's so distant."

"Adrian too," I said. "Why won't they tell us?"

"Maybe they don't know."

"Or maybe they're hiding something." Darcy looked at me.

After we ate, Tom left the head table and walked around to each of us to see how we were doing. He first went over to Sheila and the nurses, leaning on his elbows against the table as they drilled questions at him. Tom simply shook his head and shrugged. Tom ruffled Derek's hair, then came over to us.

"You all doing all right?" Tom asked us.

"Peachy," Jeremy said sarcastically.

"Yeah, we're fine," Brian said.

"Do you think Jao knows our situation?" I asked.

"I would gather they do," Tom said. "They must know something's up when they haven't heard from us in the last several days."

"Maybe this is part of Bio–CMAT's research, seeing it stands for bio–chemical mind altering test," I said. "Being shut out like this is definitely altering our minds, I'd say."

Tom gave me a curious look, and I felt Darcy's eyes on me.

"What did you say?" Tom asked carefully.

I looked up at him, confused. "Being shut out like this would…"

"No," Tom interrupted. "What did you say Bio–CMAT stood for?"

"Oh. Bio–chemical mind altering test."

Tom, Darcy, Brian, and Jeremy stared at me. The silence was thick. I hadn't thought of the acronym until now. I remember when I had learned what Bio–CMAT stood for, I was anxious to tell the others. But then I had become distracted with Adrian in the lagoon later that afternoon, and I had forgotten to tell them. I knew that Darcy, Brian, and Jeremy didn't know what Bio–CMAT stood for, but I thought surely the leaders did.

"Didn't you know?" I asked Tom, but seeing his blank face, I suddenly felt fear.

"Please come with me," Tom said.

I looked at Darcy, who looked stunned, then I stood and followed Tom to the head table. Adrian stopped talking with Grady as we approached, and they gave Tom and me a puzzling look.

"What's this?" Adrian asked Tom.

"Jamie here just told me something interesting." The men looked from Tom to me, and then back to Tom again. "She told me what Bio–CMAT stands for."

"And what would that be?" Adrian asked.

Tom looked down at me. All eyes were on me. I felt suddenly nervous, like I was standing before the principal for cheating on a test. I looked at Tom, and he gave me a single nod.

"Bio–chemical mind altering test," I said.

The men looked at each other. I couldn't read them.

"How do you know this?" Adrian asked. Oh, so *now* he pays attention to me, I thought, and shrugged.

"Why do you want to know?" I asked.

"Jamie –" Adrian said. Tom looked confused.

I turned to Tom. "I saw it in a notebook."

"What notebook?" Tom asked quickly. Oh boy, I thought, they weren't going to like this.

"In the research lab."

"In the *re*search lab?" Tom asked incredibly. Grady and Steve sat up straight.

"You were in the research center?" Adrian raised his voice at me. The others looked over at our table. "Dammit, Jamie, when?"

"Dammit yourself, Adrian!" Adrian looked surprised at me. Grady seemed amused.

"Shh," Tom said. "You two, shh!" I welcomed the silence that followed. I looked down at my feet. "When were you in the research lab, Jamie?" Tom asked me.

"Sunday," I said. Today was Wednesday.

"Jesus!" Adrian said quietly, but with anger. "Jamie, do you know how dangerous…"

"All right, all right," Tom said quickly, interrupting Adrian. I wasn't sure who Tom was trying to calm down, Adrian or himself. "Jamie, why on earth did you go over to the research center?"

I looked at their perplexed faces, except Steve's face was a stone with only a slight crease in his eyebrows.

"I didn't go there intentionally. I took a ride in the woods and… well, I fell." I didn't want to tell them I fainted and get into all that. "I was hurt. Not badly, but I couldn't stand at first. The research assistant guy found me and helped me, brought me to his lab room."

"Which research assistant guy?" Adrian asked. "Was it an older man?"

I looked at Tom to answer. "Not really. I didn't get his name."

"Marvin Maletti?" Adrian asked.

"I didn't get his name!"

"And he showed you a notebook with information?" Adrian asked.

I looked over at Adrian. "No! The man left the room, and I saw a black notebook on the counter. I opened the notebook and saw it.

Period."

"You saw what Bio–CMAT meant," Tom asked.

"Yes, that, and..." I didn't know if I should tell them.

"And?"

"Well, all your names were in there. Yours, you three security guys, Joel, and even Kane."

"Huh?" Grady piped in.

"What?" Adrian asked.

"What did it say about us?" Tom asked me. They were all talking at once.

"I didn't get the chance to read any further. The man came back in the room and I didn't want him to see me snooping."

"Let me get this straight," Adrian said. "You privately saw a notebook which was in the research lab. It said what Bio–CMAT stood for, along with our names. Did you get a chance to see anything else that was written in the notebook?"

"No. I only had a few moments."

"And this research man has no idea that you saw this," Adrian said.

"That's right," I said.

"I wonder if there were cameras in the lab," Adrian said quietly to the men as he stretched back in his chair. Steve leaned over to Adrian and said something, but I couldn't hear.

"That'll be all, Jamie," Adrian said to me. I narrowed my eyes at him.

"Thanks, Jamie," Tom said. I gathered I was being dismissed. I nodded, and then went back to my table, where Darcy and Jeremy interrogated me, and Brian did a little, too. When I looked over at the head table, the men were again huddled together, talking like agitated bees around a disturbed nest.

Kane was now leaning against the pole beam, away from us, watching, as his knife that held fruit went to his mouth. He looked so detached from the rest of us. He reminded me of the wild horses in the field who remained forever in the distance from any human, where the slightest disturbance would cause them to flee.

Friday came. We were all anxious for today's ship to arrive and bring word from the outside world. I rose early and showered quickly in the dark as Henry played in the water splashes, then headed out towards the dock. Normally, the supply ship didn't arrive until the afternoon, but I figured that maybe the ship would arrive early since they hadn't heard from us in almost a week.

As I walked the path that led to the beach with Henry struggling to keep up, I passed Kane. He was sitting on a log during the last few moments before the dark gave way to morning's light, staring straight ahead. He didn't turn his head towards me as I approached him.

"You're up early," I said, and he simply turned up the corners of his mouth into a vague smile, still looking forward. I sat with him on the log, and we sat in silence as the dark gray air turned to a light blue. The night crickets stopped their sound. Kane's little mouse peeped its head over Kane's shoe, and Henry, upon seeing the mouse, went ballistic. He ran towards Kane's shoe just as Kane scooped up the mouse, bringing it to safety.

"Kane, what's going on here?" I asked. He stared straight ahead, stroking the mouse's head with his index finger, as the blue air brightened and the birds woke and sang. Slowly, he turned his head to me.

"You'll know whom to trust," he said. I just looked at him.

"Excuse me? What do you mean?" But he didn't say anything more, and the sun emerged in the sky.

After sitting in silence with him, watching Henry paw at ants on the ground, I picked up my dog and left Kane, heading for the beach.

As I approached the dock, I saw that I wasn't alone. Tom and his twin brother Joel were already there, both with their fists in their pockets.

"Morning," I said when I stepped on the dock. I remembered arriving at this very spot exactly a month and one day ago. It seemed like a year ago.

"Morning," Tom said, and Joel lifted his chin at me. I never was confused over which twin was which anymore, as they carried themselves so differently. Tom's face was open; Joel's was hidden and he lived inside his head. It was 6:30 and the sun was rising across the ocean, sprinkling yellow and orange glitter that flickered and danced on top of the moving water.

"I was hoping the ship would arrive early today," I said.

"We were hoping the same thing," Tom said. "It sure will be a sight when we see that ship at the horizon."

"Amen," I said.

"Amen," Joel whispered.

At breakfast, spirits were hopeful. Darcy needed more shampoo, Brian was out of shaving cream, and Jim had ordered a new watch, all items that were due to arrive on the supply ship. Sheila and Alice didn't get their order requests in before our communications stopped, but didn't care, they just wanted to see the ship. Tom announced to us that once we talked with the people on the ship, all would be fine, and everything would be back to normal.

Work at the stables went on as usual. I worried that Henry would get stepped on, but he seemed to have intrinsic awareness to stay away from the ponies' hoofs. I thought I taught him not to roll in horse manure like he did on Tuesday, but he rolled in it again today. The white pony now got yancy and danced whenever I approached, acting like a dog who was excited to see their human return. I loved the white pony. Earl was quieter, and awfully jumpy, getting startled easily. I supposed that was simply missing his wife.

At lunch, we were all excited, and Tom said we could take the afternoon off and have a party on the dock. We would celebrate once the supply ship came into view. Brian suggested we blow up fireworks when we first spotted the ship, since we didn't have them for the Fourth of July. Jeremy suggested we use the flare gun. Adrian said no.

After lunch, we all trekked to the beach, all of us except for Tariq, who insisted he had to clean up our mess. As we all hiked through the woods, it reminded me of my arrival on the island when I had walked with everyone from the beach on this same path. Only this time, I fit in.

Kane was still by the log, the same log I sat on early this morning. He was chopping wood, but this time, he stopped as we walked by. He looked as if he was sending us his condolences, like we were a funeral line. His eyes locked on mine as we passed.

As we continued down the path, I heard Tom tell his twin what a scoundrel their father was for allowing them to go this long without supplies and communication from the outside world. "Dad always comes through in the end," Joel told his brother. "There's a line he doesn't cross."

"I don't know about that," Tom said.

We reached the dock, and talk was heated and excited. I leaned against the dock's thick wooden pole, watching everyone. Brian, Derek, and Jim attempted to skip flat stones, which mostly were taken in by the waves. Tom was laughing with his brother and the guys from security. I saw Tom hug Darcy. Brian, who recently confided to me he kept falling in and out of love with both Darcy and me, watched Tom hug her with a curious look on his face. Adrian looked over at me, and he winked. I gave him a small smile. I watched Jeremy as he went over to Jim, Brian, and Derek to show them how to skip rocks. When he failed, he went over to a large smooth rock, got his tin whistle out of his back pocket, sat down and played.

It was all so very perfect.

Sheila and the nurses were off by themselves, and played with their hair when Grady approached them. Derek ran to his father to tell him he actually skipped a stone, and Joel picked up his son and twirled him. Jim called over that Derek was the only one who succeeded in skipping a rock in the waves.

I wished Earl was with us. He never took meals with us in the lodge. He was working at the stables, probably wondering where I was. I had told him that if the supply ship came early and I was there, I'd be sure to tell the men on the ship to contact his wife as absolutely soon as they could, to let her know why he hadn't been able to call her. He was worried sick that she might think he was hurt, or even dead. When Earl told me his concern, I felt like hugging him to comfort him, but you don't hug Earl.

"God, it'll be good to see someone from the outside," Darcy said into the wind.

We'd been waiting for about forty–five minutes. Brian, Darcy and I were sitting on the dock with our legs dangling down towards the water, feeling the spray on our feet when the waves hit the dock.

"But still, our computers will be down," Brian said.

"But at least people on the outside will be alerted to our situation." Darcy said.

"How are they going to fix the problem when even Joel can't?" Brian asked, and Darcy and I looked at each other.

Suddenly, Jeremy yelled. "I see something! I see something!" He had stopped playing his whistle and stood on the rock on the beach. Everyone stopped what they were doing and looked out to sea. Derek jumped up and down. I hugged Darcy, and when I released her, she ran to Tom and squeezed him. I hugged Brian. Sheila and the nurses hugged each other and actually came and joined our group, giving us high–fives. The men were slapping each other on the back. I saw Grady punch Adrian's arm and laugh. Adrian hit him back, harder still. Then we all grew quiet and looked out into the vast water. We became still. I saw nothing.

"Where, Jeremy?" Jim asked. Everyone searched, some of us

cupping a hand over our eyes to shield the sun.

"Well, I..." Jeremy looked out into the ocean. "I *thought* I saw something."

By dinnertime, no ship had arrived. I felt an ache in the pit of my stomach. I think we all felt this. Sheila and the nurses were the only ones who went to dinner, and Joel asked them if they could take Derek, who claimed he wasn't hungry. Joel insisted he eat something, and pushed him along with the women. Tariq was going to be upset that only a fraction of us would be eating a meal he had prepared.

One by one, the rest of us went to our cabins. I passed the Derek garden behind my cabin, looking at the conch, the tortoise shell, the starfish, and other objects that once contained life, but no longer did. It was as if I was observing each item for the first time.

There would be no campfire tonight.

I wondered if anyone slept.

Chapter 20
FALLING OUT OF RHYTHM

I was not sleeping at all. I didn't so much mind when I seemed to need only four or five hours of sleep each night since my arrival, but now I lay in bed with primal fear, fear that we were going to die on this island, and this fear kept me staring at the wooden beams on the ceiling of my cabin as I lay in my bed at night. For the past several days, I was unsure if I had received any sleep at all, or if I had dozed for a few minutes.

How were we going to survive without supplies coming in? What would happen when our food ran out? Tom told us that we had food for about two months left. The fruit we had in storage would soon go bad and it was looking like none would be shipped in soon. However, we could get jackfruit, rambutan, bananas, pineapples, starfruit, and mangos from the island. Meat too, if need be. The security team said they could hunt if it came down to that. I was thinking now may be the time to turn vegetarian.

We discussed what supplies were luxuries, and what supplies were necessities. Supplies that the nurses, Sheila, and even Darcy, Jeremy and Brian thought were necessities like shampoo, batteries, and clothing were actually items of luxury, Adrian told us. Jim worried about medical supplies, and Adrian and Tom agreed that that was a major concern.

We flung questions at each other. Why didn't the ship come in? Did someone sabotage our computers? If so, who? Hell, for all we knew, the United States could have been bombed. We had absolutely no word from the outside world in over a week.

What was going on?

I waited until first light to get out of my small bed in the back corner of my cabin. Hearing the birds who screamed their sheer delight in a thousand harmonies every morning gave me no joy on this particular morning. After a quick shower, I walked over to the medical building. I needed to see the doctor to see if he could give me something that would allow me to actually sleep tonight. I had Henry tucked under my arm. It had rained during the night, and I didn't want his muddy paws tracking in dirt. Henry wiggled in my arms. He was starting to become willful. It didn't faze me. Not much did the past few days, as I walked around in a fog–like daze.

Just before I reached the medical building, the door banged open, and Adrian burst out, almost knocking me over. He looked worried.

"We're calling a meeting," he said. "Help me get everyone to the lodge." I stared at him, trying to make his words register; my mind was so thick from lack of sleep. "Now!" I snapped to, then hurried to the cabins to gather the others.

We were all in Central Lodge, seventeen of us jammed in the front part of the building where the couches and chairs were. Tom stood with his brother and the three security men by the fireplace, and they talked among themselves while occasionally looking out at us. Tom was waiting to start the meeting. Jim and Earl sat in chairs near the fireplace. I sat on the couch in the front–center of the room with Darcy, Brian, and Jeremy. Derek was half leaning on my shoulder, and Henry was on Derek's lap. Jeremy kept fidgeting with a rubber band until Darcy snatched it from his hands. Sheila and the two nurses sat in chairs on the other side of the room from Tom, Joel, and the security men. It was strange to see them not gabbing as they anxiously waited for the meeting to start. Tariq leaned against a pole in the center of the room, nervously tapping his spatula into his palm. Breakfast was on hold. It was odd to see Tariq not buzzing around; he wasn't even yelling at anyone. Kane stood by the entrance door. He was the only one who looked calm.

Tom cleared his throat. All became still and totally silent.

"I'm sure you're all wondering what is going on here, and why we called you to this meeting." Tom raised his eyebrows and scratched his head. I realized I had to exhale. "Folks, we have come to a very disturbing conclusion, I'm afraid." I looked at Darcy. She looked back at me. "Either the United States has been wiped off the planet, which is highly unlikely, or… " All eyes were on Tom. I heard the hum of the building when Tom paused. "Or, someone is seriously messing with us." Tom looked at Adrian, who nodded at him. "While we had our doubts before, we're sure of this now. It seems that our computer mishaps are no mistake. Joel confirmed this. Someone wishes us harm."

"What?" Darcy and one of the nurses said together. Even Kane raised his eyebrows.

"Why?" Jim asked quickly.

"Who?" I asked.

"That very bad." Tariq said, and we started talking among each other.

What in the living hell was going on here?

"We're talking about sabotage," Adrian said loudly, and we all got silent. I pressed my shoulder into Darcy. "Yes, sabotage. It seems we have an imposter." I absorbed the horror of the thought.

"Who would…" Jim started.

"Don't know, Doctor. But we have some idea."

"Who?" I asked, bewildered. We all started asking who it could be.

"Is it one of us?" Brian asked.

"When we know for sure, we'll let you all know," Adrian said. "In the meantime, we have a plan, something that will protect us all," Adrian said.

"What plan?" Darcy asked.

"We can't reveal that quite yet," Adrian said.

"Well you certainly can't reveal *much*, now can you?" Darcy asked.

I looked at her nervously, willing her to soften up a bit.

"Darcy, take it easy," Adrian said. Tom stepped towards Darcy and tried to lock eyes with her, but she stared only at Adrian.

"No, I *won't* take it easy, Adrian!" She said with narrow eyes. "Jesus Christ, we're totally locked out from the outside world, no email, no internet, no phones, no computers, no shipment, no supplies, no answers… and now we have some intruder who's… who's…"

"We're well aware of the problem, Darcy, and we're…"

"Yeah, yeah, you're *working* on it. You're *working* on it. That's all we've been hearing for a week now!" Darcy called out.

"Darcy…" Tom came over to her and put his hands on her shoulders. She started crying into her hands and he sat down and held her.

"I'm sorry for all this," Adrian said to the group, "but we are pretty sure of who's causing all this and we're definitely dealing with this situation. We should be making contact with the States again very soon. We really wish we could tell you more, but please understand that for everyone's sake, we can't. Order will be maintained soon enough. In the meantime, we'd like for you all to carry on your regular schedule as best you can." Adrian sucked in his lips and stepped down from the fireplace landing. Joel walked over to be with his son, and the security men stepped down. Tariq threw his hands in the air and stormed off to the kitchen. The meeting was over.

"What about breakfast?" Jeremy said quietly to Brian and me. I kicked him.

Leaving Henry with Derek, I went over to be with Jim. The doctor looked like he was getting less sleep than even I was. "I wonder if I'll ever see my wife again," he said. I thought of the wild przewalski horse in the field, the one who nuzzled the neck of the other horse.

Earl, who was sitting next to the doctor, looked at his hands that were clasped together in his lap, and said, "I truly don't believe I will ever see my wife again." He said this with such finality. I wanted to put my hand on his shoulder, but it was hard for me to comfort Earl. "Jamie," Earl said to me, looking up. The fire that he usually had in him was out. "Please see to the ponies tomorrow morning, if you would."

"Sure thing."

I turned to leave and saw Kane standing by the entrance door, watching everyone. He had no expression on his face.

Adrian left the lodge. "Excuse me," I said to the doctor and Earl, and I headed for the door. Henry jumped off Derek's lap and scampered after me. Adrian was walking away and I hurried to him.

"Adrian, wait up," I called to him. He stopped, but only long enough for me to catch up to him. Then he continued walking quickly and I hustled to keep up with him.

"Adrian –"

"Jamie, I've… I'm sorry. I really have serious business to take care of right now. I'm sorry I can't…"

"What the hell is going on, Adrian? It's me!"

He stopped and looked down at me. "Jamie, I really can't tell you. Wish I could."

"I just want to talk!"

"I can't right now."

"Can't, or *won't*?" I asked.

Adrian looked away and sighed. Looking back at me, he said, "Jamie, that's not fair."

"No, *this* isn't fair. This *sucks*! *You* suck! The *hell* with you!"

"Jamie –" But I had already stormed off.

I'd stormed off to the beach. Fearful of the sea's crashing flow, Henry kept his distance from the ocean, playing with sand crabs a ways from the water. I stood on the water's edge feeling the ocean spray mist my face, and wrinkled my forehead at the smell of sea fish. I let the morning sea lap towards my shoes before the ocean stole back its water, carrying back to sea each wave that merged into another wave. The ocean offered its water as an act of giving, and then with the force of greed, would recline its offer and suck its water back in. Like how this island gives fruit and game and beauty to each of us, but our sense of security is then yanked from us. The Lord giveth, the Lord taketh away. I saw no need for praise or blessings.

I had lost my composure with Adrian. The island seemed to amplify my feelings, this time swirling me out of control. My emotions swelled and ebbed like the waves, emerging, fading… rising, waning. I remembered the movements I'd seen Adrian do with Derek at the edge of the field at sunset, the forward and backward of two bodies moving in unison, a memory that seemed so very long ago when all was at peace. Now, peace was broken and was replaced by anxiety.

Moments ago I had lost control and let loose on Adrian. I realized that Adrian was trying to fix the major catastrophe that was occurring here on Jackel Island, but did he not have a free twenty seconds to slow down and look me in the eye? Did he have to repeatedly rush off without giving me so much as a glance? A notice? A word? Some kind of an acknowledgement? Did our exchange at the lagoon mean nothing to Adrian? And did any of this really matter, now that we were cut off from food, supplies, communication… now that we were cut off from humanity?

A wave rushed over my feet in a greedy gulp. I jerked backwards, but it was too late. My shoes were soaked. I would have to change into dry footwear. I walked back to my cabin in sopping shoes, calling for Henry to follow.

As I approached my cabin, I saw Brian in the clearing carrying a large burlap bag. He was heading towards my cabin.

"I have breakfast for everyone!" he called out. I stopped at my cabin door, waiting for Brian to catch up. "Tariq made these and asked me to hand them out to everyone, since people aren't really coming to the lodge for breakfast. He told me to tell everyone that's gotta' stop, that we have to come to the lodge for meals."

"Whatcha' got there?" I asked. Henry jumped on Brian's leg to smell what was in the bag. "Don't jump, Henry!"

"It's kind of an egg and cheese sandwich, with lamb," he said. "Or sausage. Or lamb sausage. Or maybe it's…"

"Brian, it doesn't matter," I said, and snatched the little wrapped sandwich that he held out for me. Henry and I went inside my cabin. I had to get out of my wet shoes. I tossed the sandwich on the table and sat on the edge of the bed, loosening my shoelaces. Henry sat politely below the table, keenly focusing on the sandwich. Brian simply stood just outside the door.

"Are you coming in? Or do you have to deliver the rest of the sandwiches?" I asked. Brian entered my room, grabbed the chair, and sat in it backwards, leaning his arms and chin on the back of the chair. I wiggled my shoe off.

"Jamie, are you kind of… scared?" I stopped pulling at the second shoe for a moment.

"Well, yeah. Of course. We all are, Brian."

"No, I mean really scared. Like we're going to maybe… like we're going to die on this island." I looked down at the shoe I held.

"That *has* crossed my mind." I looked up at Brian. "But if we run out of food, security has guns for hunting, and there's lots of fruit in the woods. I doubt we'll starve. And also, people back home know we're out here and due to come home in December. Besides, Adrian has a plan."

"What plan?"

"I don't know."

"Why aren't they telling us anything?"

"I don't know."

I don't know why the time was ripe for Brian to confide in me, but it was then when Brian revealed to me that a very Christian neighbor sexually abused him when he was eleven years old, and when he tried to tell his parents, they grounded him. Another human tragedy. Every one of us on this island seemed to have one.

"I'm not sure why I'm telling you this now," he said.

"Brian, I…"

I stared at the shoe in my hand, and Brian stared at the floor. He stood abruptly.

"Well, I better deliver the rest of these sandwiches," he said. I stood. Henry stood. I reached over towards the table and grabbed my sandwich, then tossed it at Brian, who gave me a confused look. Henry stared at Brian's hands.

"Here's an extra," I said. "I don't think I can eat it."

Chapter 21
A SPY

I reached the stables with Henry behind me, rushing to keep up. I was surprised to see Tom and the three security men in the paddock. Adrian was on his black Java pony, sitting tall and proper, and Grady was on his brown Batak, pulling a little too hard at the reins. Red–haired Steve was trying to approach the white pony, who wasn't ready for this. Steve was unable to touch the animal; every time he got close, the pony would veer away.

"Hey!" I yelled, and ran up to them. "What's going on here?"

Tom turned around and faced me. Steve ignored me and continued to approach the white pony, moving way too heavy–handedly at him. Adrian nodded a greeting at me, but looked apprehensive. I slightly lifted my chin up at him, a quick gesture of acknowledgement.

"Steve there is trying to mount your horse but is, ahh… experiencing some difficulties," Grady said, yelling the last three words at Steve to harass him. Grady's pony circled nervously.

"Well, yeah, that's because that *pony* isn't ready to be ridden by strangers yet," I said, "because maybe they'll mishandle him like you're doing right now. Ease up on the reins!"

"Well, excuse me Miss!" Grady said, amused. "Love when you talk sassy at me." Grady did, however, loosen his grip on the reins, and his pony stopped circling. Henry moved his head to the ground, his little fanny in the air, and wagged his tail wildly at the brown pony. A sound like a muffled bark came out of him.

"You need to have that white horse trained so others can ride him," Tom said to me.

"I've been working on it, Tom. But he's been spooked badly. It takes time."

"So there's no way we can get Steve to ride him today?" Tom asked.

"Not unless you want him to be bucked off," I said. "Where are you guys headed off to?"

"We'll be back well before dark," Adrian said. Annoyed, I looked off to the side and blew air out my mouth. Henry gave another muffled bark at the brown pony. For some reason, my dog had grown an affection to this mare, his first playmate. The brown pony saw Henry as a mere annoyance.

"Steve!" Adrian called over to him, keeping his black pony perfectly still. "Give up. That pony's not ready to ride yet." Steve dropped his hand, which was held out towards the white pony, and turned around.

"So how are we going to do this?" Steve asked. "Seeing there's only two horses, two's rather risky. Should we go by foot?"

"Seems we have no choice," Adrian said, and dismounted. "Now you can join us, Tom, since it seems we're walking."

"Good," Tom said. "Four's better than three, anyway."

"You just have to be careful," Adrian said. "We all have to be careful." I looked from Adrian to Tom, trying to catch what they were talking about.

Grady got off his pony and handed me the reins, giving me a creepy smile. I ignored him but took his reins, and also took the reins from Adrian.

"Seems we may not be back until almost dark."

"What, are you going out for ice cream?" I asked. But the four of them were already leaving the paddock and heading for the woods. Henry started to follow them, but could not keep up. He then turned around, saw me, and happily bounded towards me, stumbling on his feet.

The men grew smaller as they entered the woods.

I couldn't concentrate on stable chores. I went back to Main Campus and asked Darcy if she had any idea what the men were up to. Of course, she hadn't.

At lunch, I saw Earl at the buffet table, and I walked up to his side.

"Earl, do you have any idea what Tom and the security guys wanted with the ponies today?" Earl just shook his head. The fight was out of him. Normally, Earl was full of spit and vinegar, but now he just drifted in sadness. He truly believed he'd never see his wife again.

Tariq pushed between Earl and me to add steaming Bakwan Malang in a bowl on the buffet table.

"Tariq?"

Tariq grunted.

"Do you have any idea what's going on with our security guys?"

"Huh? What you ask? No one tells me nah-teeng!"

After lunch, I went into the computer room to find Joel. He had one computer hooked up to a machine that had a single light blinking.

"Joel, do you know where your brother is now?" I asked.

"He's with Adrian and the security team," Joel said, never taking his eyes off the blinking light.

"What are they doing?"

"I'm not sure."

"Really?" Joel stopped what he was doing and looked at me.

"Really."

The white pony looked up towards the woods with perked ears in the early afternoon sun, as a wind blew from the woods towards the stables. I followed the animal's gaze, but could discern nothing moving in the woods except for a bird soaring up ahead. I then continued to dump grain in the feed buckets. I stopped when I saw that the white pony was still very alerted to something in the woods. I looked again. Nothing. I stood still to listen, but heard only the bird and the wind sway the trees. I looked at the white pony and saw his nostrils twitch, and he was still focused on a spot in the distant woods. So I ran to the barn, grabbed a halter, bridle, and saddle. Henry was asleep on the hay. His feet wiggled as he slept and dreamed. Every other dog I've had woke up with the slightest sound. Not Henry.

After saddling the white pony, I climbed on and we took off for the woods to investigate. I wasn't sure if I was being foolish, because maybe it was a dangerous animal that alerted the white pony.

I wasn't far into the woods when I heard men's voices in the distance. It had to be Tom, Adrian, Grady, and Steve, returning from wherever they had gone. I stopped the white pony and dismounted quietly, tying the lead to a tree. I walked towards the voices, careful not to step on a twig or make any other noise. When I got close, I crouched down. I could barely see them through the brush, but I heard them.

"No, not that path. That one leads to the stables. It's this one."

"But this path leads to Central Lodge. We can't go there either."

"Yeah we can, it leads to Central Lodge, but it also veers off to the hut. We just have to go left when the path forks."

One of the men said something else, but I couldn't hear what it was, something about ropes.

I saw only fragments of them through the heavy foliage. I wanted to push the leaves aside so I could see better, but I risked being heard if I did so. What I *was* able to see was Grady harshly push one of the men… was it Steve? Tom? I couldn't really see. Were the men arguing or just messing around? The man being pushed side–stepped, then regained his balance, all the while keeping his hands behind his back. I often didn't understand men when they were rough with each other. I remembered in High School this one boy pushed his friend hard into his locker, and his friend had his hands in his pocket the whole time. The next day, the boy, laughing, showed us his shoulder, and it was heavily bruised.

A bug landed on my arm but I couldn't slap it due to the noise it'd make. I brushed it off me. The bug immediately returned to my arm like a yo-yo and stung me. I held back a yelp. I caught the bug in my palm and squeezed it tight, then wiped it on a tree, the rough bark scratching my palm.

I saw the men in bits and pieces as they headed down a side path, and wondered if I should follow. I was very curious, but didn't want them to know I was watching. I then caught a glimpse of something Adrian held, and when I saw what it was, my heart raced. Adrian carried a rifle! I tried to see if the other men had guns as well, but I couldn't tell. Were they hunting? Tom told us that we had enough food for almost two months, so why would they be hunting? Why all the secrecy? What was going on? I felt my bowels stir and my skin tingle.

After they were out of sight, I followed, keeping plenty of distance between them and me. I could no longer see them because the thin path twisted and turned, but I heard bits of voices every now and then, though I couldn't make out what they were saying.

The path led to a clearing, and the men left the woods. I waited a bit, then crept towards the end of the path where it opened into the clearing. I was surprised to discover that I was somewhere behind the men's showers. I never realized that there was a path here. I inched closer to the clearing and now had a clear view that was not obstructed by bushes and leaves, but did not see the men anymore. Where did they go?

Did I dare venture out in the open? I had no reason to be here on this side of Main Campus. So I headed back.

When I reached the front of the lodge, I saw Kane filling a bucket from the water bin. Henry bounded towards me, delighted that he had found me. That animal was getting the lay of the land, mastering the island's paths, and learning how to get from the stables all the way to our cabins. He tripped over his feet as he hurried, then appeared to practically have a seizure from being absolutely thrilled to see me, jumping on my leg, springing to reach my face. I scooped him up and kissed his face several times. I was actually happy to see him too, but I was considering going back to see what was going on with the men, and snooping with a puppy who was just finding his voice and learning to bark wasn't too wise.

"Kane! Can you watch Henry for a little bit?"

Kane looked confused. "Who is Henry?"

"My dog! Can you watch him and keep him from following me for just a little while?" Kane slowly nodded, and I walked over and placed Henry in Kane's arms.

"Thanks!" I walked towards the security area behind the computer building.

"Be careful," Kane called out to me, and I turned around and gave him a puzzled look.

When I reached the area by the security cabins, all was still. I went between Adrian's and Grady's cabin, feeling like I was trespassing, as if walking in someone's yard without their permission.

I remembered that the men mentioned a hut when they were in the woods, and wondered if they could mean the security shed near Steve's cabin. I now stood before it, looking at the gray timbered slab. Darcy told me that this shed was always locked, and only the security team and Tom had the keys.

The shed sat anchored in the ground, almost melting into it, and was a foreboding wooden structure. A large metal padlock was clasped to the front door screaming "KEEP OUT!" If I were Derek's age, I would guess this edifice to be haunted. I stood still, half expecting one of the men to come out. But if they were inside, the padlock would not be there, would it?

I waited. Nothing.

A breeze tickled a hair over my cheek and I smelled something sickly sweet, an island smell I'd become familiar with but could not identify. Slowly, I inched forward until I reached the shed. I tugged at the padlock, which held firm. I pressed my ear against the wood and felt a splinter almost catch my skin. I heard nothing. The men were not inside.

Still, I had to see what was in this shed.

Thinking that Darcy had a key to Tom's cabin, I ran off to her cabin and knocked. Nothing. "Darcy?" Nothing. She was most likely working in the Administration Building. She always kept her cabin unlocked, and I went in. The red walls, red curtains, and red rug always hit me like a strobe light in my face. I found keys in her top dresser drawer, and took them. I remembered she had keys to department buildings. I was hoping Tom's key was among them.

I went next door to Tom's cabin and stood at his door. I looked around. No one was within view for the moment. I knocked, and when there was no answer, I tried the door. It was locked. I tried all of Darcy's keys, but none of them opened Tom's door.

I quickly returned Darcy's keys to her dresser drawer. Back outside, I circled Toms cabin looking for an open window. I saw Joel leave the computer building, but he didn't see me. Other than Joel, no one was in visible range.

I was in luck. Tom left his back window open. Unfortunately, the Ladies Showers were behind Tom's cabin, and I'd be seen if anyone came to use the bathroom. I had to act quickly. There was a problem – I couldn't quite reach the window. I looked quickly around for something to step on. Spotting a log, I pulled at it, uncovering a zillion scurrying ants. I dragged the log over to Tom's cabin. Stepping on it, I was able to open the window, and I sprung my body up onto the ledge. I was in.

Tom's cabin was functional but not decorative, tidy, with dark green curtains and a matching pine–colored throw rug, the same exact style as Darcy's. So I could tell that Darcy ordered the curtains and rug for Tom, along with a single painting that Tom hung above his bed. I knew the painting was from Darcy because Turner was her favorite artist, and this painting had a splash of red through the middle of it. The painting showed a ship sinking in a storm, with the passengers drowning in the choppy waters.

I quickly looked for keys through Tom's drawers and his closet. Invading his privacy this way made my skin creep and my heart shiver. I felt a pang of guilt when I saw condoms in his nightstand. I was starting to come to the conclusion that Tom kept his keys in his pocket, when, on a last attempt, I found a set of keys under his mattress. Oh Tom, didn't you know that every child hides their deepest tangible secret under their mattress?

I left Tom's cabin through the back window, sliding the log back to the ants. I then hurried behind Central Lodge, avoiding the open area in front, an area that was often traveled. I passed behind Central Lodge and saw Tariq's and Brian's heads in the lodge's back window as they worked in the kitchen, and Tariq was yelling at Brian. I saw Brian's shoulders hunch up as he hurried to fulfill Tariq's orders. I reached the shed, thankful that neither of them looked out the lodge window and saw me.

The eerie structure stood chillingly against the wind, its boards rickety and uneven. Trees twisted around and behind the shed, but they were unable to camouflage the building, or protect it from sun damage. Dead–center in front was the locked door, with two long windows on either side. The silver padlock caught the sun and twinkled, almost mocking.

Taking a deep breath, I walked up to the shed, listening carefully for any noise that would alert me to bolt. All was quiet. I tried several keys, worrying over the jingling sound it made, and the third one fit like a charm. I took another deep breath and slowly opened the door.

No one was inside. It was dark with a stale and musty smell, a scent of old wood and rusted metal. It took a while for my eyes to adjust.

Shelves lined most of the walls, and on the shelves sat rope, locks, tools, a box of keys, four broken security cameras, a crowbar, six flare guns, and labeled boxes. One shelf had over two dozen flashlights, and the lower shelf had a box full of batteries. On the back wall was a ladder next to a seductive poster of a woman. Grady! I tried to read the labels on the boxes in the semi–dark. I saw that one box was labeled "MAPS", and another, "AERIAL SHOTS", and other boxes had letters like "A-C" and "D-G." One box had "EMERGENCY" written on it. Next to that was "JAO CONTACTS". I glanced at the other shelves, but nothing caught my eye. I was a little disappointed. I was hoping all my efforts would lead to some answers of what the security team was up to, but received no answers here.

I turned to leave, and felt a jolt run from my heart down my arms and legs when I spotted six rifles hung on the front wall next to the door. I remembered my Uncle Calvin shooting my horse with a 30-06 rifle after she had severely broken her leg, remembering the pointed hate and the long-lasting inexhaustible pain I carried in me for months. I let my heart calm down, and then left the security shed and locked it back up.

Chapter 22
A PRISONER

I heard a distant door close somewhere behind the men's showers, and then I heard men's voices. I bolted behind a bush at the side of the shed, my heart pounding again. I saw the three men from security and Tom emerge from the back side of the men's showers, heading my way. My heart raced. If they came to the shed, which was very likely, they would discover me hiding. They came closer. I balled my body tightly and pressed against the shed to further conceal myself, no longer worried about spiders. I held my breath as the men passed me and headed towards the clearing. When they were gone, I could breathe again.

I felt the keys in my pocket and worried that Tom would discover that they were missing. I had to return them as soon as possible. But more urgent was finding out what these men were up to.

I stood and looked around. I was not within view of anyone. I brushed dirt and possible spiders off my pants. I ventured behind the men's shower building, walked a bit further through the trees, and what I saw next made me stop in my tracks. There, somewhat hidden within overgrowth and twisted trees that gave entrance to the woods, I discovered another building, a hut. Darcy didn't tell me about this one. Did she know? This must have been where the men were. Inside surely held answers to whatever was going on here on Jackel Island.

This hut was larger than the security shed, and was more neglected, with vines and greenery clinging to its outside walls, climbing up in snake–like trails, adhering and clutching for dear life. The surrounding trees kept the hut hidden in its hardwood clutches, with a curtain of branches draped over the top of the hut, branches that shielded it from humanity. A portion of a bird's nest still remained nestled in the top corner of the A–framed roof, and what was left of an abandoned wasp nest clung to the wood above the door. The structure seemed to slightly slant wearily to one side, as if a heavy typhoon pushed at it with rage and vengeance. We had only been on the island for a year and a half, yet this building looked at least a decade old with its graying wood and its aged lean. Could this hut have been here before we arrived on the island? Two horizontal metal latches, one low, one high, held the front door in place. Vertical slabs of wood with a fat metal padlock defined the door, which stood between two head–high windows. Each window bore four thin black metal bars. A jail.

I slowly approached. Again, I pulled at the padlock, but the lock wouldn't give. I heard something kick or move inside. An animal? My skin prickled. I listened for the sound to return. It didn't. Was there a back window that was left open where an animal had gotten in?

I went around to the back of the hut to see if there was an open window. There was! I saw a small window high up, and I was pretty sure I'd barely be able to squeeze through it, but the window held vertical rusted bars which posed a problem. I thought of the crowbar back in the security shed. Perhaps I could use it to remove the jail–like bars.

It was then I heard men's voices. Oh no, they were back! I crouched down behind the hut and heard them approach. This was the third time today that I was hiding from these men. I peered around the building and saw that it was Adrian and Grady, no one else. I heard Grady say "the bastard better be a little more cooperative this time, damn poindexter."

"Easy, Grady. Let me handle this, okay?" Adrian said. They walked towards the front of the hut and out of sight. As I huddled under the window in the back of the building, I heard keys jingle and a door open, then footsteps. They had entered the hut. I heard some scutter and muddled voices inside, but couldn't make out any words. I crept along the side of the hut towards the front. Peering around the corner, I saw that they'd left the front door open. I approached the door carefully, then flattened my back against the wall and listened.

"Ouch, that looks quite painful. Hope it doesn't fester," Grady said. "You got about ten seconds to tell us, or get ready for round two."

"I can't tell you what I don't know." This voice wasn't Adrian's or Grady's!

"It'd be to everyone's benefit for you to simply tell us," Adrian said. "This is getting messy. We don't like doing this."

"Speak for yourself. I enjoy kicking this sick bastard's ass," Grady said.

"I honestly can't tell you what I don't know," the unknown voice said, somewhat strained. "Please don't do this. You'll regret it, I promise you." The voice was labored and distressed, but also strangely calm. I stretched my neck to see what was inside, and all I saw was the backs of Adrian and Grady. While the insides of the security shed looked more like a tool shed, this hut was larger and cleaner inside, contrasting with the ghostly appearance on the outside. Inside was a sitting room on the right, with two unmatched couches on an unfinished wooden floor, and a large radio on a wooden table. I strained to see the unknown man beyond Adrian and Grady, but was unable to. All I saw were Adrian and Grady facing away from me, and their bodies hid the unknown man.

"Regret this!" Suddenly, Grady exploded and struck the man hard with his foot, and I heard the man gasp. Immediately and without thinking, I gasped too from the sudden violence of it, and Adrian and Grady zipped around in an instant and saw me.

"Jamie – " Adrian was totally off guard at seeing me at the door.

"Stop hitting him! Please!" I pleaded.

"What the…" Grady said.

"Please! Just stop!" I put my hands on my face.

"Jamie, you need to leave," Adrian said harshly.

"Adrian, she can't... you know," Grady said. "What she's seen."

Grady had shifted his weight and I now saw a man sitting on the floor against a metal pole that reached from floor to ceiling. His hands were tied behind his back. His one leg was stretched out on the floor, and the other leg was bent so his foot was by his other knee. His lip and cheek were cut and swollen, and his hair was messed up. I then saw who it was! Oh my God, it was the research assistant, the man who helped me when I had fainted in the field.

"Oh no!" I said and ran to him, but Adrian stopped me.

"Adrian, it's the research assistant guy, the one I told you about. What are you *doing* to him? Why are you hurting him?"

"Research assistant my ass" Grady said. "This here is the one and only Evan Bronte."

"No," I said to Grady, then looked at Adrian. "No, he isn't." I looked down at the research assistant and he looked off into space. Had he deceived me? What was going on here?

"Christ, this clown is even lying to *her*!" Grady said. "Hey bud," Grady said as he kicked him again, to which the man let out a sound and I yelled at Grady to stop. "Do you ever tell the truth to anyone?" Grady asked the tied up man.

"Adrian, please tell Grady to stop!"

"Jamie, you shouldn't be here."

"It seems this girl has a habit of being where she's not supposed to be," the man said from the floor. I wondered how he could be sarcastic while he was in such a dire situation, while he bled.

"Who *are* you?" I asked him, and Adrian pushed me a step away from the man.

"Adrian, she can't just... go," Grady said.

"Well, what would you have me *do*, Grady?" I saw sweat form on Adrian's forehead, his eyes darting. Adrian, who was always calm and in total control, now was very agitated. I looked from Adrian's face to Grady's, trying to size up the situation. "And please, don't tell me how to handle this."

"She leaves here and she tells everyone."

"Who are you to tell me how to handle her?"

"She's a *risk*, Adrian!" Grady said. "You of all people should know this."

"Okay, so I'll tie her up next to Bronte, is *that* what you want?"

"Adrian…"

"Maybe you can kick her a couple times to make sure she…"

"All right, all right!" Grady said, holding his hands up. Adrian turned around, away from Grady and me as he ran his fingers over his head in frustration, blowing out air. I heard the man on the floor chuckle. Grady threw back his leg to kick him, then thought better of it.

"Look," Grady said, "I'm just saying that the whole thing's blown if everyone knows we've got Bronte and his brutes come looking for him tonight. I suggest we just restrain her, gently, until we're ready. Hell, give her a book to read… she can do her nails, whatever. She just won't be able to leave a room we put her in for a couple of hours, that's all."

"No." Adrian said.

"This affects us *all*, Adrian. Need I remind you of the seriousness…"

"Need I remind you who you take your orders from?" Adrian sternly said to Grady. "We don't keep our own people captive. Case closed."

"The bickering between the two of you is most amusing," the man said. "What do you think, Jamie?"

"Don't talk to her!" Adrian snapped at him, and he pulled me a few more steps away from his prisoner. I didn't like Adrian's hold on my arm, as if I, too, was his hostage. I wiggled from his grip and he let me go, but he put his body between the man and me.

"Jamie, what in God's name are you *doing* here?" Adrian peered down at me. All I could do was look at him. I had no words. I watched the two lines deepen between his eyes. Grady walked over.

"Were you spying on us, girl?" he asked me. "You had no business being in this area around the men's showers. Perhaps you needed to use the urinal." I glared at him.

"Not a word," Adrian said to me, pointing his finger in my face. His grave tone frightened me. "Not a word to anyone!" I nodded, and Adrian motioned his head to the door.

"Not so fast!" Grady said and snatched my upper arm before I could leave.

"Hey!" I yelled.

"Let her go!" Adrian said at the same time.

"Adrian, think! Use your head, not your dick!" Adrian burned his eyes at his subordinate for a second, and then pushed him hard in his chest. Grady stumbled back a step or two, releasing me, either by choice or due to the impact. The man on the floor gave a three–syllable laugh. This infuriated Grady, who in an instant transferred his anger from Adrian to the man. Grady yelled at him to shut up or he'd knock his teeth in. This caused the man to quietly laugh into his lap, and his snickering caused him to split his lip further. He winced.

"Jamie, go!" Adrian whispered to me. "I need to talk to you tonight, though."

"We're making a serious mistake letting her go," Grady said.

"It's not your call, Grady," Adrian said, then to me he said "Go!"

I tilted my head to the side to see the man on the floor. He sat conquered but not conquered, temporarily defeated by the ropes that tied him, but was very much in charge of himself. Grady and even Adrian were unable to truly defeat their prisoner. It was then I knew that this man was no assistant, that he was indeed Dr. Evan Bronte.

I felt a tinge of anger fill me, anger over being played the fool by Dr. Bronte, but I still felt saddened over seeing him cut and bruised. I remembered my Uncle Calvin whipping a horse, and in my mind's eye I again saw the thin welt that formed on the animal fill with blood. The animal had been baffled and hurt, yet kept his composure. I remembered the bruise that formed on my hip after my uncle shoved me into the table edge, and I remember hiding my bruise from the girls in the gym locker. I had shown my bruise to my aunt, who asked me how I got such a bruise, knowing damn well who caused it. And damn me for only being able to shrug at her. I hated us both for our silence, her most of all.

As I touched the door to the hut, I caught Evan Bronte's eye. "I'm sorry," I said softly to him, and Adrian gently moved me out the door, his hand pushing on my shoulder.

Chapter 23
KEEPING QUIET

Up ahead, I saw the back of Jeremy's head as he sat on the huge flat rock not far from the dock. Beyond him, ocean waves slapped the sand. I listened to him play his tin whistle, a breathy high pitch in the wind. Jeremy's soft blond hair fell on his neck and ears as his two hands worked the whistle at his mouth. He had no shirt on, and I watched the muscles in his small back move about his spine. He was twenty years old, yet Jeremy had the body of an adolescent.

I approached Jeremy from behind and climbed on the rock next to him. The whistle clicked out of his mouth, scraping his teeth, and he gave a yelp of surprise, his shoulders jerking up.

"Jesus, Jamie… scare the living hell out of me, why don't you!"

"Sorry!" I sat down on the rock next to Jeremy. Henry tried to climb the rock but could not, so he settled on pawing and biting at the tall weeds that grew at the foot of the rock. "Please, keep playing," I said. "I need to hear your music right now."

"Why?"

"Because everything's so screwed up."

"Oh yeah, that," Jeremy said, and he put the whistle back in his mouth and began playing, a soulful whisper that quieted my tense stomach.

Ten minutes prior, I had returned Tom's keys to his cabin. I could rest somewhat easier now.

Jeremy stopped playing, balanced the whistle on his lap, then leaned back on his palms against the rock.

"You know, everything's so screwed up, and everyone's so screwed up," he said.

"What do you mean?"

"Well, I was thinking how both Grady and Earl had fathers who beat them, how your parents died when you were a little kid, how Jim's sister died of leukemia, how Derek was in the car when his mother fell asleep at the wheel…"

"What's your story?" I asked.

"Me? Oh." Jeremy picked up his whistle and twirled it in his hands. "I was only punished by having to wear diapers to school when I was in second grade."

I looked at Jeremy as he brought his instrument to his lips.

Suddenly, a shadow fell across Jeremy's face. Again, Jeremy gave out a quick yell and I jumped. It was Tom, his jet–black hair almost blue in the sun. He was looking at me, his expression sad and serious. He knew.

"Come walk with me," Tom said, and he took a step back, giving me room to hop down from the rock.

"Who, me?" Jeremy asked.

"Ah, no, not you, Jeremy. Jamie." Jeremy gave me a quizzical look, and I shrugged, then jumped off the rock.

"See ya', Jamie."

"You okay?" I thought of the humiliation he must have endured in elementary school.

"Yeah."

"You sure?"

"Yeah."

Tom turned towards the water and started walking. I followed. He said nothing, and I was thinking he wanted to get out of earshot from Jeremy before he spoke. But when we were well out of hearing range, Tom still remained silent. Was he upset with me for spying? I felt a knot in my stomach tighten.

Tom turned left when he reached the water, away from the dock, away from the stables. I didn't usually travel the beach this way because of the heavy fish smell in this southern area of the island. The longer the silence grew, the more anxiety I felt. I grabbed a long stick and dragged it along the sand as we walked. Why was I now afraid of Tom, my best friend's boyfriend, our leader, my friend? Tom was just Tom, a boyish man I got drunk with one time when it was just he, Darcy and I… a man who was conflicted with his father, a fun man who saw me drop to my knees in laughter, a kind man who picked my puppy up above his head and laughed… but, also, a man whose keys I stole earlier today.

"Tom, are you mad at me?"

Tom sighed loudly. "No, Jamie, it's just unfortunate that you saw what you did. I really wish you hadn't."

"I know. I'm sorry."

"It's… not good."

"What can I say?"

"What were you doing by the security area anyway?" Tom stopped and turned to me. This was one question I did not want to answer.

"Why was Grady beating Dr. Bronte? My God!"

"That's really not your concern," Tom said. "And I want to know what you were doing by the security area?"

"Tom, it was so horrible. His face was cut and swollen! Did you see him like this? How could Grady do that?"

Tom shut his eyes for a few long seconds. When he opened them, he very slowly and calmly asked, "Jamie, what were you doing by the hut?"

I swallowed. "I was in the woods. I took a path I never took before, and it came out behind the men's showers." I wasn't lying. I was simply leaving out a few facts. "I heard a noise. It came from that hut. I never even knew that hut existed. When I got there, the door was open, and Adrian and Grady were inside with Dr. Bronte." Tom looked out at the sea and nodded. He bought it. I dug my thumbnail into my other thumbnail.

"Look, Jamie, I'm sorry you got mixed up in all this, I really am.

But it's very important that you not tell anyone here at camp what you saw, you hear me? The security team is working hard at solving the mess we have here, and we have a plan going on. If you tell anyone, it could jeopardize our safety. You understand?"

"I already told Adrian I wouldn't tell anyone, and I won't."

"Darcy is an absolute terrible liar. If you tell her, I'll know."

"Tom! I already *told* you, I'm not *tell*ing anyone, okay?"

"Okay." Tom eyed me for a moment longer, and then he turned back the way we came, and we headed towards home.

"Can I ask why you guys are holding Dr. Bronte and beating him?"

Tom sucked in his lips but said nothing.

"Is it Dr. Bronte who's causing our computer problems? Did he stop the supply ship?"

"Sorry. Can't say."

"So I guess you can't say what your plan is either, huh." I looked over at Tom and he just gave a closed–lip smile.

It took about five seconds for the blue sky to darken, and then another five seconds for the clouds to pound water down on us. I ran as fast as I could behind Tom, who stopped and turned around, reaching for my hand because visibility was about at zero. Together, we ran towards Main Campus, the rain stinging my eyes. The downpour stopped just before I reached my cabin door.

"Sorry I was a bit harsh with you earlier this afternoon, but Christ, girl!" I spun around and saw Grady standing behind me. I was at the water basin filling up my plastic bottle.

"A *bit* harsh?"

"Yeah," he said, cocking his head. The low sun caught his eye. "I was just a wee bit harsh." He pinched the air with his thumb and forefinger.

"You wanted to keep me captive, for cryin' out loud!"

"You're not still sore about *that*, are you?"

"Stay away from me. You're a thug and a kidnapper," I said.

"But I'm a *nice* kidnapper. I was going to give you a book to read on a comfortable couch," Grady said. "But if you want to see *really* harsh, I can show you."

"No, that's all right." I turned away from him and continued to fill up my water bottle.

"I *will* show you really harsh if I find out you told anyone about Bronte being held in the hut." Grady became serious.

"Thanks for the warm and fuzzy," I said, keeping my eyes on the water bottle. Then I looked up at him. "You know, I told Adrian I wouldn't say anything to anyone, I told Tom, and now I'm telling you. I'm not going to tell anyone. So relax, okay?"

"Well slap my ass and call me Sassy. Okay, enough said, Chica. We're good."

Turning away from Grady, I saw Tom and Joel walking together towards the lodge. I had left Tom dripping wet not even twenty minutes ago when we had our little talk at the beach. He had changed his clothes. The two brothers were engrossed in conversation and seemed not to notice Grady and me as they entered the lodge.

"Ahh, I'm trying to apologize here," Grady said.

"Well, you're doing a lousy job of it."

Out of the corner of my eye, I then saw Adrian and Steve also were heading towards the lodge, and wondered if this was a coincidence. Adrian saw us, Steve didn't. Adrian gave a slight nod to me and I nodded back.

"It was nothing personal," Grady said. "I just don't want you jeopardizing the security of the entire island, that's all."

"Oh is that all?" I worked at closing the water bottle but it was stuck.

"Yeah, that's all. No biggee. Just island security, you know... my job."

"Is *this* your apology?" I was putting way too much force into closing the stubborn water bottle when Grady took it from my hands, and with ease, snapped it shut. I shot him a scornful look.

"I suck at apologies. Always have. Especially with women. Well… *only* with women. I never had a need to apologize to a man before." He dangled the water bottle in front of my face with a cocky grin. I snatched it.

"You're still a creep," I said and walked towards Central Lodge.

"Does this mean we're still friends?" he called to me. I ignored him and walked up the steps to the lodge's arched door. I wanted Tariq to give me a Red Delicious apple. Tom told us to eat up the fruit before it went bad, because it might be a while until we got any fruit that didn't come from the island.

There was a note taped to the lodge door. "NO ENTRY EXCEPT FOR SECURITY AND SELECT DEPARTMENT HEADS. WILL RE-OPEN FOR DINNER."

"Wish I could escort you into this VIP meeting, but it's guys only, lil' lady," Grady said in a contrived cowboy accent. He had snuck up behind me again and I jumped.

"What's going on in there?"

"Man, you're a nosy one."

"I'm tired of all these secrets! Are we such peons you can't tell us *any*thing?"

"Jamie, seriously. It's for the best. Trust me on this one, okay?" Grady said plainly. We looked hard at each other. Grady wore his hair longer than the other men, and his sandy wisps blew in the wind. I saw that there was no mocking in his eyes and his mischievous look was gone. I rarely saw Grady when he wasn't either joking or angry, and his serious manner he now wore threw me.

"Tell me something, Chica. Why do you hang with that silly skinny boy? And also that other fat stupid one. They're just kids. A girl like you could be with a real man, any man, a man like…"

"Brian is not stupid, not at all! He's smarter and more

introspective than you could ever hope to be."

"Ooh, sassy!" Grady mocked.

"You are such a total jerk at times." Grady gave me a sober look, and I watched the lines around his eyes deepen.

"I know," he said sadly. Was he serious? "Thing is, I was trying to pay you a compliment."

"By insulting my friends?" We looked at each other again, and once more, his eyes didn't show that usual flicker of amusement, and his lips were straight instead of their perpetual turned–up curve at the ends.

"Am I really such a bad guy?"

I sighed. "You're leaving yourself pretty open here."

"I know," he said. "I mean, all I hear from Darcy is what a creep I am." He looked up at the sky. "Yeah, creep… *that's* the word she always uses. Kinda' hurts a guy's feelings. Am I really such a bad guy?"

"Are you serious?"

"Yes. I'm dead serious."

I drew a breath and looked out towards the medical building. Adrian once told me that all kidding aside, Grady was one person he could truly count on. Before my arrival on the island, Adrian said Grady worked around the clock when they suspected that someone stole Joel's watch. Adrian stressed the importance of there being no thief among us on the island while working together on this project. The watch was finally discovered under Derek's pillow, because Derek had wanted to sleep with a part of his father each night.

I thought of all the jokes Grady told around our campfire, some even made us all laugh. He *was* a character. I remembered Jeremy flailing his arms when he was head–deep in the ocean, and Grady tore into the waves to save him without a moment's thought, then almost beat him when he learned that Jeremy was just joking around.

"You're all right," I said quietly.

"What was that?"

"I *said* you're all right!"

And then Grady gave a creepy smile and went into the lodge, locking the door behind him.

The idea hit me suddenly. Seconds after I heard Grady lock the door to the lodge, I thought "now's my chance." There wouldn't be many opportunities when Tom and the security men were all in one place. They would be in their meeting until dinner, which was a little less than two hours from now.

Should I do this?

I thought of the horses that were whipped when I was a child, with me powerless to do anything. I thought of my aunt's silence when she knew of my mistreatment. I remembered a neighbor's dog left out in the severe cold, and my getting the dog at midnight, keeping it warm in my room, only to be sternly punished for it the next day when my uncle grabbed my hair and shook me. I was twelve years old. Silence kills the heart, and inaction is a cancer that festers.

I had to do this. I had to help Evan Bronte.

I had a bandana in my pocket. I often use bandanas or rags at the stables. I dampened it at the water basin, then went behind Tom's cabin.

Luckily, Tom's back window was still open. I wondered why he locked his cabin door while keeping his back window open. Once again, I dragged the log under Tom's window, carefully holding the log at the upper ends so as not to touch any ants. Stepping on the log and balancing my weight, I hoisted my body up and into his cabin. I lifted Tom's mattress and took his keys, squeezing them so they wouldn't make a sound. I looked out his back window, and when all was clear at the ladies shower, I lifted myself through the back window and hopped to the ground. I gave the log back to the ants so I wouldn't be leaving any evidence of my break–in.

I hurried through Main Campus and unlocked the security shed. I grabbed the crowbar, putting it half inside my pants so I could have two hands to drag the ladder. The metal was cold on my skin. As I dragged the ladder to the hidden hut that was concealed in the back woods, it drew two thin parallel lines in the dirt. Evidence. I made a mental note to later cover the lines with leaves.

I went around to the back of the hut and looked up at the small window. I wasn't sure I could remove the window bars with the crowbar. I quietly leaned the ladder against the back of the hut to the window and climbed up. The woods behind me enveloped me, a blanket of foliage wrapping and shielding me, keeping me hidden. I climbed up the ladder, and upon reaching the window, I looked at the four black metal bars. They were quite rusty and peeling. I grabbed a bar to test it, wiggling it, and was pleasantly surprised when it snapped loose! I tossed the bar down to the ground below me. The second bar snapped off with ease too, though I had to twist it free, the rust gritting my palm. I had to use the crowbar on the remaining two bars, but only slightly. The window was now open for me to pass through.

Leaning over the ladder, I peered inside the hut. Evan Bronte was looking up at me. He looked dirty and roughed up.

"Well hello," he called.

"Hey." I then looked down immediately below the window inside the hut. I could hop down and into the room, but I would later need something to get back up to the window when I needed to leave. I surveyed the room.

"You can use the table over there to prop yourself back up to the window when you're ready to leave," Dr. Bronte said, as if reading my mind. I looked at the wooden table, and he was right; that would work. So I finagled onto the window ledge with difficulty, having to straddle the ledge from the side in order to fit, then pushed off, landing with the thud on the floor of the hut. I stood and brushed the dust off me, then looked squarely at Evan Bronte.

"You lied to me," I said.

"Excuse me?"

"You lied to me, about who you are."

"I told you that I'm not who I seem," he said.

"You're Dr. Bronte." I brushed off more dirt off my pants. "What kind of name is Bronte anyway? Don't you think it's rather dramatic?"

"Is this why you came, to tell me my true identity, to mock my name?"

"No."

"Then why *did* you come?"

I went to him and crouched down, examining the damage to his face. The swelling on his left upper cheek near his eye was worse and turning purple, and his lip was bruised and crusting. Blood, now dried, had run down his chin and several drops had splashed on his tan shirt. I was wishing the doctor was here. Jim wouldn't like this either, our mistreating Dr. Bronte so badly. The doctor could treat Dr. Bronte better than I could; he could at least give him something for the pain. His hands were tied behind his back so he couldn't even touch his face.

"Why?" I asked.

"Why did I lie to you?"

"No. Why did they do this to you?"

"I don't know. Ask them."

"How could they... why..." I couldn't continue because I felt like crying.

"Jamie, sometimes being isolated on an island for a long while makes some people turn rather savage," he explained. "All human beings... they're commingled of good and evil."

"Like *Lord of the Flies*?"

"Like *Lord of the Flies*."

I was glad that Dr. Bronte was familiar with this novel. *Lord of the Flies* was a book about a group of young British boys stranded on an island. Ralph, made chief, wanted to run the island in a democratic way. Jack wanted to hunt and kill the beast on the island. "Maybe there is a beast... maybe it's only us."[1] After a while, the boys split, some joining Ralph, but most joining Jack for the fun of the hunt. They ended up killing each other.

If I was on this island for another year or two, how would it change me? Already, the people back in the States were becoming unreal. Life as I'd always known it seemed less important, dreamlike, hypnagogic. "The world, that understandable and lawful world, was slipping away."[2] We were all making a new life here, adapting to the island, altering to its ways, allowing it to reform us and shape us into something different. Something we were not. But in December, we were due to go "home." Perhaps.

"I got a puppy," I said, trying to show him we had a sense of virtue and that Adrian was no savage. As soon as the words left my mouth, I realized how absurd I sounded.

"Hmm?"

"Adrian gave me a... never mind."

"Adrian North? He's sweet on you, huh."

"What? *Sweet* on me?" What was this phrase? Saying someone was *sweet* on someone was something people my uncle's age would say, an outdated phrase from an old movie, from a man with cuffed pants and a fifties haircut. "No! Jeez!"

"You two are together, aren't you?"

"No!" Not after this. Not after seeing Adrian's artwork on Evan Bronte's face. "Why do you say that?"

"There were several indicators when I was watching you two interact earlier."

His astuteness surprised me. How he could pick up on what happened between us in his injured state somewhat impressed me. I was reminded that Dr. Bronte was an M.D. in psychiatry. I had to be

---

[1] *Lord of the Flies*, Chapter 5, pg. 80

[2] *Lord of the Flies*, Chapter 5, pg. 82

careful.

"Well, you're wrong," I said.

"Hmm," he grunted.

"You are, you're wrong."

"Thou doth protest too much."

"Shut up," I said softly, not in a nasty way, but not quite joking.

I took the damp bandana out of my back pocket and touched the cloth to his lip. His body jumped a little and I eased off. After he relaxed, I ever–so–lightly dabbed his lip, trying to clean the blood off. He remained relaxed while I worked at his face, all the while eying me, which unnerved me a bit. I kept my focus on his lip, not his eyes. This time, *he* was the patient and *I* was the one who was administering treatment.

"Why don't you untie me, Jamie," he whispered.

I looked at him. "I can't."

"Yes, you can."

I drew the cloth away from his face. His eyes were strong, steady, yet pleading, all the while in complete command, attempting to control. I couldn't allow myself to be stirred by another man, not again, not so soon after Adrian. Adrian's chapter had ended before it had really begun.

If Dr. Bronte were to escape, they would look to me.

"No, I really can't. I'd get in so much trouble. I would lose my job."

"I can stage it to look like I got away by myself. No one would know you had a part in it. I promise you."

"Dr. Bronte, I just can't! If they should find out…"

"They won't. Are you hearing me?"

"They would know it's me."

He drew a large breath and looked away. "So you really *are* with them. Seems you're a part of this."

"No, I'm *not*. I mean yes, I *am* with them. But no, I'm not a part of this."

"You know what they're doing is wrong." He looked strong and steady at me again, the beams from his eyes almost tangible.

"I know, but Dr. Bronte, I just *can't*." He pressed his lips together and looked off again. He looked sad, and I felt hot liquid seep inside my heart and stomach, and it burned.

"Did they feed you anything?" I asked.

He looked at me blandly.

"Well, I'll get you food then. I'll come by later tonight. Don't worry."

He drew a deep breath and stared into his lap, and I again felt the burn of guilt. How ludicrous, me telling him not to worry.

"I promise. I'll sneak back in late tonight. I'll bring you something from the kitchen." It was all I could do for him. One corner of his mouth turned up in a half smile, but his eyes were dead as they continued to stare in his lap.

"Don't you think they'll wonder how the blood was cleaned from my face?" he said into his lap. I felt a stab needle my insides. He was right. He looked up at me. "You have to think things through, Jamie, if it's so important for you not to get caught."

"Look, I'm sorry you're being held here, I really am," I said. "But it's not my doing. All I can do is try to make you comfortable."

"No, you can do more. You have the ability to let me go."

He leaned forward suddenly, but the ropes constrained him terribly. I caught myself from gasping.

"If you're worried about your job, I can assure you – that's the least of your worries, considering the situation at hand. If order is restored, believe me, I can see that Tom Gordon and the security team lose their jobs over this. I can also make sure you are still employed with Jao, if I choose to."

If he *chose* to? Was Dr. Bronte now threatening me, telling me to let him go or he would see to it that I'd lose my job along with the men?

I couldn't imagine staying on Jackel Island without Tom and Adrian, or even Grady. Did Evan Bronte really have this power? I clenched my fist.

"Why did Adrian and the guys take you like this? Do they think *you're* the reason our computers are down and our shipment didn't come in?"

"I don't know what they think, Jamie."

"Well, they wouldn't just take you for no reason." I clenched tighter.

"I'm not sure they need a reason. Heavens, sometimes people turn on each other for no reason at all other than suspicion and paranoia. Let's just say that you folks at Main Campus and I have a history." He tilted his head down and said from the tops of his green eyes which now danced, "I'm a 'badass', remember?"

I squinted my eyes and cocked my head at him, until I remembered telling someone who I thought was the research assistant that his boss, Dr. Bronte, was a "badass." This was the day I first met Evan Bronte, under false pretenses.

"Oh yeah, the day I met you and you lied to me about who you are," I said.

"Mmm."

"You told me that 'Dr. Bronte' would lock me in his basement if I trespassed again."

"Yeah, and you believed me." Again, his eyes danced as he smiled, and stretching his lip caused him to wince as he re–opened his cut. From a clean part on my bandana, I touched the cloth to his lip to help ease his pain.

Chapter 24
LATER THAT NIGHT

I lay on my bed watching the milky light from the moon coat the wooden ceiling beams white. Henry, sleeping in a ball against my thigh, sighed. Sounds of active crickets and the rustle of tree leaves in the wind gave a peaceful affectation to an island filled with turmoil and unrest. I waited.

"I'm not who I seem," Bronte had said.

Hours ago, I had left him, tied and bruised. Fortunately, the table in the hut was just tall enough for me to hoist myself up to the back window. I had leaned the rusty bars back in the window so all would seem normal if glanced at, and had returned the ladder and the crowbar back to the security shed. I even remembered to cover the lines in the dirt that the ladder had made, breezing my shoe over the affected ground.

I had not returned Tom's keys. It would be too difficult to get them from under Tom's mattress again later on tonight. I was praying that it was *Adrian's* key they used to open the hut, and not Tom's. Realizing it was quite a risk not returning them to Tom, I laid the keys on the ground outside of his cabin, covering them with a few leaves, as if the wind could have blown over them. The keys were off the main walkway so they would not be easily discovered unless you were looking for them. If Tom saw that they were missing, the keys would not be found on me or in my cabin, and when found, it would look like Tom perhaps dropped the keys out of his pocket.

Dinner was strained, like it was every night since the supply ship hadn't arrived. We still made small talk, and occasional jokes were still given here and there, but the fact that we were cut off from the outside world weighed on us like a heavy dark fog that hovered inside each of us, a black mist of doom that surrounded our hearts.

I had to be careful sneaking food out of the lodge. Saturday night, Adrian announced that he would see to it that there'd be no hoarding of food or other supplies. No one could have seconds at mealtimes, and if the supply ship failed to return on its next scheduled time, we were going to be on strict food rations. "However, we feel rather confident that our troubles will soon be ending," Adrian told us.

Tom had announced to us that our campfires would be resumed every night after dinner starting tomorrow night. I was wondering why we didn't start tonight, until I saw Tom, Adrian, Grady and Steve march off towards the security hut after dinner.

I waited in my cabin. I scooped up Henry, who fussed a bit at being wakened, and went to the window. I wanted to see if the men had returned from the hut so I could tend to Dr. Bronte. I saw no movement in the clearing. I couldn't see Tom's cabin from my window due to the sharp angle, and across Main Campus, the computer building shielded my view of any activity at Adrian's cabin or the hut. However, I could see a corner of Steve's cabin. Ten minutes ago, Steve's cabin was all dark, but now a light was on inside. The men had returned from the hut! At least Steve had, so I assumed the rest of the men had as well. Henry looked out the window and yawned.

I grabbed my shoes and sat on the edge of the bed, putting Henry down in the center of the mattress. He went to the pillows, circled, then plunked down, giving a hearty sigh before he shut his eyes. I had one shoe on when there was a rapid but quiet knock on the door. Darcy? Henry lifted his head and moofed a half bark.

When I opened my door, I was surprised to see it was Adrian, standing tall, with one arm on my doorframe with his head touching his raised hand. All I could think of was that Tom discovered that his keys were missing. I felt a quick stab of panic. My face must have shown fear or displeasure, because Adrian's jaw dropped and his eyes widened.

"I'm sorry, did I come at a bad time?"

"No, no, I…"

"If you have company, I can come another time."

"No, no one's here." His face relaxed. "Just Henry." Adrian stiffened, then took his arm off the doorframe and pulled down the bottom of his shirt.

"Henry? Who's Henry?"

"The dog you gave me?" I slowly smiled. On cue, Henry moofed again.

"Oh." Adrian smiled and looked at the ground, running his hand over his head. "Can I come in?"

"Sure." I opened the door wider for him, and his presence filled the room.

"Going somewhere?" he asked. I felt a prick in my heart. How could he know that I was planning to see his prisoner tonight? Did Bronte tell him?

"What?" He pointed to my shoes, one on, one off. "Oh!" I laughed. "No, I was actually in the process of taking my shoes *off* when you knocked."

Adrian nodded, then went to Henry who was now standing at the edge of the bed, wagging ferociously and bouncing from one front foot to the other. With his hand, Adrian ruffled the dog's head, then pulled out the chair at the table and sat down. He seemed too big for the chair. I was hoping Adrian wouldn't smell the food inside the bundled cloth. The cloth lay on the table right next to him. Earlier tonight at dinner, I'd snuck food for Dr. Bronte out of the lodge. "There'll be serious repercussions if I catch anyone hoarding food or supplies" Adrian had told all of us three days ago when we were all in Central Lodge. I joined Henry and sat at the end of the bed.

Adrian said, "I'm sure you're wondering why I'm here." This was an understatement. I folded my hands between my knees. "Jamie, we got off to a very bad start, and I'm sorry." I looked away and noticed that my sock was twisted. I reached down and fixed it, keeping my eyes down so I wouldn't be facing Adrian. "Our timing couldn't have been worse, huh."

"I suppose not," I said, my head bent towards the floor.

"Jamie, I'm afraid with all the trouble we've had on the island that I've neglected you very badly. I'm really sorry about all this. I want you to know that, ahh..." I sat up but continued to stare at my foot. He leaned forward and pushed my chin up with his finger so I would look at him and not my sock. "I want you to know that this is no reflection on how I feel about you."

I nodded. Words didn't come, probably because feelings were muddled. There was a time when I was bombarded with thoughts of Adrian. What happened? Could this be rekindled? I picked at my thumbnail. He put his hand, cold from the night air, on top of mine, so that I would stop, so that I would focus on *him*, so that I would *see* him and *feel* him. But what I felt was a need to get up and walk to the corner of the room.

"I haven't forgotten about our afternoon at the lagoon," he said.

"I haven't either." Why couldn't I feel that way again? Do we choose to feel how we feel, or are our feelings out of our control? I was conscious of his hand still over mine. He inched his chair closer to the bed.

"I'd like to see us pick up where we left off," he said quietly. I became very still. He pulled his chair closer still, then took his hand from mine and held my face in his palm. I was a statue, afraid of his feelings if I were to pull back. "I won't be so distant from now on, I promise." Now with both his hands holding my face, he drew his head to mine. I had forgotten his earthy pine taste, the thick feel of his tongue, and his arm muscles as firm as tree bark. But there was no yearning for me to press into him like I had at the lagoon, and gone was the ache to have him run his palms up and down my back. He read me immediately and pulled back.

"Is everything all right?" he asked.

"Yeah, I..." A hair strand was in my mouth and I pulled it out.

"I'm sorry, I'm afraid I'm confusing you, being hot and cold with you these past few days," Adrian said. "Now... tonight, I'm rushing you... I'll slow down."

"Adrian, it's just..." I bounced my fist on my chin.

"Just what? Tell me."

"It's just that I can't get Bronte out of my mind!" Adrian leaned back in his chair and sighed.

"I wish you would," he said.

"I just can't! What you all *did* to him!"

"Jamie, I'm not proud of this, but you don't know all the details. You don't have all the facts."

"Then tell me!" I said too loudly. The silence that followed amplified my words that echoed in the air. "Tell me," I said quietly.

"I can't." The phantom door had slammed shut.

"Then I can't... do this."

Adrian stood and turned around, showing me his back. "Well then," he said as he turned back around to face me, his eyebrows raised, his face looking blank. "I suppose that's that."

I stood. "Adrian..." I wasn't sure what I was going to say. "Adrian, seeing Dr. Bronte's face all beat up made me... I don't know... sick. I mean, we're not savages. We're not the bad guys, are we?"

"No, we're not. *He* is, Jamie! *He* is. I'm simply trying my damnedest to protect everyone on this god-forsaken island, and to tell you the truth, I'm... I'm..." He took a couple of aimless steps, looking at the dresser, the nightstand, the giraffe lamp...

"You're what?"

"I'm leaving. I should leave now." He stood still for a moment, and when I said nothing, he went to the door.

"Adrian?" He stopped and waited for me to continue. I didn't know how to say it with tact, so I just said it bluntly. "Did you come here to sleep with me?"

He kept his hand on the doorknob and I saw his knuckles turn white.

"I came here to make things right between us." He didn't say anything for a moment, and I stared at his back. "This is sad," he said, then quickly opened the door and left into the darkness of Main Campus. I felt the cold night air hit my face, but only for a moment, then it was gone.

From my window, I watched Adrian walking methodically across Main Campus, his usual perfect posture and gait now with a slight drag of defeat. He passed by the water basin, his shape growing smaller and smaller, diminishing as he went behind the computer building and towards his cabin. Adrian was gone. Things would not be the same between us again.

Had I killed a good thing?

I let more time pass before I left my cabin, clutching a flashlight in one hand, and the cloth bundle containing meat and fruit in the other. I left Henry alone in the cabin for the first time, and I heard him howl seconds after I closed the door. Great, my dog learns to give a wild beastly cry as I'm trying to be discreet. Damn dog.

A light was on in both Tom's and Darcy's cabins. Were they not together tonight? I felt foolish in front of Tom's cabin, my foot swooping the ground, feeling for the keys. If Tom were to leave his cabin for the bathroom, or even look out his window, he would see me.

Keys in hand, I felt safe behind the lodge and away from everyone's cabin, hidden within a sanctuary of darkness. I felt protected in the chamber of moonlit trees and contorted shadows, with the woods to my left, and the lodge's stone wall on my right. These two protecting walls – one solid, one earthly and permeable – gave me a sense of brief immunity from humanity. I hurried through the darkness.

I came to the campsite and stopped abruptly when I saw Kane

sitting on the ground beside the stones that now circled a mound of ashes. His mouse frantically cleaned its head with its paws like a film played on fast speed, as it stood in the middle of the powdered embers. Kane stared into the cinders and dust.

"Don't you ever sleep?" I asked him. He didn't turn to look at me. He just gazed into what was once a roaring fire.

"Hello Jamie."

I sat next to him on the dirt. "What are you doing?" I asked.

"What are *you* doing?"

He didn't take his eyes from the ashes.

"I'm looking for Henry."

"Who is Henry?"

"Why does everyone keep asking me that? Henry's my *dog*."

"Your dog is safe in your cabin. You know this," Kane said. Busted! "Where are you going with that food? Isn't this forbidden?"

Kane knew of our rationing rules now in effect on the island. I was going to play innocent, but it was no use.

"How do you know I have food?"

"I can smell ayam taliwang and salak." I hugged the cloth to my chest. I could smell nothing. "Snake fruit, taken from the palm tree." Kane said.

"It's not for me," I said.

"I know," he said.

Once again, I jumped from the high window and hit the floor of the hut hard.

"Nice of you to drop in," Dr. Bronte said. "Are you here to untie me?" I took a few steps to work out the pain in my ankle. "You okay?"

"Are you?" I asked. "Did they hit you again?" I didn't see any more injuries on his face, but his color seemed a bit drained, and his shoulders and back were slumped forward.

"Only in my stomach."

"They hit you in your *stomach*?" I hurried over to him, squatting by his side. "Are you all right? Are your ribs broken?"

"I don't believe so."

"Can I… can I see?"

"Be my guest."

I awkwardly unbuttoned his shirt from the bottom until I got half way up, and pulled part of his shirt to the side. An oval-shaped fresh wound on his ribs was starting to discolor, more red than gray, but there was no blood.

"Bad?" he asked.

"It just looks like it'll be a nasty bruise," I said. I buttoned his shirt back up.

We studied each other. He looked serious and sad, but all the while probing, taking in any information he could get, be it from me or from his surroundings. I remembered the hurt horse on his side, desperately looking for an escape as he lay in the dirt, physically incapacitated. Dr. Evan Bronte, an internationally renowned researcher who gained worldwide acclaim, was now broken and constrained to the floor and the dirt.

"Jamie, please untie me."

I sighed. "I want to, but I can't."

"Yes, you can," he said. "You're afraid of what they'll do."

"Yes."

"Well, you should be afraid of *me* if you don't."

"You don't look too frightening right now."

"Right *now* I don't," he said.

My legs ached from squatting and I stood.

"Dr. Bronte, I… I don't know how to… Listen, I can't be the one to help you with…" I took a breath of exasperation.

"Hmm? What are you saying?"

"Listen, you must…" He cocked his head and squinted his eyes at me. "Sooner or later, you're going to have to... you're going to have to go to the bathroom."

"Oh, that. That's one grace they've allowed me, with half dignity."

I nodded. I didn't want to ask him what he meant. "Did they feed you anything?" He shook his head. "Well, I brought you some food," I said, squatting down to him again, and I handed him the cloth bundle that was full of meat and fruit. He gave me a teasing look as if I was handing him a dress. I was confused. I held it out to him a few seconds more, wondering what amused him, until I realized the absurdity of my actions. "Oops," I said.

"Oops," he quietly mimicked.

I moved from my squatting position and sat cross–legged right next to him, placing the cloth in my lap. I unfolded the fabric, and with my fingers, I picked up the Lombok roasted chicken. It was rather sticky, as it was coated with palm tree sugar, olive oil, lime juice, red chili, garlic, and other gloppy ingredients. I was glad I had brought napkins. Suddenly, I felt uncomfortable. How do I feed it to him? Do I hold the chicken leg to his face?

"Are you going to feed it to me or just look at it?" he asked. My eyes went from the chicken to his face. His eyes flickered.

"You're always looking at me like that."

He tilted his head. "Like what?"

"Like that! You're doing it now. Like you want to laugh at me." He lowered his face and bit his lower lip.

I pulled a piece of meat off the bone and brought it to his mouth. He considered it as I held it in the air, but did nothing.

"Well, are you going to *eat* it, or are you going to just *look* at it?" He grinned, then opened his mouth and leaned forward a bit, but instead of putting the meat in, I jokingly held it way above his head as if feeding grapes to a Roman emperor.

"Stop!" he said, and I fed him normally.

"What's it like to be a genius in the science world?" I asked him, and he laughed by expelling a quick puff of air through his nose.

"I wouldn't exactly word it like *that*," he said.

"Well, aren't you a genius?"

"I was considered a child prodigy."

"Where are you from?"

"I was born in the United States but I was raised overseas."

"But you're American?"

"Yes."

"Are your parents American?"

"Yes."

"Why overseas?"

"Heavens, why so many questions?" he said, then he cleared his throat. "My parents, who highly valued education, believed the schooling to be of higher quality there."

"Where?"

"Finland. Place called Westend, an affluent district for the most part. My parents decided to educate me there because Finland's literacy rate ranks above… let me see… the United States, Japan, South Korea, England, and ahh… Germany and France." He slightly lurched his chin forward for the chicken. "Finland has the highest level of academic achievements for reading, mathematics and sciences."

"Thank you very much for the demographic lesson," I said robot–style. I tore off another piece of chicken as he chewed. "I don't really know anything about Finland except that it's where Santa Claus lives."

He gave me a stern school teacher look.

"What did you do growing up in Finland? What did you do for fun?"

"I did little else other than study," he said. "My parents were very strict. I was privately tutored ten hours a day, six days a week."

"How could you stand that? Didn't you ever have any *fun*?"

"As a boy, I spent summers with my mother at our summer estate in Martha's Vineyard while my father worked in Boston. Those were my fondest memories."

"So you *do* have fond memories among all that studying."

"A few." Bit by bit, I fed him the rest of the chicken.

"What did you like better, Finland or the United States?"

"Apples and oranges. I also lived in Germany for almost three years when I was a preteen."

"Could you speak German when you moved there?

"Not at the time, but I learned. I now speak Finnish, English, and enough German to get by."

The meat was gone, and I wiped the sauce off my hands. When I dabbed his mouth with a clean napkin, he cast his eyes down, either in thought, or from the humility of not being able to groom himself. Perhaps I was being overly familiar with him. I thought that this must be somewhat demeaning for him, being hand–fed like an infant or an invalid.

I took the fruit, breaking off the tip of the salak, then pealed the scaly skin from the top down.

"Seeing I spent my time studying instead of socializing like other boys, I suppose I lacked social graces." He leaned his head against the pole he was tied to. "Studying was primarily all I did."

"Sounds like a rather dull childhood." I gave him some fruit.

"It wasn't so bad. I've always enjoyed science."

"Didn't you have any friends at all?" I asked him.

"I don't remember."

"Any girlfriends?"

"Oh Jamie! Why do you ask this?"

I shrugged.

My mind went to a time months after the accident when I was nine years old. I had a friend I couldn't see, a friend who lived inside of me. We would play on the farm, in the field, the creek, around the broken down tractor. I could almost see her, her stringy blond hair in the wind as we jumped down from the loft into the hay, and I knew everything she felt. She loved and understood me and I loved and understood her. We would have in–depth conversations as we walked along the creek that divided the field behind the barn from the woods. Later, I even brought her to the new school I attended, the cold and unfamiliar school that I despised. She, too, loathed this new school, and there was comfort traveling the halls, going through the lunchroom line, and sitting at my desk in class with her. She and I were both from Wilbur Elementary before the accident, a school we both loved and missed. She had told me that she was in class with me in first, second, and third grade, though I didn't remember at the time.

They had me see the guidance counselor because of her. After I spoke with the guidance counselor in the room with the huge painting of a bowl of fruit above the plushy tan couch, I heard the counselor talking with my teacher outside in the next room, saying I had emotionally reverted to a six or seven–year–old. I remember feeling highly insulted over this, and I never spoke of my friend again. Funny how I now miss her, though of course she was never real. I think deep down, I always knew she wasn't real, even when I was nine, but I didn't really care. All I knew at the time was that she brought me comfort when no one else did, a comfort I felt from the horses at the farm in later years.

"When I was almost in High School, I liked a girl, very much," he said. " But she only liked her cat." I offered him another piece of fruit but he declined, indicating that his dinner was over. "I somehow managed to get a date with her." I drew my knees up to my chest and rested my chin on them. "I remember I, ah… I couldn't stand to see her hug and cuddle with the animal and not with me. Bear in mind, I was just a boy. Anyway, seeing her give her affections so freely to her cat but not to me drove me half insane. So I… and I'm not proud of this… I tossed the cat down a neighbor's well."

"You did *what*?"

"I tossed her cat down a well. No one ever knew." He leaned his head back on the pole and looked up at the high window. "I never told anyone this, until now. Hmm."

"That's horrible!" I squeezed my knees to my chest.

"I know. I feel sorry about it now."

"If you did that to Henry I would hate you forever."

"Who's Henry?"

"My puppy."

"Oh yes, the one Adrian North gave to you, out of sheer friendship, nothing more."

We sat in silence for a few moments. He seemed to ponder what was out the window. I shook the cloth to rid it of crumbs, then folded it.

"Does it hurt?" I asked, looking intently at the cloth.

"What? Being tied up?"

"No, your lip." I raised my head. His lip was so badly cut and swollen. A scab had caked to a blackish–red crusty vertical line on his lip. His cheek was swollen and crusted with dried blood, too. I waited, but he didn't answer me. I ran my thumb over the cloth.

"So you've never been with a girl?" I asked him.

I heard the ring of silence, and then he laughed out loud, which caused him to flinch in pain when the cut on his lip tore open for yet a third time. I wondered how he could laugh when he was tied and beaten.

"Oh Jamie, I didn't say that! Where did *that* come from?"

"Well, you said…"

"I *said* I had no time for people when I was young because I spent most all my time with my studies. Eventually, I grew up."

"So… are you married?"

"My, you're an inquisitive one. Remind me to hire you next time I need an interrogator." I gave him a blank stare. "Yes, I was married, once. Why do you want to know?" He intently looked out the window, as if he were planning an escape route.

"So you're divorced?"

"She's deceased."

"Oh. Oh." I smoothed the cloth with my palm. "I'm sorry."

"Mm."

I raised my hand and held it in the air in front of my stomach for a split second before I slowly reached over to him, and I lightly touched his lip, gently tracing my fingertip over his wound. He watched me with a poker face, but I saw his ears color slightly. I brought my hand back. He creased his eyebrows at me.

"Are we friends?" I asked him. My voice sounded weak.

He drew a breath. "Jamie, we work for the same company but in completely different capacities." And then he added with his eyebrows raised, "Actually, I'm your superior."

"Actually, you're kind of arrogant." I realized I was rude, but he had angered me by turning a tender moment into a formality.

He looked at me as if I hit a home run. "Actually, you never stop surprising me. And most people bore me." He finagled his sitting position, trying to get more comfortable, but the ropes restricted his movements. "A friend would untie me." He pressed his lips together tightly. "I have an intense ache in my shoulders from being in this position for… I can't even look at my watch… eight hours or so, a pain I almost can't bear."

"I can get you something for the pain from our doctor. I could tell him it's for me."

"You're going to have me spend the night like this?"

"I don't want to, but I have no choice."

"Yes, Jamie, you *do* have a choice."

"But I'm not your friend," I said, waiting for him to say something to the contrary, but he exhaled and said nothing.

Chapter 25
WRONG ENEMY

I had just left Dr. Bronte and was approaching the campsite when Kane emerged from the darkness out of nowhere like a bat. He grabbed me, his arm holding me against him, and I gasped.

"It's not safe!" he whispered loudly at me. He had his forearm around me just below my neck and my back was pressed against his chest and stomach. It was as if I was slammed against a metal vending machine; he was rock hard, more firm than Adrian. "They're in the woods."

"Who?" I heard nothing from the woods. He released his hold on me.

"Go now. Go to your cabin. Lock the door."

"You're scaring me. What's going…"

"Go now! That way." He pointed towards the lodge and the opening, then nudged me forward. I took a couple of steps, then looked back at him. "Go. I will watch to see that you are safe. Go now!"

When I reached the wood's edge and stood before the clearing, I saw Tom, Adrian, Grady, and Steve sitting at the base of the water basin, their backs leaning against the stone. They were holding rifles! I stopped in my tracks. Adrian rested the barrel against his bent knee as he held the forestock with one hand. Tom held his rifle with both hands, and it rested on his two bent knees, parallel to the ground. Grady and Steve had their guns on the dirt next to them, with Steve's hand resting on the trigger guard, and Grady's hand in the dirt near the stock. I turned around and looked back towards the campfire for Kane, but didn't see him.

I had two choices – one, to heed Kane's warning and walk directly to my cabin and through the clearing, which meant passing the men, or two, go behind Central Lodge to reach my cabin unseen through the woods. I was already on shaky ground with Tom and the security guys, so I headed back towards the woods, hugging the lodge to keep distance from Kane, who was nowhere in sight. I quietly kept in the shadows so as not to be seen by him or anyone else.

Kane materialized from the black air, blocking my way. He stood too close to me. All he did was point, his long finger showing the way to the men in the clearing. I was reminded of Charles Dicken's ghost of Christmas future, the spectral finger pointing to the grave.

"I don't want to go that way, Kane." He shook his outstretched finger towards the water basin, and with his other hand, he gave me a gentle push towards them.

As I approached the men, Grady and Tom, in unison, lifted their rifles in a clamored flurry, and I heard the clicks of metal and stock. I felt the corners of my mouth stretch as far back as they would go, all ten fingers stretched apart, and I felt the sour gush of adrenaline. In a fraction of a second, they realized it was only me and lowered their weapons. Adrian had lifted his rifle, but only an inch, and Steve had stood, his rifle pointing at me from his hip. In a breath, they all relaxed, and I could breathe.

"Dammit, Jamie!" Adrian exclaimed, and Steve rolled his eyes and sat back down.

"You want to get *shot?"* Grady yelled.

"You okay?" Tom asked. They were all speaking at once.

Adrian stood. "What are you doing here? It's close to midnight."

"I'm looking for Henry," I said.

"Henry?" Grady asked. "Who's…"

"My dog!" I shouted at him. "What are you guys doing with guns? What's going on here?"

"Get back to your cabin, right now!" Adrian said harshly.

"I didn't know there was an island curfew."

"Now!" Adrian's face was grim. Tom nodded at me. Steve looked away and into the woods, while Grady shook his head in disbelief. I walked past them to my cabin, and once inside, I locked my door and collapsed on my bed.

I dreamed. The air was a milky dark gray. Jeremy stood under a palm tree in the woods aiming a thick gray cylinder at me. Behind Jeremy was my uncle's farm in bright sunlight, and I saw Charlie, the horse I knew when I was ten years old, and he was tied to the fence, the rope too short, too restricting. I heard Jeremy yell "Help me!" as weeds and brush slowly overtook him, growing from his feet and around his ankles, twisting up his legs to the trunk of his body. He seemed not to notice the growth coiling around his body, but he was fearful of the cylinder he held, and I understood, as one can only understand in dreams, that he had no control of what damage he might cause with the hollow pipe that he held. We both knew danger was imminent. I tried to call out and warn him of the weeds, but no sound came from my throat. Suddenly, a miniature black cannonball slowly rolled out of the tube in Jeremy's hands, and the metal ball fell with a thud to the dirt. Strangely, the impact made a nuclear booming sound that lit up the sky with a flash of yellow. The ground shook from the black ball's collision with the soil, and I almost fell, as if trying to walk in a carnival's funhouse undulated floor. The land split near Jeremy's feet, and I watched in horror as Jeremy fell deep into the earth. The last thing I saw was his fingertips as they hovered an inch above the dirt before they slipped down into the torn earth. I tried to scream his name, but no sound came out. The harder I tried to yell, the more terrified I became. Then the ground closed up tightly so that no slit remained, a wound quickly healed. I ran to the spot where Jeremy had been swallowed, but all that remained from where he stood was the thick gray cylinder. The tube dissolved into silver molten lava, which then solidified into Jeremy's flute. I heard flute sounds though the instrument sat on the dirt without anyone playing it, three high–pitched notes, then silence, then the three high–pitched notes again, and this repeated. I heard a knock on a door from somewhere.

I woke. The light through the window above my bed was blinding, and I rubbed my eyes. It seemed that only minutes ago it was a little after midnight when I had laid down into my bed. The dream dissolved back to wherever it came from, with the flute sounds dissolving into the birds that sang outside my window. The knock was real. It came again.

"Just a minute!" I called out quickly. I shot out of bed, forgetting about Henry, who spilled to the floor, giving a quick high–pitched yelp when he hit the floor. "Oh, baby, sorry!" I went to scoop him up but saw that he had piddled, and he cowered. "Oh, sweetie, I'm so sorry!" The knock came again, more urgent this time. "Just a *minute*!" I yelled, and I rushed to clean up the mess before answering the door.

Jeremy stood at the door, breathing heavily, as blond wisps of hair fell on his raised eyebrows.

"Did you hear?"

"Hear what?" I asked.

"Kane was shot!"

"What?" A single quick moan came from my gut.

"Last night..."

"Who... who..."

"Tom. Tom shot him. By accident. Tom thought he was someone else."

"Jeremy!" I grabbed him and hugged him tightly, squeezing him, my forehead grinding into his bony shoulder.

"He's okay! He's okay!"

I rushed past Jeremy as he was saying something, running out the door, running away from Jeremy's words and the anguish they caused, leaving my cabin door wide open. I didn't know where I was running to, I just had to run, I just had to get out.

I stopped at the bottom of the clearing, the spot farthest from the lodge, and I stood pretty much at the exact center point between my cabin and Kane's. I looked around. A mangrove tree swayed in the wind above and behind Kane's dark cabin as a black–backed butcherbird landed on his roof. All else was still by his place. I turned around. Darcy, Brian and Derek stood under the large red cross just outside the Medical building's door, along with Sheila and the two nurses. Darcy called over for me, and I heard my name reverberate in the wind and in my head. I hurried to them, my friends.

Darcy stared at me, looking worried, with Brian by her side wearing the same look. Sheila and the two nurses clung to each other, and little Derek held Sheila's hand. I felt a tickle by my ankle and looked down to see Henry looking up at me. Derek let go of Sheila's hand and ran to Henry. He dropped to his knees and hugged the dog. Jeremy was soon by my side, breathing heavily.

"What's going on?" I asked. "Is Kane all right?"

"He's fine! He's fine!" Darcy said.

"He really is," Brian reassured me.

"I was trying to tell you," Jeremy said, catching his breath.

"He got shot in the arm. It just breezed him."

"Tom shot him."

"Last night."

"Just several hours ago actually."

"It was an accident."

Everyone was talking at once, and I didn't know who was saying what. My mind whirled like a shaken snowglobe.

"What happened?" I asked.

"We're not sure," Darcy said. "Tom and Adrian are holding a meeting at breakfast."

"They said they'd fill us in then," Brian added.

"If Tom and Adrian don't kill each other first," Jeremy said.

"What?" I asked.

"Yeah, Adrian is furious at Tom," Brian told me. "They're screaming at each other. They're in the medical building now."

"Adrian's calling Tom a hothead," Jeremy informed.

"It's not pleasant," Darcy said to me, shaking her head.

"I hate it," Derek softly said from the ground. He was rubbing Henry's stomach as my dog lay on his back, paws bent by his chest, neck stretched.

"Maybe Tom should let the security team do their job," Sheila said.

"Maybe you should shut your mouth!" Darcy snapped at her.

"I hate it!" Derek yelled. I knelt beside Derek and told him it was okay. Darcy crouched down next to me and rubbed Derek's back, telling him she was sorry.

"When was he shot?" I asked her.

"In the middle of the night." Darcy said. "I'm surprised you didn't hear the gun go off."

"I slept as if I were drugged," I said. "Why are you all out here?" I stood.

"They don't want us in there," Brian said, pointing his head to the medical building.

"They even kicked *us* out," said one of the nurses, and the other nurse agreed, nodding quickly. Samneric[3].

"Jim's inside bandaging Kane's arm." Darcy explained. "Joel's in there with them, trying to keep Adrian from murdering his brother."

"But Joel's no match for Adrian," Jeremy laughed.

"Yes he is!" Derek pleaded. Darcy shook his shoulder and put her forehead on his. I couldn't hear what she whispered to him.

"Hey little man," Jeremy said to Derek. "I mean no disrespect to your dad. Your dad's cool, the smartest guy on the island."

---

[3] Two twin brothers from *Lord of the Flies* who eventually were referred to as having one identity.

"Grady's in there too, holding Adrian back, trying to keep the peace along with Joel," Darcy said as she stood up.

"What is this? Everyone's tearing everyone apart!" I said. "Well, I'm going in."

"You'd better not!" Darcy warned, but it was too late.

Heads turned as I burst into the room. I'd heard Adrian say "When you're trained with weapons, only then..." but he stopped abruptly upon my sudden entrance. He and Tom leaned against two different counters at the side of the room, apart from each other. Joel stood next to Tom, and Grady, next to Adrian. Two against two. Kane sat on the metal table in the middle of the room, a man out of his element, a caged animal, as Jim tied a cloth around his bicep. He was too large for the room, literally resembling an elephant in the room. I ran to Kane and hugged him, pressing my jaw into his chest. He smelled of lightly burnt chestnuts mixed with smoke and salt. I felt a hand on my shoulder and expected it to push me off Kane and lead me away, but when I looked up, I saw that it was Jim, and he smiled down at me, a sad smile.

I released my hold. "Kane!" I said with affection and sympathy. His eyes were like melted chocolate.

"All right, you're all patched up," Jim said as he tapped Kane's shoulder, and Kane pushed himself off the metal table. "You'll be chopping wood in no time," the doctor added.

"Listen man, again... I'm sorry," Tom said to Kane. Kane gave a single nod.

Joel caught my eye. "Is Derek all right?" he asked me.

"Why don't you go out and check for yourself?" I didn't know where my anger was coming from. Joel looked to the ground.

"Jamie, can you go outside now and tell everyone to meet in the lodge?" Adrian asked me. "It's time for our meeting. Can you do that for me?"

Chapter 26
WE'RE DEAD

In the past when we all gathered for a meeting, we always sat within close proximity of each other, where we were *together*, one unit, one clan. Our meetings had always been either at mealtime when we all sat at the tables in the back of the lodge, or when we all assembled together in the sitting area at the front part of the lodge where the couches and chairs were. But now, we were all scattered throughout the room, a family divided, our clan severed and dispersed, with Tom, Joel, and the doctor by the left fireplace, and Adrian, Grady, and Steve at the other fireplace across the room.

I watched Adrian eyeing Tom across the room, but Tom wasn't looking back at Adrian, either by intention, or because Tom was lost in other thoughts. Darcy, Jeremy, Brian, Derek and I sat squeezed together on the three-cushioned couch with some of our legs interlocking with each other's like a bunch of school kids, while Sheila and the two nurses sat at the tables toward the back of the room, their heads almost touching. One of the nurses had her fingertips on the other nurse's forearm, engrossed in their conversation; Sheila listened in as she pressed towards them, twirling her hair.

Earl sat stiffly in one of the matching lodge-style mountain chairs, but though he was near us, he seemed to be away from us, alone and apart. From his grim and far–away expression, I gathered that he was thinking about his wife. At the stables where Earl was part of the scenery, where he relaxed in the pine chair in the barn, he seemed to merge and melt into the wood. Here, however, he sat stiff and rigid in the lodge's chair, apart from our structured communal living, a bear in a shopping mall. Like Kane, Earl needed to be out in the open where he could feel the wind and see the trees.

Kane now stood with his arms crossed by the window at the very front of the lodge, not far from the door. The cloth bandage he had tied around his bicep reminded me of a military armband that some soldiers wear when they belong to a violent or extreme cause. Both Earl and Kane always looked to me to be out of place in the lodge when we were all together, like a coyote and a leopard inside a ski resort.

Tariq wasn't himself when he wasn't running all around serving food like a stirred-up bee buzzing around its disturbed nest. He leaned against a table in the middle of the room, away from us, twirling a basting syringe in his hands.

The second matching chair on the other side of the couch near us remained empty.

We waited for the meeting to start.

Jeremy leg–wrestled with me, and I won. "Riding a horse develops leg muscles," I said to try to make him feel better, but it didn't seem to work. When Tom cleared his throat, I looked up at him standing by the fireplace, and Jeremy sat up.

Both Tom and Adrian spoke at the same time. I didn't hear what either of them said as their voices drowned each other's words out. They both looked at each other, and I expected them to laugh or shrug it off, but they didn't. Their faces were firm as they held each other's gaze.

"First of all, I want to apologize... I want to apologize for what happened to Kane," Tom said. Several of us looked over at Kane, who now uncrossed his arms and cast his eyes down, though he held his chin up. Kane wasn't a man who enjoyed a spotlight on him. He held no anger.

"You mean for shooting the man?" Earl called out.

"Yes, Earl, for shooting him. For accidentally shooting him," Tom said. "I take full responsibility for that." I looked over at Adrian, and he stood with his head slightly cocked, studying Tom.

"Tell us what happened, Tom," Darcy said. "Just explain to

everyone why you and the security team were out there last night with guns."

"There was a possible threat," Adrian said.

"What?"

"What threat?"

"Who?" Several spoke at once.

"Were you guys hunting?" Jeremy asked.

"Yeah, they were hunting in the clearing by Central Lodge," Darcy said sarcastically.

"We had reason to believe that some of the research team may have had cause to come to our camp last night, with not–so–kind intentions," Adrian told us.

I heard "why?" and "what intentions?" and so forth coming from Sheila's table, our couch, and from Earl. But I knew why.

"Is Dr. Bronte to blame for our computers being down and the supply ship not arriving?" I asked.

"Let me answer all *that* after I explain something first," Tom said. "First, I want you all to know that our situation isn't really as desperate as it may seem," Tom said.

"What you mean?" Tariq called out. "We don't have fresh food coming in!"

"Duh Tom, our computers are down!" Sheila said from the back.

Tom cut in. "No, what I mean is..."

"If we never leave this damn place, I'm never seeing my wife again!" Earl said sharply. "We all ain't seeing *any* of our family again!" Jim stared at the floor. Tom changed weight from one foot to the other and opened his mouth to say something, but said nothing. Joel looked intently at his twin brother. I saw Adrian raise his eyebrows and run his palm over his head.

"Earl, I'm sorry you feel this way, but you'll see your wife again," Tom said. "What I'm trying to say is..."

"You sure are sorry for a lot of things lately," Grady said.

"That's enough," Adrian said to Grady.

Grady slowly looked over to Adrian. "Now there's a switch."

"I'm kind of scared we're all going to die," Brian said out of the blue. Meek and insecure Brian who didn't usually voice his opinion now spoke out, so what he said carried heavy weight. His words echoed in my chest.

"No, Brian, no one's going to die," Tom reassured. "What I'm *trying* to tell you all is that we've got to look at what we've *got*. We've still got electricity. We have food to last a couple of months. There's plenty of game – Sumatran tigers, sun bears, rabbits and squirrels... also seafood and fruit on the island to sustain us... for as long as we need, as long as we keep our wits about us. No storm or typhoons have hit us. We all have our health..."

"*And* we have each other," Jim spoke up, taking his eyes from the floor. "We still have that. We can't turn on each other."

"Yeah, all is peachy and wonderful. We just don't have contact with the outside world," Jeremy said.

"Tom is trying to be positive," Darcy said. "Why don't you just listen to him?"

"Why don't you get your ass out of la–la land," Jeremy said. Darcy kicked him hard, and he yelled "Ouch!"

"All right, knock it off over there," Adrian said, giving us a sour look like a headmaster. Jim looked back at the floor, focusing inward.

"Derek's sitting right next to you, watch your mouth," Adrian said.

"Sorry, little man," Jeremy said.

"I've heard the word 'ass' before," Derek mumbled, but his words were only audible to us on the couch.

Tom ignored the bickering and continued. "But I'm afraid we've got some very bad news, folks." The hum in the room stilled.

Darcy and I looked at each other, both of us asking, with our eyes, if either of us knew anything. Brian nudged my shoulder and gave me the same look, and I shrugged. Jeremy and Derek stared at Tom, concerned and confused.

I looked at the others. The security guys wore no confusion; they knew what Tom was about to tell us. I couldn't tell what Jim knew, as his eyes were still fixed on the floor. Earl looked puzzled and upset, expecting the worst. Tariq, twisting the basting syringe, gave an inquisitive look at the object in his hands. I'm not sure he comprehended the situation with his poor command of the English language. I never quite knew what Tariq understood. He always seemed in his own little world, though sometimes he surprised me. Give Tariq a gold ring, and he'll give you a sour look. Give Tariq a death sentence, and he'll give you the same sour look.

Then I looked over at Kane by the front window. Standing still and calm, he wore no expression at all, the same face he wore when he was chopping wood or leaning against a tree sharpening one of his knives.

"We really don't need any more bad news," Earl spoke up.

"I agree, Earl," Tom said. "But you all need to know. We have some news regarding our computers. Joel?" Tom looked at his brother standing by his side, urging him to address the group. Joel, always the introvert, removed his hands from his pockets and opened his mouth in surprise and reserve. He said something quietly to Tom. Jim took his eyes from the floor and whispered to Tom. "Okay," Tom said, more to himself, then he looked up to address us.

"Folks," he said, "there have been a few rare occasions when Joel's computer catches a signal, but only for a few moments at a time, and then we lose the signal again. We don't know why this is. Anyway, when this happens, we get snippets of information." He stopped, hesitating to continue.

"What?" Darcy spoke up. "What have you learned?"

Again, Tom hesitated, looking at the floor, pressing his eyebrows together as he fought to find words.

"You gonna' tell them, or are you deciding whether or not to polish your shoes?" Grady asked from the other side of the room, and Tom looked over at him, his face mixed with anger and reluctance. He honestly seemed unable to proceed.

"Our assets back in the States are frozen," Adrian loudly said, finally telling us in a matter–of–fact manner. His words seemed to bounce off the walls, and after an initial silence, many of us spoke at once. We asked *whose* assets, and *why*, and *how* exactly did they know this, and could we get our life savings back. Adrian said it appeared that *all* of our assets were touched, that we were all considered penniless. He knew nothing more.

The word *penniless* reverberated in my head and thoughts rushed. We were now broke. Time to downsize. I'd have to move. No Christmas presents. Double shifts. Start over. Macaroni and cheese dinners. It'd be worse for the older guys like Adrian and Earl and especially Jim who had built up a savings over decades, a substantial nest egg. I thought about those with families. Jim, Earl, and Steve were married. I wasn't sure if Joel was even divorced. How would this affect Derek? One of the nurses started to cry.

"It gets worse," Adrian said. Faces turned to him.

"How could it possibly get any god damn worse?" Earl asked.

"Oh, it most surely does," Grady said in an animated manner. Steve, standing next to Grady, was stone–faced and looked off into space.

"We saw obituaries, on all of us." Tom called out, again taking lead, and heads snapped to him. I felt as if I were shot with a stun gun. Melinda and Jack back home thought I was dead. Did Uncle Calvin and Aunt Priscilla receive this news? If so, would they feel any pain over my death? I carried a light load back home, but my new family here on Jackel Island did not. I saw the devastation on Darcy's face, and Brian looked about ready to cry. One–word questions and longer exclamations along with a few comments were fired at Tom. "It's in the newspapers back home. We've all hit the national headlines. In fact, we're the top stories," Tom said. "Supposedly, some kind of brutal storm swept through the island and killed us all. There were no survivors. We're all dead."

There were no survivors. We were all considered dead.

He let it sink in as we spoke among ourselves, and we threw more questions at Tom. Why? Who? How? When? But mostly *why?*

"We have reason to believe it's Evan Bronte who's causing us our troubles," Adrian said, and for a second, it seemed as if he had spoken through a microphone. Everyone started talking at once with no one being heard, and Adrian held up his palm until it was quiet. "It's a puzzle we're piecing together, and we don't have all the pieces, but so far, what we speculate fits."

Adrian stepped down from the ankle–high fireplace landing, and grabbing a chair from one of the tables, he pulled it back near the fireplace and sat down backwards in the chair, his forearms and hands dangling in front of him from the back of the chair. Grady sat down on the stone landing, and Steve leaned on one shoulder against the fireplace. Tom, his brother, and the doctor grabbed chairs and pulled them closer. I leaned forward, resting my elbows on my knees.

Adrian looked at me. "It was something Jamie said exactly one week ago that got us all thinking," Adrian said, and I felt my ears get hot. "She told us what bio–CMAT stood for. *Bio–Chemical Mind Altering Test.* Thing is, that's not what we were told. And I got to thinking… why would Jao lie to us? Why would they lie to the Chief of Security, and even to our Administration Head, the owner's son? Why is Evan Bronte the only one on the island who knows what our project stands for?"

"So *Jao* lied to us." I said.

"Not necessarily," Adrian said. "Our employee information packages could have been tampered with."

"But didn't it come out in the interviews with Jao, what bio–CMAT stood for?" I asked.

"Does anyone remember being told this directly by anyone in Jao?"

Adrian asked the room. No one spoke up.

"With all due respect, this doesn't really prove anything solid," the doctor said.

"You're right," Adrian said. "Again, these are all pieces that don't carry any weight when viewed alone. But put the pieces together, and you start to see a picture."

"What picture?" Earl asked.

"Well, another piece of the puzzle is that Jamie saw a notebook over at the research center." I felt eyes burn on me, but I stared straight ahead, my eyes fixed on Adrian.

Earl turned to me. "What were you doing over in the research center?"

"Yeah, what was she doing over there?" Sheila asked. I kept my eyes locked on Adrian, silently willing him to speak to move the focus back on him and not on me.

"Let's stay on topic." Adrian said. "Jamie saw six names in Dr. Bronte's notebook – my name, Grady's, Steve's, Tom's, Joel's and Kane's."

"*Kane's* name?" Jeremy asked. "Not mine?"

"No Jeremy, your name wasn't in there," Adrian said facetiously.

"They had the *maintenance* guy in there?" Jeremy asked incredibly. He turned to Kane. "Why was *your* name listed?" Kane slowly turned his head to Jeremy and gave him a blank stare.

"Another piece of the puzzle is that last week, shortly after we learned that our phones and computers were down, I rode out to the research center to ask if *their* computers were down as well," Adrian said. "I was told, by Dr. Bronte, that they were. A couple of days later, we found out that wasn't the case."

"How'd you find out?" Darcy asked.

"Steve and I rode out there one night to check," Grady said.

"You *spied* on them?" Darcy asked.

"Sneaky little devils, aren't we?" Grady said. "When things weren't adding up and life here was going down the toilet, yeah, we did." Grady scratched his head. "You have a problem with that, Missy?" Adrian gave him a disapproving look. Grady shrugged.

"The biggest and most disturbing piece of the puzzle is this." Adrian stood, keeping one hand on the back of the chair. His face went cold. He looked over at Tom. "We have reason to believe that we're being used for biological testing."

The silence that followed stabbed each of us, and I felt the jittery rush of epinephrine flood my veins. What was this? Were they coming in the night sneaking needles into us? I felt dirty, contaminated. But my health seemed fine. Excellent, in fact. I felt confused.

"That's preposterous!" Earl said.

"No way! That can't be!" Jeremy cried out.

"We would know!" Shelia said. "Wouldn't we?"

"How would they be able to do this?" Darcy asked. "And *why* would they do this?"

"It's not preposterous; it's quite possible," the doctor said. "You can definitely be unaware that you're being drugged, if the drug is administered in small enough doses over time where the body slowly becomes accustomed to it. Think of how we all have been experiencing heightened senses. Think of how we all are getting by on very little sleep."

I thought about my only needing about four hours of sleep a night, my heightened senses, *all* of our heightened senses. I remembered my second night here on the island when Darcy told me how everyone's feelings were intensified. I thought of how I could detect smells in the air like never before, how food had such taste, the intense stirrings I felt towards Adrian which was out of character for me, how quickly it took for me to become so close to these people I worked along side with here on Jackel Island. So was all this real? Were my affections towards these people genuine, or due to a chemical, a drug?

"The doctor has taken a sample of blood from the security team, my brother, and from me," Tom said.

"And?" Darcy asked.

"Results should be coming in two days," Jim said.

"How can anyone drug us without our knowing it?" Jeremy asked.

"Easily," the doctor said. "Through our water, our food... it can even be through a particular contact, or it can be airborne."

"If the tests come back positive," Adrian said, "we're going to have to beef up security. We'll start by boiling our water, eating only food that comes from the island, and we'll also have to take further precautions."

"Why would anyone drug us?" I asked.

"For biological testing," Adrian said, and he drummed his fingertips on the back of the chair. "There's huge money in pharmaceuticals. Here Jao has roughly twenty human test subjects, quite isolated, out of U.S. jurisdiction, and now all assumed dead. Very convenient for them."

"Why do you think it's Dr. Bronte?" I asked.

Adrian said, "Who other than a man with a Ph.D. in biochemistry and neurophysiology, a man who passionately studies human brain cells, a man who's written texts on bio-molecular altering consciousness, has such motive to do this?"

"Also, the guy doesn't seem to have high regard for people," Tom said. "His arrogance is off the scale. He gets paid six figures for his research. And following protocol in human decency takes time when one is impatient."

"Well, what are we going to do about this Bronte guy?" Earl asked. Tom looked at Adrian. It was then when Adrian told the group that we were holding Evan Bronte.

The room seemed to spin on an unseen axis.

I wanted to shout to everyone how wrong this was, how wrong they were and that they had no proof, that Dr. Bronte was a decent person who had no friends when he was a child, whose wife died, who was cut and bruised. A man who's lips I'd traced with my fingertips.

"I'm not who I seem," Bronte had told me.

Faces on the couch drained. How much more could they take? I wondered how much shocking news in one sitting people could absorb. To be told "*you lost all your money, and everyone you knew at home thinks you're dead, and oh, one more thing... strange chemicals are being put into your blood*" isn't an easy pill to swallow. Brian gave me a troubled look; he was so lost right now. Just then, I could picture what he must have looked like when he was Derek's age. I reached over and put my palm on his cheek, and he pressed his face into my hand as he let go a hot single tear.

Adrian explained that the reason they were keeping Bronte was so he couldn't do any more damage, and also to right the wrong he's caused here on Jackel Island. The plan was that we would release Bronte when he released his hold on our computers, our shipments, and when he would reveal to us how he was using us as human test subjects. Adrian made it seem easy.

"He can't be working alone," Adrian said. "We don't know if he's working with someone dirty at Jao, from the military, or even with someone crooked in our government."

"What if he doesn't confess?" Earl asked.

"Oh, he'll confess all right," Grady said. "We'll make sure of that." Grady, too, made it seem so easy. What if the guy was innocent, you fool? You can't force blood out of a rock.

"So you see everyone, we have a plan in action," Adrian said. "I assure you, no harm will come to any of you. I feel confident that our phones and computers will soon be working again, and word will be released to the States that we're all alive and well. Dr. Bronte is a very wealthy man, so we should have all our assets returned to us. However, it looks like Dr. Bronte will be... *out of commission* once the authorities know all that he's done. This will most likely mean the end of our project so we'll probably be returning home sooner than planned, but we'll all be fine. I'll see to that."

The nurses looked quizzically at each other, and Jim looked over at us and gave us a weak smile. Joel patted his brother's shoulder. I'm not sure we were all one hundred percent convinced that we would be fine.

"See, so that's why we were out there with guns last night," Tom told us. "We knew Bronte's people would come looking for him. We're trying to keep everyone safe."

"But oh my God, Tom, you shot the wrong guy," I said. "You and the security team almost shot *me* last night. We're shooting our own people."

Chapter 27
SNAKES IN THE NIGHT

Tariq served a light breakfast after the meeting, and most of us just picked at our food. I saw Kane carry his plate outside, and I followed him out to the water basin. He sat on the dirt and leaned against the stone. I plopped down next to him, our shoulders almost touching. I saw that his plate was filled with fruit.

"Does your arm hurt?" I asked him. Seeing that I hadn't brought food out for myself, he held his plate out to me. I took a slice of water apple. I looked up at him, waiting for him to answer. I watched as he chewed, and with a serene face, he looked straight out into the clearing.

"It's kind of annoying when you don't answer questions directed at you." He stopped chewing and looked down at me. For the first time, I saw surprise, or was it amusement, in his eyes, eyes that usually lacked any emotion and showed only calmness.

"You rely too much on spoken word," he said.

Touché!

Then he continued, "This surprises me because you are so keen with animals." I dealt with animals on a different level, going more by intuition. I made a mental note to pay more attention to the non-verbal, to work on communicating with people the way I do with horses.

"Kane, why did you tell me it wasn't safe in the woods last night?"

"Because it was not safe."

"Why?"

"There were others near us, coming towards us, people who had dark thoughts."

"Who?" He said nothing. "People from the research team?" Again, he said nothing. I looked for non-verbal clues. "How do you know this?" I put the last bit of water apple in my mouth. "How do you know what they were thinking?"

"They were hidden. They were masked. They were like snakes in the night," Kane said. "They ran when they heard the guns." Kane picked up a piece of fruit. "But they'll be back."

Chapter 28
JUDAS KISS

"Why?" I asked Dr. Bronte, towering over him with one hand on my hip, looking down at him as he sat tied to the ground. It was more than an hour after dinner. I had once again sneaked inside his hut with mouthwash and hand towels folded in my backpack, and two canteens around my neck, one of soapy water, and one of just plain water. I was thinking I may clean him up a bit, but was unsure if I wanted to touch him, considering that this morning I'd learned that he might be a swiney beast demon.

"Why are you doing this to us?" I asked him.

"Once again, I'm not."

"Once again, who else would?"

"Who else would *what*?" He was annoyed. "Are we talking about your downed computers? The supply ship that didn't come? Or perhaps your frozen assets? Your obituaries? And what was the last one… being drugged? What is it, Jamie? What is it that you think I've done?"

He looked pitiful sitting on the dusty floor, one leg bent up and the other straight, his arms pulled back behind him. His bruises had purpled while his face was drained of color, muted to an anemic pale gray. His eyes and hair had lost their luster, and he now looked out from dim ashen eyes under matted hair. His only comfort was the hard pole he leaned against. Dusky whiskers poked from his jaw, under his nose, and around his chin. Life that was once sharp in him was now hazy. He was a ghastly sight. I could tell that another week of this would smother the life out of him completely.

"Never mind. You're not going to admit it anyway." I knelt beside him. "I came to clean you up a little." I took the canteens off my neck and slid the backpack off my back and laid them on the floor of the hut.

"Why would you wash me if you think I'm some kind of monster?"

"Because I'm an idiot." He exhaled a laugh that was just a breath. Unscrewing the soapy canteen lid, I firmly held a towel over the opening and tipped the canteen upside–down.

"Would you believe me if I told you that I'm actually trying to protect all of you?" Bronte said.

"No." However, I half believed him, because I *wanted* to, though I wasn't sure what he was capable of. I dabbed the soapy towel on his face, avoiding his injuries. Still, his eyes watered, though he didn't flinch this time, and his head and mouth remained fixed. He tried to look strong, but his vigor was slowly draining from him. With another wet towel, I washed the soap from his skin that now began to show a hint of color. I put a towel to his neck and he lifted his chin for me. I cleaned his neck, and some water dripped down into his shirt and chest.

"If you can put a cool cloth to my wrists..." he asked quietly. With my knees, I maneuvered around behind him to where he was tied to the pole. I lifted his shirt cuff to soap up his hands, and what I saw made me gasp. His wrists were rubbed raw, as angry, festering red gouges cut into his skin from the ropes that tied him. Part of the rope was abraded in the skin and pus seeped around the edges of his wounds.

"Oh God! Dr. Bronte..."

I had to stand up. I had to get away, as if his hands contained wasps. I felt light–headed when I stood, then suddenly nauseous. I feared I was going to vomit. I dropped to my knees near him, unable to see his face as I was still behind him. I looked at the floor, waiting for the unpleasant feeling to pass.

"Do you still think *I'm* the bad guy here, Jamie?" he whispered. I softly laid a fresh towel on his foul wrists. With a sudden and drastic drain of strength, I fell forward onto him, my forehead on his shoulder, and I cried. I cried for what we had done to this man, the decay of health. I cried for our paradisal life that had turned to perdition. I cried for suddenly being impoverished, for having no place in a world that thought we were dead, for our altered DNA. It was the first time I had cried since I sobbed on Adrian days after my arrival to Jackel Island, since our world had turned upside–down. Here I was, crouched close behind him, my eyes wetting the shoulder of this beaten man, this Evan Bronte, who could be the cause of all this.

"You all right?" he asked. I felt slight vibrations from his shoulder blade as he spoke. I backed off him and gathered myself. "Really, Jamie, I should be the one crying," he said sarcastically.

"I know."

"Why are you crying?"

"I don't know. Your wrists…"

"That's nothing compared to the ache I feel in my shoulders."

"Sorry," I said. "All I can do is… this."

"There's more you can do. You can untie me." He moved as much as the ropes allowed, trying unsuccessfully to get comfortable. "Three times you denied me this. The first time was yesterday afternoon when you washed the blood from my face with a washcloth. The second time was last night when you brought me food. And now this."

"I can't let you go… I can't betray them like this."

"You really care what they think?"

"Of course I do."

"So you allow them, your friends, to treat me like this?" he asked. The hum of the room stopped. I lay my forehead on his back and shut my eyes.

"I'm sorry," I said. We are all faulted.

After some silence, he said, "I could arrange it so they'd never know it was you. Jamie, I told you this before."

"They'd figure it out," I said. I took a deep breath and lifted my head off his back. "Dr. Bronte, I brought mouthwash. I figured, since you spent last night here…"

"Thank you."

I moved over so that I was once again in front of him and reached for my backpack. Fishing the plastic jar of mouthwash from my backpack, I awkwardly poured some in his mouth, trying not to spill any down his chin. It must have stung the cut on his lip because he winced a bit. After he swished, he looked quizzically at me, and I looked quizzically back at him. I started to realize my mistake. He couldn't ask with a mouth full of liquid. He raised his eyebrows. I shrugged and said "sorry!" and with a gush of force, he spit the mouthwash out to his right side by the back wall. I had to laugh, and ever–so–slightly I saw the corners of his mouth turn up and his eyes lightened.

"Listen, I gotta' go."

I saw slight amusement in his eyes as I stood. I admired him for being able to find humor while he was in such a dire situation, but didn't know what he found amusing.

"Dr. Bronte, don't worry. They've got to let you go sooner or later. They can't keep you here forever."

"Mm hmm." He looked at me as if my pants were unzipped, and I turned away. I looked for the table that I used to reach the window. It wasn't where it always was against the front wall of the hut. I took a quick glance around the room. No table.

"Where's the table?" I asked quickly. I spun around. There was no table.

There was no table.

"Oh yeah, they took it," Dr. Bronte calmly said. I then remembered, earlier today… was it after lunch?... seeing the same wooden table with sawdust and some sort of project they were building on it just outside of Central Lodge. At the time, I thought it was odd, but didn't connect that it was the table from this hidden hut. I never gave it a second thought. Until now.

"No!" I desperately looked around the room, thinking I'd eventually see it. "No, it can't be!"

"Oh yeah, they took it," he said. "They took it this afternoon."

"Why didn't you tell me?" I said as my eyes darted around the room. It finally dawned on me that the table was most definitely gone. I looked at him and shouted at him, "Why didn't you tell me before I jumped down from the window? Why didn't you warn me? How am I supposed to leave now?"

"Gee, I don't know," he said calmly. Sarcastically. For a split moment, I felt hate.

"Why didn't you tell me?" I pleaded. "Why didn't you tell me?"

"Why didn't you untie me?" I stood there looking down at him, breathing hard. "Looks like you have to now."

"I don't have to do *any*thing," I said. "Do you realize what you've done?"

"Oh yeah."

"No, I don't think you do. I can't leave now. I can't…"

"I know." I stared at him with an open jaw, starting to realize.

"You *meant* for me to be stuck here with you," I said. "You *meant* for this to happen. This was intentional. You planned this."

"I didn't plan this. I don't know why they took the table, but when they *did*, I knew that the next time you came, you wouldn't be able to leave. It got me thinking." I waited, but he said no more.

"So this is revenge because I didn't untie you?"

"No, Jamie. It truly is not. However, this will now force you to untie me."

"I don't think so."

"Oh, I think so." He nodded quickly.

He said no more and watched me squirm as I looked around the room. There had to be something I could use to hoist myself up to the window, one of the worn couches, the large radio… But nothing was tall enough. There was nothing. I was stuck.

"They'll find me in here," I rapidly said, trying not to panic.

"Mm hmm."

"When they come next, they'll find me."

"Mm hmm."

"Why do you want this? Why do you hate me?"

"I don't hate you. I need you to untie me."

"I can't."

"Okay then. We'll just wait."

I looked around the room.

"I can hide. I'll hide behind the couch when they come."

"And after they leave and lock up? What then?" He paused, as if he got delight in having me fully realize the situation. My hand went to the top of my head.

"Dr. Bronte –" I didn't know what to do. Like a fool, I jumped up towards the window. Twice. Double fool. "Dr. Bronte –"

"For heaven's sake, relax. I can get you out. But you need to untie me."

I turned to him. I parted my mouth and squinted my eyes at him. "So *this* is why you didn't warn me. *This* is why."

"Yes Jamie, *this* is why. You see, you have no choice now but to untie me."

"I won't."

"Okay then, be discovered by your friends. They'll surely wonder what you're doing here."

"Why do you hate me?"

"I don't hate you. Quite the contrary. I just need to get out. Untie me and I'll lift you up to the window."

"Then… how will *you* get out?"

"Oh, you'll have to get the keys and unlock the door."

"What? I don't think so." I gave a little laugh.

"Oh, I do. Because if they find me in here untied, it won't go so well for you."

"You'd tell?" I asked, and he slowly nodded.

He had this all thought out. I had no choice.

"But when they discover that you're gone, they'll think it's me. I will have betrayed them."

"No, they'll think it's my people. I can back it up for you later."

I learned how to play a bad hand thirteen years ago, the inevitability of it. He had won. Dr. Bronte would have to be released.

I went behind him and tugged at his ropes, careful not to have them touch his injured wrists.

"You'll need a knife," he said. Ignoring him, I tried to work the knot loose with my fingers, but was unable to. "You'll need a knife," he said again, slowly. I pulled harder, to no avail. "I know they keep a Ka–bar bowie knife on the top shelf over there." He moved his head toward the direction of the shelf. "Behind the atlas and the whiskey bottles. Did you know that your security friends drink here on occasion? Seems this is their own little party room."

I got the knife and dropped to my knees behind him. I told him not to move as I held the blade to the rope and pulled up. Nothing. I pulled harder. The rope was too thick.

"You have to saw the blade back and forth," he said extremely slowly and methodically, as if talking to a two–year–old. I wasn't thinking straight. I hit the back of his head with my fingertips.

I moved the knife forwards and backwards against the rope until it gave, and when it did, Dr. Bronte gave a quick "ahh!" of relief. He immediately brought his hands in front of him and rubbed them. He massaged his shoulders and moved them.

"Thank you!" he said with heavy emotion, and awkwardly tried to stand. He didn't seem to have the strength, coordination, or balance at first, and it took him several wobbly tries. I thought of Tawny from my childhood, a foal, remembering the animal's first attempt to stand soon after she was born. I stood. I tried to help him by putting my hand under his upper arm, but he gently pushed me back with a closed–lip smile.

He reached and took the knife from my hand.

"Hey!" I said. "That's not yours!" He ignored me and slowly paced around the room. His first steps were painful, and he limped as he tried to walk the soreness out. It looked as though pain shot through his ankles and hip. I remembered a television show where a man was tied to a chair in a basement for days, and upon his release, he had instant strength. Dr. Bronte's movements eventually became smoother, but he was weakened. I wondered how he was going to lift me up to the window.

Standing directly under the window at the back of the hut, he turned to me.

"Come here," he said quickly.

"You okay?" I asked.

"Yeah. Come here." I went to him, and he interlocked his fingers and held them low for me to step on. Unsure, I looked him in the eye, and he jounced his head, indicating for me to get a move on it, quickly. Putting one hand on the wall and the other on his shoulder, I slipped one foot onto his hands.

It was then we heard the jingle of metal at the door, before I had a chance to put any weight in his hands. Someone was here!

"Damn!" he whispered, and I froze. "I didn't anticipate..." He didn't get to finish his sentence. Adrian came bursting inside, stopping short when he saw us. Tom was behind him, and he almost bumped into Adrian's back when Adrian stopped so suddenly. Fresh night air slapped me. The look of shock on their faces shot a rush of adrenaline in my gut. All four of us froze for a split second.

It was Adrian and Bronte who broke the spell. Adrian rushed at Bronte at about the same time as Bronte grabbed me in a flash. I'm not sure who acted first. It was all a blurred scuffle. Bronte held me tightly against him, his forearm too hard on my collarbone. His right hand held the knife at my jaw. What was he doing?

"Don't do it," Bronte warned Adrian, and I felt his choking grip tighten. I wasn't sure if my legs could support me from leaning back into him at this awkward angle. I also wasn't sure if I was going to throw up from the adrenaline rush.

Adrian stopped in his tracks.

"Good evening, gentlemen," Bronte said.

Adrian quickly gained his composure, pulling the bottom of his shirt down. "A fine time to leave our guns behind, huh Tom," he half–joked, but Tom was still stunned, as was I. "Though we didn't think guns were needed. We surely didn't anticipate this. Hello, Jamie."

I couldn't speak.

"What the… Let her go!" Tom shouted. He leaned slightly forward.

"Oh, you're not in any position to fling orders," Bronte said. I was held so tightly I couldn't even squirm without risk of hurting my neck. My legs gave out from the ground's contact, and he supported my weight by holding my upper chest. He finagled so that I could once again use my legs to support my weight.

"You're not exactly holding the trump card," Adrian said.

"Really? I believe that I am," Bronte coolly said.

"Let her go!" Tom shouted again, but Adrian and Bronte ignored him and stared each other down, both of them displaying an eerie calmness. As I watched the two of them, it became strangely clear to me that at another time, another place, these two could become close allies. Friends even. They were evenly matched.

"So we're to let you go or you'll hurt her, is that it?" Adrian asked.

"That's it." Bronte said in a sing–song tone. Their smooth manner spooked me. Would Bronte really hurt me? It dawned on me that they were right all along about him. "*I'm not who I seem.*"

"Then what?" Adrian asked with raised eyebrows.

"You won't take that chance," Bronte told him.

"Neither will you," Adrian answered.

Without giving him a chance to think about it, Bronte maneuvered away from the back of the hut towards the door, traveling with me held tightly against him. Awkwardly, my legs labored to match his steps. I looked at Adrian, but he looked only at Bronte. I saw the internal struggle and then defeat in Adrian's eyes as he stepped to the side to let us pass.

As we passed Adrian, Bronte leaned towards him and said quietly, but with reserved anger, "You took something sweet from me – my freedom. Now I'm taking something sweet from you."

Adrian lost his command. His face dropped in surprise and concern. I saw in his face that my future was grave, but I couldn't fully comprehend.

"Don't worry, I'll return her in the morning when I'm done with her."

Adrian eyes became red venom. He charged at Bronte, but stopped short, for Bronte had squeezed his grip on me so very badly that I yelped. I felt the knife's blade touch my jaw. Adrian halted, his face full of abhorrence and scorn. Bronte had once again won. He eased his grip on me a bit and pulled me towards the door, passing Tom, who took a step back.

Just then, as we were at the door, Grady appeared, entering the hut as if this were a soda shop. When he saw us, his expression went from aloof to shock to action, and with a fumbled clutter, he raised his rifle. Before Grady could position his weapon, Bronte, with urgent speed, violently shot his arm up and pierced Grady's hand with the knife in a single movement, pinning Grady's hand in a hellish way against the wooden door. There was a half a second's pause before a heavy stream of blood drooled out. Grady instantly cried out, and it took a second for me to realize that I was screaming, too. Tom stepped in but didn't dare approach Bronte, because his fingers held me under my chin, twisting my neck in an unnatural way.

"Try to stop me, try to get her during the night, and the show's over for her," Bronte said. "I mean it. You now know I mean business. Don't step one foot in our compound!" Then he casually said, "You'll get her back in the morning."

Tom stood by the door blocking our way, and I could see Bronte out of the corner of my eye glaring at him. Tom anxiously looked to Adrian and struggled almost frantically with indecision.

"Easy, Tom," Adrian said.

"Don't do it!" Bronte warned.

I heard Grady moan as he was pinned to the door with a raised hand, and it looked like a pitcher of black–red blood was poured over his hand and down his arm, pooling on the floor. Adrian was at Grady's side, gingerly working the knife out as Grady gave mournful sounds of agony. Bronte gave me a quick squeeze which made me grunt. Tom then succumbed and stepped away, allowing us to pass through the door.

PART THREE

Chapter 29
ESCAPE

Immediately after we left the hut and entered the night air, Bronte released his chokehold on me, though he grabbed my upper arm and rushed me through the woods. I believe I was in shock and was surprised my legs functioned at all. I ran on auto–pilot. Black tree limbs bent wildly down at us from every angle under the charcoal sky, twisting towards us in a haunting and violent manner, and I swatted them from my face as we ran. I tripped on a tree root, but his hold held me up, though I stumbled horribly, and he continued to rush me further into the black woods.

I hadn't had time to think or access the situation. My mind now touched upon what had just happened in the hut, with disturbing thoughts and images of knives and rage and blood and betrayal. I couldn't do more than merely brush over these reflections.

"You're a monster," I told him as we hurried through the woods.

We ran roughly fifty yards deeper into the woods before we stopped. Bronte bent forward with his hands on his knees and breathed heavily.

"Don't run off, I don't want to chase you," he labored to say. I thought of running away from him; I had better stamina, but was afraid. He would push past his pain to catch me. I feared leaving him and I feared being with him. This man who I had fed and cleaned, this man who spit mouthwash over his shoulder and made me laugh, had held a knife near my throat not even ten minutes prior. And he had put a knife through Grady's hand.

"My energy is gone," he said more to himself, seeming to be surprised. His breathing eased. "I'm sorry, Jamie. I truly am. I never intended to harm you. I'm glad Mr. Adrian North didn't call my bluff."

"So can I go?" I sounded weak.

"No. Not yet."

"Why not?"

He lightly took my arm and we continued walking away from our cabins, away from my home, towards the east side of the island, towards his world.

The woods gradually became more visible as my eyes adjusted to the darkness. Our feet rustled through some scattered dried up leaves. I thought of a fearful Halloween night when my parents were still alive, kicking leaves along the sidewalk that followed the black iron fence as we went from house to house. Ten-year-old Eddie told us he saw a wolf beyond the fence, and I remembered the terror I felt. Weeks ago, Adrian told me to stay on the path and not venture into the woods where wild animals were prominent. Bronte, keeping to the side of the trail near the black trees, occasionally looked behind us, checking.

"Why can't I go? You're free now. You don't need me." I asked. He did not answer.

I began to remember more of what transpired in the hut. I remembered the rage in Adrian's face, and Tom frantically trying to prevent the inevitable.

I looked over at Bronte and saw that he was sweating profusely. He looked totally drained, like he was going to drop. But he trudged on.

Could I run from him in his weakened state without him catching me? I thought of running for all I was worth. But when I prepared to almost do this, my heart raced and I was sick with fear. Too many times I had witnessed a horse near death give a sudden burst of profound energy when threatened.

I remembered Bronte's words to Adrian. A fear twisted in me, like a snake coiling around my intestines.

"I was kind to you. I brought you food, I cleaned you up. So why are you doing this to me? Why don't you just let me go?"

"Adrian North needs to sweat," Bronte said.

"But he's going to think... all night long, he'll think..."

"That's the idea."

Oh my God. "You won't really..."

"Relax. You'll be fine tonight. You can go back in the morning."

"But I need to go *now*."

"You can't."

"This is kidnapping."

"Call it what you will."

"It is. It's kidnapping. It's a federal crime."

"Call the police."

We descended through night air and evergreens like fallen gods of the forest, a jungle that concealed and asphyxiated its horizons, where the odor was one of ominous tombs and decay. I spotted a seedling sprouting from the middle of a cracked round stump. We passed fungi clinging to a log... life from death, growth from decay. It seemed that nothing of color or beauty could blossom here during the pinnacle of this night. I felt unseen nettles whipping my pants, sharp switches that caught cloth and occasionally stung as it also caught my face. The former sanity and amenity that existed on this island was now gone, and I listened to the dull and hollow sound of our feet scuffling through the dirt path littered with leaves and wild overgrowth from this foreign place on the other side of the world.

"You're a monster," I again told him.

"I suppose I can be when I need to be," he said, then mumbled, "I sometimes slowly lose hold of my original and better self, and become slowly incorporated with my second and worse."

"Huh?"

"That's a quote from..."

Suddenly, there was a quick shuffle of brush and Kane was upon us! Before I knew it, six–foot–six Kane had Bronte on the ground, despite the injuries he'd sustained from his arm. Kane had his knee on Bronte's chest, holding him down. Bronte looked small in comparison.

"Kane!" I ran to him and hugged his back as he held Bronte down. Bronte didn't even struggle. His palms faced the sky as he held them up by his face.

"Kane!" I said again into his back.

Kane turned his head back towards me. "I only came to tell you this. You will go with this man. He will not harm you. You are the only one who can unify the two sides."

"What two sides? What?"

Kane took his knee off Bronte and stood. With effort, Bronte got to his feet and looked with amazement at Kane. I'm not sure who was more baffled, Bronte or I. Bronte's palms rested on his thighs as he bent forward.

"I must go now. Know that you are safe with this man."

"I'm going with you!" I said, astonished. "You can't leave me, Kane."

"This brings me pain, but it is our only chance," Kane said.

"Chance at what? Kane? Kane!"

But he was gone, slipping into the night like a shadow.

"What just happened?" I asked myself out loud. Bronte brushed himself off.

"Mr. Jabari is one very strange man," he said. "Come on."

We trekked on. A blue mist from the sky passed through the trees casting a soft milky glow on branches and on Bronte's shoulders. I felt a light sheet of humidity coat my skin. I could derive little sense from Kane's words, though I played them over repeatedly in my head. How could he leave me with Bronte? How could he leave me? The night air entered my lungs and stung my insides, as if the blue glitter was a poison. Insect and animal sounds close by shrilled and howled, spooking me. I saw that I was pressing my shoulder into Bronte's arm for comfort from the night and from being taken as we hurried down the trail, and when I realized this, I pulled away from him.

I did this as a child soon after my parents were killed, pressing my cheek against my fourth grade teacher's ribs in the playground, feeling her soft coat against my skin... leaning against my cousin who was two years older than I, until he shoved me away and said "eww!" I remembered my minor car accident three years ago, finding myself shaking and holding the cop's shoulder for no reason. I hadn't even realized I was doing this until the officer touched my arm and assured me all was okay, that it was only a fender bender.

I am damaged and defaced, and I go through life with a scarred soul, an internal blemish which no one can see, until times like this when I am exposed for what I am, for what I've become. Bronte seemed oblivious, or if he noticed my impairment, he said nothing. How could he *not* have noticed? Like Kane, he must also find me very strange indeed.

Twice, Bronte had to stop, bending forward at the hip, and I saw sweat drop from his forehead and nose. What was the matter? I seriously thought of running, but fear weighed me down. I couldn't stop seeing Grady's dark blood, the horror of it.

Bronte heard it first. He stopped abruptly and thrust his arm out like a sword, stopping me. Then I heard it, a ruffle of leaves up ahead, coming towards us.

"Is it an animal?" I whispered. *There were others coming towards us, people who had dark thoughts. They moved like snakes in the night. And they'll be back.*

"No, shh!" he quickly whispered back. He crouched down and pulled my arm so I squatted next to him. He surprised me when he put a hand over my mouth, pushing my head into his chest. His body was moist with sweat. If it was Tom or Adrian or the others coming for me, they wouldn't be coming from further out in the woods. They'd be coming from behind us. Or would they? Could they have circled around as a tactical ploy? I grew hopeful. I squirmed, and Bronte jerked a tight squeeze that hurt. When I was still, he eased up some.

The sounds got closer, and with it, we heard men's voices. Suddenly, Bronte absent–mindedly released me, as his focus was now fixed on the voices. He stood with ease and turned up a corner of his mouth. Confused, I slowly stood, and I heard Bronte call out to the voices.

"Mr. Hyde! Mr. Edwards! I see you finally made it."

"Dr. Bronte?" one of the men called out in a low–pitched tone, and they rushed over.

"Yes, it's me." Two iron–built men dressed in dark clothing stood before us wearing steel expressions. I saw a pistol on one of their belts, as moonlight caught the metal, glinting like Christmas tinsel. I couldn't see the other man's waist. Dr. Bronte stood firmly before these two steel men who did not in any way look like research geeks. Breathing easier, Bronte seemed to gain strength with their presence, and he smiled.

"We came to free you, Dr. Bronte," the other man reported.

"You're a tad late, gentlemen," Bronte said sarcastically.

"We came last night, but they shot at us."

"They didn't know *what* they were shooting at," Bronte said to himself, exasperated. "Listen, I'm afraid I'm in a weakened state. I have a fever, and it's sapping my energy. I may be a bit slow getting to the center." He ran his palm over his forehead and looked at his hand. "Oh, and keep an eye on this one." When I saw them looking at me, I realized who he meant. "Don't harm her, just see that she stays with us. She actually aided me while I was being held."

They looked blandly down at me, two tin soldiers. I should have run when I had the chance. I don't do well with strangers who hold a darkness, another consequence of my tainted past.

I remembered Darcy telling me about the two men who protected Bronte the day Tom and the security team stormed into their camp a year prior to my arrival on Jackel Island. I believe she referred to them as *thugs*. She said they looked more like bodyguards than research assistants, and I knew without a doubt that these two combat gorillas were the same two thugs to whom Darcy had referred. They unnerved me. I realized once again that I was pressing against Bronte's shoulder. I quickly moved off him.

"Let's go," Dr. Bronte commanded, and the four of us headed through the woods to the east side of the island.

We walked most of the way in silence, though Bronte murmured a few comments here and there to his guards, words I couldn't hear. Three times, Bronte had to stop to catch his breath. When one of the guards tried to assist him by offering a supportive arm, Dr. Bronte brushed him off in annoyance, then had us continue on our way.

Chapter 30
BRONTE'S WORLD

It must have been not much before midnight when we arrived at the black iron fence that encircled the research center. I could hear the sea smashing against sand and rock in the not too far distance on our left. One of the iron men hit buttons on a metal keypad that was attached to the iron post, and he opened the gate for us. Fear gripped me; I did not want to enter. I wasn't sure why, but I stood paralyzed. Since I was a child, I felt sudden fear when first presented with a new and unfamiliar place.

"Come on," Bronte told me when he realized I was no longer walking with him. He held out his arm towards me. Like a stubborn horse, I wouldn't budge. "Come on," he said again, wiggling his fingers.

"Dr. Bronte, I don't want to… I don't want to go in there."

"Heavens! Come on!" he said for a third time, and reached over for my arm and gently pulled me as one of the thugs pushed my shoulder from behind. "I got her," Bronte told his thug. Reluctantly, I followed him inside.

Their area was lit with tall thin European–styled lampposts that stabbed the sky, and the light cast a soft yellow shadow on our faces and on the open grounds that spread graciously in their little community. We followed a pristine redbrick footpath that led past a small picnic area under a huge waringin tree. I saw that the brick path continued towards their homes, branching out to several pastel–colored stucco cottages.

Four people rushed out of one of the peach–toned cottages, hurrying our way. Two men and two women eagerly approached, and Bronte stopped and gave a closed–lipped smile at them. As lamp–light caught their faces, I identified these four from the Jao employee profile. The two thugs were not in the employee handbook.

"Dr. Bronte! We were so worried!" I recognized the dark haired woman. Two Sundays ago, she brought a tray with a needle on it, a needle that Dr. Bronte later injected into my arm.

"You're safe," the younger light haired woman said to Bronte. I sensed she wanted to hug him but held back.

"That I am," Dr. Bronte said. His eyes warmed to these people, and he actually looked sweet. I found it hard to believe that a little more than an hour ago, he had held a knife to me and pinned Grady's hand to the door. One of the men, a scrawny balding man, playfully slapped Bronte's arm, and the larger older man smiled at him and nodded. A happy reunion. These people were family, excluding myself and the two emotionless robots who stood at Bronte's side. We three were the outsiders. This small close–knit family was not much unlike our own at the other side of the island. But I sensed that Bronte kept people at arm's length. He would not physically embrace them, nor would he allow anyone to get too familiar with him.

"You're hurt!" the dark haired woman said. I remembered her name was Pauline.

"Oh, your face!" the other woman said.

"What the hell did they do to you?" the larger man said.

"Nothing that a hot shower and a little medicine won't fix," Bronte said.

"You're sweating," Pauline noticed.

"I have a high fever, probably from infection," and he held out his wrists to her. She made a face. "I'm afraid it's taken its toll on me."

"I'll bring something by for it."

Pauline looked at me, causing the others to also turn to me. She looked at Bronte with questions in her eyes. There was an awkward pause, and I took a step back, bumping into one of the thugs.

"She helped me while her security team had me tied and bound in one of their less than desirable dwellings," was all Bronte revealed to her, though she wasn't satisfied. The larger man winked at me, and I didn't know how to react. I felt terribly ill at ease. Did they realize what a swine their Dr. Bronte really was? Should I tell them? I picked at my thumbnail.

Bronte chuckled. "Jamie, meet Philip, Marvin, and Sandra. I believe you've already met Pauline."

The women studied me while the older man who had winked at me now nodded. The younger birdlike man held out his hand and I just looked at it, feeling nine years old again, hesitant, too stuck inside myself to react. I finally took the funny man's hand in a clumsy manner, and Bronte gave another muffled laugh as I shook hands.

"Well then, now that the amenities are over with, I suggest we all get some rest. Jamie?" He held out an arm to lead the way for me, raising his eyebrows. When I didn't comply, he took a step towards me and I was afraid. But he went past me to his bodyguards and said something to them in low tones. The two research men and the blond woman turned and walked to their cottages while Bronte was still discussing something with his guards. The light from the lampposts cast a yellow glow on their homes, and I saw that the cottages all had matching dark green shutters. I thought of *The Stepford Wives.*

Pauline told Bronte that she'd be by later with an antibiotic and something for the pain, that he should get started on it right away. She then headed towards the large grey–stone building with Greek columns that sat to the left of the cottages. The two thugs went off in another direction between the stone building and the sea. Bronte placed his palm on my back and led me through the lamp–lit darkness to his home.

I did not want to step inside. I felt my familiar anxiety and reserve as I froze in consternation at Dr. Bronte's front door. He was now standing next to me, holding the door open for me to pass through.

"Go on, it's all right." He smiled slightly. Hesitantly, I stepped inside.

The door led to his stylish living room. He was neat, uncluttered, and his fine tastes were almost but not quite exquisite. I was surprised that a science man living alone would fix up his place this way. The room was tastefully decorated in a handsome manner, too masculine in style to be elegant. The colors were mostly earth tones – tans, browns, and grays, giving the room a cultivated and natural feel.

"Make yourself comfortable, Jamie. I'm going to wash up. I'm a bit overdue." He walked deeper into the room as I stood by the door. "Oh, and not to bring up unpleasantries, but please don't try to leave. My two men are watching the house." Dr. Bronte stood at the end of the room where his living room flowed into the dining room. He waited for me to respond, and when I did not, he veered off to the left into another room, shutting the door.

Slowly, I took a few steps into the living room. A square gray marbled coffee table sat in the center of the room, and on it was a vase with barley–colored bristly ferns, and a worn thick book with many bookmarks sticking out of it. I picked up the book and read the title – '*Human Cortical Cellular Neurophysiology, Institute of Bio-molecular Science*.' I immediately put the book back down.

A beige couch and two matching chairs shaped an arch around the coffee table. I ran my palm over the posh dark brown pillow on the couch. Did Dr. Bronte ever lie down on the couch the way Jeremy lay sprawled out, or did he always sit properly the way Jim did? A classy tan throw rug lay under the coffee table, couch, and chairs, and under that, a plush wine–colored rug spread out on the wooden floor. I didn't see one speck of dirt or debris on the rug.

The walls were a very light gray with white trim. A dark gray marble fireplace was set flat into the wall, and I wondered why he had a fireplace when we were in the tropics. On one side of the mantel ledge sat two maroon vases, one large and one small, and their muted color matched the plush rug. On the other side of the mantel were two thick brass candlesticks with white beeswax candles. The wicks were brand new, never used. An exquisite mantel clock sat dead center on the fireplace ledge, under a neo-classical landscape painting done in oils, mounted in a thick gold elaborate frame. I walked up to the painting and studied it. The picture showed a rocky coastal landscape with castle on a slanted cliff, with a gangly and twisted brown tree under a pale blue sky, where a storm was approaching on the right. The painting looked like an original, the way it shone from a small round ceiling light aimed directly at it. I wondered why Dr. Bronte took such efforts to decorate his temporary home when he would only be staying here for two years, and why would he bring such an expensive work of art here on the island, but I suppose if one had his kind of money, one could do anything one wanted.

A stylish bookcase stood flat against the wall near the front door, a bookshelf that reached the ceiling, each shelf filled with thick hard–covered books. Walking over to the books, I noticed that the books on the left were science texts similar in nature to the book on the coffee table, and the books on the right carried lighter works, mostly fiction. I scanned titles I recognized – *Paradise Lost* (many volumes), *The Iliad and the Odyssey*, *Heart of Darkness*, *The Art of War*, and *Crime and Punishment*. I pulled *Crime and Punishment* out, but didn't open the book, because my focus fell on a human anatomy model that showed the skeletal system, nerves, and blood vessels. A small thin metal pole was inserted into the model, supporting it. It sat on the end of a high shelf.

"Do you believe that murder is permissible in pursuit of a higher purpose?" Bronte asked, startling me. I spun around. This was the second time he had approached me from behind without my hearing him. The first time was a little over a month ago when I had first met Dr. Bronte, only I didn't know it was *The* Dr. Bronte. He had posed as a lesser man. "*I'm not who I seem.*"

Dr. Bronte was transformed. He stood before me drying his hair with a thick beige hand towel. He had washed the excess blood off his face as best he could, a face that was no longer smeared with grime and sweat, a face that was now more pink than gray. He had shaved and thus looked younger, less rugged. He stood before me clad in clean clothes – dark blue baggy casual pants, perhaps for working out or sleeping in, that tied in front, a soft white cotton shirt, and gray socks with no shoes. He looked like anyone's father, not a world–renowned man of science who stuck knives through people's hands when they threatened him.

"The book you're holding – *Crime and Punishment*."

"Oh." I had forgotten his question, distracted from his transformation from dirty villain to clean human. He looked almost cuddly after his shower, approachable, and my mind stumbled. I asked him to repeat his question, and when he did, I answered, "No. No, I don't."

"Really? We do it all the time; we've done it throughout time, through our wars and our judiciary systems. We say it's justified when…"

Just then there was a quiet rapid knock on the door. Dr. Bronte excused himself and answered the door. I could see Pauline through the crack in the door as I stood by the bookcase, and I caught a few words – "every six hours" and "red streaking in the skin", all the while as she tried to peer inside. Clearly, she wanted Dr. Bronte to let her in. Clearly, he wasn't going to. "Let me at least dress your wounds," I heard her say, and he assured her it was not necessary, though he thanked her. His repeated quick "thank yous" were dismissals, and she eventually left.

Shutting the door, he turned to me holding a small white bag in one hand, and a Tupperware container in another. He approached me, walking right at me as if making a romantic overture, and I felt a solid rush of cowardly discomposure. But he passed me by and went to a small dining table in back. Did he do this on purpose, or was his sense of personal space amiss?

I slowly walked towards the back of the cottage and into his dining room. His living room, dining room, and kitchen were all one big room, defined only by furniture and not by any dividing walls, with the kitchen being in the very back. Dr. Bronte held out a chair for me at his dining room table, and I sat. The table's wood was dark, perhaps mahogany or cherry. I saw a science book on the table, and didn't bother to read the long title. Four black placemats were neatly placed on the table by each of the four chairs, perfectly in place, and Dr. Bronte sat in the chair with his back to the kitchen. A crystal Waterford vase with delicate wispy ferns sat in the center of the table, a stylish centerpiece.

Dr. Bronte placed the white bag and the Tupperware container on the table. Opening the bag, he took out three pill bottles, gauze, a baggie filled with a few cotton balls, and a small jar of ointment. I watched him open the ointment jar, wet the cotton with its contents, and then dab the cotton on his wounds. I watched his face for pain but he showed none. He raised his eyelids and caught me looking at his face. I looked down at the pill bottles.

"I need you to wrap my wrists, if you would," he said, and held the gauze out to me. I did not take it.

"Why should I do that? You held a knife to my throat."

"Because I didn't really hurt you."

"What do you call giving someone a heart attack?"

He continued to hold the gauze at me, and still, I wouldn't take it.

"I don't even want to be here," I mumbled. When he didn't put his arm back, I rolled my eyes and finally took the gauze from his hands. Pulling out a length of the cloth, I looked on the table for something to cut it with.

"Are there scissors?" I asked, and he took the gauze from my hand, pulled out a longer stretch, and roughly ripped the cloth, making two long bands. He handed me the gauze strips, and I bandaged his wrists, wondering if there was any other person on the planet who would willingly bandage the injuries of a man who had just kidnapped them.

He took pills from the bottles, and without water, swallowed them.

"Are you hungry? This is still warm." He held up the Tupperware. I shook my head. "You sure?" I nodded. "Well, if you don't mind. I haven't eaten since you brought me food last... when was it... last night around ten o'clock?"

"Tom or Adrian didn't feed you anything all day today?"

"I'm afraid not," he said. "Nice friends you have, huh."

He opened the lid, and I saw that Pauline had packed him a thick black plastic spoon, as if he didn't have a spoon in his kitchen. She apparently gave him every convenience. She even included a napkin! Mother Hen. She had prepared for him some kind of hearty soup with a red broth. It did smell good. I looked away as he ate, looking over into the kitchen to my left.

In the middle of his kitchen, just behind Dr. Bronte, stood a gray marble–topped island with dark wood below the granite counter. The wood under the counter matched the dining room table's wood exactly, intertwining the two rooms. I stood, glancing at him quickly before I entered his kitchen, half expecting him to tell me to remain seated.

Though no walls divided the living room from the dining room and kitchen, each had its own feel. When I entered the kitchen, I entered a new world. Iron pots and pans hung from the ceiling above the island. Did he cook? The dark gray floor was of polished terrazzo that shone reflections and shadows, as if he never wore shoes on this floor, and cleaned it routinely. Perhaps Pauline did.

Hung on the back brick wall by the stove was a mounted rack of knives, framed like a showpiece in the same dark wood that was used for the dining table, the island, and the kitchen cabinets. Dr. Bronte seemed to need everything to join together. Looking at the knives, I thought of Kane, though Kane would never frame his knives for show.

Walking further into the kitchen, I noticed that his gray pewter refrigerator matched his oven, which matched his microwave. Again, he intertwined and connected his world. The cabinet handles were made of an elaborate black iron of intricate design. Like his living room, this earthy kitchen had no clutter, and the only thing he had on his countertops, besides a few appliances, was a plant, a thick white candle placed in a tasteful iron candle holder, and a black wiry basket of oranges.

Venturing back to the dining room, I looked over his shoulder and noticed that he had finished his soup. He sat back and glanced up at me, turning his head. I became uneasy over what was to happen next.

"It's late Jamie. Let me get you settled in." I grew more nervous.

He stood and put the Tupperware in the sink, then led me towards the area where he had washed up earlier. It was his bedroom. I felt a tightness grip inside me.

"What are you going to do?" I asked quickly.

"I'm going to go to sleep, how about you?" He patted his shirt pocket and removed a small key, then placed it on his dresser near the bedroom door. The tightness in my intestines grew to a sharp pain.

"Relax, Jamie," he gave a quick two–beat laugh. "You can sleep here. I'm sleeping out on the couch."

The tightness eased and I felt my shoulders drop.

I gave a quick look around the beige–walled room. His bed on the far side of the room was neatly made with layers of tan, white, and dark–brown decorative blankets and sheets. Did he actually sleep under all those sheets, here in the tropics? Or perhaps it was a look he was accustomed to from his life in the States. Maybe Dr. Bronte needed familiarity.

I saw a gold–framed African painting above his bed, or perhaps it was a painting from India. The painting showed abstract red stick people with black spears and straight black poles for legs. He had a nightstand by his bed, a small bookcase with even *more* books, a leather chair in the corner of the room with a downbridge tiffany floor lamp next to it, and a knee–high black vase containing cattails and foxtail grasses that poked up towards the ceiling. All of this harmoniously sat on a camel–colored wool sisal rug.

Dr. Bronte went to the bed and grabbed a pillow and one of the blankets.

"Wait," I said. "Why don't you sleep in your own bed? I can take the couch."

"Believe me, the couch will feel like a palace bed compared to how I spent last night," he said, and headed across the room towards the door. "Besides, I don't want you too close to the front door. Should you get the idea to leave during the night, I want you to have to pass me to get to the door. I'm a very light sleeper."

"I thought you said your thugs were outside."

"My *thugs*? Yes, the two men who work for me, Mr. Hyde and Mr. Edwards, are outside. Added precaution." Dr. Bronte put his hand on the doorknob, then turned to face me again. "Pleasant dreams," he said, and started to leave the room.

"Dr. Bronte…" I said, and he stopped. When I said nothing, he turned around. "Why did you take me? I mean, why did you take me like this after all I did for you, after I brought you food, after I cleaned you up… risking everything. Why are you doing this to me?"

He looked to the floor. "I already told you why."

"To get back at Adrian?"

"Yes, there's that. That's partly it."

"What else?"

He brought his eyes off the floor and looked at me. "Good–night, Jamie." He turned to leave.

"Why didn't you take Adrian instead of me?" I asked, then added, "if it was him who you were after."

Bronte stopped. "I had literally less than a second to act. You were right beside me, and…" he turned around and faced me, "you are quite a bit easier to hold than Mr. Adrian North. He would have been most challenging in my weakened state."

Anger hit me. I had no idea why.

"Adrian can take you on your best day."

"Your admiration of my fighting abilities is most flattering, Jamie."

"He can, you know."

"I hope it never comes to that," he said. "Good–night, Jamie."

Dr. Bronte left me alone in his room.

Chapter 31
SUNRISE IN THE EAST

I barely slept. I laid in Bronte's large plush bed, listening to the sea waves in the distance and wondering if I should attempt to leave. Thoughts flooded me. Surely, he would be sleeping soundly after the ordeal he had endured the last twenty-four plus hours. What did I have to lose should I get caught escaping? Dr. Bronte said he wouldn't harm me.

Or would he?

Roughly five hours ago, he had held a knife to my throat and then had rammed the very same knife through poor Grady's hand. Over and over again in my mind's eye, I saw the dark blood cake his fingernails. Tom and Adrian, men whom I loved, believed that our blocked communication was Dr. Bronte's doing. He had kidnapped me. Yet he really hadn't hurt me. And, he was so charming. Kane told me that I could trust this man. Could I?

Oh my God, what if Kane was in on all this?

I would be quiet. I could listen for Bronte's breathing on the couch. Would he wake to the sound of the front door being unlocked? If I successfully made it outside, were his thugs really watching? Or was it a bluff? Dr. Bronte bluffed Adrian, twice. He led Adrian to believe he would kill me if Adrian had overtaken him in the hut. He led Adrian to believe that he was taking liberties with me tonight. What kind of man was Dr. Bronte? He was a man full of lies. Perhaps there were no guards outside in the night. They were most likely sleeping at this hour, anyway.

If I made it outside, the grounds would be wide open, so I'd be quite visible. There would be no place to hide. If Bronte or his thugs were alerted, I would surely be caught in the exposed spread of land. But if not, I could make it to the woods, and then I would be safe. If I heard them coming after me in the woods, I could hide in the brush. Then again, Bronte had a habit of sneaking up on me unheard. How did he do that?

If I was successful, it would be a three-mile hike to Main Campus, to my own bed, to the people I loved.

But oh my God, Adrian and Tom and the others would be so very upset with me. Words like traitor, Benedict Arnold, and betrayal came to mind. They would ask me why I was in the hut with Bronte in the first place, and what would I tell them? They would hate me. I perhaps had lost the only family I ever had since I was nine years old.

With these thoughts, I drifted to sleep, dreaming dark images of red stick men stabbing me with their spears as I lay on a rocky coastal cliff under a Wizard of Oz apple tree, a tree with gnarly arms that grabbed at me. The sky, blackened with evil flying monkeys, as a tornado brewed on the horizon.

I smelled coffee and opened my eyes. Disoriented, the light outside surprised me. I was confused… the window was at a different location, and the room was larger. It dawned on me that this wasn't my cabin. In a flash, I remembered where I was. I heard the light clunking of metal pots and cabinet doors softly shutting in the kitchen. I hurried out of his bed.

I felt ill–at–ease using Dr. Bronte's bathroom, like I was invading his personal space, as if I was being too familiar with him. Glass and counters shined with cleanliness, and I saw more vases with wheat–colored ferns along with jade-colored glass soap holders. Was he really this meticulous? I quickly washed up, using my finger as a toothbrush.

"Good morning," he said without turning around when I walked into the kitchen. Do I say good morning back to a man who held me against my will? When the silence became too awkward, I bid him a good morning, but refused coffee or sliced oranges when he offered. He held out the small plate of oranges a bit too long after I'd said "No thanks," and I saw his un–bandaged raw wrists exposed in the kitchen light.

True to his word, he told me I could go home. I was immediately ready, and feeling somewhat upbeat, I sarcastically told him "it's been nice." I welcomed the thought of a long solitary walk through the morning woods, but he insisted on taking me back most of the way to ensure I would arrive safely. I assured him it wasn't needed, that I was perfectly capable of walking through the woods by myself in the light of day. He insisted, saying to do otherwise was not gentlemanly. I disagreed, I argued, then I lost the argument. We traveled the three-mile stretch on his pony.

"If you had given me the white pony that is rightfully mine, we wouldn't have to share a pony," he said.

"The white pony isn't ready for you," I said.

"You've had ample time to train him for me."

"I don't give you deadlines for your job. Please don't give me deadlines for mine," I said. This made him laugh.

Roughly a hundred yards from our campfire, Dr. Bronte let me off his pony, holding onto my arm as I dismounted. When my feet hit the ground on safe soil, I felt a breeze of freedom, but he held onto my wrist for a few seconds too long. Was he changing his mind on letting me go? I looked up at him, at his bruised and scabbed face, at his light brown hair that shown gold at the ends where the morning sun hit it, at his sad expression. He let me go. I squinted up at him for only a moment longer before I rushed off towards my home.

Chapter 32
JAMIE'S WORLD

I opened the door to Central Lodge. They were all there, my family, seated at their regular spots at the tables in the back of the lodge. Tom was engrossed in conversation with Adrian, Steve, and Grady, who picked at the thick white bandage on his hand. Joel was drawing something on a napkin for Jim and Earl; Jim was nodding and Earl looked confused. Darcy had her arm around Derek, explaining something to him, and she repeatedly pushed Jeremy's head away each time after he leaned it on Derek's head, with Derek laughing and Brian staring at Darcy the whole time. Sheila and the two nurses huddled together, picking at their food with a fork, as Tariq walked about the room, plopping food on people's plates while mumbling irritations.

I took it all in.

Darcy shrieked when she saw me standing at the front door. Conversations ceased as heads turned my way. Darcy stood abruptly, and in doing so, knocked over her chair. Others quickly stood from their chairs, looking at me as if I'd risen from the dead. Tariq yelled at Darcy for knocking the chair over, but she didn't hear him because she was running across the room to me.

She embraced me in a bear hug. I squeezed her back. I then felt hands patting my back, and someone roughed up my hair. When I opened my eyes and turned around, I saw everyone standing around me, everyone except for Tariq, who was wondering what all the fuss was about. And Kane, who wasn't present in the room.

Adrian clasped me by the shoulders and turned me to him, giving me a dead serious look as he leaned down towards me.

"Did he hurt you? Are you hurt?"

I saw Tom, Jim, and Brian aching with concern as they searched my eyes for the answer. Grady was steaming with anger, either at me or at Dr. Bronte, I couldn't tell which, and Earl wouldn't look at me.

"No! No, I'm fine. Really!" Adrian seemed a bit perplexed and looked at Jim, who cocked his head and squinted his eyes at me. "Adrian, are you mad at me?"

"No, Jamie, no. I was sick with worry."

I looked at everyone. "Are you guys mad at me?"

I heard many murmurs to the contrary.

"Dear girl, why should we be mad at you?" the doctor asked.

"*Mad* at you?" Jeremy was bewildered. "I'm fuckin' happy as hell to..." Tom kicked him, hard. "Ahh! Jesus!"

"My nephew... watch your mouth!" Tom said. I saw Derek roll his eyes.

"Jamie, did he... did he..." Darcy asked in my ear.

"No!" I told her.

"You can tell us," Tom, who held Darcy's shoulders, said. "Because if he did, we'll..."

"Tom, are you upset with me?" I asked.

"I'm just glad you're back, safe," Tom said. "We all are."

Derek tugged at my arm sleeve. "They said Dr. Bronte hurt you," Derek said. "How? You seem okay."

"I *am* okay."

"Now that she's back safe let's go kill the bastard," Grady said. "Perhaps we can start by putting knives through parts of his body, particularly one part, then go from there."

"Enough," Adrian said, but he said it quietly, and he put a hand on Grady's shoulder. I wanted to apologize to Grady seeing it was mostly my fault his hand was bandaged, but everyone was talking at once.

"I'm with Grady. I'll come help put the asshole away," Jeremy said.

Grady said, "Boy, you need to eat some spinach before you..."

"Guys, my son," Joel spoke at the same time Grady did, putting his arm around Derek. Joel didn't usually speak up in a crowd.

I looked behind to see who was rubbing my back. It was Brian, looking at me like he wanted to cry. I smiled at him.

"I say we go get him," Earl said, still avoiding looking at me. Why wouldn't he look at me?

"We'll get him," Tom said. "We'll surely…"

With a rush of emotion, Adrian, who was always composed, sprung forward and clutched my head and shoulders to his chest. "I thought you were… damaged beyond... I was so… " We all got quiet seeing Adrian show such emotion like this.

"I'm okay. He didn't do anything bad to me. I'm really okay!" My voice was muffled, coming from his chest.

Then Adrian picked me up a few inches and twirled me around, and I heard some of the others laugh. I felt his familiar muscles, hard as tree bark, and smelled his forest smell, and my mind went back to our late afternoon at the lagoon a week and a half ago. It seemed like a year and a half ago.

They didn't hate me.

When Adrian put me down, Tom swooped me right back up, swinging me around just like Adrian did. I heard laughing, my own laughing blending in with the others. When Tom put me down, I said "No more, please! I'm dizzy."

I saw Adrian talking in whispers with the doctor. They both were looking at me.

"Jamie, let's head to my office, all right?" the doctor said as if I had a scorpion on my foot and he was trying to keep me calm. He put his arm across my shoulder and we headed out the door. The others called out their "byes" and "stop by laters." Earl told me not to forget I had work to do at the stables, and the fact that I was held at knifepoint and kidnapped certainly didn't mean I could slack off.

"She need to eat!" Tariq called out, rushing to us as he held out mie goring with egg on a ladle from a bowl.

"Just prepare a plate and bring it to the Medical building, if you would," the doctor told him. I saw Jim shoot Tom and Adrian a knowing look, as if they shared a secret.

"I not a cater. Wat da matter with her eating here?" Tariq complained. "Wat da' matter with you all?"

"Thank you, Tariq!" Jim called as we went down the stone stairs and onto the dirt clearing.

Chapter 33
INTERROGATION

Jim kept his arm across my shoulder as we walked across Main Campus to the Medical building.

"I'm okay, Jim. He didn't hurt me," I assured him.

"We just want to be sure," Jim said.

Once inside, I stopped at the door.

"Doctor, I'm not getting on the exam table," I said.

"Okay. There's no need for that. I just want to talk." Jim said. "Have a seat." He pointed to the light brown vinyl chair.

"That's your chair!" I said, and pulled another chair over to his. He eased into his chair, crossed his legs, and leaned back, interlocking his fingers and putting them behind his head. He gave me a troubled smile and an extended look, as if I could now truly confide in him. The thing was, I already had.

"Jamie, you need to realize that there's no shame in being victimized, in having someone overpower you."

"I know, I…"

"Please let me finish," he said. "Now, I'm your doctor, and it's very important that you let me know if Dr. Bronte violated you in any way. I need to know for health reasons. Surely you understand this. Remember, there's no shame on your end, none whatsoever. I can keep this confidential if you prefer. Unlike the others, I don't seek retribution. Just physical and mental health."

I sighed. I held my hands out for emphasis, as if holding a big rubber ball. "Jim, really. Nothing happened. I swear. I would tell you. I wouldn't be this calm. He didn't touch me."

Jim looked at me a few more moments, then smiled sincerely.

"I believe you," he said. "Oh thank God, I believe you. Dear

Jamie…" Jim swung his chair left and right to expel some energy. Then he stilled his chair and took a breath. "What exactly happened last night?"

"Well… I'm sure Tom and Adrian told you how Dr. Bronte grabbed me… and Grady's poor hand…"

"Yes, yes, after that."

"Let me see… He took me into the woods." I chose not to tell him about Kane, how Kane allowed me to go with Dr. Bronte. How could they understand and justify Kane when even *I* could not. "His thugs met up with us there in the woods."

"His *thugs*?"

"His guards, or whoever they are," I said. "Jim, those two aren't even in the Jao Employee Profile. What's up with that?"

"I don't know. That's something to discuss with Tom and Adrian," Jim said. "Go on."

"Well…"

Just then the door opened, and Tom entered with Adrian. Jim held up a palm to them, and they stayed quietly by the door.

"Go on."

I now had to be a little more careful with my story. "Dr. Bronte was weak and had to stop a lot to catch his breath."

"Was Dr. Bronte or the guards rough with you? Did the guards hold a gun to you?"

"No. No, they didn't. So I guess I really should have made a run for it, but I was… scared." I looked over at Tom and Adrian, wondering if they'd find fault with me for not running when I had the chance.

"Jamie, look here at me. What happened next?"

"Well, when we reached the research center, his staff was happy to see him. Really, they're kind of like us, how we are together… maybe not quite as warm, but… They were worried about him, concerned when they saw his injuries."

"What happened with *you*? How'd he treat *you*?"

"Fine."

"Jamie…" He exhaled. "What happened next?"

"I don't know. He brought me to his house. I didn't want to go in there, but…" Adrian took a step forward and Jim again held out his hand to stop him. "He said if I tried to leave, his two thugs, the guards, would catch me."

"Those are the same two guards that…" Tom started, but Jim gave him a look and he stopped.

"Jamie," the doctor said and I looked back at him. "Go on."

"Well, Dr. Bronte went off to clean himself up a bit. One of the nurses came by with food and medicine for him."

"Were you tied up?"

"Oh God, no."

"Was he holding you with a knife or a gun, or just holding you?"

"No, nothing like that."

"You were free to move about in his house?"

"Yes."

"Go on."

"Well, he gave me his room to sleep in and he slept on the couch. That's about it."

"That's it?"

"Yeah."

"And you were free to go this morning?"

"Yeah."

We looked at each other with raised eyebrows, then Jim looked over at Tom and Adrian. Jim said "excuse me for a moment" to me, got up and walked over to them, then said something to them in low tones.

"If I may…" Adrian said, and he walked over to me, followed by Tom and Jim. Adrian pulled a chair over as Jim sat back in his vinyl swivel chair. Tom leaned on the counter near us.

"Jamie," Adrian said, "did Bronte say anything about the computers or the supply ship, anything like that?"

"No."

"You two didn't talk at *all* about that?" Adrian asked.

"Well, I asked if he had anything to do with our troubles on the island, and he said no," I said.

"Well of course," Tom said.

"Wait, so Bronte *did* mention the computers." Adrian said.

"Well, yeah, after I asked him about it."

"I see," Adrian said, and Jim creased his eyebrows. "What did you two talk about?"

I started to feel like I was being cross–examined.

"I don't know. I really don't remember."

Adrian and Tom kept looking at me, wanting more from me, and I grew uneasy.

"Nothing important. He mentioned *Crime and Punishment*."

"*Crime and Punishment*?" Adrian asked.

"Hmm?" asked Tom.

"The book," I said. "Never mind."

"I'm aware that it's a book. Why were you discussing it?" Adrian asked.

"I don't know. It was on his shelf."

"So things were a little cordial between you two." Adrian said.

"Yeah, real sweet and friendly!" I said loudly. I stood. "He took me! We didn't have a tea party! I wanted to go home and I…"

"All right, all right," the doctor said. Tom held his forehead. "Adrian –"

"Okay, I'm sorry, I'm sorry." Adrian said. "Just trying to figure out why… why he changed his mind. I'm certainly glad he did, but…" He ran his two palms through his cropped hair.

"He *didn't* change his mind. He never *intended* to harm me," I said. "He only wanted to *scare* you."

"How do you know this?" Adrian asked at the same time Tom spoke.

"He *told* you this?" Tom asked. I nodded.

"So again, Bronte deceived us," Tom told Adrian.

"But he didn't hurt her," the doctor said.

Adrian looked up at him gravely. "He took her from us. He took her against her will, and held her overnight." The doctor nodded and looked to the floor. He sighed.

Adrian leaned forward in his chair. "Jamie, I have to ask." I waited as he fought to find the words, or fought to find the courage to ask. "Why were you in the hut with Bronte?"

Everything stopped. I felt the pulse throb in my neck. Jim changed his weight, and looked stunned. So Jim didn't know! Apparently, Tom, Adrian, and Grady didn't tell the others that I had broken into the hut. I had to answer. I felt like crying.

"I... I couldn't stand to see... him cut up like that, tied up, bruised... you guys didn't even feed him."

The doctor crossed his arms. Adrian leaned way back in his chair and looked off in space. My throat felt like it grew a large solid tumor.

"I'm sorry," I said.

Tom pushed off the counter and crouched down near me. "Jamie, I'm sorry you had to see all that, but you really shouldn't have done what you did. I know your intentions were good, but you jeopardized..."

"I think she realizes this, Tom," the doctor said. "Why don't we wrap up here?"

Adrian brought his focus back to me. "How did you get in the hut?" he asked. I felt water form in my eyes and hoped it wouldn't drip down my cheek.

"Does it really matter now?" the doctor asked.

"I'm afraid it does," Adrian said. "We need to be secure with our keys. Tom, Darcy doesn't have access to any of your keys, does she?"

"Darcy? No." Tom was insulted.

Adrian looked back at me. "Did you get a key from Darcy?"

"No! I didn't use a key to the hut."

"Then how'd you get in?"

"Through the back window."

"There are bars on the windows."

"They're rusted out. Go look."

"How'd you reach the window?"

My eye could no longer hold the water and it fell in a burning line down my face.

"How'd you get in the window?" Adrian asked again. I licked my lips. Then he asked very quietly, "Did you untie him, Jamie?"

I cried in my hands. "I didn't want to! I never intended to! He made me! He said if I didn't, he'd… he'd…" I removed my hands from my face. "I told him he was a monster. I told him you could beat him any time. I told him…"

"But you untied him." I again covered my face with my hands.

"All right, this is enough. Let's end this *now*," the doctor said. "Turning on each other accomplishes nothing."

"I agree, Doctor. I agree." Adrian said, and he stood. "But I'm afraid this is war. When we are blocked from contact with our world, when we are denied supplies and are robbed of all our capital, it's war. It's not what I want, it's not what any of us wants, but it's here. And war is ugly. It's not for the meek to handle. My job is to protect us all, with the help of my team. I can't have… I can't have *this*." He pointed four fingers at me.

"And my job is to protect the physical and mental health of the people on this island," Jim said sternly. "Jamie just returned from…" Jim scratched his head. "I'm going to ask you to leave my patient. Now." He stood, and the Chief of Security looked eye–to–eye with the doctor for several long seconds. Tom nervously looked from face to face at the two men who were squaring off. Adrian finally backed down, breaking the stare, taking a step back.

Water will eventually wear down a hard rock. *"Softness triumphs over hardness, feebleness over strength."*[4] Our meek and mild doctor had triumphed over our Chief of Security.

"I'm sorry doctor," Adrian said. "It seems we're both trying to do our jobs the best way we know how."

"I believe that to be the case," Jim said.

Adrian turned to leave, but not before we both said we were sorry to each other. Tom wiggled his fingertips in my hair before following Adrian to the door. I told Tom I was sorry, too. Tom's only reply was "ditto," and the two men left the Medical building.

"I think a warm cup of strong coffee is in order," Jim said. "What do you think?" I agreed whole–heartedly. He got up to make a fresh pot.

"Jim, all I do on this island is cry. I haven't cried in years, but then I come here to Jackel Island and I just… I cry all the time. I hate it!"

"It's the drugs we're being subjected to," Jim said over his shoulder as he filled the glass container with water. "Everyone's feeling more intense, but it affects each person differently." Jim pulled out a paper coffee filter. "Grady came in here asking for a 'sex–nullifier' drug. Said he couldn't focus."

"I think you just breeched doctor–patient confidentiality."

"I think I may have done just that." He turned to me and chuckled as the coffee brewed.

"What's a 'sex–nullifier' drug?"

"Don't ask."

"Did it work?"

"No."

As Jim walked over to sit in his treasured tan vinyl swivel chair next to me, Brian banged in the door, bringing me Henry! Henry had a

---

[4]Lao–Tsu

conniption fit when greeting me, all tongue and tail and jumps. I let him lick my face as if my skin were honey, and I scrumpled my hand all over his fur. I held his wiggly face between my hands and kissed him between the eyes.

"Who took care of Henry?" I asked, losing my fingers in his fur.

"Little Man." Brian told me.

"Derek?"

"Yeah."

"'Cause I wasn't sure if you meant Jeremy." I smiled, and put Henry on the floor.

"Ooh! Verbal attack!" Brian said. "No, I meant Derek, the *other* Little Man. Derek took care of Henry this morning, though he slept with Kane last night."

"*Derek* slept with *Kane*?"

"No! *Henry* slept with Kane!"

"How'd that happen?" I asked.

"I don't know… ask Henry. Ask Kane."

"That'd be like asking a tree why it grows."

Brian got up to bring me something in a picnic basket (Tariq!), and when I stood to get it, Brian grabbed me in a tight one–armed bear hug and twirled me around in a circle, my feet skimming the ground. I wailed, and I heard the doctor, who was getting coffee, laugh. Henry gave puppy barks of excitement.

"Had to give you round three!" Brian said, and put me down. "Gee, I was so worried about you! Love you."

"Love you too. But enough already!" I saw Jim smile as he looked down into his coffee and stirred.

"I was scared that Dr. Bronte really hurt you," Brian said.

"If he tried, I'd kick his ass."

"Yeah, from all those *breathing* exercises Adrian taught you," Brian said. "All you'd have to do is give him a Ninja chi–breath. He'd be at your mercy."

"Yeah, right."

"Here's breakfast from Tariq," Brian said as he handed me the picnic basket. He sat down looking at the doctor and me. When Jim and I said nothing and I didn't eat, and when the three of us were just looking at each other, Brian slapped his hands on his thighs and announced he should leave.

"Come visit me at the stables later," I told him as he went through the door.

"Sure thing!"

As I had breakfast and coffee with the doctor, we told each other of our earliest memories of playful food fights in our elementary classrooms back home.

Chapter 34
THE BLACK VULTURE

Jeremy sat on the steps at Central Lodge with a big blue bowl between his knees, pinching off spinach, one leaf at a time. Brian leaned against the stair's railing with his fists jammed in his pockets, whistling, and Darcy leaned on the opposite railing twirling Jeremy's tin whistle in her hands. Both looked amused.

"What is this, a game of Monkey in the Middle?" I asked as I walked up to them. I had come to Central Lodge to return my breakfast plate before heading off to the stables.

"Ha–Ha, very funny," Jeremy said.

"What are you doing?" I asked.

"Tariq's making him pull off the stems of each spinach leaf for complaining about stems in the salad," Darcy said with a grin.

"Why don't you guys help me?" Jeremy pleaded.

"'Cause you're doing just fine by yourself, buddy," Brian said.

"Oh, go eat another donut!" Jeremy said. Henry put his nose near the bowl, and Jeremy gently pushed him away.

"Gee Jare, it looks like there's over a thousand spinach leaves," I said, leaning forward towards the bowl.

"Gee Jame, maybe it'd go *faster* if you were to *help* me." Jeremy said.

"Gee Jare, I just can't do that right now. I'm in a delicate state having just been kidnapped." Darcy high–fived me. Henry kind of barked.

"Ooh, you work it, Girl, play it for all it's worth!" Darcy said.

"I bet even Bronte didn't have you de–stem spinach leaves." Jeremy sounded pitiful.

"Nope. Can't say that he did," I said.

Joel appeared and he hopped up the steps with a pad of paper in his hand. He didn't notice Henry wagging at him.

"What are you doing there, Jeremy?" Joel asked.

"Nothing," Jeremy said. Darcy and Brian laughed.

"Hmm." Joel said, puzzled, but only for a second. He then went on inside.

"Listen guys, don't say anything to anyone," Jeremy pleaded.

"Yeah, like you told everyone about Mr. Dody," I said.

"Who's Mr. Dody?" Jeremy asked.

Just then Tom appeared. He bent to pet Henry. "What's going on?" he asked.

"Nothing," Jeremy said loudly. Brian looked to the sky and whistled more loudly. Darcy did the same. Then I followed suit.

"You all need to just shut up," Jeremy said.

"We didn't say a word," Darcy said, and she, Brian and I laughed.

Tom shook his head and went on into the lodge.

Kane was chopping wood in his regular spot in the woods behind my cabin, and it was only yesterday when his arm was shot. Jim had said that the bullet only breezed his arm, but still… If I stopped to speak with Kane, I'd be even more late getting to the stables, but figured Earl would only fuss for just a little bit.

"If you stayed on this island for five more years, there'd be no more trees left," I told Kane as he balanced a log on a tree stump. He showed no sign that he heard me. "Make that two more years," I added as he gripped his ax. He looked to the sky but not at me. "Kane I'm kidding. I don't know if you know that I'm just kidding, but I'm… kidding." It was then I heard and saw the elang bondol raptor bird come into view. Kane and I watched it soar until it went out of sight behind the trees.

"Thank you for watching Henry."

"Henry?" I pointed down at Henry by his feet. Something about Kane's shoelaces intrigued my dog, but Henry became even more intrigued when he saw Kane's mouse peep his head out of his pocket, a height Henry couldn't reach. Kane let his ax fall on the log. Henry darted away in fear. "A puppy should never sleep alone."

"Words to live by. Kane, I came to ask you a favor." Kane turned to me. I sat on a nearby log, watching Henry forget about his fear and return right back to Kane. He jumped up on Kane's leg with total focus on his pocket. "Henry's collar is getting too tight. Can you make him a new one?" Kane looked down at the dog and nodded. "I mean, I see you carving with your knives and skinning animals, so I figure you're crafty like that. Do you mind?" Kane shook his head and turned his focus to his ax and the log.

"Kane?" Kane, who had his ax full peak in the air, stopped what he was doing and calmly looked at me again. Anyone else would have been annoyed at the interruption. "Are you friends with Dr. Bronte?" He brought his ax high in the air and let it fall again. Once more, Henry bolted. "I hate when you don't answer me," I said, and he sniffed the air, wiping his nose with his hand. He turned to look at me. "I know, I know… I'm too verbal." Henry retuned to Kane's leg. "I mean, how did you know that Dr. Bronte wouldn't harm me?"

"If I was not completely sure, I would not have allowed you to be with him."

"But how did you know?" Kane positioned another log on the base. "Did you two talk?" He raised his ax in the air. "How did you know?"

"How come you did not?" he asked, and the ax fell.

I got Brian up on the white pony! It was the first time anyone but me was able to mount him. The white pony took to Brian like syrup to pancake.

"That damn beast will let anyone on 'em except for real men," Earl snarled as he walked by us in the paddock, carrying grain in a burlap bag. He headed for the barn.

"I love you too, Earl!" Brian said from the saddle.

"He's just jealous because this pony still won't let Earl near him," I said. I didn't know if the white pony would ever trust Earl, but the fact that he let Brian mount him showed that he would most likely allow Dr. Bronte to mount him as well.

"I'm afraid this animal is now ready for Dr. Bronte." I said. "Looks like I'm going to lose him."

"Yeah, but if you kidnap the horse trainer, you lose your riding rights," Brian said.

"I like that. I'll go with that."

"So now the white pony is yours. Problem solved," Brian said as he started to quickly dismount, spooking the pony.

"Easy! Easy! Move slowly with him."

Intuitively, Brian stayed quiet on the animal until both were calm, then he gently dismounted, patting the pony after his feet hit ground.

"Jamie, can I ask you something?"

"Hmm?" I handed the reins to Brian and we started to walk around the paddock's perimeter. I wanted the pony to get used to someone else leading him.

"Do I really seem gay?"

"I don't know, but what does it matter, Brian?"

"It really bothers me," he said. "A lot."

"You're just more in touch with how you feel. No offense, but most guys are clueless. I mean, look at Jeremy."

"Am I like... super weird?"

I looked out at the mountains beyond the paddock, mountains that gave background like a stage backdrop, mountains that formed a barrier between the woods and the sea. "Brian, who isn't weird? Name one person on this island who isn't weird in their own way."

"Well, we can rule out Jeremy," he said.

"And Tariq," I said.

"Git out ah da way!" Brian mimicked.

"And Earl," I said.

"Howdee Cowboy!" Brian said in a John Wayne voice. "Go clean the muck outa' dem dar stables!"

"Grady! Do Grady!"

"Hey there, little Missy!" Brian shot up his eyebrows in three quick successions. I laughed at Brian's attempt to be seductive. He looked more like Pee Wee Herman.

"What about Sheila and Company?" I asked.

"Ooohey Ooohey," Brian said in an exaggerated girly–girl tone.

"What about Kane? Is he weird?"

"*Very* weird, the weirdest one on the island."

"But very cool too," I said.

"Yes, very cool."

"See! *Every*one's weird!"

"Except Jim and Derek."

"Yeah, well okay. They're the only two on the island who aren't weird."

"And Darcy… she's not weird," Brian said.

"Are you kidding me? Little Miss Fireball? I love her like a sister, but she may even be weirder than *I* am."

"Not really."

"Shut up!"

Earl came out from the barn and yelled for me to quit yakking and get to work, that this wasn't social hour. I told him I needed Brian to help tame the white pony. Earl snarled, then focused on his work.

"Jamie, do you think we'll ever make it off this island?"

"I do. I really do. I don't know how, but I think we will."

"I'm not so sure," Brian said. "I mean, at home, everyone thinks we're all *dead*!"

"When we get our communications back, we'll fix that."

"*If* we get our communications back."

"I just don't know why there's all these secrets," I said. "Why doesn't the security team tell us stuff? I mean, we're big boys and girls. Why all the secrecy?"

"Isn't government like that?"

Brian and I stopped talking when Tom and Grady walked towards us, an odd sight, considering Tom rarely came to the stables, and I rarely saw Tom and Grady together without Adrian. Grady came often enough to ride his pony. We said our hellos and gave a little bit of small talk, but something specific was on their mind.

"Brian, do you mind if we talk with Jamie?" Tom asked.

"God, that's twice today when I'm dismissed," Brian said, and he headed out to the fields towards Main Campus.

"What the hell is this, cocktail hour?" Earl called over from the fence.

"This is important, Earl," Tom called out. "We need to discuss something with Jamie for a little bit."

"If there's a bartender anywhere near, order me a beer!" Grady hollered.

Earl opened his mouth and looked like he was going to yell back something nasty, but then looked agreeable, making his eyes big and closing his mouth. "A shot of Jack would be more like it," he said as he dumped grain in the feed buckets.

"Ha! Good man!" Grady smiled big.

Brian, attempting to fit in with the guys, turned to us and yelled "And order me a Margarita!"

"Oh Jesus!" Grady said under his breath.

"Jamie, come over here with us for a second," Tom said. The three of us walked to the far end of the paddock, and we leaned against the fence. Tom gave me a serious hard look. The humor was even gone from Grady's face, which always scared me.

"Look, Grady, I'm really sorry about your hand," I said. "I truly am. I know I had something to do..."

Tom held up his hand at me. "We're not here to talk about Grady's hand." I looked square at Tom, cocking my head. "I'll get right to the point. We need information. We were very close to breaking Bronte down and finding out how to get our communication back with the States, and set things right."

"But that just didn't happen," Grady said.

"Look, I'm sorry! I…"

"What's done is done," Tom said. "What we need now is…"

"Just have a beer with me, little lady, and all is forgiven."

"Grady!" Tom said. I sighed and looked back at Tom. "What we need now is to get information from Bronte, to know what he knows."

"Okay," I said with trepidation. "I don't follow you. What's this have to do with me? Are you planning to kidnap him again?"

"That's an appealing option," Grady said, raising his eyebrows at Tom. "I got voted down on that one." Grady scorned Tom.

"Grady, enough!" Tom said quickly, then looked back to me again. "It'd be difficult to grab him while he and his guards are now alerted. But we'll fall back on that if our initial plan doesn't work."

"Initial plan?" I asked.

"That's where you fit in," Grady said. I heard Adrian's black Java pony neigh, and a jasmine breeze washed over us, but I remained fixed on Tom and Grady.

"Bronte didn't harm you," Tom said. "He's already proven that. Grady, Steve and I are sure of it."

"*Steve's* in on this?" I asked.

"Yes, he agrees with Grady and me," Tom said.

"What about Adrian?" I asked.

"Here we go!" Grady said looking up at the mountains.

"Listen," Tom said as he held out his fingers to me. "We need you to go visit with Bronte, get familiar with him, gain his confidence, find out what you can."

"Are you kidding me?"

"No, we're dead serious," Tom said. Grady raised his eyebrows and nodded.

"How am I supposed to do that?"

"Find any excuse to go visit with him," Tom said.

"I have no excuse to see him. None what–so–ever," I said.

"Find one," Grady said. "Hell, a girl like you trotting over... he'll appreciate it, unless he's gay."

"Grady..." Tom said with annoyance.

"Man, Grady!" I said. "Tom, I work with *horses*, not with James *Bond*. I can't do this!"

"Yes you can! You have to!" Tom said. "We very much need this, Jamie. Please help us. There's little risk to you."

"Are you kidding?" I said loudly. "He'll see through me. He's got a M.D. in psychiatry."

"Don't let that happen," Tom said.

"Oh, okay," I said in a mocked cartoon voice.

"See, she may screw this up," Grady said. "I say we just take the slimy bastard. Our team with you, your brother, even Earl... put Kane in with us, if we can get him to come. Bronte and his two apes don't stand a chance."

"Grady, we voted!" Tom said slowly, shutting his eyes. "Jamie, you can do this."

"Be coy. You women are good at that," Grady said.

"Shut up, Grady," I said. "Tom, I'm not good at this. Bronte will wonder what I'm doing."

"He'll just think you're visiting him," Tom said. "The only risk might be getting caught when you're looking through his notebook. So just... be careful. See to it that you don't get caught."

"Oh, now you want me to look through his notebook *too*?"

"Yeah, we do."

"Oh wow," I said, and I slumped down, sitting on the dirt and scattered hay, leaning against the fencepost. Some kind of black vulture flew in a large circle in the sky. I watched him, and wondered about all this. Tom sat down next to me. I looked out in the middle of the paddock and saw Earl once again attempt to approach the white pony. The white pony wasn't so forgiving.

"Will you do this for us?" Tom asked.

"Tom…" His face was kind, beseeching. "I'll think about it. That's the best I can do."

"That's all I can ask," Tom said. "There's one more thing." He brought his knees up, interlocking his fingers around them. "Adrian's not exactly warm to this idea."

"What do you mean?"

"Let's just say… he's not to know. In fact, no one's to know except for the three of us, and Steve."

"Oh, great," I said.

"It's our little secret," Grady said with a creepy grin.

I worked the rest of the morning at the stables, going through the motions of scrubbing the water bucket, cleaning the saddle, spreading hay, and sweeping out the barn. My mind was beyond the paddock, the woods, the mountains, the east side of the island… beyond the sea, turning over and over, trying desperately to decide whether or not I should be a damn spy.

A damn spy.

During my lunch break, I stopped behind my cabin to look at Derek's garden of lifeless signs of life – a bird's nest, a conch, fossils, disintegrating snakeskin held under a rock where it blew in the wind like tissue paper… Each item had held life. Each life had moved on.

At lunch, Tom announced that the results of the blood work would be ready tomorrow, and this would determine whether or not we were being human guinea pigs for some biological test. I saw Jeremy cross his arms and run his fingertips up and down his upper arms. What foreign matter was inside us?

I passed Steve by the water fountain and he seemed preoccupied. He didn't acknowledge me in the slightest, except when I was almost completely past him, I saw him looking at me out of the corner of his eye with a stern expression.

I avoided looking at Tom or Grady because I had not yet decided whether or not I would, or could, help them. I wanted to support our side, but sincerely didn't know if I could pull this off. I also had mixed emotions about Dr. Bronte. Signs surely pointed to his guilt at hijacking our island – his computers worked while ours did not; he lied to me about who he was when I first met him; he lied to the others about his computer working; we seemed to be human subjects in some kind of biological test; only *he* knew what bio-CMAT truly stood for while our team was lied to regarding its true meaning; he had secret profiles of our department heads in a notebook he hid in his lab; his low regard for us demonstrated multiple times in various ways... by turning off our electricity to prove his point, impaling a knife through Grady's hand, not to mention kidnapping me. One should read red flags, and a fleet of flags was waving here, blaring a flashing brilliance, parading blood red. Yes, I should betray this man without any guilt. Yet, why did my heart go out to this villain, a villain who Kane said wouldn't harm me, a dangerous man who could also be so charming? Was I such a fool who could so easily be completely played?

Adrian stood next to me at the drink counter and we said our polite hellos. When I looked at him a little too long, he asked "What?", to which I answered "Nothing!" All the while, I could detect Tom's eyes on us like a hawk.

Back at the stables for the rest of the afternoon, I lost myself in my chores.

Dinners had not been the same since the supply ship hadn't arrived six days ago. Gone was the convivial static and loud laughter that had once filled the lodge's walls. We weren't yet on rations, but servings were only a little more than meager. I sneaked some of my food to

Brian, who seemed to need it more than I.

Our campfires weren't the same either. Before, they were carefree and upbeat. Now, they were strained and somewhat tense, and we were trying to force our former happiness.

The next day came, Friday the thirteenth, the day we were waiting for. This was the day the test results for the blood work were in. Tom somberly announced at breakfast that the results came back positive. There were indeed contaminants in the blood of Tom, Adrian, Grady, Steve, and Joel, foreign chemicals in their veins, which meant impurities within the fiber of each of us. The thought of a possible poison within the core of my being, adulterants infesting within the hull of my gut, toxins within the nucleus of my lifeblood, made me want to crawl out of my skin and run.

It was then I decided to visit Dr. Evan Bronte under false pretenses.

Chapter 35
GETTING INSIDE

The next morning, I rode through the woods towards the east side of the island where the land spread and unfolded allowing more sunlight, and where the sea grew rougher revealing rocky cliffs and bouldered earth which shielded the research center from the harsh sea. I played the scenario out in my head. I would knock on Dr. Bronte's door. If he didn't shut the door in my face, he'd ask what it was I wanted. He'd be skeptical. Why would I return to a man who kidnapped me? My plan was to tell him that I came to establish peace between our two sides. Maybe that was even the truth. At that point, he'd most likely tell me to take a hike, in which case, I'd ride back to our west side, and our plan would be one of failure. If he decided to hear me out, I would have to tell him *how* I planned to create peace between us. That was where things were a little hazy in my head. I would tell him it would be no easy task, but our attitudes would have to change, and we'd have to establish regular and cordial communications, for starters. I wondered how Geneva did this.

Tom and Grady thought that this plan would initially get me in to see Dr. Bronte, but told me to work on building his trust and establishing some kind of feigned friendship with him for repeated visits. What I didn't tell Tom or Grady was that I was sincerely going to work on establishing peace for both sides. What I wasn't going to tell Dr. Bronte was that Tom and Grady were in on this, and that I was trying to get information from him to discover the truth for myself.

I passed the vast east field where the przewalski horses grazed. I stopped the white pony and looked over the field, golden with swaying straw–like foliage. When I saw no signs of the herd, I rode on.

I stopped my pony at the black iron fence that encircled the research center, dismounted, and tried the gate. It was locked. It surprised me how quickly the two thugs appeared, pounding the dirt as they came from the ocean side of the center. For a moment, I considered getting back on the white pony and heading back, but they were at the gate before I could think it through. The meaner looking thug pounded numbers on the gate's keypad and loudly opened the gate with harsh metal clunking, and motioned for me to come in. Their faces were hard.

"It's okay, I'll come back later," I said.

"It's not an option," the mean thug said, and reached for me, pulling me inside by my upper arm. When the gate slammed shut, I jumped.

"My pony…"

"The animal stays here," the other thug said, and he reached for the rein and quickly tied it too tightly to the gate. The meaner thug patted around my waist and socks, and then got slightly too familiar for my comfort. When I brushed his arm off me, he roughly swatted at my hand with a force that made me shudder. I thought of the apple tree in the Wizard of Oz when a tree roughly grabbed Dorothy – my recent dream.

"Clean," said the thug to the other.

They allowed me to see Dr. Bronte, but I couldn't go unescorted. I felt my chest tighten as they led me to his cottage. Thugs were not in my plan.

Dr. Bronte opened the door, holding a pen and paper with chemical equations scribbled on it. He was dressed in tan khakis and a dark blue button–down shirt, and his mouth parted slightly when he saw me. For a second, I was at a loss for words.

"Jamie Ella!" he said, and I wondered how he knew my middle name. It was not listed on the Jao profile.

"She's clean, Sir," Thug number one said.

"That'll be all, thank you." Dr. Bronte told them, and the air got a little fresher after the two of them left. "Sorry about the frisk, Jamie. They were simply doing as instructed. I suppose our hackles are up on both sides. Please, come in."

'Please come in'? I didn't expect this congeniality.

Nervously, I entered his living room. He invited me to have a seat. "Coffee?" he asked. I thought of Jim.

"No thank you."

"To what do I owe the pleasure of your unexpected visit?" He sat on the couch, placing an ankle on his knee and his arm on the back of the couch. I saw that his wrist wasn't quite as raw from the ropes that tied him four days ago, and his wounds were scabbing over. The surrounding skin was still an angry red.

To tell him I came seeking peace just didn't sound right.

"Well, I'm trying to establish... some kind of truce here between us."

"Between you and me?" He seemed amused.

"No! Between your department and ours."

"Oh, really? How do you hope to accomplish this?"

"Me? I can't accomplish this by myself. It's up to you and Tom and our Security team. You're the ones who are feuding so terribly."

"I see. So why have *you* come here? I mean, why you? What is your part in this?"

"Well, hopefully I can arrange for you all to meet with each other, though making peace with Grady... that'll be a hard one."

"And why should I do this?" Dr. Bronte interlocked his fingers and put them behind his head. His body language was very open and overly confident.

"Ah –" I said in exasperation. "Don't you want things better between us?"

"Define better."

He was being difficult. I looked at the ceiling and tapped my leg with my index finger, thinking. "Peaceful," I said, looking back down at him. "Don't you want things more peaceful between us?"

"Between you and me?" He looked as if he were having fun with all this and wasn't taking me seriously at all.

"Stop it!"

He grew serious and removed his hands from behind his head. "Did your security team put you up to this?" Did he know?

"Adrian doesn't even know I'm here."

Dr. Bronte sighed. "Jamie Ella Robinson… Peacemaker."

"How do you know my middle name?"

"Oh, I know all about you," he said as he slowly shook his head.

"You don't really know me."

"Oh, but I do!"

"You don't know me, other than what I've told you, other than what you read on my employee profile."

"Well you see… that's not entirely true," Dr. Bronte said, still shaking his head. "Let me see… with the exception of fourth grade when you moved in with your Aunt and Uncle, you made very good grades. You did exceptionally well in mathematics and English, which is rare because most people lean one way or the other with those two polar subjects. You were pretty much a loner in school, spending time with your studies and your work training animals." I looked at him with cold amazement. "Early on, your Aunt voiced some concern when you had an imaginary friend immediately following your parents' death, which can be expected when a child…"

"Wait a minute, how…"

"…when a child experiences such a monumental loss. Later on, when you were fifteen, you had a small local business, training dogs and horses. You did not attend your High School Prom. You…"

"How did you know that? How do you know all this?" He held up his hand.

"…you went to Colby College, a fairly accredited school though I personally believe you could have done better, Jamie."

"What do you mean? Colby's rated very..."

"You chose a local school so you could continue training your horses. You joined no clubs or organizations in college, engaged in no extracurricular activities, didn't frequent the college bars, and had the same boyfriend, a Daniel Larrabee I believe, for three out of the four years you attended Colby. Other than this boy, you pretty much kept to yourself. You earned a 3.6 grade average. Good job, Jamie!"

"*How* do you know all *this*?" I was astonished. And angry.

He held up one finger so I would allow him to finish. "However, you are a bit of an underachiever. Getting paid to train horses is fine, but again, you can do better, don't you think? Consider utilizing your mathematical abilities... you would yield much higher financial results."

"I suppose you know my annual salary on the job I had before Jao."

"Yes I do."

"I wasn't serious, Dr. Bronte."

"I am," he said, and he stood and walked to the fireplace. "After college, you lived alone. You chose a modest apartment at the edge of town on Utterson Street. You lived there for almost a year until you upgraded to the small but quaint house you now rent on Hastie Lane, or *did* rent... Anyway, besides work and training horses, you do little else other than read. Your activity at the local library is quite heavy. I find your selection of books quite interesting, especially your interest in the classics, Taoist thought and the idea of balance. You have minimal contact with your Aunt and Uncle, if any, and you..."

"All right, enough!"

Dr. Bronte turned to me. "Heavens, did I upset you? I'm sorry." He adjusted a candlestick on his fireplace mantle. "So you see, Jamie, I *do* know you. You said I don't, but I most surely do."

"You just may be even creepier than Grady!"

He played further with the candlestick. "I don't care to discuss Grady Galinger," he said, and went towards the kitchen. "Are you sure I can't interest you in a cup of coffee? I'm getting one for myself."

Without waiting for my answer, he went in the kitchen, and I followed him. I was festering over his invasion into my personal life and didn't want to stew on it alone in his living room. I needed to throw some verbal injury his way to abate my own. I leaned on the refrigerator watching him spoon coffee grains into a filter. I folded my arms tightly across my chest.

"That stuff was personal," I said through my teeth.

"Oh?" He continued to add spoonfuls of coffee into the filter. His playful tone after his encroachment made me boil, but I kept my voice calm and even.

"I know a *lot* of very personal stuff about *you*," I said, forcing my voice to remain steady and not quiver with anger. I was not going to hold back. I was going to give it to him full throttle. I saw him pause, if only for a half second, and this brought me mild satisfaction. He then calmly added the last teaspoon of coffee into the filter and slid it into the coffee pot.

"You do?" His voice was overly upbeat as if talking to a toddler, which caused my boiling blood to bubble. He turned to me and leaned against the kitchen island with his hands in his pockets, looking amused.

"Well, let me see..." I began, looking at the ceiling. "You got excellent grades in elementary school, because... well... all you did was study. You had no life." He smiled. "In fact, you had no friends. In High School, no one would be friends with you because word got around that you killed a cat." His smile faded a bit and his eyes were still. "You killed all your girlfriends' puppies and kittens because... because you're a jealous guy." Bronte removed his hands from his pocket and slowly crossed them over his chest. We both stood cross–armed and glarred at each other. "You could have done better socially, don't you think? But you just didn't."

"Jamie..." He said softly, looking at the floor.

"Let me finish." I said in a high tone, sarcastically, holding one finger up at him. "You're very accomplished, scientifically speaking, but only scientifically speaking. In science you get an A+. In human decency, you get a D minus." Bronte sighed as he continued to stare at the floor. He opened his mouth to say something, but I cut him off, uncrossing my arms and using my hands for emphasis. "You get a D minus in human decency because you lie about who you are!" He gave a one–beat air laugh and looked up at me, looking sad. "You lie about your research computers being down when they're really working, and you lie about what bio-CMAT means." His face changed as if he'd received a small electric shock in his chin. He uncrossed his arms. I realized my mistake immediately, but the only thing I could do was continue, and hopefully blow over my error. "You kill our computers, our phones... stop our supplies from reaching us..." he shook his head, "...you freeze our assets, you let everyone think we're dead..."

"No, Jamie..."

"And then you biologically insert *things* in us!" I hadn't realized that I was yelling. My words were still in the air, and they stung. After some time of looking at each other in confusion, my eyes went to the floor. More time passed until he softly spoke.

"Jamie, why are you here?"

I clasped my hands together and put my two fists on my forehead. "I don't know," I whispered.

"This isn't exactly the best way to establish a truce with me."

I had to laugh, letting out some tension. I slid to the floor and brought my knees up to my chest. He moved closer to me, but remained standing.

"I think you misunderstood me," he said. "I wasn't attacking you earlier. I didn't find anything about your past... distasteful. I never cared much for loud or popular people and always preferred the quiet loners. I meant no insult to you or your past."

"You were toying with me," I said, barely moving my mouth.

He exhaled loudly. "I suppose I was a bit, but not in a cruel way, I assure you."

I picked at my fingernails. "You knew such private things about me!"

"Jamie, I'm in research. That's what I do. I know even more details about all the top staff here on the island," he said. "About you, I was simply… curious."

I wanted to apologize but didn't know how. "I can be full of venom," I said.

"That you can." He smiled.

"So how'd it go?" Grady asked me.

"Horribly,"

Grady sat on his brown Batak pony as the animal side stepped on the wood's path. Grady had a hard time keeping his animal still, holding the reins too tightly. I rested firmly in the saddle on the stationary white pony. We were near the campfire.

"Hey, ease up on the reins!"

"He's not on to you, is he?" Grady asked as his pony lifted her head and backed up a few steps.

"No, but I told Bronte that he had no life, no friends, and that he's a liar and a puppy killer."

"You said all that to him?" Grady smiled as he jerked the reins, and I feared his animal was going to raise her front feet.

"And more. I told him he was the jealous type who lacked human decency. I told him he was guilty of everything wrong that's occurring here on the island."

"Way to go to build trust and establish peace, little Chica!" Grady said. "We don't need rifles, we have you!"

"You really need to loosen your reins."

Grady eased up on the reins slightly, but not enough. His pony calmed down somewhat.

"Did you get the notebook?" he asked.

"I wasn't even in the lab."

"Well, find a way to get in there."

"That'll be really hard."

"We didn't say this would be easy," Grady said. "You now have three reasons to visit Bronte again." I raised my eyebrows at him. "One, we need that notebook. Two, you need to warn him that Adrian's coming for him tomorrow night."

Grady filled me in on details. Naturally, Adrian needed to act, unaware that we already were. Grady and Tom had been subtly putting Adrian off as long as they could, but were no longer able to, because Adrian was ultimately responsible for our safety. I was instructed to warn Bronte of this ambush under the condition that Bronte would not harm Adrian, or anyone else riding with him. "Including yours truly," Grady added. I was to talk to Tom for further instructions.

"What's the third reason?" I asked. "You said there were three."

"You also should really apologize to Bronte for calling him a puppy killer."

Chapter 36

WORLD OF SILENCE

The next morning, I rode out to the east side of the island, filled with trepidation and dread. I did not want to face Bronte or his thugs, but I *did* need to warn him about Adrian's approach tonight, whether it be a sincere warning, or part of my betrayal.

I remembered "Mission: Impossible" and other spy shows I watched as a child, but what they never revealed was how afraid and guilty the spy may have felt, and how perhaps the spy may have had humane feelings towards the person they were deceiving.

I rode over two miles through the woods to where the clearing opened up to the vast meadow. I stopped the white pony at the edge of the woods and looked out to the gold field before me.

I was surprised to see Dr. Bronte about fifty yards out.

He stood tall next to his off–white pony, watching the wild horses in the distance well beyond both of us. It was fortunate I didn't have to face his thugs at the research gate for my visit this time. This meeting would be on neutral territory.

I noiselessly dismounted and tied my pony to a tree. As quietly as I could, I walked across the field towards Dr. Bronte's back, figuring it was my turn to sneak up on him. I was careful not to rustle the barley straw as I crept through the meadow, moving only when there was a breeze. When I was not even twenty feet from him, he said "Hello, Jamie," without turning around. I stopped abruptly, but only momentarily. I then walked normally up to him, swishing through the pasture's weeds.

I stood next to him, and together, we watched the wild horses beyond us. One horse rolled on his back in the bristly grass. I recognized the horse I had freed exactly two weeks ago today, the young stallion that got his leg caught in the log, the horse I touched, human contact with the wild. I watched him nuzzle the neck of another horse the way I'd seen him do many times in the past.

"Hopefully, this visit will be a bit more pleasant than the last," Dr. Bronte said, still not turning to me. I gave a small chuckle. "Are you here to finally give me my white pony?"

"No, afraid not."

"So why the visit?" He looked down at me, but I kept my gaze on the animals in the field, and after a few moments, he turned his head to watch them too. I recognized the horse who frequently trotted with a pleasant bounce as he mingled with his peers. This stallion always amused me.

"I came to warn you about something, and to apologize about something."

One horse lifted his muzzle and emitted a loud and lazy neigh. These wild animals were family to one another, comfortable with each other, and didn't worry about being cut off from any other living thing. They had each other, and that was enough for them.

"I'm listening."

I looked up at him. "I'm sorry I called you a cat killer, Dr. Bronte."

He laughed. "Is that all you're sorry about?" He looked at me.

"No."

I looked back at the animals. The przewalskis had no need for supply ships, as they received all they needed from Jackel Island. This island fed and nourished them, sustained and nurtured them until all they knew was the moment, never hoarding, never worrying, never planning or scheming. They felt no threat of betrayal among each other. They had no concept of war. Threat came from outside predators, never from within. Their world was a vastly different one from our own.

"What did you come to warn me about?"

"If I tell you, can you promise one thing?"

"Perhaps."

"Promise me you won't hurt Adrian, or any of my friends."

"Ha, well that depends," Dr. Bronte said. "I will defend myself, if need be."

"Can't you defend yourself without hurting them?"

"Jamie, what did you come to warn me about?"

"Your word first." I said. "Or I won't warn you."

"For heaven's sake, you drive a hard bargain," he smiled.

"You always say *heavens*. Only old British men in bad gothic movies say *heavens*."

"Is that a fact?" he asked. "I'll tell you what. I'll resort to injuries as the absolute last result. I always do."

"Listen, I really don't want anyone hurt at *all*, okay? That means no blood, no bruises, not even a paper cut. Okay?" I said. "I don't want anyone hurt."

"I don't either."

"Okay then."

Taking a deep sigh, I slid down to sit in the field, letting the tall grass hide me among its wisps. Dr. Bronte leaned against his pony, facing me. I proceeded to tell him about Adrian's plan to ambush him tonight, and as I did, heavy feelings of disloyalty and unfaithfulness pecked at me. I wondered what I was honestly doing to Adrian. It only gave me mild comfort knowing that Grady, Tom, and Steve had initiated this plan of action. In their minds, my revealing this information was a way to ensure trust between Bronte and me, so he would be more apt to impart information to me. In my mind, it was a way to prevent either Bronte or Adrian from getting hurt.

"Why are you telling me all this?" he asked. "This surprises me, that you reveal this to me."

"Well, maybe because I don't want you *killed*." I said, as if it were blaringly obvious, phrasing my words to the tone of a question. I picked off a long weed and ran my finger along it. "Also, maybe because I'm a real jerk," I said under my breath, staring at the weed in my hand.

"Hm, they won't be able to kill me." Dr. Bronte sat in the grassy field between his pony and me. "As to the latter, I don't believe that to be the case."

We watched the horses in silence for what seemed to be about twenty minutes. There weren't many people with whom I felt I could be silent and still feel comfortable. Brian was one. I used to be able to enjoy silence with Adrian when he trained me in the field between the stables and the woods behind my cabin, and when we used to ride together along the sea. But now there seemed to be a rift between us, a barrier like there was between the east and the west here on Jackel Island. Kane existed in silence and serenity, breathing, moving and living in a peaceful stillness, and he let the world around him fill him with color and vitality. Earl and I often worked along side each other at the stables without saying anything, but we had the chores to fill the space between us, and without the chores, we'd fill the gap with chatter, or would go on about our business independently. I never enjoyed silence with Earl, though he was a man of the earth. Darcy was a chatterbox and we would ramble on and on. Besides his whistle that calmed him, Jeremy was also filled with words. Joel and Steve kept to themselves, and didn't allow anyone into their world of silence. Tom and Grady were filled with words, but I suspected they spent their quiet times only with themselves. Tom perhaps shared this serene time with Darcy, if she would ever be verbally still enough to listen. Derek wasn't filled with words, but was filled with the wonders of the island, always showing me a starfish, an interesting rock which glistened when the sun hit it just right, or a colorful bird's feather that he found along his solo travels. Derek was intrigued with the treasures of the island. He continued to give me such gifts, and I continued to add them to the Derek garden, a garden that lay like a shrine, or perhaps a grave behind my cabin. Calmness and placidity surrounded Jim, but there was a special kind of silence that could only be felt outside and in the open among the breezes, and Jim mostly kept within the confines of the medical building. I often felt the open silence with dogs and horses.

I now shared this special silence with Dr. Bronte.

After a while, he stood and stretched his legs. I looked up at him, and he offered me his hand. Rising, I brushed the earth from my pants.

"Allow me to walk you home," he said, "at least most of the way. I'll have to stop a good distance before we reach Main Campus. It wouldn't go over too well for you or for me if anyone saw us together."

We walked nearly two and a half miles along the beach, holding our animals by lead when the terrain allowed. At first, it was rough going along the rocky and narrow bank with the turbulent waves crashing too close to our feet. I sometimes had to use both hands on the rough wet rocks as we trekked along the coastline, rocks that were light gray in their natural state, but now blackened by the sea. The ponies had some difficulty, but managed, often choosing to travel in the water rather than by rocky land. The terrain eventually unfolded to smoother and wider turf as we headed west.

When we reached flatter ground and could breathe easier, Dr. Bronte said, "You never fully answered my question."

"What question was that?"

"Do you believe that murder is acceptable when pursuing a necessary objective?"

I stopped and turned around to look at him, trying to read any amusement on his face. There was none. He was serious. I heard the gulls call and smelled the salty fish air from the sea. The sun touched his cheek and hair. His bruises were healing.

"What are you, some kind of intellectual geek?"

"*Crime and Punishment,*" he said.

"Yes, I remember, and no, I don't believe that."

"Then you don't believe in lethal self–defense, in capital punishment, or the justification of any war."

"I didn't say that."

"Yes, you did, actually."

"Well, who makes these decisions of who lives and who dies?" I asked.

"Exactly," Dr. Bronte said. "Some believe that if, collectively, a group of people or a society as a whole agrees to a set of laws, then murder is justified." We walked along in silence for almost a minute. The seabirds' cries became louder, almost piercing, as one white bird dove into the ocean for a catch, and was rewarded. "I wonder if ever an individual whose intelligence supercedes society as a whole can be in a better position to decide the life or death of another."

"Wow. Heavy stuff. Do *you* believe that murder is ever justified?" I asked.

"Murder is justified much of the time in our society."

"Yeah, but do *you* believe that it's right?" I asked. "Because it kind of sounds like you do."

"I might surprise you."

Chapter 37
THE EAST SIDE

Adrian's ambush went wrong, as planned. As planned, Adrian and his team headed out to the research center in the night, and as planned, Bronte and his guys were waiting for him. Apparently rifles were drawn, but no one was hurt. According to Tom, it was rather a standoff. Tom revealed no other details to me, but told me that it was imperative that I get to the notebook in Bronte's lab.

"No problem, Tom. I'll just tell him I prefer to take our coffee in the lab."

"Do what you can, and quickly."

The third time I headed out to the east side to be Tom's *super spy*, I found Dr. Bronte training with his thugs in the center's clearing near the picnic area. I stood just outside the black iron gate, watching, as Dr. Bronte would hold a thug by his shoulders, then roll him over his hip to take him to the ground. Next, a thug would do the same to Dr. Bronte. They repeated this action over and over with each other.

Dr. Bronte spotted me, and stopped. He grabbed a towel that lay at the base of a large banyan tree and wrapped it behind his neck. Holding the ends of the towel over his shoulders with two fists, he approached me, with sweat darkening and twisting his hair into small single lock clusters. His thugs followed close behind him.

Dr. Bronte tapped buttons on the gate's keypad and opened the gate for me. One of his thugs immediately stepped in, standing like an iron barrier between Dr. Bronte and me. I took a step back.

"It's all right, Mr. Hyde," Dr. Bronte said in a low tone. Mr. Hyde gave Dr. Bronte a questioning look, and Dr. Bronte returned this look with a harsh look of his own. "The moment I choose, I can be rid of you, Mr. Hyde." Mr. Hyde stepped back and allowed me to enter the research center.

"That'll be all, gentlemen," Dr. Bronte said. "Remember to check the perimeter and the grounds in back." In unison, the two thugs gave a subtle nod and walked away. Again, I was reminded of 'Samneric' from *Lord of the Flies*, twin brothers named Sam and Eric, where their nickname inherently implies the taking away of the boys' individuality, where brother eventually turned against brother, where they eventually turned towards the savage side of society.

"Is that for me?" Dr. Bronte asked. I was confused. He pointed with his chin to the white pony, who was tied to the gate.

"Not yet. Be patient."

"How patient?"

"Actually, you lost your rights to this animal when you held a knife to my neck."

"Oh, did I?"

"Yeah, you did. Endanger the horse trainer, lose the horse."

"Hmm, raw deal." He stepped back to give me room to enter, spreading his arm towards the center of the cleared area. "Come on in."

"Thank you."

He patted his face with the towel as we walked together towards the picnic area in the center of the clearing.

"You're becoming quite the familiar sight. This is three days in a row now where you charm me with your visits. I'm afraid, however, I'm not dressed for a guest." He had on athletic pants and a light grey T-shirt..

"I hope my coming doesn't interfere with your work," I said.

"Not at all. I'm simply waiting for... some cultures to develop. What brings you here today?"

"Well, apparently you're still alive," I said.

"Apparently." He smiled.

"I saw no bruises on Adrian last night, and there's no bruises on you now."

"Mm hmm."

"No one got hurt last night, so obviously, you kept your word. Thank you."

"So you came to thank me, is that it?" He stopped at the picnic table and turned to look at me. "Jamie, if I may ask… while I find your visits gracious, I'm also puzzled. Why do you repeatedly come to see me?"

"Dr. Bronte, I'm trying to keep the peace here between us, remember?"

"Well, that's just it, Jamie." He scratched his head, somewhat squinching his face. "If that were the case, wouldn't you be more focused on setting a time and place for me to meet with your security team, or with Mr. Gordon? Why are you instead spending so much *time* with me instead of getting to the point? Why do you speak to me of such personal matters? It makes me wonder."

"Wonder what?"

"Your intentions." I looked up at him and had no words. Fear began to grip me. Did he know? "If you're here to distract me while your friends are hidden nearby, know that we always take security measures. If this is some kind of crush you have on me, know that I, of course, cannot act on this. It would be inappropriate; you're too young for me. I wouldn't have my daughter be with a man sixteen years her senior. Or perhaps you are being instructed to come get information from me. If you indeed are, know that I am careful about what I reveal."

My jaw dropped. "I'm not planning any ambush – I train horses, for cryin' out loud! As far as having a crush on you, eww."

He put two hands on my shoulders and slowly pushed down so that I sat on the picnic table behind me. He then put one foot on the seat next to my hip, almost touching me with his foot, and leaned an elbow on his knee, one hand holding his wrist. He leaned into me, his face too close to mine.

"Jamie, tell me how you know what bio–CMAT means."

"What do you mean?" I wanted to push him away.

"You know what I mean."

"No, I don't."

"Two days ago, you told me that I was lying about what bio–CMAT means. What did you mean by that?"

"I don't know."

"Yes, you do. Tell me, please." He leaned in even closer still. I smelled his aftershave and noticed a single fallen eyelash just below his left eye. I couldn't lean back anymore because my back was already digging into the edge of the picnic table. The urge to push him away grew to be insurmountable. "Tell me." I leaned to my right, away from his knee, but he immediately put out his arm to stop me. "I'm waiting," he whispered.

"Well, go ahead and wait until you die and rot away!"

"Jamie..."

I gave him a cold stare as he eyed me with a blank but serious face. I thought I could outstare him, but grew increasingly uncomfortable, as he remained fixed. When I had ridden out here, I was confidently whistling the theme of "The Pink Panther" through my teeth as a joke to myself, thinking it humorous how I was playing the part of a spy. Now, losing my composure, it seemed I was playing the part of a coward. I was scared to move. Minutes ago, he'd thrown large men to the ground. All I knew to do now was to be still. I was the rabbit hiding still in the field, and he, the snake, waiting for my next move. One twitch of a muscle, and he could pounce.

Dr. Bronte was balanced on one leg. I thought of pushing him away. He was military trained; it was probably not a good idea to shove a man who threw thugs over his hip.

But one thing I knew and I knew well – I could read animals. I knew body language. Kane said I should rely more on the non-verbal. I studied Dr. Bronte. When afraid, an animal will lower its stance, flare its nose, keep its tail down or tucked, pin its ears back, will look away or unfocused, and the whites of its eyes will show. Dr. Bronte breathed easily, leaned comfortably forward with relaxed muscles and confident eyes, and was very focused. He held no fear. I noticed I had been holding my breath, the muscles around my jaw and eyes were strained, and the picnic table's edge dug into my back from my leaning back so strongly. I realized I was unable to hold my stare any longer. I'd lost this battle, though I could not tell him what he wanted to know – that I sneaked a look into his lab notebook while he was away.

"I'm still waiting, Jamie. Tell me."

"The security team, they knew," I said quickly, hating myself.

"Who? Who knew?" I looked down at my fingernail and picked at it until he placed a hand on mine, stopping me, making me focus on him again. Without uttering a sound, he mouthed "who?" while raising his eyebrows.

"Steve."

"Steven Taylor?"

"Mm hmm."

Bronte then pushed back from the picnic table and stood, releasing his intimidating posture. He ran his palm over the top of his head and looked off towards the sea.

"How does Mr. Taylor know this?" Bronte asked.

"I don't know." He looked at me. "I really don't!" He sighed.

"Do your friends or co–workers know that you visit me?"

"No."

"No? So you visit me in private, while you attempt to establish peace with our two sides? Why the silence with your people? This doesn't make sense."

He and I stared at each other for several long seconds.

"I want to leave now." I said. He looked at me with wide eyes, and for a moment, I thought he wasn't going to let me leave. But then his face relaxed and softened.

"I'm sorry, Jamie. This was a security matter. You're free to go."

Now that I was no longer trapped and was released from intimidation, courage replaced fear, and anger replaced defeat.

"Well, thank you very much, Warden!" I said sarcastically as I stood. "Nice of you to allow your prisoner to leave. You know, you are so very arrogant!"

"So I've been told," he said quietly.

I took a few steps past him towards the gate. Then I stopped and turned around.

"Wait a minute, you have a daughter?"

He slowly sat on the picnic table and leaned forward, interlocking his fingers between his knees. He said nothing. I waited. Finally, he spoke.

"I said you were free to go."

He didn't mention his daughter on my next visit, and I didn't pry. Instead, I asked for a specific date for him to meet with Adrian to discuss peaceful coexistence on the island, to which he flatly refused. So we discussed classic literature instead, a common interest outside of our professions, as we slowly rode our ponies in the field, side–by–side, their muzzles and cheeks inches from each other as they walked.

We started with *Brave New World,* where we discussed the idea of chemically–driven happiness or an *engineered paradise*, and wondered about the morality of using bio–technology to change our DNA. Next, we talked about the dehumanization of the characters in *Heart of Darkness*, where darkness exists within every human being, and every human being is capable of committing heinous acts of evil. Bronte asked, "When man is isolated from society, and when moral boundaries begin to fade in one's community, when even 'civilized' man loses his foundation, let alone the 'savage' man, it's a short step to losing one's mind, don't you think?"

"I thought that a person's genetic make–up determines whether or not they'll go mad," I responded. "I mean, a person doesn't go mad due to a situation, or do they?"

"Fascinating subject. Funny you should ask. So you're asking if psychosis is caused by heredity or environmental factors, right? It's the age-old question of how and why one goes mad," Dr. Bronte said as his pony blew air out his nose. "When one is isolated in the wildness of the wilderness, could this possibly induce madness?"

At the end of our ride in the field, Dr. Bronte invited me to his cottage so he could lend me a few of the classics to re–read and discuss with him at a later date. I rode home with *Of Mice and Men*, *For Whom the Bell Tolls*, and *Catch 22* inside my saddlebag. I planned to read through these books quickly and was eager to later talk about the ideas behind the writing.

After living on this island, these books had a totally new meaning, a message that was always there within the pages, but one that I was blind to in the past when I went about my life in Maine's school halls and farmland. The books spoke, but I had only listened intermittently. In the wilderness and wildness of Jackel's jungle, the books' messages became alive and relevant. They took root and formed a life of their own.

Chapter 38
THE WEST SIDE

At home, Tom and especially Grady grew increasingly frustrated with me over not bringing them any information on Dr. Bronte.

"Did he tell you *any*thing of importance, anything at *all*?" Tom asked. I tried to make up information to appease him, but my focus now weighed more on literature with ideas of a chemically–derived utopia from *Brave New World*, along with allowing wild and twisted foliage to overtake one's mind, and less on our survival on this island. It was easier to think of an ideal society, however false, than to dwell on our isolation from outside voices, from needed supplies, and from our harsh reality. It was more comforting to escape to a world of pseudo–realistic happiness, even if it *was* a drug–induced euphoria, than to brutally face a world of separation and deceit.

"You need to get the notebook, Chica."

"I know, I'm trying."

"Well try harder!"

Darcy and Brian asked why I was often disappearing. I told them I needed time alone, considering our dire situation. Derek was delighted to be in charge of Henry while I was on the other side of the island. Earl screamed at me for missing work for hours on end, and I told him I saw no point anymore. "We have to keep on going, we have to keep on working," Earl said.

When again the ship didn't appear from the sea's horizon, we grimly accepted our fate, and strict food rations began. We all began losing weight, Brian most noticeably.

Tom, Grady, and even Adrian were intent on revenge, and it was aimed at Bronte. They wanted blood. Jeremy, too, joined in on this hate, and seemed to adopt a bit of a savage look. He badly needed a haircut and his eyes lacked focus, often darting from the hollock trees to the sea, then to the betel nut palms in the forest as he spit out words. He lost his sense of humor and his boyish clumsiness. I missed this, and his strange new look frightened me. I found his tin whistle discarded by a rock on the beach, rusting and full of sand.

Darcy, who was always feisty and full spirited, cried a lot. Brian did too.

Derek began acting very childish and clung to Joel, and sometimes to me too. I couldn't back up without bumping into him or stepping on his foot when he was around me. He hoarded items from the island, keeping starfish and snakeskin and fossils inside his cabin, and he even slept with a bird's nest on his pillow, until Joel finally yelled that he had enough, causing Derek to run into the woods and stay there for hours. I later found Derek huddled under a jackfruit tree, crying, as he hugged his knees to his chest. I got down on the ground next to Derek and held him, rocking back and forth with him in my arms, until his whimpering eventually stopped.

Joel stayed busy in the computer room, and Earl, in the stables. Sheila and the nurses huddled together, shutting the rest of us out, and Steve, always the introvert, seemed to grow more watchful of us. He grew a red stubble along his jaw, and his hair, which was always cropped short in military fashion, now hung loose and unkempt. He spoke only to Adrian and Grady, sometimes to Tom. He unnerved me.

Tariq still complained, but it was more in a manner of quibbling to himself under his breath. He looked like a madman, pacing and complaining in low tones, words that were aimed at no one, words that no one could hear.

Only Kane remained the same.

We became sick often — petty things like headaches, diarrhea, nausea, and dizziness — and Jim kept busy tending to our ailments. Jim seemed to age a couple of years in a matter of weeks, where his eyes dulled and sunk into his skin, and his hairline receded. He told me the ache he felt for his wife was a chronic pain in his gut, always twisting.

We were now totally on our own, where the world outside Jackel Island faded into dust and memory, like a movie where you only remember bits and pieces, all the while knowing that it's unreal. I lost myself in the words, ideas, and meanings of my books.

Chapter 39
THE EAST SIDE REVISITED

I don't remember exactly when Evan's guards no longer frisked me when I came to the east side. While Mr. Hyde and Mr. Edwards would never be my *buddies*, they no longer pounded the ground as they stormed over to me upon my arrival, and they no longer caused me to stand erect with my shoulders stiff and high. I could now breathe normally around them, and I was now able to tell them apart. Of the two, Mr. Hyde was the nastier one. Like our security guard Steve, Mr. Hyde now gave me a stone–faced single nod when he saw me, warm when compared to his former rough treatment, while Mr. Edwards actually raised a corner of his mouth at me, even if it *was* just a bit. Since they were so god–awfully serious like two tin soldiers, for my personal amusement, I asked them "Hey! Where does a snowman keep his money?" They looked at me oddly, puzzled. Derek had asked me the same bizarre question yesterday. When they didn't respond, I said, "In a snow bank!" Their faces didn't change. They held the same confused look. "Get it?" They looked at each other. "Mr. Edwards, do you get it?" I asked again. I found humor not in the foolish joke, but in their reactions to it. Silently, they walked off, Mr. Edwards shaking his head, Mr. Hyde already forgetting my joke.

I don't remember exactly when the others from the research team dissolved their silent and careful treatment towards me and began to smile or wave at me. Besides Evan and the two guards, there were only four others on the east side of the island – two men and two women. Philip, the older man, would say "Hello there!" to me when he opened the gate to let me in. Philip seemed to be the only one on the research team with whom Evan even remotely let his hair down. Marvin, the silly looking man with pigeon–like mannerisms, got all flustered when he punched in the code on the keypad to let me in today, frantically pecking at the buttons with such urgency, muttering "Darn! Darn! Darn!" when the gate would not open. I feared he would break a finger. To put him at ease, I told him my snowman joke, and he stopped smashing the keypad, looked squarely at me, then laughed too loudly and too hard at this joke which a ten–year–old would consider juvenile.

I no longer needed an escort when I was once inside the research compound; I was free to walk about. The guards and the two women left me alone. When Philip saw me, he'd tipped an invisible top hat to me in an exaggerated gentlemanly manner, or gave me a mock military salute. Last week, I gave him a Roman centurion salute back as I pushed my eyebrows into my eyes and puckered my lips. This made Philip laugh. Now, whenever I see him, I give him a centurion salute.

Days ago, Marvin spastically waved at me across the yard with a huge grin. At first, I thought he was trying to be humorous, so I waved back in the same ridiculous manner. Evan later told me not to mock him, that the poor fellow was serious; that this was simply Marvin's mannerism.

Forty–something–year–old Pauline, the medical researcher and physician assistant, hovered around Evan, constantly bringing him reports, cool drinks, news of a storm coming, or a sandwich. She'd sometimes linger after setting a dish down beside Evan, and I worried she aimed to dab his mouth with a napkin after he took a bite, though she never did. At first, it was just *one* drink or *one* sandwich, and I felt invisible. I wondered if these two had something going on, but he paid her no mind; he would just utter a cool "thanks" without looking at her. I wondered if he was being discreet, or if this was merely a one–way infatuation. Or perhaps it was nothing at all. He never ate, drank or acknowledged her offerings, and he ignored the cup or the plate she brought as we discussed the classics. Last week, however, Pauline brought *two* drinks, and yesterday, *two* sandwiches. It was then when I noticed that Evan would sip at the iced tea, or take a bite when I spoke. I was tenderly moved by his consideration, but said nothing, and appeared not to notice his courtesy.

When Philip came by to see Evan, which wasn't too often, Evan would excuse himself and go over to him. The two would briefly talk in hushed and serious tones. Philip had eighteen years on Evan, though Evan clearly held the reins. During my last visit, just after he was finished talking with Evan, Philip winked at me when he left, and I gave a soft and vague Roman salute. This puzzled Evan, as his eyes moved from his friend to me, but he said nothing.

Sandra, the younger of the two women, frequently seemed flustered or overwhelmed, often lost in her thoughts. I sometimes saw her rushing about carrying too many documents and texts, looking as if she were trying to memorize the federal budget. She sometimes came to Evan, and when she stood before him, she would forget what she had wanted to tell him. When she forgot something, she would make an "O" with her mouth while lifting up one finger. Evan would wait for her, then would shrug and resume whatever it was he was doing. I would watch her march off, her blond hair bouncing on her back.

Today, the first day of August, Evan and I sat at the picnic table under the hot sun as Sandra came up to us and asked Evan if she wanted him to log the glucose test information. He simply looked at her without any expression.

"Oh, that's right, you told me to log it. I'm sss... sorry, I forgot. I'll log it," she said. Evan gave a faint smile, and she turned to leave. Then she turned around and said, "Jamie, are you staying for the chess game this afternoon? It's this afternoon, right Dr. Bronte?" Evan gave a single nod. "You can watch Dr. Bronte slaughter Marvin."

"Chess game?" I asked Evan.

"We periodically play," Evan said. "Every now and then, one of my team challenges me to a game. Believe it or not, Marvin is my most challenging opponent. You're welcome to stay and watch."

"Dr. Bronte's never lost a game," Sandra told me. "Or have you? No, you haven't. Of course you haven't."

"That's because he's never played *me*," I said, smiling. I was completely and absolutely joking. Sandra looked nervously at Evan, who slowly raised his head up to me and cocked one eyebrow.

"I'm kidding," I said.

"I'm going to hold you to your challenge." Evan asked calmly, though his eyes danced.

"Uh–oh," I said.

"Uh–oh is right," Sandra said.

"You learn so much about a person when you play chess with them," he said.

"Listen, while I'd love to stay and watch the slaughter, I can't. I have to get to the stables this afternoon."

"Nice seeing you, Jamie," Sandra said, and then she bounced away. As I watched her leave, I was thinking how I was instructed to only *pretend* to be friends with the people on the research team, these people on the other side of the island, people whom I was told to betray. People whom I was, in reality, beginning to like.

"It's good that you're getting close with them," Tom had told me days ago. "It's your ticket into the lab. You have to get in the *lab*, Jamie. You have to get the notebook, remember? And *soon*!"

I pushed Tom's voice from my head as I sat next to Evan, focusing instead on Heller's premise that anyone who goes out of their way to avoid a sure death must surely be sane, though only being found insane would grant you life. Catch 22. If I was to be compassionate to the people on one side of this island, I must be cruel to the people on the other. Which side do I take? Am I a compassionate or a cruel person? Can I be both? How can I not? Who was I exactly?

"Jamie?" Evan asked. I hadn't registered what he was saying.

"Oh! What? Sorry."

Just then, Marvin came rushing up to us, overdressed in this heat. Poor Marvin… he had a few hairs growing from age spots on his skull, and his teeth were filed down, apparently from constant nervous grinding. His eyes and ears were tiny, almost freakishly so, and the poor man had pimples even though he was middle–aged. Jeremy once told me that if you see a man with pimples, it's because he doesn't have enough sex. I really wished Jeremy had never told me that, because I didn't want to look at Marvin and think in those terms.

Marvin frequently interrupted Evan and me, always needing his boss's input, which annoyed Evan to no end. This privately amused me, though I gave no indication, either to Evan or to Marvin.

"The culture simply isn't reacting!" Marvin said with too much concern, pecking each word, nervously rubbing his fingernails together in front of his chest as he waited for Evan's response.

"Give it time," Evan said without even looking at the wimpish man. Staring at his shoes, Evan patiently waited for Marvin to leave so that he and I could continue our discussion on *Catch 22*'s corruption and lack of morality in society's upper levels, where the bureaucrats often discreetly eliminated their subordinates.

"But you predicted that the culture would…"

"Give it *time*, Marvin!" Evan said slowly and methodically, appearing calm, but I now knew Evan well enough to see that he struggled to keep control over his frequent exasperations. If this bird–like man uttered another sentence, Evan would surely snap at him. Marvin's feelings were easily bruised, and so Evan fought hard to keep a lid on his frustration. I looked to the ground and sucked in my lips, pushing back a smile. Marvin knew better than to pester his boss any longer, and so he left, flittering away. I saw Evan shut his eyes for a second or two.

"Where were we?" Evan asked. I had to smile. Seeing this, Evan said, "If he wasn't so damn thorough and devoted to his work, I would have sent him off the island a year ago." And then he added under his breath, "... in a body bag."

I laughed. "Cut him some slack. He's just your typical geek," I said. "You know... those science types."

Evan looked squarely at me. "I'll let that go." He cleared his throat and crossed his legs. "So where were we?"

"The no–win situation of *Catch 22*, where the only way to survive an insane system is to be insane oneself."

"Ah, yes." Evan opened his mouth to say more, but I then interrupted him.

"And then you were going to tell me about your daughter."

Evan slowly let his mouth shut and gave me the look he often gave me lately when I was a smart ass, cocking his head a little to the side, squinting his eyes. "Oh, was I?"

"You never say anything about her." He continued to give me the look. "You're not going to tell me about your daughter?"

His face fell, and he looked away. "I have a son, too. Twins. I have never laid eyes on either my son or daughter. My wife and I separated before her pregnancy started showing." He uncrossed his legs and leaned back, crossing his arms over his chest. "I learned only recently, three years ago, that I in fact *had* children." He sighed, staring at the ground. "They'd be thirteen–years–old now. I was just a couple of years older than you are now when they were born, though their mother never told me of... of their birth. My son is quiet, studious, compassionate... was easy to raise, from what I hear. Wants to be a geneticist. I dare say, my daughter is a feisty one, full of fire. She tells her brother to stay away from me, and he adores her, so he complies. She wants nothing to do with me or my money." Evan uncrossed his arms and laid his elbows behind him on the picnic table ledge. "Imagine that," he said flatly.

Chapter 40
CUTTING INTO THE GROUND

We were getting cranky with one–another. Earl continued to scream at me for taking mornings or afternoons off from the stables. I knew I couldn't get in trouble with Tom, because he was the one who sent me on these so called "spy" missions, which were turning out to be social visits filled with interesting literary discussions and escape from the turmoil at home.

"Where in God's heaven do you go off to, Girl?" Earl asked as he bore his shovel into the dirt, taking his anger out on the earth, cutting into the ground with spite and vengeance.

"I just have to get away sometimes, Earl."

"You have a job to do here!"

"Well then fire me!"

"I will!"

"Go ahead!"

"I will!"

"Fine!"

"Fine! Get out of my sight!"

"I will."

"Wait! Come back here!"

Tom now had to take careful inventory control, and Darcy assisted with counting and recording numbers. A list of items were posted on the wall inside Central Lodge – matches, lighter fluid, batteries, coffee, fishing line, laundry detergent, dishwashing soap, body soap, shampoo, pens and pencils, and ammunition, which was listed in red – and next to each item were numbers that indicated the quantity we had remaining.

These numbers were continually crossed off, and a lesser number was written in. I panicked at the thought of my riding shoes wearing out. Jim's blood went cold over the thought of no more coffee. One of the nurses, Brittany, I think, got upset with Sheila over some ridiculous thing, and so for revenge, Brittany told Tom that Sheila hid five shampoo bottles in her closet. The crazy thing was that Brittany was hoarding soap herself!

Grady and Steve argued over whose meat rations were larger. Steve told Grady he'd stab his good hand if he didn't get it away from his plate. Darcy yelled at Sheila for using up the hot water in the shower, and they shoved each other. Tom and Darcy began sleeping apart more and more. Tom constantly wore a worried look and started to get lines around his eyes as he reassured us during the dinner hour that help would surely be on its way. Joel became even more of a hermit, frequently locked in the computer building, never socializing with any of us any more. Joel also took long walks alone along the beach. He neglected his son, who was starved for his attention.

Brian found Jeremy sleeping outside behind his cabin among the leaves, and when Brian suggested he sleep inside in case a snake sought the warmth of his body during the night, Jeremy sneered, "Shut up, you faggot!" This was not like Jeremy. It was also not like Brian to then push Jeremy's thin body in the dirt.

"I'm sorry!" Brian was horrified over what he had done. "I'm sorry, brother! I'm sorry!"

"Shut up, you fag!"

Jeremy stopped brushing his teeth, and his blond stringy hair grew past his green eyes and over his ears, giving his face an even more pointed look. Grady threatened to hold him down and cut his hair, and secretly, I wished he would. "You look like a damn girl!" Grady told him. Jeremy punched Grady with all the might that his skinny adolescent body would allow, and Grady just laughed, then shoved him away with his fingertips. Jeremy's quizzical and amused look was gone, along with his youthful demeanor. In its place, he now carried the look of a coke addict, living only within the tedious thoughts of his mind, distracted, impatient, unaware of surroundings, nervously licking his lips. When Derek asked Jeremy what was wrong, Jeremy told him, "Don't know, Bud. What the hell's wrong with you?"

Derek began asking me repeatedly if he could sleep with Henry. The problem was… *I* needed to sleep with Henry. I gave Derek my stuffed animal, Mr. Dody (who was now missing an eye which Henry had apparently gnawed off). When this didn't suffice, I finally allowed Derek to sleep with Henry and me in my bed, though little Henry, who slept between us parallel to the bed's headboard, took up most of the space. This left Derek crammed against the wall, as I dangled an arm over the edge of the bed. Derek wanted to sleep like this every night, and I thought he was crazy for this. I didn't know how to tell this little boy "no". When I told him that there was no room on the bed for the three of us, he started to almost throw a tantrum like a two–year–old.

"I bet Kane would allow me to sleep with him!" Derek protested. "Kane's nicer than you!"

"Then go ask him," I said.

"But I want to sleep with you and Henry."

"There's no *room*, Derek," I argued. "Go sleep with your father."

"He says I'm too big, and it's not appropriate." He mispronounced 'appropriate', giving it three syllables instead of four. Talking baby talk was a new thing for Derek.

"Go ask Adrian. You two are tight. Don't you two train any more?

"No. Adrian's mean now. Everyone's mean now."

"Oh, all right, but only for tonight, Derek. Just one night." I told him. I would allow this, but upon further thought, I actually welcomed this, or perhaps even needed this human contact. "I mean it, Derek… just this one time!" That was over a week ago, and I was now used to waking with a dog's tail or a child's hand across my face.

Tariq continued to mutter to himself. I now realized that preparing lavish meals for us in the past had given him purpose, and now that was taken away. Fruit and half–stale bread served as breakfast, while lifeless and limp appetizer–sized portions were our lunches and dinners. It was never enough. Brian, whose weight loss showed most noticeably in his narrowing face, said he always had a hunger headache, and Jeremy's skin stretched thinly over his bones, now more pronounced than ever.

"I think this is it," Brian told me as he put the last spoonful in his mouth. As his face became more defined, I noticed that he could be quite handsome, with red cheeks, visible cheekbones that were no longer simply a round mound, full lips, and thick eyebrows.

"I'm sorry there's no more food, Brian. You can have mine, if you'd like," I had told him. "There's not much..."

"No, I mean I think this is it. For us, I mean. There's nothing left. This is what life will be like from now on. Nothing more."

I continued to go to Jim for comfort, but it seemed at times that the doctor had pretty much spent all the affection he had, with little left to give. In the past, Jim would offer his coffee and his solace to me. Now, during some of my visits when I sought warmth and repose, the only thing I received from the doctor was distraction and a lack of focus. He would just stare out the window with his mind far away, perhaps on his wife, perhaps on our dark outlook, or perhaps on our dwindling medical supplies. Other times, he was the same old compassionate and kind–hearted Jim.

I was due for my monthly blood test, but Jim said we were doing away with blood tests for the time being. Security decided to stop delivering our blood to research for analysis for obvious reasons. Instead of me giving blood, Jim gave me coffee.

"Where is it you go off to, Jamie?"

After some thought, I revealed, "I go to visit with Dr. Bronte."

"Wha-a-at?" Jim asked, dragging out the word, ending in a high tone. He set his coffee down. "Now why would you do that?"

"He's become my friend, Jim."

"Your *friend* prevents me from any contact with my wife!" Jim spat out the words. I rarely saw Jim angry.

"You don't know that for sure. You don't know that it's him."

After some time, Jim softly said, "You're right." He sipped coffee from his mug. "You're absolutely right. I need to keep telling myself that."

"Please don't tell anyone that I go over there."

He put his arm around me. "Trust me, I won't." He rocked me a bit. "It wouldn't go well for you at all if anyone knew."

The thing was, I had told Brian. I had been finding it increasingly difficult to keep this secret. Brian got angry with me and didn't speak to me for two days, which surprised me. I thought that of all people on this god–forsaken island, Brian would be the one who'd understand. "Because of your new *friend*, we're now all going to die here, do you understand that? Do you? Why don't you just go live with *them* now, give them all a big fat kiss, then pound the final nail in all our coffins!"

Darcy was my best friend, but I couldn't tell her that the research team was just a group of people, people like we were. We were lead to believe that there existed two separate entities here on Jackel Island, when actually, we were one. When you have an east side and a west side, the only thing that separates the two is air. Just air. The thing is – it is air that binds us. If I told Darcy that Evan Bronte was my friend, her volcanic reaction would make Brian's reaction seem like a molehill in comparison. She could possibly turn to hate me. I believe Jeremy would kill me with his fingers around my throat. So outside of Tom and Grady, who instructed me to visit with Evan Bronte, only Brian and now Jim knew that I was doing this. And Kane. Kane knew.

Tom and Grady grew increasingly impatient with me, understandably. Grady once rested his two palms, even his injured one, against the wall on either side of my head, trapping me, scaring me, demanding to know what I was doing over there if I wasn't getting information.

"Oh, we're having tea and crumpets, Grady!" Thing was, my sarcasm wasn't too far from the truth. Tom would ask me the same question in so many words, and then would throw his hands in the air in exasperation when I had nothing to tell him. Yesterday, I began telling them that I overheard Dr. Bronte talking with one of his guards, telling him details about an attack they were planning on us.

"What is this?" Tom asked, with Grady cocking his head, and I proceeded to give specific details. It didn't take them long to learn that I was making everything up. Grady grabbed my ear and moved my head back and forth, I think in jest, though it did hurt a bit. Tom simply stared at me with an open mouth, in disbelief.

"Ow, Grady, dammit! I'm just telling you what you want to hear," I said.

Adrian worried me most of all. He grew a bedraggled stubble, which soon grew to an unkempt beard. His fingernails, which were always trimmed and groomed when we used to train in the field, and when he ran them over my arms in the lagoon, were now neglected and gangly. Looking at him now, I cringed with the memory that I once allowed him to touch me romantically. He spent days in the jungle. Half the time, we couldn't find him; but then again, half the time, Earl, Darcy, Brian, Derek, and the others could no longer find me. If I wasn't at the stables, I was either with Evan, or I'd lock myself in my cabin with a book, or I'd ride off some place near the sea or deep in the woods where no one could find me, so I could escape in a book.

Yesterday morning when I entered the showers, I called Sheila by another name. Sharon, I think. She snarled at me and called me Janet. Worse, when I passed one of the nurses by the water basin and attempted to say hello, I had forgotten her name.

On a good note, Adrian started returning from the jungle with meat. At first it was squirrels and rabbits, which Sheila and I had a hard time eating. Then Adrian brought back Javan pig, Bawean deer, Banteng, and Babirusa hog. Kane showed Adrian, Grady, and Steve how to cut and prepare the meat. I looked away as they skinned an anoa on the beach. Kane told Adrian to make sure that he shot the animal when he was grazing, not running.

"A running animal has adrenaline, and when adrenaline gets into the meat, it tastes sour and is tough," Kane said, adding that it was imperative to make a perfect shot so that the animal will bleed less. "If blood seeps into the muscle, it gives it a gamey taste. Also, there are the moral issues for the animal, and for yourself, to consider."

The only other time I'd heard Kane speak so much was when he was explaining his religion to me. Perhaps hunting was his edge.

Kane showed Adrian how to field dress the animal as soon as possible by removing all the vital organs. "Bacteria begins to grow immediately, so keeping the carcass cool is important. Skin the carcass to help cool the meat, especially with the heat of the island."

I couldn't bear any more of this talk, so I turned to leave. As I did, I heard Adrian tell Kane, "Tariq says the refrigeration unit may be on the blink. If it goes, we're in trouble. It's not like we can get appliance parts anymore."

Tariq wouldn't allow Kane to cook the meat; this was his job and his job alone. I found it amusing that wiry sixty–four year old scraggly Tariq pushed giant Kane away from the kitchen, and from the look on his face, Kane was amused over this, too. Kane allowed Tariq to push him without lifting a hand, and left Tariq alone to do his job. I heard Tariq hum as he carved up the meat.

We began to have cookouts around the campfire, and I was hoping it would be like old times. Tom, Grady, and Steve offered to hunt with Adrian, but Adrian preferred to hunt solo. Jeremy asked Adrian if he needed an assistant, someone to carry stuff while he hunted, and Adrian didn't even answer him. Jeremy glared at Adrian. Adrian did not notice. Kane rested a hand on Jeremy's shoulder, and as brief as a glimpse, I saw Jeremy soften, something I hadn't seen in him in weeks.

Joel was having difficulties as he attempted to trap and gather seafood by himself. Tom, Jim, and Earl joined Joel at the beach, but their nets and fishing poles came back empty. Kane showed them how to extract shrimp, demersal fish, crab, mussels, rainbow fish, mackerel, and pelagic fish from the sea, and so we began having fresh seafood for lunch and dinner.

Darcy, Brian, Derek and I gathered fruit. Kane silently came to us and dumped a burlap cloth at our feet, and joyously, papayas, star fruit, and mangos rolled out over the soil, giving color and delight to our senses. Derek ran up to the huge man and hugged his legs, burying his face in Kane's stomach. I gave in, burst forward, and hugged the other side of him, as Darcy and Brian watched us in wonder. When I felt Kane's warm arm rest on my back, it soothed like honey on a sore throat. I opened my eyes from Kane's chest and saw that his other hand was on Derek's head.

Chapter 41

A GAME OF CHESS

Evan never lost a game of chess, ever.

Two days after our *Catch-22* discussion, I rode over to the research center to watch him play against Philip. Mr. Edwards, the guard whose smile I could perhaps detect if I had a microscope, silently let me in the gate, and as I walked through the open grounds of the research center, I saw a white card table just outside the main stone building, the building that contained the lab. At the card table, Evan and Philip sat across from each other with the chessboard between them, with Evan on my right as I approached. The remaining three from the research team settled around them, watching the game.

"Hello, Jamie!" Marvin gave me a grin that was too wide, exposing off–white corn–kernel teeth, and an over–eager wave. I knew better than to wave back in the same manner.

"Hey!" I said to everyone when I reached them.

The game had already started. Two folding chairs sat near the card table, one between Philip and the stone building, and the other by Evan, on his left side. Pauline was seated in the chair near Philip, and it was angled to face Evan. Sandra stood out of the sun and up on the porch in the shade, where the thick stone somewhat cooled the air around her. She leaned against the thick Greek Doric column that extended from floor to ceiling. The porch led down to the manicured ground, where the rest of us were standing. Marvin hovered too close to Evan, breathing on his head, his back to the stone building.

Pauline smiled at me while Sandra called hello from the porch. Philip, who was focused on the board, broke his focus to tip an imaginary hat to me. I saluted him. Evan rested an elbow on the table with his hand dangling in the air by his face. I looked at his wrist and saw that it was finally healing, though the three–week wound left a raised scar and was still pink, like a wrinkled night crawler on his skin. Evan vaguely shot up his index finger and gave me a quick glance that acted as a hello to me. I raised a hand to return his gesture, but he was already watching Philip. I took the empty chair and watched them play.

Philip rested his elbows on the table, his fingertips holding his forehead as he concentrated on the game. Evan studied Philip. Philip sweated. Philip seemed to calculate every offense and every possible counter attack before he would move one of his chess pieces. He was slow and deliberate. As soon as Philip moved, Evan would counter. Philip would then deliberate over every piece on the board again. Marvin gasped when Philip made his next move, and everyone looked at Marvin, causing him to sink his chin and scratch his eyebrow. I examined the board to see what mistake Philip had made. Evan immediately took Philip's rook.

"Damn!" Philip said.

I was among five science people who were able to hold their interest in this strategic and analytical game, but I grew increasingly restless after several minutes. I played chess in middle school, and was actually quite good at it, but found it mentally taxing and stressful. Playing chess was more a grueling and tedious chore than something that brought me pleasure. Thus, I never enjoyed the game.

As the chess match silently continued, my mind wandered to the other side of the island. I realized that lately, I felt more relaxed here with the research team than at home among my friends on the west side. I thought of our food rations and dwindling supplies, Joel neglecting his son, Brian's weight loss, Jeremy's wild look and Adrian's savage ways, and I no longer considered that place safe.

Marvin gasped again, and I snapped into focus. As I watched the two men play chess with their team close by, I felt like an outsider in this small tight–knit group of people, these people who had not, as yet, turned on each other. We on the west side were tainted; these people were not. The dirt had settled on and perhaps in me, in my pores and in my being, but these people were clean. I was jaded. I was indeed an outsider looking in, wanting in, but dirtied.

I suddenly needed something unidentifiable, something similar to attention, acknowledgement, kind consideration, or familiarity, and I needed it immediately. I could not name what it was that I yearned for, this faceless and urgent hunger, nor did I understand my emotions. All I knew was that I needed to act. I did not know how or why.

I slowly got up from the chair. I was on Evan's left side and a little behind him, and he didn't seem to notice when I stood, engrossed in the game as he was. Nor did Philip, who was fixed on the chessboard. Sandra now sat on the stone steps, and she scribbled something onto a pad of paper in her lap. Pauline glanced up at me, and Marvin looked over at me, confused, but I ignored them. Stuffing my hands in my pockets, I eased about the grounds, drifting away from the group a little. I needed to quench this strange hunger I had and fill this black void, this aching desire to be clean once again, to finally fit in once again.

I looked for a distraction and I found it. A long white PVC pipe lay propped against the far right side of the stone building. I took it and twirled it in my hands, then looked over at the people by the game.

Slowly, I walked back to them. Marvin eyed me, puzzled. Pauline glanced up. I crept up behind Evan's back, lifted the PVC pipe to my mouth, and quietly extended the other end of the pipe behind Evan's left ear. I then, with full alacrity and gusto, blasted a sound as loud as I absolutely could, a sudden "AHHHH!" from my lungs directly into Evan's ear. He jumped, which was putting it mildly. Philip looked up at me, displaying total shock and disbelief. Sandra had her fingers over her mouth, and Pauline paled. I had surprised even myself. Marvin's eyes darted from me to Evan, then back to me, as his fingers from one hand dug into the next. He wore a look of apprehension. Philip then gave a loud and uncontrolled belly laugh, and couldn't stop. I waited curiously for Evan's reaction.

Evan slowly turned around in his chair to face me. I was a little afraid, but more curious. I wanted him to laugh, and if he did, I would too, and everyone would follow. But he didn't laugh. In fact, his somber face scared me. My face fell.

"Quiet!" he yelled at Philip. Philip immediately stopped laughing. "And for heaven's sake, get off me!" Evan pushed Marvin away from him. "Game's over."

Evan stood, calmly and slowly adjusted his shirt over his hips, then with a rush of anger and fervor, shoved the card table over. All the chess pieces, along with the table itself, fell on Philip. Philip turned gray. We all froze.

Evan turned to me. "You certainly take liberties with me, young lady," he said calmly as if he were telling me it was a sunny day. Then he, with a poised collectedness, straightened his shirt again and walked off to his cottage, leaving us all looking at each other in still silence. Their eyes finally fell on me.

"I'm sorry! I'm sorry!" I said. "I really am. I meant it as a joke, that was all. I don't know why I did it."

"It wasn't just you, Jamie," Marvin said. "His game was slightly off today. He was making mistakes I've never seen him make." Marvin fastidiously licked his lips like a lizard. "He's a far superior player than I am, and I've never seen him make mistakes like this before. His focus was off." Marvin spoke too quickly. He grew excited. "I think anger from something else, perhaps the game, was building in him." He nodded in rapid succession. "Yes, that's what I think."

"But why'd he get so mad?" I asked. "I've never seen him like that."

"Oh we have," Pauline said, and Sandra nodded.

"We most certainly have," Philip said.

"He gets angry at *me* all the time," Marvin chirped.

"That's because you're so god damn annoying, Marvin." Philip said, only he was smiling. "But we love ya', brother, even though you're a royal pain in the ass."

"Fuck you very much too, Philipé," Marvin said. I was surprised such a nerdy fellow would use such language. I couldn't tell if he was joking.

"You don't cross Dr. Bronte." Sandra said from the porch. She was now standing. "Not ever!"

I looked baffled.

"Sweetheart, you made him lose his composure," Pauline explained. "That's the worst thing you could do to the doctor. Even if it was just for a split second, you startled him. You caught him off guard. You don't do that to this man."

"Why not?" I was very confused.

"I still think it was the game, or something else, and not Jamie," Marvin tweeted, speaking quickly in high pitch. "His focus in general has been off lately. Have you all noticed? His anger seems to have been building. Have you all noticed?" No one answered him.

"I have not laughed like that in two years," Philip said. "I thought the good doctor was going to blow a gasket. Well, he actually did, didn't he?" Philip chucked. "I was hoping you'd run for your life, Miss. The brilliant Dr. Bronte and his temper tantrums… I thought I was going to rip my gut open, laughing so hard. I still can't believe you did that, to *him* of all people! What possessed you?" Philip laughed harder, and Marvin nervously joined in. Pauline and Sandra looked confused at each other. I remained frozen, bewildered by all of them. Philip's laughing dwindled down. "Ooh boy, the surprises here on Jackel Island! I tell you!"

My astonishment over Evan's behavior slowly turned to anger. My need, which was so humungous and colossal that I felt compelled to shout it from my gut directly into his ear, was invalidated and negated. I had needed his affirmation and acceptance in order to feel somewhat joined with these people, and I had badly needed to quench this nameless desire for admission, to be received, to feel clean once again.

Instead, he had rudely shoved the card table over, and in doing so, he kept me dirty and detached.

"I need to go," I quietly told them, more like a whisper.

"Sure, honey," Pauline said softly.

"Sandra, before I do, can I borrow a piece of paper and a pen?"

"Huh? Oh, sure." She ripped a piece of paper from her pad and handed it to me, along with her pen.

"You okay?" Philip asked, cocking his head.

Without answering him, I left through the gate and reached my white pony. From my saddlebag, I got the book that I had borrowed from Evan. I hadn't yet read *Of Mice and Men*, but I sure as hell wasn't going to read it now.

I went off by myself to the picnic table, and under the August sun, I wrote the most heartfelt, romantic, and intense love letter to Evan Bronte. Then I signed Pauline's name. Folding the paper in thirds, I walked over to Evan's cottage, relieved somewhat that the four others had dispersed. Upon reaching Evan's home, I put the letter under a rock by his door, along with his book, which I left just outside his door in the dirt.

"I'm not going back," I told Tom and Grady. Upon my return from the ravaged chess game, I had found our leader and our over–sexed security guard in the open paddock. Tom was helping Grady saddle up his brown female Batak for a ride. As I watched her rub her muzzle on Grady's shoulder, I could swear this docile but spirited animal was flirting with Grady. Her choice in males left much to be desired. A month ago, I was thinking how much I would miss my special white Sandalwood pony who finally let me, a human, in. I would also miss Grady's slender and sweet Batak pony who carried her tail, her spirits, and her pride high, and Adrian's black Java, a tough boy with such soft expression in his eyes. I was thinking how much I would miss them when I left for the States in December. Now, I realized that

I perhaps would be spending the rest of my days with these animals. Bittersweet.

"What do you mean, you're not going back?" Tom turned to me, squinting. "Why the hell not? What happened?"

Grady spoke at the same time, telling me that yes indeed I was going back, like it or not. He pulled the girth too tightly on his pony's belly and I cringed.

"Evan said I'm not allowed back."

"Oh, it's *Evan* now, is it?" Grady asked sarcastically.

"Dr. Bronte I mean. He said I can't come back."

"And why not, Miss Stockholm?" Grady asked.

"What happened, Jamie?" Tom asked.

"I'm just not going back. It's over!" I led the white pony to the other side of the paddock to feed, away from these men. "I've had enough."

I lay in my small bed that night, facing the cabin's wood–logged wall under the open window, with Henry's back tucked against my chest and his head under my chin. My arm lay over Derek's shoulder. I willed sleep to come, but instead, I listened to the night crickets, the wind swaying the jambul trees, and the boy's breathing in synchronization with the dog's. I thought of how I would miss Evan Bronte, and wondered how I could miss someone who I now hated with passion. I wondered if a person could hate someone they never loved in the first place. I supposed it happened all the time in cases of sheer abuse, but love that turned to hate held its distinguished spice. I would never see Evan again. I would also miss Philip, the sweet yet solid older man who once told me he got a kick out of me, whatever that meant. I would even miss nurturing Pauline, scatter–brained Sandra, and also Marvin, the funny looking man whose name so very much fit him, who, according to Evan, was close to genius.

As I looked at the milky white smear that the moon cast on Derek's black hair, I knew that love starts as a creamy white purity, and hate soured this purity into a muddy brown haze. I watched my breath slightly wiggle Henry's ear. I drifted.

I dreamed that I was kneeling on stony damp grounds, shouting through a sewer pipe that started at a river's edge and extended through the air to a distant mountain. I stuck my head in the opening of the pipe and yelled as loudly as I could, and then pulled away from the pipe. As I gazed past the pipe, I watched the barley that grew between the river and mountains sway in the thick blue breeze. When I stood, I felt filth ooze from my hair down my face, while the sun illuminated the barley into a brilliant gold.

The next morning, as Derek slept on, I opened my cabin door to let Henry out. He stopped briefly to sniff an object on the ground just outside the door, then ran out to do his business. Looking down, I discovered two items by my feet. The book *Of Mice and Men* lay by the foot of the door, and next to it, a piece of paper lay folded in thirds under a rock. I feared it was the love letter I had forged, and wondered if there'd be an angry note scribbled below my handwriting, but when I reached down for the paper and opened it, I saw that it was a totally new and different handwritten note:

Dear Jamie,

I most humbly apologize for my inexcusable behavior yesterday.

Please reconsider and read Of Mice and Men. Steinbeck writes of loneliness and isolation, and how people are unable to attain true attachments due to their human frailties and weaknesses. We all have them, Jamie. Steinbeck's characters are rendered helpless by their isolation from one another, yet they

Seek to hurt and destroy each other. Isolation, be it on an island or on a remote ranch, makes people return to their instincts, fighting to Survive, while companionship keeps us civilized.

I would love to discuss this with you Sometime Soon.

Affectionately,
~Evan Bronte

I forgave him completely! I felt happy and relieved, quite thrilled, actually, to have the boulder off my soul. I felt an urge to see him soon, to show that I harbored no grudge.

"What the hell are you whistling about?" Darcy asked me in the showers. "Did you have sex or something last night?"

"Oh yeah, right."

"Not that I remember what *that's* like," Darcy said. I ignored her and continued to whistle. "Are you back with Adrian or *what*?"

"Sorry, I'm not into Neanderthals these days," I said.

"Yeah, he *has* turned into quite the Neanderthal lately, hasn't he. That scraggly beard!"

"That, and I'm not too fond of the long curly yellowing finger nails."

"Eww!" We both laughed.

"Next he'll have blood from his killed animals dripping down from his teeth."

"Eww again! Oh, Jamie!"

"When he starts walking on all fours, we're *really* in trouble!"

At breakfast, Tom again asked us how we were all holding up, and assured us that rescue from the States must surely be on its way. He went over our list of dwindling supplies, and thanked everyone for our sacrifices and our rationing. Derek mumbled that he was tired of fruit, that it made him go to the bathroom all the time, and that meat was hard to chew. I put my arm around him and wiggled his shoulder as I eagerly told him that when we get back to the States, I would promptly take him out to breakfast where we'd each eat a dozen pancakes with thick gooey maple syrup. Darcy and Brian looked at me as though I were crazy.

I went through the rest of the morning working hard at the stables, whistling as I swept and polished, with Earl often glancing my way with a suspicious look.

I read *Of Mice and Men* through lunch, not hearing Brian and Darcy as they sat on either side of me, quibbling over whatever it was they were quibbling about.

"Earth to Jamie! Earth to Jamie!" Brian said.

"She's just pretending to read so she can daydream about her Neanderthal man," Darcy said.

"Huh?" Brian asked.

I ignored them, though I did jab my elbow into Darcy's shoulder.

I took extra time to read in the gold field before returning to work.

"You're late!" Earl said when he saw me. "Again!"

Before and after dinner, and well into the night, I read *Of Mice and Men*, with Derek grumbling for me to turn off the giraffe lamp. I propped Henry on my stomach to use him as a pillow to lay my book against. He was fine with that, though he weighted my stomach down. He was also growing at an alarming rate.

The next morning, Earl eyed me as I entered the paddock.

"Mornin'!" I called to him.

"Mm hmm. How long you sticking around this time?"

I checked the hay supply by the gate, checked to see that the water bucket was fresh and full, then went into the barn to get a saddle, bridle, and the rest of the tack. Back outside, I began tacking up the white pony, whose ears pricked into the air in anxious anticipation of a ride through the woods.

"Uh–uh, oh no. You're not going off for another joy ride again. You've got work to do here, and plenty of it!"

"I'll make it up to you, Earl," I said as I climbed up on the saddle. "I'll work double–hard this afternoon."

"Don't you dare leave! Girl, don't you *dare*!" His voice was low and rough.

"Guess you gotta' fire me," I said as I turned my pony around. "That, or call the police." I kicked the animal's lower belly as Earl shook his fist at me, and dust rose in his face as I trotted off. I heard him venomously yell at me, threatening me, as he stood by himself in the center of the paddock, but his voice faded as I got farther away.

I did not ride through the dense and dark humid woods. Instead, I chose the unimpeded open air along the beach, the bare space that extended naked and exposed for several long thin miles. Birds called from above while waves roared from the left, and the sounds blended with the huffs from the pony's nostrils, the soft bounce in the saddle, and the breath of the wind, all of which unraveled and loosened my soul. I rode on.

Unbarred sand that sparkled in the sun eventually gave way to rocks as I approached the east side of the island, so I cut a hard right, leaving the beach. I climbed up and into the jungle. As I entered the forest, I walked the pony around trees and over the woodland's thick brushwood full of ferns, briar, thicket, and scrappy bushes, trying to find the path. The woods breathed and whispered life in surround sound, giving pulse and cadence to the rhythm of the jungle. I had forgotten what being so alive felt like.

Inside the gate, I saw Evan with Marvin under the lamppost that rose into the sky, reaching for the heavens. Marvin held papers, and they were reviewing the contents as I walked up to them. Marvin jabbed his finger into the paper as he asked Evan questions, his eyes puzzled and frustrated, with Evan calmly reassuring him. Marvin saw me first and grew nervous, his eyes darting between his boss and me. Evan looked up from the paper to Marvin's face, then over to me.

"Well now!" Evan said loudly, and he grinned. It was rare when he gave a full exposed grin, and it always stabbed me with a certain pleasure when he did. I had to smile, considering the way we'd left things… what I did, what he did, then what I did.

"That'll be all, Marvin."

"But the results just don't make sense, I tell you. It shouldn't have reacted that way. The chemicals…"

"That'll be *all*, Marvin."

"Oh, okay, Sir. Yeah, okay. Hey, Jamie."

"Hey Marvin." He attempted a cocky grin before he faced the gate, then did a one–eighty towards the stone building and headed that way. Evan gave a voiceless laugh through his nose. We watched Marvin leave, then turned to each other.

"A pleasure to see you!" he said. "Though I'm afraid this will have to be a quick visit."

"Oh?"

"Yes, I have to, ahh, prepare for my *date* with *Pauline*."

For a second, I believed him, and he gave a tight grin with a silent laugh, and when he was done, he winked at me. Again, I felt the familiar emotional stab. It traveled like melted wax from my stomach down my upper legs.

"Did Pauline see the letter?" I asked. "Did you show her?"

"Well, you know I have to get you back. I seem to remember that you challenged me to a game of chess."

"I didn't."

"You did!" He motioned me to follow him by wiggling his index finger. "Follow me. The chess set is inside."

"Evan, I just came to discuss *Of Mice and Men*, not to play chess!"

I followed him inside the stone building, where it was instantly cooler. He opened a glass cabinet door just above his head and reached for a rectangular leather case.

"Care for a cool drink?" he asked over his shoulder.

"No thanks. I'm good," I said. "I mean it, I'm not playing."

"Are you sure you don't want a drink? After that three mile ride? And now, we're about to sit in the sun." He laid the leather case by a lamp on a black table that sat just inside the entrance door. Turning the tiny gold knob, he opened the case and took out a stiff folded board, revealing many chess pieces.

"The refrigerator's in the small rec room around the corner on the left, across from the lab," Evan said. "Please, if you would, pour me something… all right?"

"All right," I said. "But I don't know why you brought out the chess set. I told you, I'm not playing."

"And for heaven's sake, get a drink for yourself!" he called to me.

"You always say *heaven*!"

I returned from the rec room holding two cups. He was examining a rosewood chess piece. Each chessman lay in their separate red velvet compartment like a row of open coffins. I handed him his cup and took another gulp. It'd been too long since I had anything to drink that wasn't juice or water. He brought his cup to his lips, then abruptly stopped.

"Oh my God, Jamie… Did you drink the mango juice or the coke from the refrigerator?" His urgency startled me.

"What?"

"Did you drink the juice or the Coke? Just tell me!"

"The Coke. Why?"

"Oh for heaven's sake, let me see… You'll be okay, at least I hope." He paced around nervously. This was so out of character for him. My skin started to feel prickly.

"What?" I leaned forward. "You told me to get a drink. I did! You didn't tell me not to drink the Coke."

He placed his palm on his forehead and left it there. His thoughts appeared to race. "Listen to me, Jamie. You have to come with me right away."

"Why? Where? What's going on?"

"The Coke wasn't for drinking. We were growing a culture… never mind. I think you'll be okay."

"You *think*?"

"Come here," he said, and he led me to the lab in back, the same room I was in over a month ago after I had fainted in the field. He filled a cup of water, and while his back was to me, I saw the spot on the counter where the black notebook sat, but it was no longer there. At this point, I didn't really care. I was now feeling quite hot and anxious.

"Here, sit down. Drink this water. Keep drinking. You need to be as hydrated as possible." I drank, and he made a phone call. I drank again. "Pauline. How quickly can you prepare for surgery?"

"Surgery!?"

"Shhh," he said to me, then focused on his phone. I kept drinking, trying desperately to flush out the Coke. "Uh huh. Come soon as you can. Bring everything you need. Get the others here to assist."

"Evan –" He shooed me away with his hand, finished his call, and came to me. I drank more water. "Jamie, we need to act fast, okay? Don't be alarmed."

"Well of *course* I'm alarmed. What the… what's…"

"Just listen. We need to prep you for surgery. You ingested some very harmful chemicals."

"What chemicals? Surgery?!"

"In a moment, I'll need to put you out. When you wake up, it'll all be over, and recovery will only take about a month."

"A month!"

"Don't worry. You'll be fine. The scar will be minimal."

"Scar?"

He looked squarely at me, then said, "I got you back."

"Well, I'm glad you've got my back, but Evan, I really don't know what's..."

"No, I got you back." He smiled. In an instant, I knew I had been had. "I told you I would. I'm good at this, better than you."

What little water I had left in my cup, I threw at him, but he quickly dodged it and remained dry, though the floor did not.

"Now how about a game of chess?" he asked smugly.

Against my protests, Evan told the others to set up a game. Philip whistled as he unfolded the white card table and set it just outside the stone building, the same spot where it was two days ago. Philip set the board on the table, and Evan, who was smirking the whole while, arranged the chessman in their proper squares. Marvin, exiting the stone building, carried two chairs on either side of his body, and tripped over himself. I walked close to Evan.

"Evan, I don't want to play chess," I said in his ear.

"Mm hmm." He set a rook down at the corner of the board, still smirking.

"I can't face Pauline. Does she know? If she knows about the note, I can't face her."

"You ready?" he asked after all the chessmen were all in place. Then he took a seat at the card table and motioned for me to do the same. His eyes danced.

It was a quick game. Marvin stood inches from Evan, one hand holding his elbow, the other, his chin. Philip sat next to me, and he and Marvin coached me a bit, until Evan told them to stop. Sandra came soon after the game started, and sat in the remaining chair. She had on a straw sun hat with an orange chiffon ribbon.

Like Philip two days prior, I contemplated all possibilities before I finally made my move, after which, Evan immediately placed his move, then would look at me with that same damn smirk. He had two of my pawns and was quickly setting me up and locking me in for a sudden checkmate. I could see his strategy, but only when it was too late.

When Pauline came, I tensed. Evan looked up when he heard her approach, then looked at me and smirked. His face fell to concern when he looked at her again. She marched directly to Evan and said something in his ear, then handed him a note. He quickly read the note, stared at the paper for several seconds, then looked up at her, dead serious. Pauline looked worried. He nodded and she left. Philip studied Evan. Marvin studied the game. Sandra had given this transaction little notice and studied her nails.

"I'm afraid I'm unable to finish the game." Evan stood. Sandra looked up.

"But now we'll never know who would've won," I said, hoping he knew I was joking, but he wasn't paying attention to me.

"Well, actually," Marvin said, "you do have a slight chance of maybe turning it around, just maybe, if you would just position your knights, and castle your king and rook." Marvin proceeded to explain how, in perfect detail, to strategically maneuver my men so that I possibly had a chance of winning the game. No one was listening. Sandra was watching Evan climb the stairs to the stone building, while Philip put the game back in the leather case.

"What was that all about?" I asked, interrupting Marvin.

"I don't know," Philip said to me, then more to himself, "I honestly don't know." He folded the card table as Marvin continued discussing how knights can protect rooks. I thought it might be a good time to leave and head back to the stables. I stood.

"Seems he got some alarming news that he had to deal with," Philip said, interrupting Marvin.

"Does Dr. Bronte always interrupt his chess games?" I asked.

"Oh no, not always." Sandra said. She had taken me literally.

"Most of the time, he plays the game all the way through," Marvin said, taking me literally too.

"So what's up with him?"

"He's a moody man, Jamie." Philip said.

"I wonder if he was like this before his wife died," Sandra asked. "Do you know, Philip? You're the only one who knew him before we arrived here on the island."

"He lost his temper before his wife died, but only rarely." Philip said. "When we worked together in the States years ago, everyone respected the brilliant Dr. Bronte, and you know, he's calm and charming most of the time. But no one knew when he was going to blow up. No one knew when the good doctor would switch to his other self."

"Getting back to chess," Marvin said. 'Jamie, on your fourth move when you set your pawn out..."

"It must change a man to have his wife die on him," Sandra said under her hat.

"When did she die?" I asked.

"Three years ago."

I stopped dead. Three years ago. Three years ago.

Three years ago.

Chapter 42
THE NOTEBOOK

It was three years ago when Evan learned that he had a son and a daughter, twins, information his wife kept from him. I can only imagine what that might do to a parent, to learn that thirteen years of your children's lives have been kept from you. Then, coincidently, his wife died the same time he learned that she had deprived him of his children. The same time. Thoughts poured over me – thoughts of Evan suddenly shoving the card table over in a blast of rage, his co-workers talking about his uncontrolled temper, how he had lied about his identity when I first met him, Evan stabbing Grady's hand, Evan holding me with a knife to my neck, and how he had taken me against my will, which is called kidnapping, which is a serious crime, I do believe. He had even killed a cat! Had I been blind? Evan Bronte must have killed his wife!

How could Tom and Grady allow me to be alone with this dangerous man? My leader and my protector threw me to this wolf who dressed like a polished man. Now, here we were, without communication to the outside world, while Evan's computers were working just fine. Didn't that alone prove his guilt? Tom and the security men and everyone else at Main Campus were right; our sabotage had to be at the hands of this scientist all along. Why couldn't I see this? The worst matter of all was that the blood tests proved that we were being used for biological testing, and it was so very obvious to me at that very moment, as I stood with his team under the lamppost that jabbed into the sky, poking a hole in the heavens, that Evan Bronte had an evil side.

"Jamie, are you all right?" Philip asked.

"Philip, how did Dr. Bronte's wife die?" I asked slowly. "Wasn't she rather young?"

"It was an accident. She fell down a flight of stairs."

I now saw my chance to finally attempt to get to the notebook while Evan was distracted, while I had an excuse to enter the lab. I would simply go in and check on him, acting as if I were concerned after his abrupt departure from our game. The difficult part would be getting into the lab room alone and not getting caught as I read the contents of the notebook. I couldn't exactly carry the large heavy book out of the stone building, across the grounds, and through the gate.

I told the others that I wished to make sure that Dr. Bronte was all right. Philip assured me he was fine, that he always quickly bounced back to his well–mannered and enchanting self in due time, and suggested I give him space. Sandra agreed. Marvin cautioned to stay out of a possible attack zone, but I insisted.

Inside the stone building, my shoes echoed as I walked down the hallway, which stirred a beehive in my stomach. Walking more quietly, I entered the lab. I was alone.

Here it was, the fifth of August, when back on the first day of July, I had seen this lab room for the first time, waking up here in this very room after my strange fainting spell. I looked at the cot against the wall, the place where I had awakened over a month ago. The light green blanket that had covered me was now folded at the foot of the cot. That day seemed like an era ago when the tide and the trees and the wind were all carefree. The sounds and sights brought back the memory of the low drilling hum and the pulsating white in the room, the faint ammonia smell, the gray walls, and the cold sterile feel. The plastic human anatomy model seemed to suspiciously watch me as I walked across the room under the surgical's spotlight to the formica counter where the black notebook had been over a month ago. It was no longer there.

It was gone.

My eyes breezed over graph paper, a calculator, pencils, small glass tubes filled with muddy liquid, and a microscope… items that were scattered haphazardly on the counter. I looked behind the small plastic globe. Nothing. The black notebook was simply gone.

Crouching down, I tried the cabinet door that sat close to the floor, but it was locked. I wiggled the handle desperately.

"What are you doing?"

I jerked up, hitting my head hard against the counter. "Ow!"

"What are you doing?" It was Evan. Wife–murderer. His face was one of pure perplexity. I had only seconds until he became aware.

"I was looking for… I'm looking for…" He squinted his eyes in confusion. I couldn't think! I couldn't think! "… my glasses."

"Jamie, you don't wear…" That moment, his face fell from perplexity to grave seriousness, then stern displeasure. He briskly walked over to me.

"Get up!" he said.

With a gush of adrenaline that sickened my stomach, I sprang up and started to dart around him, trying to bolt away. He grabbed my upper arm as I was almost past him and yanked me back. His bottom lip protruded in anger. Now holding both my shoulders, he gave me two rough shakes. I thought of my Uncle Calvin.

"How could you betray me like this!" He gave me a final harsh shake as he yelled "How?"

"You killed your wife!" I half screamed.

"What?"

"I know you did!"

"Heaven forbid, how long have you been thinking this ridiculous absurdity?"

"I pieced it together today. I know it's true. You can't lie to me anymore!" I tried to wiggle free, and almost succeeded because for a moment, his bewilderment clouded his focus. "You killed your wife, just like you stabbed Grady's hand, just like you put a knife to my neck!

You even killed a cat! You act all nice and polite, but deep down, you're a monster. I see the monster in you more and more; it's so blatantly obvious now. You can't hide it from me anymore. I know that it was *you* who stranded us on this island, took down our computers while *yours* are still working, and you're biologically experimenting on us, which is sick! You hear me, Evan? It's *sick*! You're sick!"

We looked at each other, me breathing hard, and him staring at me in amazement.

"Are you quite done?" he asked, strangely calm. I was catching my breath.

"Quite."

"So you've decided, huh? You're prosecutor, jury, and judge, is that it? I don't even get a trial? What about *your* crimes?"

I realized then that I might have made a mistake, revealing to him that I knew of his guilt. I thought that with Philip and the others just outside, I was safe. Perhaps I thought wrong. I had to get out. I twisted to free myself, but he held on tightly, then with some effort, lifted me on the counter that was behind me, placing his hip in–between my knees, leaning in. I was trapped.

"I'm afraid I may have to keep you here with us for a while, Jamie, considering you tried to get at my personal log, which, I may add, I keep locked away. Careless of me not to have locked it away last month when you were here, don't you think?" I was sitting on either a pencil or the small flat calculator.

"Evan, please, I have to go home."

"Considering how you deceived me, I don't think I'm going to let you go. I'll rather enjoy sending a message to your friends who sent you on this little mission." He released his hand that was leaning on the counter too close to my hip and scratched his cheek. "It's a shame, because I had been growing quite fond of you." He placed his hand back down. "Tell me – all our talks and discussions… were they just to get inside my head, to get at my log?"

"Tell me – do you think you're going to get away with all this?"

After a couple seconds of looking at me with absolutely no emotion, he turned up a corner of his mouth.

"Hmm," he half laughed. "Well, this is quite a shame, Jamie. It truly is sad. I need to know… why did you do this?"

"Why? You're asking me *why*?" I tried to hop down from the counter but his body was in the way. "Listen, I never wanted this! I never truly suspected you, despite the fact that everyone else knew it was you, but I myself was never sure. I really wasn't. Maybe I kept visiting you because I enjoyed talking with you, liked being with you. I hated how they wanted me to get to your stupid notebook, I really did. I couldn't have cared less about your damn notebook. I never even tried to get to it, until it dawned on me, not even an hour ago, that you killed your wife."

"I killed my wife? You think I killed my wife? How in heavens did you get this into your head?"

"Three years ago, you learned that you had a son and a daughter, that she kept these twins from you. Three years ago, she dies. Falling down the stairs… yeah, right!"

Evan shut his eyes. "I loved my wife. Still do. I'm not going to discuss this with you."

"You held a knife to my throat, Evan!"

"Oh, for heaven's sake… We've been over this. I would never have hurt you, not in the least. Did I hurt you at all?" He tilted his head slightly. "I'm a survivor, Jamie. I did what it took to get away. If they had called my bluff while I held you, I still would not have hurt you, though I would have been at their mercy."

"I don't believe you."

"Believe what you will. I'm actually trying to help you and your friends."

"Right. By turning off our electricity. By stabbing Grady. By being a kidnapper. I still say you're some kind of monster."

"I suppose I have anger issues at times, and yes, I can be arrogant and rash. I do what I have to do. But I'm no monster, Jamie. I'm a good man."

He backed up from me, giving me space, and didn't stop me when I hopped down from the counter. However, he put his body in my way when I tried to pass him. I sighed and put a hand on my hip in exasperation.

"So what do I do with you?" he asked. "Do I simply let you go, after what you've done here? Do I ignore this, or do I take action against you and your co-workers? Do I let it go, like I've ignored your toying with me all along?"

"What are you talking about? I don't *toy* with you!"

"You sometimes say the most provocative and suggestive things to me."

"I do not! Never! Like what?" I was sincerely bewildered.

"At first I thought you were unaware of the double meaning you gave. Like the time you leaned your body on me."

"Oh that, oh God, I can explain." I shook my head in disbelief. "Since the accident, I have this… this *problem*. When I get…"

"What about when you leaned so close to me where your cheek almost touched mine, where your hair fell on my arm?"

"When? I never did that!"

"When we were discussing *The Good Earth*."

"I was just looking at the text you were pointing at! You held the book in your lap! How was I supposed to see the tiny print? My God!"

"And the time you were climbing onto your saddle. You… I'm not going to say this, Jamie."

"What?"

"Anyway, I let all this go, never acting on this out of respect for you. I chose to be appropriate, respectful. But should I respect you now? Should I, after what you've done here? After what you've done to me?" His eyelids moved as he looked me up and down. "An attractive young girl like you running your finger along my lip when I was tied in the hut… surely you knew what you were doing." He sucked in his lips and stared at my stomach. "I would strongly suggest that you get out of here before I truly turn into a monster."

He stepped aside, looking off into space, and I eyed him as I eased around him, then I ran for the door.

Chapter 43

INVADERS

Leaving the light of the research compound and passing beyond its iron gate, I entered the aphotic woods, which besieged me now, as briar and thicket consumed air and space. Tree branches dipped down towards me from the twisted sky, weaving and coiling, reaching as if to wrap around my marrow, suffocating me. I felt invaded.

Just then, there was a rustle of bush just off the path ahead of me. Startled, the white pony neighed and sprung his two front legs into the air, causing me to nearly lose my balance. As his two hooves hit ground, I saw a man grimy from dirt and sweat emerge from the woodland vines. It was Adrian! I almost didn't recognize him, with his neglected hair over weather–beaten and sallow skin, and his chiseled, angular features from recent weight loss, all of which gave him a rather untamed and bestial look. Losing weight and his sense of security turned his muscular body to a wiry one, though he was still quite fit. I noticed the way his pants fit around his waist. Once snug and sturdy, his pants now hung loose with the end of his belt strap hanging down. He viewed me from watery, half–primal and squinting eyes, and with vaguely feral movements, Adrian advanced towards me. The white pony sensed me, sensed Adrian, and backed up, as I hugged my legs around his firm belly. Adrian took the reins with his familiar sure command to steady my pony, as his other hand held a rifle against his sweat–stained shirt.

"Adrian!"

"What have you been doing?" His tone was sinister.

"Out riding. Are you okay? Why are you way out here?"

"Why are *you*?" The white pony jerked, but Adrian held him steady. "What have you done?"

"What? Nothing! Adrian? Are you all right?"

"Get down!" I looked down at him, stupefied. "Now!"

Stunned, I dismounted, and he roughly took the reins from me. I gasped. The sun caught his rifle and flashed a sparkle on the tip of the barrel. Adrian smelled bad. I started to lean on the white pony for support and comfort, and to create distance from Adrian, but the animal side–stepped to also get away from this man.

"Adrian, you're scaring me!"

"Jamie, I know about you," he said in a guttural voice. "I saw you! I saw you enter the research gate as if you have done so a hundred times before. You marched right up to our enemy as if they were your cousins. What are you doing with these people? What have you done?"

"I… Adrian…"

"Is it you?"

"Is *what* me?"

"Do you have something to do with the hell that's going on here?"

"What?"

"Are you working with them, Jamie?" He spoke from the sepulchral pit of his stomach.

"Me? Oh my God! No!"

"Come with me."

He let go of the reins to seize my upper arm, while his other hand still grasped the rifle. I was able to get the reins he had dropped before he tugged me on. We walked, with me leading the white pony.

"Adrian, I…"

"Quiet!"

We said nothing as we walked a couple of miles though the cheerless jungle. Even the birds were silent. The trees pushed their roots gravely into the soil, while their top trunks and limbs reached coldly into the dispirited sky. When we came to the path that veered off to the lagoon, he mockingly asked me if I wanted to go for a swim. I felt like crying. The Adrian I knew in the lagoon roughly one month ago no longer existed.

Adrian silently led me the rest of the way through the woods and back to our home on the west side of Jackel Island.

As we approached the campfire pit just behind Central Lodge, I saw Kane showing Derek the motions of chopping wood. The giant man merged with the little boy as an ax glistened in the sun between them. Henry was not far from their feet, pawing the sawdust. It took the pup a moment to detect me, and when he did, he bounded towards me. I tried to bend down to scoop my dog up, but was unable to because Adrian was holding my upper arm. Now early afternoon, Henry seemed to have grown since I'd left early this morning. I ached to hold my dog.

Kane stopped when we approached and straightened, looking concerned. Derek looked over. I appeared to be Adrian's prisoner and was close to tears, while Adrian was a ghastly sight, looking like a wild man or crazed soldier who had lost his way in the jungle.

Without stopping, Adrian gave a single nod to Kane as we passed. Not seeing Kane's mouse, Adrian nearly stepped on it as the mouse scurried away just in time. Derek muttered an inaudible question, and Kane covered the boy's shoulder with his large hand. I gave Kane a pleading look, and his return was one of affliction, anguish, and heartache.

"Man, Mr. Hankey, you need a shower!" Grady said when he saw us. He had just emerged from the men's showers and was drying his hair with a towel. I assumed he was referring to Adrian.

"Hey there, Chica! Don't get too close to Mr. Peccary here, it may be contagious." His smile faded. "Hey, what's the matter with you two?"

"Get Steve and Tom, now!" Adrian commanded.

"Yes, Sir!" Grady said emphatically, and he hurried off, but not before he turned to give us a surprised and curious look.

Grady soon returned with our island's leader, who was untangling fishing line as he approached, and with somber-looking Steve who marched right alongside Tom.

"What's up?" Tom asked Adrian when he got within earshot. He looked up from his fishing line, and when he saw our filthy and angry Chief of Security holding me as I was scared and uncertain, he let the fishing line drop to his hip. Tom looked at Grady, who shrugged. Steve gave me a quick glance, then looked at Adrian with his head slightly cocked. He held no expression.

"What the devil is going on here?" Tom asked.

"Ask her!" Adrian said, and he pushed me forward, finally releasing my upper arm, which had gone numb from its circulation squeezed off for so long. I imagined I would be wearing a gray imprint of Adrian's fingers on my arm for days.

"What do you mean, ask her?" Tom asked.

"You're saying that Jamie's a Mata Hari?" Grady asked.

"Seems she's a familiar sight over at the research center," Adrian said. "Seems she and Bronte are no strangers to each other."

Tom spun on his heels and exhaled through puffed cheeks, looking at the treetops, while Grady raised his eyebrows and scratched his head, giving a "we're in trouble" look. Steve merely creased his eyebrows.

"You didn't tell him?" Tom turned back around to ask me. I shook my head.

"Tell me what?" Adrian demanded, leaning his head to the side, now suspicious of Tom. He looked at his two assistants with the same dark suspicion. Steve remained poker-faced while Grady gave an exaggerated innocent little boy look, which made me almost smile in spite the situation, though Adrian did not see the humor in this.

"All right, Adrian, it's time you knew," Tom began.

"Oh, here come the fireworks," Grady predicted, but he underestimated the explosion which followed.

Tom began to explain to Adrian that he had directed me to spy on Bronte to get to the notebook, how it was our only course of action, an action that he realized Adrian would never have approved of.

"Damn right I would not have approved of this!"

"It was my call," Tom said. "I didn't need your approval."

"Like hell you didn't! Who's in charge of everyone's safety here, huh? Who?"

"Watch it, Adrian!"

"How long have these shenanigans been going on BEHIND MY DAMN BACK!" Adrian then shoved Tom, and Tom almost fell backwards, as his feet took many back–steps too quickly.

"Whoa Nellie," Grady said holding his hands out towards his boss. Even Steve was alerted, stepping forward while raising his hands a few inches.

"*That* was for arranging this behind my back," Adrian sneered at Tom, then shoved him again, hard. "And *that* was for putting Jamie in grave danger, you coward. Would you put Darcy between you and an assailant?" Tom immediately swung a fist at Adrian, but missed when Adrian dodged his strike.

I was surprised that it mattered to Adrian whether or not I was in a compromising situation, considering Adrian's fury with me the last hour. As soon as Tom gained his balance, he came again at Adrian, who was ready for him. Adrian struck Tom in the mouth. Tom fell back and staggered.

"How can I do my job and keep everyone safe when you're so reckless?" Adrian shouted. "I'm going insane, trying my absolute damnest to keep everyone secure, and failing miserably, because you pull stunts like this behind my back!"

There was further shouting and shoving about who was in charge of what, and Tom got the worst of it, because his punches rarely landed. Adrian's did. Adrian dodged most of Tom's swings, then would immediately counter, one of which caught Tom under his chin and lifted him off the ground for a split second before he fell. Poor Tom picked himself up off the soil, wiggling his jaw and spitting blood into the dirt.

"Did you know?" Adrian turned to Grady.

"Who, me?" Grady asked, then looked at Tom, who eyed him from the tops of his eyes. "Ah, yeah." With a pop, Adrian struck Grady in the face. Grady looked stunned, then said "Oh, shit!" just as his nose began to bleed.

"Did you know?" Adrian asked Steve.

Just then, Tom darted towards Adrian, grabbing him in a football tackle to take him down. He was unsuccessful; Adrian remained standing. Adrian began pounding Tom in the ribs and back until finally Grady and Steve rushed to Adrian and held him back, for Tom had had enough.

"Man, you stink!" Grady said, and I saw Steve lean his head away, either from Adrian's flailing arms or from his smell.

Adrian struggled to free himself from his two assistants, while Tom breathed heavily as he leaned forward, unable to stand straight, resting his hands on his knees for support. He dabbed his bleeding lip with the back of his hand. I went to Tom and put my hand on his arm. Grady, holding Adrian by his upper arm, looked over his shoulder and told me that this was not a pretty sight and suggested I leave. I did.

Word spread quickly about the fight between Tom and Adrian. Brian wondered if Tom was going to fire Adrian, and Jeremy told him how ridiculous that was.

"Yeah, he's going to have Adrian go stand in the corner, you moron," Jeremy said to his best friend. "As if we don't need our top security guy. As if Tom could stand a chance against Adrian."

"But Tom's our leader," Brian argued.

"We ain't got a leader any more," Jeremy said. "Don't you get it? We're all on our own."

"That's not true, Jeremy," I said.

"Yeah, that's not true," Brian said.

The doctor treated Tom, asking what this was all about, but Tom said little. Joel was by his brother's side, while Darcy held his hand.

"It was kind of my fault," I told Jim.

"*You* beat Tom up?" Jim asked.

"No, I… No!" I said. Jim winked at me. Tom started to smile but moving the skin on his face hurt him. Darcy reached over and swatted me with the back of her fingers.

"Jamie was following my instructions, though Adrian didn't exactly *appreciate* my instructions," was all Tom told the doctor. Tom had difficulty speaking, as his jaw wasn't working too well.

"Shh, honey," Darcy told him, rubbing the top of his hand. "Don't talk if it hurts."

"*Adrian* did this?" Joel asked.

"Adrian…" Jim said more to himself, and he continued treating Tom. Joel asked his brother what those instructions were exactly, but Tom did not answer. Joel looked at me, and I shrugged. It was up to Tom to tell his brother. Besides, I wasn't too proud of what I was made to do. I wasn't sure how it was going to be received by the others.

When Jim finished treating Tom, he took a final swallow of his coffee, firmly clunked the cup down on the table, then said he needed to give our Chief of Security a piece of his mind. He headed for the door.

Go Jim!

"Don't! Leave it alone!" Tom called out to him, cringing a bit from his pain, but Tom was unable to stop the doctor. We heard the door slam.

"Well I'll be damned, our good doctor!" Darcy said.

I wondered what it would be like to be reprimanded by Jim. More so, I wondered how Adrian would receive this, as Adrian deeply respected our doctor.

As we were gathering outside Central Lodge for dinner, Earl stood with Tom by the water basin and was showing him how to jab–cross–hook. Tom playfully pushed Earl away, saying to leave him alone, that he already knew how to fight.

"Apparently not, son!" Earl told him.

"Want me to prove it?" Tom asked with wide eyes, smiling as best he could.

"You don't want that, boy, not in your condition," Earl said. "Besides, I've been in a few scrapes or two in my day. I was a prett-tty fair fighter, if I do say so myself."

"If your fists are as ornery as your mouth, I bet you were."

Preferring to eat alone this evening and many other evenings, Kane sat on the soil and leaned against the far side of the water basin with a wooden bowl of fruit, not reacting in any way to Earl's fighting lesson and their bantering back and forth. An hour ago, I was with Kane, showing him how big Henry was getting, asking if there was any way to make it stop. I preferred he stay a puppy. Kane's answer to me was just a smirk as he held the basin's ladle an inch from his mouth. He was about to take a drink when Tom stumbled by. This was the first time Kane had seen Tom's injured body. He had stopped moving the ladle towards his mouth and gazed with dejection. Now, Kane sat rooted into the earth by our leader's feet, popping mangos and lychees into his mouth. I wondered if this gentle giant knew how to fight, and figured that he could give better advice than Earl about any jab–cross–hook or such, though Kane preferred to keep his mouth shut.

Tom had entered Central Lodge very slowly with a bend to his back, and his face had purpled. Sheila and the nurses were the only ones who hadn't heard the news and stared imprudently at Tom, then whispered among themselves.

For no reason we knew of, a pewter cup sat at each of the seventeen place settings on the table. Before the room buzzed too loudly with questions about the cups, Tariq announced that we were having wine with dinner tonight, something he'd only done on holidays or when the men from the supply ships used to visit. One by one, Tariq poured red wine into each of our cups as we silently looked up at him in wonder. He even poured a swallow into Derek's cup and instructed the boy to sip, always sip wine, not gulp, or he'd knock him in the head. Derek looked up at the master cook wide–eyed with fear. With Tariq preoccupied, Jeremy got up to take the extra wine cup that was set aside for Kane, but Grady beat him too it, smiling. Grady drank every bit that was in the cup, all the while staring right at Jeremy. Jeremy was not amused. Darcy and I looked at each other and laughed.

Tom sat at one side of the head table with his brother, the doctor, and Earl. Adrian, Grady, and Steve sat together at the other end of the head table, and two empty seats formed a great divide between the two sides like the Berlin Wall. I noticed that Tom and Adrian never looked at each other. I supposed that was better than both of them glaring at each other. I also noticed that Adrian had showered and wore a clean shirt, though he hadn't shaved.

"What's going on?" Derek asked.

"Shhh, baby, nothing," Darcy told him.

"Why aren't they sitting in their normal seats?" Derek asked.

"They're just having a little disagreement, that's all," Darcy said.

"Yeah, they just want to kill each other," Jeremy said, returning to our table.

"Shut up, Jeremy!" Darcy said.

"You shut up!"

"No, *you* shut up!"

"No, *you* shut up!"

Derek covered his ears, and Brian asked them to please stop.

Shifting Henry from my lap to Derek's, I got up from the table to get more juice from the beverage table at the back of the room. Lately, Derek and I had been smuggling Henry in during the dinner hour. No one cared except for Tariq and Earl, who both agreed that a dining room was no place for a dog. I disagreed, and actually, there was no place that Henry would rather be, and he ate well at Central Lodge now that Adrian had supplied us with a surplus of meat. The problem was that Henry was getting too big to smuggle, and definitely too big for our laps. Derek said that if he didn't eat so much he wouldn't be getting so big so fast. He had a point. Sheila said that it was gross that dog slobber was in the same room where we all ate, but she never did tell Tariq on me, so I didn't tell her that Henry's slobber was way cleaner than her own.

As I poured juice into my glass, I heard Adrian tell Steve that someone present in the room had betrayed him. Evan had used the same word, and I felt a sting in my intestines at the thought of it. I wondered if Adrian had purposely meant for me to hear his words as a stab at me, a hurtful puncture like Grady's knife wound, or if he was referring to Tom. I thought of how Adrian had denied our possible budding relationship during the days following our encounter at the lagoon, when all our troubles on the island had just begun. I now denied Adrian my heart. I no longer knew this Adrian. Adrian denied me, then I denied Adrian, and later Evan and I denied each other. Perhaps Evan had denied all of us any human decency the whole time. Pretending I didn't hear Adrian, and without looking at him, I left the drink table and went back to join Darcy, Brian, Jeremy, and Derek.

Jeremy pumped me for details on the fight. I told him to get a haircut. Jeremy persisted, despite Darcy and Brian telling him to leave me alone. When he refused, I left our table and headed for the fruit counter.

I joined Tom and Earl by the assorted fruits, and Earl told Tom to keep his elbows down as he punched to cover his ribs, and to tuck his chin to protect his neck. Tom response was "yeah, yeah, yeah." I saw Tom wince when he reached for the star fruit, so I pushed Tom's hand back, and I dropped pieces of star fruit on his plate. Tom silently mouthed "thank you" to me, which again made him wince in pain, either from his cut lip or his injured jaw. Evan crept into my mind again, the image of his cut lip, the image of me breezing my finger over the crust of his wound and the curve of his lip, touching a washcloth on his skin, feeding him. I never knew how all this had made him feel, or what it was exactly I felt. Then a strong surge of guilt, his and mine, crashed on me. I could not process this, or deal with the strange ache it caused deep inside. Once again, I cast Evan out of my thoughts and down into my own personal hell.

Tariq proudly carried a heaping roasted babirusa hog on a large pewter platter in front of his chest, with pineapple scattered along the perimeter of the platter. Setting the platter down in the middle of the head table in front of the empty seats, he told us to remain seated because he had another special surprise, and disappeared into his kitchen. The hum of conversation stopped as we quietly waited. Tariq quickly returned with a long wooden bowl that held a lavish loaf of bread, and he placed it by the hog. Bread! Our diets had consisted mostly of meat and fruit, so bread was most welcomed. Adrian, Grady, Jim, Earl, Darcy, and Jeremy rose from their seats and went to get either meat or bread. I wondered if we had now mostly used up our reserves of flour, yeast, sugar, and other ingredients. I also wondered what had gotten into Tariq, offering us bread and wine when there was no special occasion, when this was not a special supper.

That night as I slept in my bed, my dream changed to where the bed was shaking, and then a large hand softly shaking my shoulder awakened me. I felt Henry's tail thumping on my face. I opened my eyes and saw Kane standing over me in the dark. I shot up.

"You must come! There's danger!"

"Hmm?"

He put his hand behind my head and gently led me off the bed. The clock read 4:07. Derek stirred, and Kane scooped him up.

"What's going on?" I asked.

"Follow me. Quickly!" Kane said, holding Derek. Derek squirmed a bit in Kane's arms and miraculously fell back asleep.

"Kane, I need to change my clothes."

"No time. Just put on shoes, and pull a shirt over your sleeping clothes to warm you against the night air. Come, we must go!"

Outside, the black air chilled and invigorated me as we hurried over the hard ground towards Central Lodge. We cut behind the Medical and the Administration building. Kane traveled in the shadows, holding Derek against his chest and keeping me close. Henry followed by our feet.

When he opened the heavy lodge door with his free arm, the light inside Central Lodge hurt my eyes. Tom, Darcy, Joel, and Jim were already inside by the fireplace. Then I noticed that Sheila and the two nurses were here too, huddled together in the back of the room by the tables, separate from the others.

"What's going on?" I asked. Kane had told me nothing. Tom, Jim, and Darcy hurried to me as Kane gently set Derek, who was amazingly still asleep, down on the couch. It was comforting to see that Tom had on his pajama pants like I did, though he pulled a regular shirt on, and Darcy wore a nightie with a red button–down shirt thrown over her shoulders. I didn't feel so ridiculous.

"Kane spotted a boat," Tom said. His face was even more discolored than it was at dinner, and he now spoke with a slight slur from a swollen jaw.

"That's fantastic!" I said with a big smile, only they weren't smiling. "Isn't it? What…"

I heard the front door shut and saw that Kane had left the building, heading back outside and into the black night.

"Where's he going?" I asked. "What's going on?"

"Jamie, sit down," the doctor said, and I sat on the couch between Jim and Darcy. Tom sat in one of the chairs, while Joel remained standing near the door, looking nervously out the window.

"Kane went to get the others to bring them here to safety. We're all gathering here," Jim explained. "Kane's acting as a scout."

"Why?" I asked. "What's going on? What about this boat?"

"Jamie, it's not good!" Darcy said.

Before Darcy could answer, Joel, who was standing by the window, quickly said, "I see something!" Forgetting his injured state, Tom sprung to his feet and Jim dashed to the window. This made my heart jump. Darcy took my hand and squeezed it. Then Joel said, "Oh, it's nothing. It's just the wind. It moved a twig behind the computer building. I thought…"

Jim and Tom sat back down, but not before Tom swatted his brother's chest with the back of his hand.

"Jamie, a boat has arrived on the island," Jim explained. "Kane spotted it not even twenty minutes ago. It must mean a ship is further out."

"Well, that's great, isn't it?" I said. "Isn't this what we've been waiting for?"

"It's not a supply ship, Jamie," Tom said.

"Well, what is it then?" I asked. No one answered. I looked at them all one by one, and they all looked at Tom.

"It appears to be a boat full of soldiers."

Piecing together what Tom and Jim told me, I learned that Kane saw a boat docking during the dead hour of the night. Roughly a dozen men, all in some kind of dark uniform, slipped out of the boat and traveled into the woods and towards the east side. No one knew if these men were under the direction of Evan Bronte, another crazy man or woman here on Jackel Island, Jao Institute, a fanatical group, the United States military, or even a foreign military.

"We're assuming their intentions are not good, but we're not even sure of this," Tom had said. "Considering all that's happened, we can only assume the worst."

Adrian, Grady, and Steve had set out into the woods to learn what they could, and to protect us, if they were able to. They planned to see where the soldiers were, and to find out if the boat was guarded, to see if we could possibly escape off the island. They had rifles. "This is profoundly dangerous for them," the doctor said.

I heard what sounded like a quick shriek of laughter from the back of the room. We turned our heads to Sheila and her two friends, and the sound came again. It wasn't any shriek of laughter, it was hysterical crying.

"Excuse me," Jim said calmly, and headed towards the women.

"Kane's got everyone from the cabins on Admin side and has brought them here," Tom said, "only we can't find Earl."

"He sometimes sleeps in the stables," I said.

"We haven't been able to get Tariq, Brian, or Jeremy yet," Darcy said. "We have to get those three."

Ten minutes later, Kane returned, but only with Brian. Brian rushed to Darcy and me, and we embraced him. I saw Brian rest his forehead on Darcy's, and they held on like this for several seconds. Joel watched us from the window, unable to connect, but wanting to, I think. I felt a pang of affection and sorrow for him. Brian, stupefied like I had been earlier, asked the same questions I had asked, and they filled him in.

Tariq had refused to come with Kane and had stayed in his bed, saying this whole matter was ridiculous. Jeremy was not in his cabin and was nowhere to be found. He and Earl were missing.

"What are we going to do, Tom?" I asked.

"I don't know," Tom said. "I don't know."

Chapter 44
SECURITY RETURNS

All was quiet in Central Lodge during the two hours before dawn. We had settled down. Brian and I had joined Derek and Henry on the couch to try to get an hour or two more of sleep. Brian had just started to gain weight again due to Adrian's hunting, and the couch allowed only so much room for all four of us. Sleeping was near impossible; there were too many legs sticking in too many directions.

Tom sat in a chair with Darcy on his lap, and she softly snored. I couldn't tell if Tom was sleeping. His eyes were shut but his breathing wasn't relaxed.

Jim sat in the other chair, but every time I looked at him, his eyes were open. Half the time he was staring off into space, probably thinking about his wife. Or us. Other times, he caught me checking on him, and he'd turn up a corner of his mouth in a half smile, while his eyes remained sympathetic and sad.

The faint crying from the girls in the back of the room eventually ceased. Joel settled down under the window, leaning against the wall.

An eerie sense of contentment, peacefulness, and well–being softly poured over me, and I realized that I could easily get used to all of us sleeping in the same room, providing I wasn't sharing a couch with Brian's elbows. I wondered if it was primal human nature to sleep as a group and not alone. As I faded, I thought of the expression, "it's always calm before the dawn," or was it "it's always the darkest before a storm." I couldn't remember.

I drifted in and out.

A blast of dim morning light pierced my eyelids as the lodge door opened. Cool fresh air caressed my face. I pushed Brian's arm off me and sat up, rubbing my eyes. Henry jumped off my legs and scampered to the door, wagging at Grady and Steve's feet as they stood at the lodge's entrance. They each held rifles, objects that were wrong and out of place, like muddy boots in a church. Tom and Joel were already by their side, and Jim was slowly rising from the chair. Brian stirred. Derek slept.

"Where are the men from the boat?" Tom asked.

"Where's Adrian?" the doctor asked at the same time.

"Is everything all right?" Joel asked.

Grady held up his hands to slow the questions down. Steve surveyed the room behind Tom's back. Our eyes locked, and for a split second, he scared me.

"Whoa all you inquisitive Nellies!" Grady said. "The situation is under control, for the moment." His upbeat Grady–style casualness relaxed me a bit.

"They're stationed behind the research center," Steve quietly said to Tom. "Two of them are guarding the boat. We couldn't get too close."

"Are they communicating with Bronte?"

"Couldn't tell. Probably." Steve said.

"Sick bastard's probably having tea with the soldiers," Grady said. "Chica, you've got to clean this up!"

For a second, I thought Grady meant that it was up to me to clean up this dire situation we were in. But then I noticed that in his excitement, Henry had piddled near the door by Grady's feet. I thought he had outgrown peeing upon seeing men for the first time. The two security men gingerly stepped around the puddle and entered the room. Grady looked about the room.

"Damn, I missed a slumber party," he said.

Darcy stretched in her chair, not quite awake yet.

"Where's Adrian?" Jim asked again. "He's okay, I take it."

"Oh, yeah. He went to wash up." Grady said. "Lord knows, he's been needing to. Whew!" Grady walked over to waking Darcy and bent down to stick his face near hers so he'd be her first sight upon waking. She pushed him away with her foot. "We need to round up some guys to transfer the rest of the rifles from the hut to here," Grady said as he stood and walked towards the couch. "Where's Earl? Shining his cowboy boots or twirling his lasso? Where's that skinny boy?"

"That's what we'd like to know," Tom said. "And did you see Kane?"

"Yeah. He's outside in back, keeping an eye on the woods,"

I went in the women's bathroom to get damp paper towels to wipe up the mess Henry made. Tom told us weeks ago to use paper products sparingly, to use cloth instead, but this warranted paper, not cloth to be washed and reused. Darcy entered the women's room, still half asleep. I handed her the wet paper towel and asked her if she wanted to wipe up Henry's pee, and she pushed me away with a moan and dragged herself to the sink with half–closed eyes.

When I returned to the others, Grady and Steve now sat on the couch with Derek between them. How this boy could *sleep* during all this was beyond me. The way the two security men sunk in the couch reminded me that they hadn't slept. Tom and Jim had returned to the chairs. Stiff from his injuries, Tom was moving slowly, and his face was an array of stormy colors. Brian wasn't in the room anymore, and I heard noise from the men's bathroom. Sheila and the two nurses had joined us up front, dragging chairs. One of the nurses came up to Grady, and he stood. They hugged, and I saw Grady's face become serious and tender.

As I cleaned up the mess, I heard Grady tell Tom that Adrian suggested they take shifts, along with Joel, Kane, and Earl, to secure the perimeter of Central Lodge.

"Don't exclude me here," Jim said.

"It's dangerous," Tom said. "We may very much need a doctor."

Jim was a healer, not a warrior.

With no seats open, I sat on the floor and leaned against the couch, partially against one of Grady's legs. Normally, I avoided any physical contact whatsoever with Grady, but he, Steve, and Adrian had risked themselves for us during the night

Just then, the lodge door opened, and Adrian stood silhouetted at the entrance. When he stepped inside, I couldn't believe what I saw. Tom stood. Brian came out from the men's room and stopped in his tracks. The others looked up, astonished.

"Well now, Handsome, welcome to the world of the civilized!" Grady said with a big grin.

Adrian stood before us clean–shaven with cropped hair and groomed fingernails, dressed and polished in clean clothes. I stood up from the floor, and his eyes met mine. He smiled.

Adrian had returned to us.

Adrian owned the room as he stepped towards us and fully entered the space, once again, taking his former accustomed command. He went over to Tom and patted his arm in a friendly manner, then made a sour face. "Ooh, that must hurt!" he said playfully. Tom just squinted and shook his head at him.

We all took our seats, with Adrian picking up Derek, who was starting to wake up, and putting him on his lap as he sat in the middle of the couch. I sat back on the floor with Grady's leg on one side of me, and Adrian's on the other. Adrian gently pushed his leg into my side and I felt a slight stirring, and then it was gone.

Jim asked Adrian if he saw Jeremy, Earl or Kane this morning.

"Only Kane. He was by the campfire, watching out in the woods. Are the other two missing?"

"Yeah, I'm starting to get a little concerned," the doctor said. I told Jim that Earl often slept in the barn and skipped breakfast. Brian told him that Jeremy had become a bit of a hermit as of late, sometimes out roaming all night and sleeping during the day. Adrian said he and Kane would venture out to look for Jeremy and also go to the stables to get Earl. He also told us to get Tariq's cantankerous ass in here, as none of us should be alone.

On queue, Tariq pounded in the lodge and stopped abruptly when he saw us all camped out about the room.

"What you all doing? You all go back to your homes, now, and stop this foolish thing. I have a meal to prepare. Now git!" When we all just gaped at him without moving, he threw his hands in the air and moaned, then muttered something inaudible about our sensibilities as he walked past us towards the kitchen.

Adrian gave Tom ideas for securing Central Lodge, mapping out where our men would be placed outside for optimal security of Main Campus, with shifts which would allow them time to rest and eat at intervals. Tom agreed to Adrian's plan. I saw Jim catch Adrian's eye, and he nodded, and I knew that there was an understanding between the two of them.

Jeremy's timing was impeccable. With rumpled clothes and hair in his eyes, Jeremy crashed through the lodge door seconds before breakfast was served. Even the old Jeremy didn't ever simply *enter* a room, he always burst in. We had much to tell him, as he hadn't heard about the boat that had landed on our beach, and the men from some army that had intruded on our island. We filled him in. He, of course, had many questions.

Earl had joined us a half hour ago, arriving through the doors with Kane and Adrian. Like we thought, they'd found him in the stables. Adrian was a bit upset with us because no one had retrieved Earl during the night while the security team was scouting in the woods. He said that it had been unsafe for Earl to be alone. Tom told him he'd considered venturing to the stables with Kane and his brother before dawn, but it was too much of a risk with soldiers, or whoever they were, lurking somewhere. Adrian considered this, and nodded. After we told Earl all that had happened, Earl was ready to "kick some army butt," as he put it.

Tom told us that we should all stay in Central Lodge as much as we could, but if we had to leave the building to get clothes or any item from our cabins, for whatever reason, we had to travel with a partner and make sure at least three people knew our whereabouts. Also, we had to return within fifteen minutes or someone would go out looking for us. The men were to start their guard duty immediately after breakfast.

"If we stick together, we will get through this," Tom said.

"But what's to stop the soldiers from annihilating us, even if we're all together?" Brian asked.

"If the soldiers come to Main Campus, we'll deal with it," Adrian said. "Trust us."

"Why aren't *I* included in guard duty?" Jeremy loudly asked. Several of us turned our heads to look at him, as his tone was rather belligerent.

"You have no training, Jeremy" Tom said.

"Neither do you!" Jeremy shouted. "Look how beat up you are."

"Watch your mouth!" Adrian told him.

"Joel and Earl have no training either. Neither does Kane, I bet." Jeremy pleaded. Joel looked at the floor, while Earl glared at him. Kane, who was standing by the fruit, calmly brought watermelon from the tip of his kīlaya knife to his mouth and looked emotionlessly at Jeremy as he chewed.

"Jeremy, you're not the only male who won't be patrolling Central Lodge," Jim said. "Tariq, Brian, and I won't be either." The doctor attempted to console Jeremy, but Jeremy's face was bitter.

"Or Derek!" I said. My humor was not well–received by Jeremy.

"I won't be doing what?" Derek asked, and looked around. When no one answered, he asked, "What won't I be doing?"

"You should be glad, Jeremy." Brian said. "It's dangerous."

Jeremy mouthed "faggot", and Jim immediately yelled his name in stern disapproval.

"Can't have a boy do a man's job," Grady said. "Hell, Darcy weighs more than you, kiddo!"

"Thanks a lot!" Darcy said.

"Fuck you all!" Jeremy said. He shot up from the table, and headed for the door, but Adrian was on him in a minute, and he pinned Jeremy against the wall with his forearm under his chin.

"You watch your mouth, young man! There are ladies and a small child in the room. Have a shred of honor! Now apologize to everyone for that worthless sailor's tongue you got."

"I won't!"

"You will!" Adrian tightened his grip and brought his face close to Jeremy's. Jeremy squirmed. Adrian did not let up, and Jeremy's face turned red. It was painful to watch – Adrian, who was built like a drill sergeant, roughing up Jeremy, who was built like a frail teenager, a fate that gnawed at Jeremy to no end.

"I've got all day, boy!" Adrian said, drilling his eyes into him.

Jeremy, who was butter in Adrian's hands, finally gave in, muttering his apologies. When Adrian made him say it louder, I had to look away, as did Brian and Darcy, though Grady laughed, and Earl said the boy got what he deserved. Derek dug his face into my shirt and I held him tightly.

Sometimes, I did not understand the harsh and unrelenting ways of men, or of boys wanting to become men.

Chapter 45
THE WAITING GAME

All day, we waited. We waited for any sign of the intruders to appear at our Main Campus. We waited for one of our men to come rushing to us with terrifying news, or worse, not to come back at all. We waited for the boat to depart with the soldiers so we could continue our desperate lives here on Jackel Island. We waited for another boat to arrive, be it good or evil. We waited for help that we knew would never arrive. We waited in quiet chaos, in controlled panic.

The first time any of us ventured outside after breakfast was a bit frightening, even in the light of day. Several of us left the security of the lodge and each other to either change out of our nightclothes, to shower, or to grab a book or any object of interest from our cabins. I imagined snipers hiding behind trees, or soldiers crouching in the brush. Tom, Joel, Earl, Kane, and the three security men didn't appear to be frightened like this as they set out to patrol our area. Tariq denied there was a threatening situation as he paraded to his cabin, fussing when Grady insisted on accompanying him. Jeremy claimed not to be afraid and frequently left the lodge without asking for an escort, spiting authority. Through the lodge window I could see Kane following several paces behind Jeremy, keeping watch on him.

Grady and Steve carried a heavy wooden crate with black metal latches into the lodge. Appearing like a miniature coffin, the men set it against the wall under the front window. The crate contained weapons. Jeremy was inches from Steve just after the two security men had set the crate down, and Jeremy asked Steve if he could hold one of the rifles. Derek, who stood several feet away, asked if he could hold one, too.

Steve pushed Jeremy out of his way with the side of his pinky and headed for the men's room. Joel took his son by the shoulders and told him not to go near the crate, under any circumstances.

Kane came into Central Lodge, working with something in his hands. He leaned against the pole, and I saw that he was polishing Jeremy's tin whistle with a chestnut–colored felt cloth. He had rubbed out several of the rust spots. Kane looked over at Jeremy who was leaning forward in his chair, idly bouncing a small rubber ball between his knees without focusing on it or anything in particular. He seemed to be pouting. Kane slowly walked over to Jeremy, then handed him his former beloved instrument. Jeremy stopped bouncing the ball, looked at the whistle, then looked up at Kane.

"What the hell am I supposed to do with that thing anymore?"

"Simply accept it. Hold it in your hand," Kane said. When Jeremy didn't move, Kane added, "Please."

Jeremy looked at the tin whistle for several moments, then slowly took it. He twirled it in his hands.

"Why don't you play it?" I asked. Jeremy looked at me as though I was crazy. "Remember you used to play for me on the rock by the beach?" Jeremy used to soothe me when he played his tin whistle. Now he just made me sad.

By mid–morning, I was quite bored, and decided to take Henry for a short walk in the clearing by the water basin. Having just returned from first shift, Adrian asked if he could escort me. "Why? You need a body guard?" I asked Adrian.

"That's exactly it," Adrian responded.

Actually, I welcomed the added protection from our finest protector.

We walked the grounds in silence for a spell before either of us spoke.

"Jamie, I'm afraid I've been a bit of an ass."

"Mm. Perhaps a bit boorish." After a couple seconds of silence, we laughed. "I am sooooo glad you shaved, Adrian. And those nails, my word!"

"Mm hmm. I *did* let myself go, didn't I," he said. "Listen Jamie, I owe you an apology."

"Hey… don't."

"No, I'd really like to make amends. For a lot of things. To you, in particular." We stopped walking. Adrian traced his shoe along the dirt, then looked up into the sky, squinting. "Jamie, I was in a bad place. In my head, I mean. When things turned sour here, I felt pretty desperate to… to fix the situation, and when I couldn't… well… I'm afraid I let myself go, and I let you go, among other things. It really tore me up inside that I couldn't keep everyone safe, more than you know." He again drew his shoe along the dirt. "I was too thick–brained to see the tender things. I only saw the hell." He looked up at me. "I let you slip through my fingers."

I watched Henry dig frantically, shove his nose in the earth and get very still, expel air loudly, then dig frantically again. Sometimes we can only see things that are just an inch in front of us. We don't raise our head and see the horizon.

"Well, when everything started falling apart, you were just… preoccupied." I said.

"I should have been there for you, for everyone, *especially* in a crisis. Instead, I frantically tried to fix the situation. And when I couldn't, I retreated, from you, from the others… from myself…"

We continued walking. Henry ran on ahead. Curious, I thought, how a dog *follows* you, but is *ahead* of you. Sometimes I was unclear when I myself was leading or following.

"It still doesn't sit right with me that Tom and Grady sent you over to the wolves, putting you at such risk."

"Actually, Evan was most charming. He's guilty as sin, and he's a fraud, but he's a charming fraud, I can tell you that."

"*Evan* is it? Hmm." I said nothing. "He treated you all right, then?"

"Mm hmm. I mean, he never thrust any more knives at my neck or anything like that," I said.

"Well, that's always good."

"Yeah, that's a good thing," I said. "Strange thing is... his team... the other research guys? They seem to be really nice, just regular ordinary people."

We turned around and headed back. Henry soon caught wind of this and ran ahead of us.

"Hypothetical question here," Adrian said in an upbeat manner, starting a fresh topic. "If you had to choose... if you had to choose between killing Evan to get off this island, or letting him live which would mean we remain here the rest of our lives... what would you choose?"

"Oh, now *there's* a fun and cheery question!" I said. "Gee, let me consider..."

"Seriously, though, what would you choose?"

"I just hope it doesn't come to that."

Chapter 46
SUSPICION

In the afternoon, heavy winds swept the island, swaying the trees and emitting a long and low swishing whistle in the air. Then things changed among us.

Most of us were in Central Lodge, except for Tom, Joel, Steve, and Kane, who were on patrol around the perimeter of Central Lodge. We were scattered around the room, and we considered ourselves lucky if we had the couch or a lodge chair, because otherwise, we had to sit on one of the hard dining chairs, or the floor. Tariq was clanking plates, pots, pans, and bowls in the kitchen, cleaning up after lunch. We heard him humming.

"What's *he* so happy about?" Darcy asked.

"Damned if I know," Grady said. "It's annoying."

"Not as annoying as your mouth!" said one of the nurses. Darcy and I turned and looked at her. Grady slowly turned his head.

"Ouch, little lady!" Grady said. "Thought I was forgiven." He tried to look pitiful.

"Never!"

"Do we really have to hear about your lovers' quarrel?" Darcy asked. "I mean, gross."

"Why don't you ladies put a lid on it," Adrian said, then flipped a page from the gun magazine he was reading.

"Why don't you go hunt a bear or something, Adrian," Darcy said. Adrian looked up. "And besides, it was your precious assistant who started all this."

"Me?" Grady asked. "What the hell did *I* do?"

"You? You keep secrets, from what I hear," Earl said as he was playing with a rope, tying various knots. Grady shot me a look, and I shook my head, raising my palms to the ceiling.

"What secrets? What are you talking about?" Grady asked.

Just then, the winds picked up, and lightening illuminated the lodge in neon white for a split second. Henry started shaking.

"Whoa!" Brian commented on the approaching storm.

"Speaking of secrets, Earl," Grady continued, "I want to know why you spend so much time alone, why you skip out at meals, where you go at night, especially *last* night."

"What are you getting at?" Earl asked, and stood.

"You challenging me, old man?" Grady asked, and he stood as well.

"Enough!" Jim, who was looking through some of his old medical journals, said. Grady sat back down. Earl eyed him coldly.

Thunder cracked and vibrated in our chests, then another blast of lightening. The lodge lights flickered.

"Henry's terrified," I said.

"Who the hell's Henry?" Grady asked.

Oblivious, Tariq's humming from the kitchen grew louder.

"Sit back down, Earl," Adrian said.

"Not until this hooligan tells me what the hell he was implying." Earl tossed the rope down on the fireplace landing.

"Sit back *down*, Earl!" Adrian said again.

"It's just that it was strange that you were missing all night," Grady said. "What were you doing, out chasing buffalo? Does anyone else find the fact that Earl was gone all night a wee bit strange, especially when a group of men in uniforms shipped the same night?"

"But Earl always sleeps in the barn," I said.

"How do *you* know?" Grady asked me, giving his eyebrows two separate and distinct raises, Groucho Marx style.

Just then, I felt an instant chill, and then rain pounded the roof.

"The little pip–squeak guy with the flute was missing all night, too." Earl grabbed the rope and sat back down on the fireplace landing. "Ask *that* little twerp where *he* was."

"Shut up!" Jeremy said. He stopped bouncing his rubber ball.

"You telling me to shut up?" Earl said. "Come here, boy."

"Yeah, Jeremy. Where do you go off to at night?" Brian asked from the floor.

"I said shut up!" Jeremy commanded.

"Guys, please!" Jim said, keeping his eyes in his magazine.

It sounded as if the rain was going to pound through the roof, and it felt as if my blood was going to pound through my temples. Tariq simply kept humming through all this. I wanted to smash him.

"I just think it's really weird that you wander around at night, that's all." Brian said.

"Well, I think *you're* really weird." Jeremy said, and then he flung his ball at Brian, hitting him in the shoulder.

"Hey!" Brian yelped.

"Quit being an asshole!" Darcy snapped at Jeremy.

"People!" Jim set his journal down.

"Knock it off! All of you!" Adrian said, then got up, grabbed the ball from the floor, and tossed it to Derek, who caught it and looked confused. Jeremy mumbled something. "What was that?" Adrian spun around and loudly asked Jeremy, glaring at him.

"Nothing!" Jeremy said. Adrian eyed Jeremy a bit longer, then walked back to his seat.

Tariq's humming intensified as he reached several high notes.

"Will someone shut that guy *up*?" Darcy said.

"Jamie, are you telling Earl that I have secrets?" Grady asked.

"No!" I said.

"Then who is?" Grady asked.

"How the hell do I know?" I said.

"Since when do *you* swear?" Jeremy asked me.

"Jamie's not around long enough to tell me anything," Earl said. "Anyway, she didn't *have* to tell me, I already knew. We all know."

"Know *what*?" Grady asked. "*What* secrets? What are you talking about?"

"Seems you send a mere girl out to do your dirty spy work."

Grady slammed his fist down, his good hand. Derek jumped, and all side conversation ceased, amplifying the rain. We looked aghast at Grady.

"Adrian! You *told* them?" Grady said through his teeth.

"Calm down, I said nothing." Adrian said to Grady.

"Well, someone certainly did, and it wasn't Mother Theresa!"

"Mother Theresa?" Darcy said. "What's she have to do with the price of tea in China?"

"Who's Mother Theresa?" Derek asked.

"Shh, baby," Darcy told Derek.

"Where'd you hear this?" Adrian asked Earl.

One of the nurses laughed. "Grady, you say too much when you drink. You also talk in your sleep."

"Oh, do I now?" Grady said.

"Seems we found our leak," Adrian smiled. Grady was not amused.

"You know, Adrian, it used to be you, me, Steve, and even Tom drinkin' in the hut," Grady said. "Lately, it's been just me, Steve, and Tom. Where've you been?"

"You guys drink in the hut?" Darcy asked. "Tom never told me. I wonder why he never told me!"

"Adrian's been spending a lot of time alone in the woods," Jeremy said. "I've been noticing that. It's kinda' weird."

"What exactly were you doing by the research center yesterday, Adrian?" Grady asked. "When you discovered Jamie over there, why were you there yourself? Hmm? Were you fixing their plumbing?"

"Grady, you're out of line," Adrian said. "Way out of line!"

"How often do you guys drink in the hut?" Darcy asked.

"I think Jamie's the one with the most secrets," Sheila said.

"Me?" I asked.

"You were spending all this time over at the research center with Bronte. That's pretty weird, isn't it? I mean, *someone* brought our computers down, stopped the supply ships, froze our assets, and someone's using us as guinea pigs… and we all know who. It's Bronte!"

"Don't you think he has to have someone working for him? Someone who's stationed over here on Main Campus?" the other nurse said. "I mean, he can't do it all by himself from over there, right?"

"What are you two talking about?" I asked.

"I think you're working for Bronte," Sheila said. "Plain and simple."

"I think so, too," the other nurse said.

"Oh, for cryin' out loud!" Adrian said.

"Girls, please stop it," Jim said.

"Seriously, you guys drink in the hut?" Darcy asked again.

The sky brought another blast of light into the lodge.

"Really, Jamie, what exactly *were* you doing over in research all that time?" Jeremy asked. Jeremy's question was bad enough, but what really stung was when Darcy and Brian looked over at me, waiting for me to answer. I stood, thinking about escaping to the ladies room, or even out in the rain to be alone in my cabin. I took a couple steps towards the door. Jim looked at me, too, and I couldn't tell if he wanted to hear my answer, or if he was simply reading me to see how I was taking all this.

"Was that guy your friend?" Derek innocently asked me.

"Yeah, was Bronte your buddy?" Jeremy asked. "Huh?" Then Jeremy stood and came over to me. He looked calm, softer, and he was half smiling. I eased, thinking he was about to apologize. Had the old Jeremy returned, just as the old Adrian had returned to us? He got close to me and put his mouth to my ear. I leaned my head a little over to him, welcoming the closeness of the Jeremy I used to know.

"Is Bronte now your fuck buddy?" he whispered in my ear.

Jeremy eased his face back from my ear, and I stared at him in disbelief. All that was in me froze.

Jeremy was dead to me forever.

"What's going on over there?" Adrian asked; I *think* it was Adrian… perhaps it was Jim.

Our faces were inches from each other. His face changed from one of smug satisfaction to slight surprise, and then to realization.

"I'm sorry," Jeremy quickly said to me, looking almost frightened. "I'm… Jamie, I'm…"

A single syllable sound came out of me, some sort of cry, and I turned to the door.

"*What* did you *say* to her?" I heard Darcy ask.

A couple of people called my name just as I reached the door, and I heard scurrying, like some of them were coming to me, but I didn't turn around to look back. I just wanted everyone to leave me the hell alone.

"She's not going out there in this weather, is she?" I heard one of the nurses ask as I pulled the heavy lodge door. I felt Jeremy's hands on my arms, perhaps others' hands, but I shook them off me. I heard Jim yell my name, and Adrian called for me not to go out there. But it was too late. I ran. I didn't care if it was pouring outside. In fact, I welcomed it. I wanted the water to pound on me, to drown me, to dent me. I needed to feel something else that was stronger than what I was feeling.

I ran through the loud rain, running around the lodge towards the woods in back. My clothes were soon plastered to my skin like clinging burlap, and the cold rain stung my eyes so badly I could barely see. My skin shriveled with a deep chill. I ran on. I zigzagged around trees to lose anyone who may have been following me, as their voices faded in the pounding rain, in the slosh of my feet through the mud, and in the crack of thunder. I ran.

Chapter 47
MAD SCIENTIST

I ran through the woods, running as the leaves and mist breezed my face, running from my pain and anguish, running on and on until everything became a green and gray blur. Tears mixed with rain. I ran until there was no more run in me, no more *any*thing in me, where my breath pounded through my chest and my blood pushed through my torso, arms, and legs. My knees fell into the mud as I gasped for air, almost choking on it.

The rain died down to a trickle.

Without consciously realizing where I had been running to, it dawned on me, as I knelt in the mud with labored breathing, that I had been heading towards the lagoon. Emerald Lagoon, my small jade lagoon with the waterfall at the far corner that spewed a prism of colors, was the slice of paradise that I had once claimed as my own, once upon a time. I had not been to Emerald Lagoon since the first of July, which was over a month ago, which seemed a lifetime ago.

As soon as I once again set eyes on the lagoon, the sun came out, roaring in its glory, as if God was a conductor who began a grand visual symphony of joy. Before my feet, smooth tan sand and rock gave way to pine–green water, which led to the soft blue, purple, and maroon mists of the waterfall in back. With the new sun, birds sang after their lull during the rain, calling above the waterfall's calming rumble. Trees with their lush green surrounded and blanketed the lagoon, wrapping their maternal arms and wings around the water, tickling and embracing this treasure of a place.

I shivered. Dressed in shorts and a sleeveless shirt, my crinkled clothes stuck to my skin like wet leaves to pavement. My knees were coated in wet mud. Fully clothed, I entered the womb of the lagoon for its warmth.

"Fancy meeting you here."

I jerked my head to the voice. Adrian? No, it was Evan, standing tall with his shoulders back, his chin up, as one hand held his other wrist in front of his hips. He looked noble. He, too, had been caught in the rain, as his hair lay plastered to his head like ivy to brick, and his clothes hung drenched and darkened on his body. My first instinct was to swim to the waterfall for protection.

"What are you doing here?" I asked quickly.

"I'm wondering the same thing about you," he said. "Actually, I've come to warn you."

"Warn me what? How did you know I was here?"

"I know where all of you are, Jamie," Evan said. "I know that most of you have spent half of last night and all of today in your lodge, with the exception of Kane Jabari, who spends most of his time hidden in the woods. I know that your security team and a few other men patrol the area in two hour shifts."

"How do you know this?" I asked. Evan simply smiled. I waited. I heard the long drawn out fizzle of an insect directly above us. "How do you know this?" I asked again.

"We keep track of your whereabouts."

"We? Those men who came on the boat… they're with you?"

Evan stood very still watching me as I stood chest–deep in the water, water that acted as a barrier between Evan and me. I noticed water drip from his hair, the cuffs of his short–sleeved shirt, and the bottom of his long pants. He didn't shiver. In fact, it did not seem to bother him to be standing there in soaked clothes. I felt the sun on my face and shoulders, but still, I knew that if I left the protection of the warm lagoon, I would shiver.

Throughout time, there have been barriers, barriers that divide and isolate people, barriers that disconnect and sever the human heart. The Gates of Alexander, the Great Wall of China, the Berlin Wall, the Iron Curtain, the Israeli Gaza Strip, to name a few. The Belfast "Peace

Lines" separate Catholics from Protestants; Vietnam's 17th parallel separates the north from the south; Korea's north/south border divides the country; the United States–Mexican border separates Americans from Americans… all these amputate the human race, dividing soul from soul. In literature, it was the division between the Jets and the Sharks in *West Side Story*, Shakespeare's division between the Capulets and the Montagues, and the Socs and the Greasers in *The Outsiders*. With each example, there was an other side, an "*us*" and a "*them*". A "we" and a "they." There always seems to be an enemy, but no one ever claims to be an enemy himself. Here on Jackel Island, it was east versus west, security versus research. Now, a body of serene aquamarine water stood as a physical and psychological barrier between Evan Bronte and me, with me inside, and Evan, outside.

"Yes, they're with me. A scout keeps track of your whereabouts and reports to me."

"So you hired an army against us?"

"Heavens, no! Not a whole army. Just a squad."

"You would really do this? So it's come to this?" I asked. Evan said nothing, and he looked down. "Evan, are you going to hurt me?"

Evan slightly squinted his eyes. A slender-billed crow called from a tree limb that swooped down towards the lagoon, seeming to laugh at us.

"No," he said.

"Are you going to hurt any of us?"

Evan dropped his shoulders a bit and sighed. He walked towards me and crouched down at the edge of the lagoon, resting his elbows on his knees. Water nipped at the toes of his shoes as he studied the water.

"You've been experimenting on us, haven't you?" I asked.

Evan looked down at his hands. "Not me," he said. "Not exactly." Bringing his head up, he looked squarely at me. He was somewhat silhouetted, as the sun was behind him.

"Richard Gordon is not a moral man, Jamie."

"You mean Tom and Joel's father?"

"That's right. As you know, Mr. Gordon is CEO of Jao Institute, but on paper only. He supposedly oversees our bio–CMAT project."

"Well, doesn't he?"

"Technically, yes. At least that's what the public thinks." Taking stress off his legs from crouching, Evan sat in the sand, wrapping his arms around his knees. "There are three others who have rather… taken over the company. They used to be Mr. Gordon's right hand aides. The three of them, along with Mr. Gordon, had quite a covert operation going, until Mr. Gordon learned that his two sons' lives were in danger here on the island. His grandson, too. That's when he backpedaled, causing the other three to squeeze him out." Evan sighed. "Blackmail is quite powerful, especially when you have billions to lose."

I took a few steps through the water towards him.

"Are you one of the three?"

"Me?" He laughed a little. "Heavens, no." Evan unwrapped his arms from his knees and placed them behind him, leaning back. "Though perhaps I have more influence over Jao Institute than Mr. Gordon or the other three gentlemen would wish." A wind swept by, bringing a sweet smell. "I'm rather the brains behind their entire operation. Without me, well… there'd be no operation, no research. Up until now, that is."

"What is it that Jao's doing?"

"Bingo. That's the million dollar question." Evan looked up at the sky. "Under the guise of studying sleep deprivation, and under the guise of strictly adhering to legal parameters, mind you, our bio-CMAT project is *actually* studying whether or not *dissociative identity disorder* truly exists, and they're doing so under rather… illegal circumstances. *Extremely* illegal circumstances, I should say."

"Illegal? How? And what's dissociative identity disorder?"

Evan took his eyes from the sky and looked down at me. "You might know it as Multiple Personality Disorder."

I walked out of the water and sat next to him, dripping in the sand. I asked, "Is that what the movie *Sybil* ..."

"This condition is where the presence of two or more distinct identities or personalities exist in one person, usually caused, or believed to be caused by a severe traumatic event in one's childhood." I shivered.

"That's ironic, because we all were talking at our campfire one night, and we discovered that each of us had something pretty intense happen to us when we were kids." I brought my knees to my chest for warmth.

"That's no accident, Jamie. That was one criterion Jao Institute mandated in order to hire each of you. A severe childhood trauma acts as a trigger for this condition."

"I don't understand."

Evan drew on oval in the sand. "When an intense traumatic event occurs, the brain, to protect itself, sometimes can be thought to divide, in a sense." Evan drew a harsh line through the oval in the sand. "This occurs when the corpus callosum, which is the bridge between brain hemispheres, is suppressed." Evan then drew a squiggly line over his harsh line. "The neural memory traces become isolated from one another, where portions of the brain become isolated or compartmentalized." Evan drew small ovals within his big oval. I had no idea what he was drawing and had little understanding of what he was saying. I focused on the fading scar on his wrist. "It's a physical isolation of neural networks within the brain. With extreme and long–lasting stress, repeated compartmentalization," and he drew more small ovals, "can lead to deep–rooted changes in the neural circuitry, which could lead to a phenomena called '*split brain*'." Evan drew another harsh dividing line. I looked up at him. "With severe stress and trauma, chemical substances are released, causing the increased production of several neurotransmitters, including norepinephrine, opiates, dopamine and serotonin." I think Evan was used to writing on a drawing board, because he wrote the letters "N, O, D, and S" in the sand, each letter under the other. "Although the increased release of these substances is beneficial for short-term intervals, the long term effects of these substances are detrimental. Chronic stress can cause the death of neurons." He then wiped out his entire sand illustration with a swipe of his palm. "Thus, the disorder."

"Well thank you very much for the lecture, Dr. Bronte!" I said sarcastically. He cocked his head. "Evan, I never took biochemics 401. I have no idea what you're saying."

"Hmm." Evan looked down, then sighed before looking back at me. "And *biochemics* is not a word. Anyway, this disorder is one of the most controversial of all psychiatric diagnoses. The question remains – do multiple personalities exist?"

"I don't know."

"I… I'm not saying that you *do* know." I think he then rolled his eyes, if I read him correctly. "The debate still rages within the scientific community." Evan wiggled into his weight and became very focused. "If it were to be proved that multiple personalities do in fact exist, and a company such as Jao Institute were to prove this, then create a drug to alter its damaging effects, imagine the revenue this would bring."

"So does it exist?"

"Well, one thing's clear – it's not nearly as common as people thought a decade ago. A growing majority of mental health professionals believe that multiple personality disorder has been grossly over–diagnosed, a so-called "fad" diagnosis, due in part to the broadcast you mentioned, *Sybil.* Before *Sybil* aired in 1976, fewer than 200 cases were reported. Since *Sybil,* more than 20,000 cases were reported."

"So why does Jao waste time creating a drug for a disorder that maybe doesn't even exist?"

"Ahh, but Jao Institute is so very close to proving that it *does* in fact exist. That's where you all fit in."

"Us?" I shivered.

"That's right. If studies were allowed to use human subjects without following legal and moral protocol, research time could be cut by decades. The financial savings are staggering. To have you killed off and appear to be dead to the outside world is to their advantage. It's nothing personal on their end, I assure you."

"My God, are they trying to create alternate personalities in us?" My teeth chattered from my wet clothes.

"They're attempting to. But they're not successful. Still, the side effects are heightened senses, shortened sleep cycles, a tingling sensation, frequent feelings of euphoria intermixed with elevated stress levels, where people seem to be overreacting. Sound familiar?"

"So all that's been from a drug?" I quivered. "How… How have they been infecting us?" My body trembled.

"It's in the soap. Are you all right? Here, face the sun, let it warm you, try to relax."

"The soap?"

"Yes, the soap. Remember when you fainted and I brought you into the lab? When you tried to rub your rash off in the shower?" I nodded. "By rubbing and rubbing, especially when your rash made your skin more permeable, you, in essence, gave yourself an overdose. The injection I administered to you neutralized the effects."

"Evan, they aren't experimenting on you, are they?"

"No."

"So you *knew* all this was going on. You *knew* they were harming us, and you did nothing."

"Actually, I was working around the clock to develop an antidote, a counteragent that would nullify the effects. And I've been successful." Evan stood. "Jamie, had I come forward earlier, they would have killed me, and there would be no antidote."

He held out a hand and helped me up.

"They wouldn't have killed you. They need you. You even said… you're the brains in the company."

"Believe me, if it came to my revealing their actions…"

"But you're revealing information now. To me. Why?"

"Because this has to stop. The cat's out of the bag now."

"I don't know if you're telling me the truth, Evan. Some things still don't add up. Why were *our* computers down while *yours* were working?"

"They're not stupid. Jao wanted us to fight among ourselves, to make you all think I was the enemy instead of them. They purposely created a physical divide on the island from the beginning, placing a less equipped Main Campus on the west side, and our more luxurious Research Center on the east side."

Evan began slowly walking away from the lagoon. I followed him.

"I could no longer hide the fact from them that I was protecting all of you. I could only defer for so long before they caught on. I recently learned that they now have plans to either kill me or imprison me, because I know too much and am therefore a threat. They want me to comply and conduct my research for them under lock and key, where I'd be little more than a prisoner under their thumb for the rest of my life." Evan stopped walking and looked down at me. "I can't do that, Jamie. Thus, my squad. Former military friends. I, ahh, have connections." He looked up at the trees. "Jao is not fully aware of my resources. They underestimate me."

"Are they aware of your arrogance?" Looking back down at me, he was momentarily puzzled, then made a face, looking at me out of the corner of his squinted eye.

"Philip, Marvin, Pauline, Sandra… do they know all this?" I asked.

"Hmm." Evan continued walking, heading to the side path that led away from Main Campus, away from my home. "Up until this morning, my team knew nothing. Philip suspected, but to protect him, I never told him what was going on. My team was quite innocent. But now they know. They're quite concerned, actually."

"Kane – he seems to know. He always seems to know. Did you tell him?"

"Mr. Jabari? That fellow is an enigma to me. I've told him nothing."

"Why are you telling me all this now?"

Evan stopped.

"Because tonight, my squad is coming to your camp. Tonight, everything will be revealed. It may get a little sticky."

"Why are they coming? What are they going to do to us?"

"All of you need to be given the antidote, tonight." Evan said.

"What? Why?"

Evan held up a finger in front of my nose. "We need to act quickly before Jao learns that fifteen of my, uh, military friends have come to this island. I'm afraid that tonight may not go too smoothly if your people protest, which I suspect they will. I may have a hard time convincing your security team and your administrator that our intent is a moral one. There may be a bit of a… conflict."

"Evan, I don't think they'll believe you. They're going to put up a fight if you wish to vaccinate us all."

"Jamie, you need to come back with me. Things may be hairy tonight. I want you to stay with Philip and Pauline, out of harm's way when all of this is going down."

"I can't. I need to stay with my…"

"You must. You really must. I don't want you around when things get complicated. The squad is with me, but they're strictly military, and their methods can seem… harsh. They're armed, and they're prepared to use force, if necessary."

Chapter 48
THE RAID

I didn't go with Evan. I didn't go back to my side of the island either, at least not initially.

It took some doing to break from Evan, whose urging was borderline forceful. However, in the end, he let me go, with trepidation. I could see he was still doubtful, so I left quickly before he changed his mind.

I wandered through the wet woods, passing through the dense green of the verdant leaves and the opulent pine, tender in their sprouting, wondering where to go, where was home, and what was right. The jungle was profusely ripe, alive with bud and bloom, crawling with sap and viridian blood, with wet apple smells and olive sea colors. I thought of Kane who told me to listen to my heart, but I couldn't hear it, unless it spoke of trust and tenderness. Logic dictated otherwise. Do I follow my head or my heart? Was I being a fool to comply with Evan, to consider all he had told me, to even feel something similar to affection and tenderness for him? Logic and rationale pointed to his guilt, his crimes, his sins, and to allow him consideration, to let him into my heart was to play the fool, to lose touch with reality, and to lose my sense of sanity. I would perhaps even be putting the others at risk. But I felt the *being* of Evan, his presence, his entity, and his soul was kind and valid. At least maybe it was. I wasn't sure.

I passed through flower and blossom split and divided.

Suddenly, there was a rustle of brush, and two men clad in dark green uniforms were on me. Before I could utter a sound, the dark man grabbed me from behind and clamped my arm still against his ribs, while the lighter–colored man, quick as a snake, produced a needle, and with a bitter prick, forced it into my arm. He held it there for some seconds as he pushed down with his thumb. I could not move even a half–inch because the dark man had me locked in a vice grip. I whimpered, more from fear and alarm, and then they were gone, slithering back into the night as quickly as they had come out from it.

I shivered in the steaming stillness, from damp clothes, from shock, and from being sinfully invaded. I was like a card in the hand, used momentarily, and then discarded, dropped away. Was this attack Evan's doing? Was this black violation part of Evan's reprehensible plan? What did they put in me?

WHAT DID THEY PUT IN ME?

Half crying, I staggered through the woods towards home.

As if waiting for me, Kane sat on the ground leaning against a hollock tree in the woods just outside our campfire area, carving a piece of wood. I saw the mouse by his side. He stood when he saw me, letting his hand and the carving knife he was holding drop to his side. His clothes were dry, and I vaguely wondered where he was when the storm hit the island. I ran to him and hugged him, burying my face in his chest.

"You will be all right," he said. "You will be all right."

"Kane, I…"

"Go to the others now."

I looked up at him, puzzled. I wasn't entirely sure if he meant Tom and everyone, or Evan and his research team.

"Go to the others, now."

Steve saw me before Tom did. I had been heading to Central Lodge, and the two men were guarding our area, with Steve leaning his hip against a tree, watching, and Tom with his foot propped up on a stump fumbling with his shoelaces. I went to them.

"You need to run along now," Steve said. "Go on in the lodge."

Tom zipped around and called my name, pounding the word *Jamie* in the air. I ran to him and took his two hands in mine, looking up into his swollen purple face.

"Tom! The army guys… they got me!" I couldn't get the words out fast enough. "Dr. Bronte says that it's Jao's people who've been putting chemicals in us… from the soap! It's from our soap!"

"Huh? Slow down." Tom stepped back to look at me better, and Steve's mouth dropped open a little.

"Two of the army guys… they grabbed me in the woods. They injected me! With a needle! They *put* something in me, Tom! And, and… they're coming… tonight! The army. Tom –"

Tom looked at me in disbelief as Steve looked over our shoulders and into the woods.

"Jamie, I am so very sorry!"

Jeremy grabbed me in a bear hug. When he released me and stared in my face, I saw that he had a swollen eye that was starting to color into a dim purple. Jackel Island – land of the injured men! First Evan with his cut face and raw wrists, then Kane's arm, then Grady's hand, then Tom's face, and now Jeremy's eye.

"Who did this to you?" I asked. I wondered if it was Adrian, or perhaps it was Grady. Earl! It had to have been Earl. No, it was probably Adrian. Or maybe it was Tom.

"It doesn't matter who," Jeremy said. "I guess I deserved it. God Jamie, what I said to you… it was so horrible. I am truly sorry. I really am, okay?"

"That's okay, Jeremy. I'm just glad you're back. You've just got to stay with us, okay?" I said. Did he know what I meant? "Don't leave us again, like Adrian did, all right?" I cocked my head. "Did Adrian do this? My God!" I lightly touched his eye with my finger pad.

"No. It was Darcy," he whispered.

Jeremy and I were standing on the stairs and entered Central Lodge together. Adrian, Jim, Darcy, Brian, Derek, and even Earl rushed to me, all talking at once, scolding, concerned and curious. From the fireplace, Grady bellowed out "Next time you want to go dancing in the rain, just ask!" He was leaning a shoulder against the mantel with his arms crossed, his eyes shimmering. They'd all spoken at once, with Adrian telling me that with all his tracking experience, he could not find me, though the pounding rain didn't help matters. Jim was telling me how dangerous it was to venture out while there was lightning, while Earl was telling me what a complete idiot I was. Joel stood over by Grady, and he lifted his chin at me, raising and wiggling his fingers by his hip towards me in a shy hello. Tariq thought I needed a sandwich, figuring that would cure any affliction I may have felt. Brian was rubbing my shoulder while Derek slid his hand in mine, and Darcy was telling me to never *ever* pay *any* mind to anything, *any*thing Jeremy had to say.

I'd had no chance to tell them of my attack, or of my encounter with Dr. Bronte, and when I finally did, Adrian sat me down on the couch and everyone fired questions at me. Was I hurt? Did I feel sick at all? Did I feel any effects whatsoever? Did Bronte say who exactly was experimenting on us, and did I honestly believe him? Multiple personality disorder *WHAT*? So it was in the *soap* all along? The *soap*?? How will we clean ourselves from now on? (Sheila wanted to know). And what was this about Richard Gordon, Tom's father, CEO of Jao Institute, and should we tell Tom? How did Bronte get these soldiers on the island? Could we possibly sneak everyone onto their boat and return home? How did Bronte know about our whereabouts today? Did Tom or Adrian or any of the security men notice Bronte or his men watching us? Was I sure that the soldiers didn't follow me here? Was I all right?

Adrian held up a hand and commanded everyone to be quiet. "One question at a time, please," Adrian said. "Jamie, direct your answers to me." With two fingers, he moved my chin so that I would face him. I answered all of his questions as best I could, telling him all I knew.

"Adrian, Dr. Bronte just might be telling the truth," I said to him, but his face was hard, disbelieving.

Adrian stepped away from me to think, rubbing his chin and looking out the side window by the fireplace. We all looked at him.

"We need to beef up security outside while leaving at least two men inside Central Lodge at all times," Adrian announced. "Earl, you and I will go outside in a moment; we'll join Tom and Steve to see what's what out there." Earl blandly nodded, then grabbed a rifle. "Grady, Joel – you two stay here in case our new guests decide to pay the lodge a visit." Grady leaned back and smiled contently. Seemed he was pleased with his cushiony job. "Jim – can you give Jamie a blood test to perhaps determine what in God's name she was injected with?"

"Will try," the doctor said. "It'll take at least a day, maybe two, before I can determine anything, *if* I *can* determine anything. Can't make any promises."

"Just do what you can." Adrian said. "Grady, you might want to escort the doctor and Jamie to the medial building."

Grady rose and cracked his knuckles. Darcy told him he was gross.

"So far, I don't feel anything different," I said. "I feel fine."

"That's good, Jamie," said the doctor, trying a little too hard to sound upbeat. He held out an arm for me to walk with him out the door.

"Well, let's get a move on it," Adrian said. "It'll be dark soon."

A gunshot pierced the night air. One of the nurses let out a yell as Grady stood abruptly. Joel, Jim, and Darcy stood as well. A second gunshot rang, then silence. Grady grabbed a rifle from the wooden box.

"What in the blazes…" Jim said.

"Here!" Grady tossed a rifle over to Joel, who awkwardly bent to catch it after it arched in the air. Grady looked over at the doctor. "You ever use one of these, farm boy?" Grady asked Jim, holding out another rifle, a harsh vertical line cutting the air.

"Point and shoot, right?" Jim asked, and Grady threw the rifle his way. The doctor caught it more smoothly than Joel had, which surprised me. Hands that healed now held a tool of human destruction.

"I know how to use a gun," Jeremy stepped up.

Grady looked out the front window, scanning the yard, as Joel searched the area from the side window. I could hear the winds picking up outside and saw the trees sway as I looked above Joel's head and out the side window.

"See anything?" Grady asked Joel. Joel shook his head.

Sheila and the nurses huddled in the back of the large room near the head table, as Darcy smoothed Derek's hair, his head pressed against her chest. I now realized I was holding Brian's hand and had to let go because he was squeezing too hard.

"Was that gunshot from us, or from the soldiers?" Darcy asked.

"I don't know," Grady said.

"You don't know the sound your own rifle makes?" Darcy asked, and Grady made a face at her.

"The soldiers won't come here, will they?" Brian asked.

"I don't know," Grady said.

"Well, what *do* you know?" Darcy asked him. Another face.

By my ankle, Henry shook from the gunshot sounds. Tariq stormed out of the back kitchen. "What goes on?" he asked as he stood with his hands on his hips.

"We got it under control," Grady told him. "Go... Go cook something!"

"Think we should go out there?" Joel asked Grady. "They may need our help."

"We gotta' stay here. We can't leave them unprotected."

"Why don't just I go out? You can stay with Jim," Joel said. "Grady, my brother's out there."

Grady looked out the window. The trees seemed to take human form and howled in the early night wind, their boney arms and fingers stretching towards us.

"Go!" Grady said, and Joel hurried to the door with his rifle, holding it unnaturally, like a man holding his wife's purse. It endeared him to me. Joel was a computer geek, not an outlaw with a gun.

Before Joel had his hand on the door latch, Derek was at his father's side, holding his arm, looking up. Joel paused, put his palm behind his son's head, parted his mouth to say something, then left through the door.

We waited. We watched Grady as he moved to the side window and peered out. Jim moved to the front window. We stood in apprehension and fear, as if sitting were a luxury we couldn't afford right now.

Just then, the door burst open as greedy air rushed in, riding on a hungry wind. Joel hurried in and slammed the door shut, then leaned on the door. Breathing heavily, he held the top part of the barrel as the butt of the rifle rested on the floor. Derek rushed to his side, and Joel pressed his son's head against his ribs.

"They're out there," Joel said. "They've got Tom, Adrian, Steve, and Earl at gunpoint with their hands on their heads." I looked at Darcy and Brian. Jeremy stepped forward. "I think one of them may've seen me as I rushed away."

"How many?" Grady asked.

"About a dozen, maybe more."

"Where are they?" Grady rapidly asked.

"Along the back side of the lodge, by the campfire."

"Did you see Kane?" the doctor asked.

"No," Joel said, turning to the doctor. Joel seemed surprised, as if it just dawned on him that Kane was missing.

"What are we going to do?" Darcy asked desperately.

"I'm thinking!" Grady snapped back at her. "There's only three of us with rifles. Ain't good odds."

"Four!" Jeremy said, puffing his chest out at Grady.

"Oh Christ… go grab a rifle, pip squeak. And don't shoot your toe off," Grady said, giving in. A surprised and eager Jeremy hurried to the rifle box. "Or mine either, for that matter."

"There can be five of us," Darcy said, pointing an index finger to her chest. "Six, if you count Tariq. We can all help! If you include Brian and Jamie, that makes eight. We're not lame, Grady, as much as your pig–headed male chauvinistic mind thinks. There'd even be eleven of us, if you count Sheila, Alice, and Brittany. It'd be an even match. Well, almost."

"Oh Lord, have mercy!" Grady said.

"Is that a yes?" Darcy asked.

"No! That's a no!" Grady said. Brian, who stood next to me, exhaled loudly. One of the nurses looked at Darcy as if she swallowed a light bulb. Jeremy trailed his finger along the neck of the rifle he held.

"Do you want to give the soldiers out there a good hardy laugh? Is that it?" Grady asked Darcy. "Hell, let's send Derek out there with a rifle."

"Daddy, I don't want to go out there!"

"He's joking." Joel rubbed the back of his son's head.

Just then, there was a harsh and urgent knock on the door. Brian jumped as Grady immediately brought his rifle to his eye, aiming at the door. In a flash, Jim followed suit. Joel pushed Derek to me and stepped away from the door, bringing his rifle to his shoulder, aiming at the door. Jeremy armed his weapon as well. Jim whispered to Jeremy to take the safety off. As a panicked Jeremy searched his weapon and asked how to do this three times in quick succession, Jim reached over and briefly adjusted something on Jeremy's rifle. Jim never took his eye from the door.

"Open the door!" It was Evan's voice from outside. He was yelling. "We've got your guys. We mean no harm, but we need you to hear what we have to say."

"We can hear just fine from in here!" Grady yelled back.

"Open the door!" Evan persisted.

"What do you want?" Grady called out.

"For you to open the door," Evan said with exaggerated patience.

"Ain't gonna' happen, sweetheart!"

Silence. A weighted dark stillness hovered around us, as an apathetic wind washed over the roof. I listened to Brian's breathing until I realized it was my own.

A crack of gunshot rang out from just outside the lodge, making us all jump. Sheila or one of the nurses shrieked, as Henry ran under the couch.

"What the…" Grady was heated.

"Open the door, Mr. Galinger," Evan warned.

"Or you'll *kill* us?" Grady asked. "Is that it?"

"Not kill. Perhaps injure," Evan said. "By the way, how's your hand healing?"

"Asshole!" Grady said under his breath, then he called out, "Very well, thank you for asking. Thoughtful of you."

Adrian yelled, "Grady, don't…" then we heard Adrian give a loud and painful "oof".

"Mr. Galinger, we just want to talk. Please come out." Evan tried again.

"Are you hurting our people, Dr. Bronte?" Jim called out.

"Not entirely," Evan answered. "And who may you be?"

"We're not coming out!" Grady yelled to the outside.

"You know we vastly outnumber you," Evan reasoned. Silence. Evan tried a new tactic. "You realize we can come in and get you."

"Then why don't you?" Grady called back.

"We want to do this peacefully," Evan said.

"No, you don't want a bullet through your head if you open the door."

"Mr. Galinger, you have a child in there, do you not? And women?"

Grady turned around to read us, but we returned blank faces. Grady was sincerely at a loss over what to do. He asked Joel and the doctor if we should wait it out. Jim suggested we hear what they have to say.

"Mr. Galinger, my squad here is becoming quite impatient," Evan said. "I don't know if I want to hold them back too much longer. Please, I just want you to hear what's been going on here. We don't want this to get unpleasant."

Grady impatiently drummed his fingernails against the forestock of his rifle. "Oh dammit," he said, then went to the door.

Once we were all outside, Evan's soldiers quickly confiscated rifles from Grady, Joel, and from the doctor. Looking about, Grady and Jim exchanged a confused look, vaguely looking around for Jeremy. They hadn't noticed that Jeremy had hid inside the fireplace as the rest of us were leaving the lodge. The soldier who gave a quick look through the lodge hadn't noticed either. But Darcy and I had. With pleading eyes, Darcy had beckoned Jeremy to come with us, but he remained squatted in the fireplace, giving her a desperate look in response to her urging look. Tom, Adrian, Steve, and Earl, who had been with Evan and his men all this time, each had someone holding a gun to their head. One of the soldiers put a gun to Grady's head.

Where was Kane?

We were instructed to sit in a semicircle on the ground by the water basin. If we didn't move quickly enough, we were pushed. Evan forbade anyone to speak except for the security men, Tom, and the doctor. Tariq fussed the whole time, even when one of the soldiers rammed the butt of his rifle into Tariq's upper arm to quiet him. I locked eyes with Evan just before I sat in the dirt, but only for a second until his eyes darted away. Tom, Adrian, Steve, and Earl were pushed to the ground with us. An angry Earl started to bounce back up off the ground until a gun was pointed about two inches from his skull. He reluctantly settled back down. Darcy rushed over to Tom, half crawling, and she buried her face in his shoulder.

Adrian leaned in to us and told us that they had plans to inject us, and that Bronte gave them some incredible story. He was quickly silenced with a boot from one of the uniformed men.

"I need you all to listen," Evan said. "We really haven't much time. We'd originally planned to get you all off this island early this morning, but the other ship was held up with equipment failure. It was supposed to arrive with the squad boat. The transport ship should be arriving some time tonight. Actually, it's overdue."

"Don't believe him," Adrian said, and he got kicked.

"I don't," Grady said. He got kicked too. "Ow! Dammit!"

"Gentlemen! Don't anger the soldiers, please," Evan said. "You *will* believe me, I trust, when you see the ship. However, you may find it hard to believe that I've been protecting you all along." Earl snarled. Evan leaned his leg against the water basin. "You realize by now that you've been subjects for biological testing. Mr. Gordon – you, your brother, and your nephew were to be spared, but when that no longer was the plan, your father opted out of the rather illegal operation that he and three of his Jao associates were running."

"My father had nothing to do with any of this!" Tom said.

"Oh, but he did, I assure you."

"Please leave our father out of it," Joel spoke up.

"Your father, Mr. Gordon, would have made millions of dollars using human test subjects to bypass all the legal and moral parameters. His temptation was quite high," Evan said to Joel. "And you were not given permission to speak."

Joel looked at his hands and vaguely shook his head.

"This is all nonsense," Tom said. "We know it was you all along."

"Why would I lie now? I have you all under my thumb."

"Because that's what you do, Dr. Bronte," Adrian said. Evan turned to him, as did the rest of us. "You lie and you deceive."

I thought of when I first met Evan, how he told me he was a mere research assistant, and played that role for quite some time. I thought about how all the while we were discussing literature, he never shed light that all this was going on. I thought of his ramming a knife through Grady's hand, kidnapping me, his wife's death, his unleashed anger during the chess game. Kane said to listen to your heart, that it contained all the answers. But I couldn't hear it, for Evan's charm didn't quite mask his violent demeanor.

Where was Kane?

"Mm hmm," Evan said. "Well, long story short, we need to get you all vaccinated. It's overdue. We haven't much time before they try to stop us. You see, some of you are already showing signs of seeing things that aren't really there due to the effects of this drug."

"What are you talking about?" Tom asked.

"Dissociative identity disorder, Mr. Gordon."

"Multiple personality disorder?" the doctor asked. "It's highly unlikely that this disorder even exists."

"Jao Institute intends to prove that it in fact *does* exist. And they plan to have a cure for the public. Do you know what this means, dollar wise?"

"That means you'll get very rich if you inject us with harmful micro organisms for one of your sick tests," Adrian said.

Evan sighed. "For the past year and a half, you all have had microorganisms and chemicals introduced into your bloodstream, hence your heightened senses and animal instincts, shortened sleep cycles, and erratic behavior at times. It can even act as an hallucinogen. It has been administered through the soap Jao supplied. What a perfect way to monitor dosage levels – larger people need a larger dose, thus more soap that covers a larger body. But I'm afraid your condition will only get worse. There may be a point of no return. You'll start to see people who don't exist and create a full identity in your mind. You must let us vaccinate you, now."

"I don't think so," Tom said. "If you get us back to the States, we'll look into it then."

"It will be too late by then," Evan said. "If this plan goes wrong, which is a distinct possibility, you won't have a chance to be vaccinated, ever, and you'll all be… lost. If they should intercept our ship as it travels back…"

"If there are ill effects with your so called vaccination, it'll be too late for us," Adrian said.

"There will be no ill effects," Evan said. "Judge for yourselves – Miss Robinson here has already been vaccinated, and you see no ill effects with her, do you?" Evan leaned forward towards me. "Jamie, how do you feel?"

"She feels marvelous," Grady said before I could answer.

"You could have injected her with a placebo," Jim said. "Or there may be some ill effects that haven't displayed yet."

"I assure you, it was no placebo, and…"

"You're not injecting us, Dr. Bronte," Adrian said.

"I'm afraid you have no choice." Evan said. "I was hoping you would comply. I really don't want a scene, but it looks like we may have to resort to one." Evan looked at his squad who stood waiting for his call.

"This doesn't add up," Adrian said. "So you're saying Jao, or a few people from Jao, planned to use us as test subjects to make big bucks on some hushed mega biological project, right? Thus we had chemicals put into us. Okay then, biologically speaking, how do they know it's working?"

"Your monthly blood tests."

"How have they been observing our *behavior*?" Adrian asked. "Since this is a human study on behavior and effect, how did Jao see how it was effecting us? Who reported back to the people at Jao?"

Evan moved his head to the side to look at Steve.

"You used your own soap, didn't you, Mr. Taylor."

Chapter 49
THREE HUMAN ERRORS

Our eyes shot to Steve like daggers. Steve would not look at us. He looked off with absolutely no expression on his face. I hated him.

We did not comply with Evan and his men. Evan looked to the ground as if deep in thought, tightened his lips together, then nodded to one of his soldiers. His single quiet nod set off a chain reaction. Suddenly, there was a rush of commotion and organized movement as a dozen soldiers rushed at us, while the remaining three soldiers made a single clinking noise as they brought their weapons to their faces, aiming directly at us. It was as if they were linked by an internal computer signal, a sudden switch turned on giving a universal command to this network of fifteen mechanical soldiers. It was code red.

They were on us in a heartbeat.

They rushed to our security team, and to Tom. They swiftly and efficiently pulled Darcy off Tom. Adrian, Grady, and Tom each had four soldiers on them, pinning them to the ground, restraining their chest and arms in a secure hold that totally and thoroughly immobilized them. Tom, still recovering from yesterday's fight with Adrian, called out in pain. Adrian swung his legs up to take them and was struck in the face, then a soldier pinned his legs down. The three remaining soldiers aimed their rifles at us. I never had a gun pointed at me before, and it was as if I stood in a boulder's path, unable to move, with someone at the other end ready to push. We were at their total mercy. I felt the grip of an internal choke around my lungs.

Evan squatted by Grady and eased the needle into Grady's arm, with Grady spitting out every cuss word he could think of. When Evan was done, he stood and looked at Tom.

Tariq began to yell in his own language while the nurses cried. A uniformed man kicked Tariq, but Tariq wouldn't stop carrying on. He was kicked harder. Like a stirred bee's nest, Tariq's agitated words rang more rapidly in the air, now in higher pitch. Ignoring this, Evan crouched down to Tom.

Tom tried to struggle but was held so firmly, he could not budge. Tariq finally stopped barking, and watched in horror as our leader was injected. Darcy wailed.

Evan approached Adrian. As he stood over him and looked down at our Head of Security, I saw in Evan sympathy instead of the victorious look of a conqueror. Adrian bit his lip as the chemicals were forced into him, all the while glaring into Evan's eyes. I had to turn my head away.

The soldiers next took Joel, Earl, Tariq and Jim, three against one this time, pinning them to the dirt. Rape is a forceful act that need not be sexual. Two of the standing soldiers stepped in and aimed their guns specifically at Adrian, Grady, and Steve. A single soldier kept his rifle aimed at the rest of us while the hellish needles were going into the men's veins. Earl resisted physically with all his might, but he was only able to move his neck. Tariq fought just as hard, only verbally. Joel took his medicine in silence, while the doctor was frighteningly calm.

I knew who would soon be next – Darcy, Brian, and oh my God... Derek. Sheila and the nurses, too. Brian started making guttural sounds as Evan stuck the needle into Joel, who shut his eyes during the short procedure.

"Stop!" A voice rang out from the lodge. Heads turned. It was Jeremy, standing proud in front of the open door. He held a rifle, and aimed it at Evan. Evan slowly stood. As one, Evan's soldiers stood and aimed their guns at Jeremy, a single unified movement. Three soldiers continued to control us on the ground.

"Easy, boy," Evan said.

"I said stop!" Jeremy yelled. "I'm not a boy."

"Put your weapon down, son." Evan said.

"I'm not your damn son!"

"Jeremy, for god's sake, put your rifle down!" Adrian commanded.

"No Sir! Not gonna' happen," Jeremy said. "I can do this. I got control of the situation."

"Like hell you do!" Grady said. "Don't be an idiot."

"Jeremy, twelve rifles are pointed at you," Evan said in a controlled calm voice. "Think about it."

"Yeah, but I got one bullet aimed at you," Jeremy told him, and he raised his shoulders, ready to fire.

Where was Kane?

"Jeremy, please!" Darcy pleaded one last time.

I'm not sure, even now, years later, the exact sequence of what happened next. As if on cue, as if it were a divine plan to grab them back to the abyss where they started before they were born, yanking the innocent from us, from this island, Derek ran to Jeremy. His fists were like pistons pushing back and forth along his side as he ran. I think he ran to protect Jeremy, to stop all this, the way he tried so intently to stop some of us from bickering in the past, the way he'd cover his ears when we'd banter back and forth. Darcy and Joel screamed "Nooo!" at the same time, almost in octave harmony, as Darcy sprang up and ran to get Derek. Joel jolted, I remember that, and Adrian and Jim stood too, I believe. Tom perhaps, too. The soldiers stopped the men. There was a scuttle of guns and motion and sound, then a blur of red and gray. This flash all took place within two seconds, perhaps three, the time it took for Jeremy to raise his shoulders, inhale, and prepare to fire.

But he never got the chance.

In an alarmed voice, Evan yelled "Hold your fire!" But it was too late. Before his last word was uttered, there was a loud crack, then a series of two or three cracks that shattered the air, the island, and my soul, as Derek reached Jeremy and Darcy reached Derek, four arms around each other as Jeremy still held the gun. Silence followed, as smoke thinly coiled up into the night air like a dancing snake. Darcy fell first in a surreal surrender of body and being. Derek slowly turned to us, looked confused, and then red bubbled out of his chest as he fell on Darcy. There was a long white stillness as we held our breath in disbelief and red terror. I hadn't realized an owl had been calling until it stopped. I smelled jasmine along with cordite. Jeremy let gravity drop his weapon down to his hip, then it slipped from his hand to the ground. He looked at us wide–eyed, until his knees gave way and he fell straight down. When he gave his last exhale, a line of blood dribbled from his nose and down his lips and chin.

Joel was on them. He squeezed Derek to his chest, wailing, getting his shirt soaked in his son's blood. "I'm sorry, I'm sorry, I'm sorry, I'm sorry!" he repeated, rocking back and forth as he squeezed his son in a way that would have hurt him. The doctor was right there too, taking pulses, then looked back at us in horror, defeated. Evan looked lost and bewildered; he had surrendered. Some of the soldiers brought down their guns. Adrian looked from Evan to the bodies on the ground.

I thought of Darcy's red walls, red curtains, and red rug in her room, as she now lay in her own red blood. I thought of a discarded flute in the sand, succumbing to the elements, later to be rescued and polished, perhaps to be played again, bringing music to the island and to our hearts. I thought of Derek's garden behind my cabin, the seashells, the butterfly wings, the snake skin, the tortoise shell… all signs of life passed on, living things which had thrived, only to perish. I remembered one night at campfire a lifetime ago, when Derek held a live banyan tree frog in his cupped hands, and when he tried to pass it to me, the frog jumped, slipping from his hands. Now, Derek's life had slipped from him into the unknown. "No, Joel, you had it backwards," I thought. "You asked me to watch your son in case anything happened to *you*. Well, who watches him now?"

"Who watches him now!" Heads turned to me. A hand warmed my

shoulder. I looked up, and it was Kane.

"Where were you!?"

"I was always with you. All of you."

"Then why didn't you stop all this?"

"I was unable to."

I looked at the scene before me and it was as if the sound were turned off. I only saw fuzzy movement, a commotion of people over three dead humans, and I stood frozen, watching. I had absolutely no idea why, among all this abomination, despondency, and heartache, I thought of the white pony. I saw him clearly just then, a pure white creature who finally learned to trust after he was so very broken. I had gained his trust by intuition, heart, and compassion, not from anything I was taught, not by anything I had read… not from any manual, not from any holy book. I thought of the fallen wild horse lying on his side with his foot caught in a log, and was perplexed that these thoughts and these images came to me among all this anguish, remorse, and suffering. Like the horse, we were trapped and saw no way out. The fallen horse was a wild animal on a wild island, freed only by human touch.

YEARS LATER

YEARS LATER

Looking back, I know that what we had on Jackel Island was an inexplicable, enchanted, and somewhat magical world, a life that could never be experienced again, not by us, not by anyone else. The island left us with an almost unearthly feel, yet the place was so very much of this earth with its lush jungles and warm waters, and was so abundant with life. Our times together were mixed with sweetness and pain, bitterness and love.

Sixteen years have passed. I have not been back to the island. And even if I had, it wouldn't be the same. Jackel Island will forever exist only as it had during that short window of time sixteen years ago. And that's okay. If all the cabins were exactly as we'd left them, if Central Lodge remained the same, the Medical Building, the stables, the huts… if every tree and rock remained untouched and the lagoon still sparkled every bit as emerald, it still wouldn't be the same. We'd be strangers, and the sand and the dirt and the trees and the water wouldn't embrace us as they had when we lived there during that special time in our lives.

No one in the States would ever know it the way Tom, Adrian, Jim, Darcy, Brian, and the others knew it. No one in the grocery store, the library, the gym, or the other places I now frequent would ever truly comprehend the compassion and unity we felt, the fear and suspicion, the panic, the conflict, and the deep–rooted love we all experienced on Jackel Island.

The ship did arrive on that hellish last night, and it took us away from what we thought, at the time, was a damned and wicked island. It was a somber voyage to India before we boarded the plane that would take us home, a voyage mixed with tears pulled from the gut, silences, depression, bewilderment, empty stomachs that couldn't eat, and long–lasting whispers into the night between two or three of us. We tried desperately to make sense of what had happened as we moved over the cold waters and felt the sea breeze sting our face.

Loved ones greeted us as we stepped on United States soil, with squeezing hugs and wails of joy over people thought dead. My Uncle Calvin and Aunt Priscilla were not there. I don't know why I had looked for them. I stood on the large concrete loading area among my fellow island survivors and their families. News media with their blinking cameras and white news vans, policemen holding a crowd behind stretched yellow tape, a band playing "America the Beautiful" like you hear at Fourth of July parades, and Marine personnel who welcomed us with a white–gloved military welcome surrounded us as I watched the scene. I felt very apart from everyone, more alone than I had ever felt on the island. Seeing me standing by myself, Jim called me over and introduced me to his wife, who was now in a wheelchair suffering from the later stages of Parkinson's disease. I immediately warmed to her. Jim took me home that night, told me I could stay until I got settled. I stayed for almost three years.

I was quite happy living with Jim, his wife Ellen, and Henry in their large house. I had my own living area upstairs as Jim and Ellen slept in the master bedroom on the main floor. I cooked meals and helped care for Jim's dear wife until she died eleven months later. Jim was heartbroken and I helped him heal from his pain, as I healed from my own, having early morning coffee on the porch with him every day, calling him every afternoon, and spending dinner and reading time with him in the evenings. Jim was every bit a father to me.

Brian became my best friend, living nine miles away in the less affluent but fun town of Lanely. Friday nights were our nights to grab pizza and a beer, go to the movies, or just enjoy coffee until the staff kicked us out because they had to lock up. It was sacrilegious for us to spend a Friday night apart. That was, until Brian met his life partner, Kyle Klemmons. They remain happy together.

Earl's wife, believing him dead, had moved on and was engaged at the time of our return. She chose to be with her fiancé. Earl took it hard. He never re-married and now lives alone. But he has a nice farm in Colorado and spends his time outdoors. Last time we spoke, he told me that he had expanded the farm and had hired staff who "don't work worth a damn." Earl calls me every Christmas, and last Christmas he told me that his new passion is rodeos.

Drawn out proceedings and a long trial followed for two years, where many of us had to re–live the gut wrenching events on Jackel Island, and worse, to see the facts twisted into a horror show on the news. We all received hundreds of letters and emails per week the first year or two, and one night, Brian, Jim and I sat in the living room laughing over some of the letters. We became celebrities. During the two to three years after our return, my life was interwoven with the trial, taking care of poor Ellen, and training dogs and horses, a business which boomed partly due to my short–lived life as an island–survivor celebrity.

Court lacks the drama that it has on television or in movies. I was bored much of the time, and so I would sit in the courtroom sketching horses with a pencil. A couple of times when I looked up from my scribbles, I'd catch Evan looking at me from the mahogany table on the other side of the room. His eyes would dart away soon after my eyes met his.

Evan had been a stranger on the ship as we had traveled to India, and also on the plane, keeping to himself. He had bodyguards, which was probably wise. I don't know if we blamed him for the deaths of Jeremy, Darcy, and Derek, or if we honored him for getting us home. We were all in such a gray state. We learned quickly that the antidote he administered gave us no ill effects, and many extensive medical tests during the months that followed proved that we were fine. I tried to see Evan in his cabin on the ship, but he wouldn't respond to my knocks. I saw him on the upper deck during our second-to-last night on board. It was close to midnight, and unusually cold, and he was leaning on the thick ropes where the rough sea was directly below. His bodyguards wouldn't let me get close to him, and he never turned around, even when I called his name. "Evan, you still have thugs!" I called out, and one of the guards blocked me with his body. Evan never even turned around. I tried to contact him about two months after I had settled in with Jim and Ellen, but I couldn't get through to him. Court was where I first saw him since our voyage home two years prior.

Evan Bronte was acquitted of all charges. After grueling investigations, proceedings, and dialogues in court, Evan was proven, well beyond a shadow of a doubt, to have been trying to help and protect us when we were on the island. He very easily could have been charged with assault for stabbing Grady's hand. Grady, however, did not press charges. And then there was my overnight kidnapping, but I did not press charges either. And then I suppose there was his illegal use of firearms, and his little imported army… But I suppose the human heart has a great capacity for forgiveness, at times.

Steve, however, wasn't so lucky. He was found guilty of conspiracy, fraud, and criminal purpose and was sentenced to twelve years of prison. Tom's father and the three men who ran Jao Institute were charged with numerous accounts, including unlawful restraint, kidnapping, pharmaceutical drug trafficking, conspiracy, perjury, fraud, physical injury, extreme psychological injury, unlawful interstate transportation, possession with intent to distribute, abuse of position of trust… and they were indirectly responsible for three human deaths. They were sentenced to life.

During the trials, Evan had been stone–faced and factual, similar to his hidden behavior when he was a recluse in his cabin on the ship's voyage home. I thought at the time that his heart had calcified, perhaps due to the deaths of the innocent. When the trial was finally over, I saw Tom and Adrian shake Evan's hand. This was healing to me, like a warm washcloth on a wound. Grady shook Evan's hand too, begrudgingly. Evan kept hold of Grady's hand and turned it around, making an exaggerated "ooh!" face when he saw Grady's scar. They laughed. I swear, I will never understand the ways of men.

As I walked down the white stone steps from the courthouse, Evan, who had been for the past two years surrounded by people in business suits carrying briefcases and folders, called to me from the top of the stairs. "Jamie Ella!" He asked me out for coffee. We sat at a small table against the window that looked out at people hurrying on their cell phones, women pushing strollers, and shoppers carrying earth-friendly burlap bags. Evan apologized for his past silence. He told me that he was plagued by guilt during our voyage back to the States, and immediately upon our arrival home, had been advised by his attorneys to say nothing to anyone from the island, until the trial was over. "Now I wish to make up for lost time. Have you been happy, Jamie? What are you reading?"

We were married a year later when I was twenty–five years old.

He had this silly vague grin during the whole wedding, a grin I never noticed on the island, except the time when he was setting up the chessboard for us to play. Evan bought a small island off Canada as a wedding present for me. We go there every summer. Later, we moved further out in the country where he built a beautiful stable for me, and he bought me two fine horses. "There you go," he said, "even though you never *did* give me the white pony from Jackel Island." Then he grinned. I still tease him about that grin, because he says he doesn't know what I'm talking about when I say "there it is, you're grinning right now!" He denies that he's grinning at all. Then he grins.

His twins were sixteen years old when we married, and they were living with their grandparents. I always wondered why he didn't have custody, as he was the biological father. Evan said he easily could have obtained custody, but chose not to force them, and felt that they were happier with their grandparents. However, he desperately wanted them to be part of his life. As the years passed, his daughter still refused to see him, communicate with him, or accept any money. To this day it's like that. His son, however, sees him regularly, and they now have a loving relationship. They spend a couple of weeks together every spring, traveling to a different country each year.

Evan developed a friendship with Adrian. He told me he always respected and admired Adrian for his strength, honor, and sense of command, even when he was Adrian's prisoner. "He's a fine soldier," Evan says. I sometimes forget that Evan, too, was in the military. Once a year, Evan's military friends go on a winter hunting trip in the Catskills, and he now takes Adrian with him. Every September, Adrian invites Evan along with some other guys to a cabin by a lake in Alaska, where they grill elk, drink beer, and fish off their row boats.

At times when Adrian would stay for dinner at our house, I'd catch him looking at me with creased eyebrows and a focused sadness. I, too, sometimes wonder what could have been.

Adrian eventually married a retired park ranger. He was most devoted to her, and she to him. We went to their outdoor wedding.

Tom took a long time to recover from Darcy and Derek's death. He grew a ponytail (which looked disgusting) and drank too much for several years, until he met Betty. Betty was almost five-foot-three with wild auburn hair, a zillion freckles, and an Irish temper. Betty protested, often screamed, with the entire muster that her small frame could dish out, demanding he clean up his act. And he did. They were married in a small white church at Casawasco Lake, and I hear they're having their third child.

Joel didn't fare so well. I think of Joel now and feel a black lump in the pit of my stomach. He never recovered from the death of his young son, and died twelve years ago after he ran his Honda into the brick side of Saul's Drug store at 55 miles per hour. We went to his funeral.

Grady married. Four times in fourteen years. Then he said that that was enough, and told us he preferred chasing women as opposed to marrying them. He chased women all over the world. His new security job with KaTel involved quite a bit of travel, which he loved for many reasons. We received Christmas cards from him, cards that frequently announced his wedding plans, assuring us that this one was *The One*. Other cards told of his divorce. As the years passed, we heard from Grady less and less. Last I heard, he was a financial advisor, of all things, over in Nebraska, of all places.

Tariq also sends me Christmas cards every year. He hasn't missed one year. He's a chef in New York City, and he complains about his boss and the customers in every Christmas card. But I think he loves these people. He continues to ask me why I married that crazy man, and used to ask when I was going to have children, adding that he hoped they look like me and not like that lunatic research man. Every year, Tariq signs the card, "Love you very much, Master Chef Tariq." He underlines the word "very."

Henry is the only living thing that was untouched by the horrors of the island. I speak of such horrors, but I don't forget the wonder and the beauty of the place, too. Jackel Island was the first place, since I was nine years old, where I found people who were like family to me. Henry was a happy puppy on Jackel Island and a happy dog in the States. He was delighted to live with Jim and Ellen, and he stayed by Ellen's side right up until her end. Henry was also delighted to live with Evan and me in our large house, often taking over the bed as he pressed his back against me and stuck his paws over Evan's chest and legs. Evan told me the dog couldn't sleep with us, but I fussed, and Evan always gave in to me. I shared a bed with Evan and Henry until we had to put my dear dog down last year. He was fifteen years old. I like to think he's with Derek now.

We get Christmas cards from Philip, Marvin, and Paula. Lord knows whatever happened to Sandra; she didn't stay in touch with anyone. Philip remembers my birthday but forgets Evan's, and calls me every January 6th. He calls me his little Centurion and asks if I've whipped Evan's ass in chess lately. He now joins Evan and Adrian on their manly–man weekends at the cabin every September. Marvin made it big, heading the biological team at Sesse Institute of Pharmaceuticals, and is becoming quite well known in science circles, almost up there with Evan.

"Is Marvin as much of a big shot as you are?" I asked Evan when we were reading together in the den, my legs across his lap.

"Heavens, no."

"You always say 'heavens.' That's a word for an eighty–year–old stodgy rich guy who drinks brandy."

"I drink scotch."

I wiggled my heel into his leg.

"Is there anyone who's as much as a big shot as you are?"

"Heaven's no." He never took his eyes from his book.

Marvin once went on a business trip with Evan, and from Evan's nightly phone calls, I could tell that Marvin still drove Evan bonkers. "He won't shut up, Jamie!" Evan told me. "And he stands a half inch from my face as he goes on and on!"

Pauline sends Evan homemade cakes on his birthday.

Kane never made it off the island with the rest of us that night. No one ever found him. Seems he disappeared. Brian didn't like me talking about Kane for some reason, and Jim denied he even existed. But then again, Jim is now 72, and memories cloud with age. Evan becomes frustrated when I mention Kane. Kane's involvement in the trial was kept from me, so I gather they all know something that they think is best I not know. Some of the material that they uncovered in the trial was quite disturbing – what they had put in us, how it had changed us without us knowing, how it could cause permanent damage in some, and perhaps cause some of us to eventually lose our minds. What they had planned to do with us in the end was most disturbing. I do remember Kane Jabari's name being mentioned in the black notebook in the science lab, so whatever involvement he had, I don't know. I only know that it was positive and good. It had to be. I knew it with every fiber in my heart. There were times on the island when I thought I could not emotionally survive had it not been for Kane.

I can become quite troubled over the past. Evan suspects that I received some cruel treatment from my uncle that I've repressed, but I don't believe that I am the repressing type. I can't seem to talk about or think about my best friend Darcy, or little Derek, who will forever be nine years old. I was at an outdoor music festival, and when someone played a raspy wind instrument, I had to leave. I had dropped to my knees and cried in my hands, thinking of Jeremy playing his tin whistle for me on the rock not far from the crashing waves. In spite of these memories, for the most part, I'm rather happy with Evan and with my animals. I just can't think about the three people we left behind on the island. Four, actually.

Adjusting to Evan's financial lifestyle was difficult and foreign for me. Evan hires people to do…. well… *every*thing. He was mortified when he found me scrubbing down our porch with a bucket of soapy water, and he was dumbfounded when he returned from a meeting to find me cleaning the glass by the entrance door. He told me to stop, that he didn't want his wife doing this sort of thing. I told him I didn't want a husband telling me what I could and could not do. He continued to look dumbfounded at me, while I simply continued to scrub.

Evan and I have a good marriage, overall. He gets quiet at times when something's upsetting him, and he doesn't share his business dealings with me, but I can tell I am the highlight of his world, and he, mine. Evan still has a temper, but he has never directed it at me, heaven forbid. One time, in a fit of rage, he fired a whole team who had been working on one of his projects. Another time he slammed the phone down and yelled "Idiots! Everyone's an idiot!" and was silent throughout our dinner, the first time I made shepherd's pie. After, when I reached for the dessert in the refrigerator, he came up behind me, hugged me, and whispered "sorry" in my ear.

Sometimes I test his limits, tempting him, taunting him. I don't know why I do this. When he's in the den trying to work, I sometimes sneak up to him and scream his name through the rolled cardboard that holds wrapping paper, yelling in his ear when he's so focused on his research. He gets very still and shuts his eyes when I do this. He once grabbed the cardboard from me and bopped me over the head with it. But he's never toppled his desk over, and he's never yelled at me in his life, nor has he ever stayed angry with me overnight. I hear that this is miraculous in a marriage.

We had a bit of a rocky spell in the beginning of our marriage when I pleaded for a child, and he insisted he was too old at forty-one. Evan says he can never say no to me and that I always get my way, though I disagree. We had a baby boy two years after we were married. This boy is my world. Evan's too. He is now eleven years old and is extremely intelligent, sensitive, and claims he wants to be a veterinarian. He also has this amazing temper. Evan says he's not sure where he gets this from. We named him Derek. Derek J. Bronte.

Discussion Questions & Reading Guide for Jackel Island

May contain spoilers

Life on Jackel Island can be thought of as a miniature society. Of the 21 people on Jackel Island, who represented democracy? Who represented the working class or the common people? The elite? The innocent? Who were the misfits?

What are the differences between the east side and the west? What does each side represent in today's world?

Who, or what, was truly the enemy on Jackel Island?

The following is a quote from the *Mad Scientist* chapter: "Throughout time, there have been barriers, barriers that divide and isolate people, barriers that disconnect and sever the human heart. The Gates of Alexander, the Great Wall of China, the Berlin Wall, and the Iron Curtain, to name a few." What was the author trying to say about physical and psychological barriers and borders?

Which characters, if any, fell to savagery when conditions begin to sour on the island? Which characters kept their humanity?

What are the spiritual overtones in this novel?

Tom is, in essence, the leader of the group on the west side of the island. What are his strengths? What are his weaknesses? Are these typical characteristics of world leaders?

What was Adrian's internal struggle when things started going wrong?

Why does Evan Bronte, an extremely accomplished, controlled, and polished man, have a temper?

What is the theme of Jackel Island? Is it about our isolation, how a society can crumble when people don't bond or connect? Is it about returning to our instincts, whether that be savagery or being civilized? Or is it about the frailty and darkness of the human heart?

Evan and Jamie discuss literary classics such as *Crime and Punishment*, *Lord of the Flies*, *Heart of Darkness*, *Catch 22*, *Brave New World*, *and Of Mice and Men.* Why were these particular works of fiction mentioned, and how do they relate to the theme of Jackel Island?

Often, readers find it difficult to keep track of all the characters in a novel. Also, when a novel is made into a movie, viewers often disagree with how the cast was selected. In Jackel Island, the author drew each of the characters, and wrote a blurb as to their position. This is typically not done. Did this aid or hinder the story?

What references are made to Jekyll and Hyde, and why the reference to Lord of the Flies 'Sam-n-Eric' as one person? Tom and Joel were twins, yet opposite, with Tom being outgoing and full spirited, and Joel, introverted and calm. How does all this relate to the theme of the story?

Does Jamie deal with reality, or does she escape?

Each character enters the west side of the island with an emotional tragedy from their past. What was Jamie's? Tom's? Adrian's? Darcy's? Jeremy's? Some of the others? How did their tragedies affect them?

Who was Kane? What did he represent? Was he real?

How does Jamie change by the end of the novel?

Who were the three characters that faced such tragedy at the end? Were any of them leaders? What was the author trying to say about the innocent dying for reasons caused by the not so innocent?

REFERENCES & BIBLIOGRAPHY

Anderson, Stephen. Neurophysics of Human Psychology and Human Behavior. Chicago, IL. 2011.

Baintree, Andrew. Human Brain Cells and Human Consciousness: Exploring the Network of the Psychology of the Brain. New York, NY. 2008.

Brown, M.T. Multiple Personality and Personal Identity: Philosophical Psychology, 14, 435-448. 2007.

Carson, Benjamin. Bio-molecular Altering Consciousness: A Study of the Interface Between Mind and Behavior. Boca Raton, Florida. 2011.

Cormier, J.F. & Thelen M.H. Professional Skepticism of Multiple Personality Disorder. 2011.

Federal Sentencing Guidelines.

Hayes, J.A., & Mitchell, J.C. Mental Health Professionals' Skepticism about Multiple Personality Disorder. Professional Psychology: Research and Practice, 25, 410-415. 2009.

Hopfe, Lewis M. Religions of the World, sixth edition. Macmillan College Publishing Company, New York, NY. Maxwell Macmillan International, New York, Oxford, Singapore, Sydney. 1994.

Jenkins, T.W. Przewalski Horses, the Last Survivors. Indianapolis, IN. 2010.

Kennett, J., & Matthews, S. The Case of Dissociative Identity Disorder. Philosophical Psychology, 15, 509-527.

Kihlstrom, J.F., Glisky, M.L., & Angiulo, M.J. Dissociative Tendencies and Dissociative Disorders. Journal of Abnormal Psychology, 103, 117-124. 2012.

Marcel, Kirk. Separation Barriers in History. Cambridge, Massachusetts. 2003.

Razvan, Gary Jr. How to Prepare Game Meat. Toronto, Canada. 2006.

Reid, Stephanie. Wild Horses of Indonesia. 2008.

Richardson, Thomas. Indonesian Life, Culture, and Diet. 2006.

Spanos, N.P. Multiple Identity Enactments and Multiple Personality Disorder: A Sociocognitive Perspective. Psychological Bulletin, 116, 143-165. 2009.

Yadav, Kumar. Life and Living in India. Jaico Publishing House, Mumbai, India. 2002.

The fortune cookie from *King's Wok Chinese Restaurant* in Raleigh, North Carolina, for giving me the snowman joke.

About the Author

Amy L. Benevento was born in Syracuse, New York. She graduated from Oswego State University of New York with honors, majoring in English and art. She is a fifth degree black belt and has owned Red Sun Academy of Martial Arts for 23 years, teaching Jo Kwon Chi and Tai Chi. Amy Benevento lives in Raleigh, North Carolina with her husband, Rob, and her dog, Pony.

Sa. Institute - Rx firm

- Joni - main character - horse trainer
- Tom - head of tall thin man Administrator - Leader
- Joel - Toms computer Joel brother - Twin - Derek - Joels son
- Adrian - Chief of Security - kind of fat
- Grady - worked under Adrian - security
- Earl - Joni's supervisor
- Jim - the Dr.
- Darcy - Admin
- Sheila - runs admin under Tom
- Tariq - main cook

Mr Dody - Joni's stuffed Dog

Brian
Jeremy > Brother - soft gentle young thin wirery

Kane - Head of mt - Big Black GBY - Jeremys Best

Made in the USA
Coppell, TX
28 June 2021

58226250R00260